It's Always Darkest

By LISA MARTINEZ

PUBLISHER'S NOTE

This is a work of fiction. Names, characters, places, and incidents either are the product of the author's imagination or are used fictitiously, and any resemblance to actual persons, living or dead, business establishments, events, or locales is entirely coincidental.

DEDICATION

This book is dedicated to the loving memory of my Grandma Nettie (I will treasure you always), my Auntie Dorothy (thanks for the chocolate chip cookie and life lesson, you were taken from us too soon and too quickly), and Paul Van Dresar (who succumbed to the ravages of bipolar disorder...I wish I had known.)

If you suspect that you, or someone you know, may have bipolar, or any other mental illness, PLEASE, seek help immediately. It is not your fault and help is available.

PROLOGUE

HOW CAN YOU tell the difference between a good person and a bad one? Is it when they grab your dinner plate and toss your food in the trash because you didn't have a grateful enough expression when you said thank you? Or is it when they bring you breakfast in bed the next day—a double-sized slice of chocolate cake, *thank you very much,* with sprinkles on top because they are oh-so-sorry they lost their temper and sent you to bed hungry last night?

Or maybe it's when they come home late, reeking of whiskey and mayhem, smack your mother around a bit and then come looking for you or your sister. Or when they show up at your high school, a wide smile painted on their face as they take a casual stance, leaning against a cherry-red Porsche 911, then toss you the keys just as the cheerleading squad is sashaying by.

The point is, sometimes it's a fine line. One fine, fucking confusing line.

And I walked that line all my life, wondering, was it him or me? After what happened to my sister that day, well, I know it was definitely him…but sometimes I worry…I think it's me too.

CHAPTER ONE

"UNMENTIONABLES?"

"Yes. Unmentionables."

"And then what did he say?"

"He told me if I wouldn't mention what was stolen he couldn't help me. Then he hung up. I don't think the Seattle PD would approve of an officer hanging up on an innocent, law-abiding citizen."

"Why wouldn't you just *mention* it, dear?"

"Mom. What was I going to say? 'Hi, I'd like to report a stolen box of panties. Oh—and bras too. Yes, Officer, lacy bits, thongs, one pair of ex-boyfriend boxers, and, since we're being completely honest, three pairs of granny panties.' Oh my God, how could I?"

Lilli's mother laughed. "Well, I wouldn't go that far. Not even your mother needs that much information. What is it they call that?"

"TMI, Mom." She groaned and swept a hand through her hair. "Anyway, you see my point. I know I don't seem like it, but sometimes I'm still that shy little girl. The confidence thing—it's an intricately balanced lie."

"You don't lie, Lilli."

"You're missing the point, Mother."

"And what is that, dear Daughter?"

"My Victoria's Secrets are no longer secret."

"But you get to go shopping now."

"Who has the time?" Lilli reached up and began placing more coffee mugs in the cabinet. "I suppose it's my own fault for packing my unmentionables in my computer monitor box, and leaving the back of my Jeep open."

"Stop beating yourself up, you do that too much."

"Anyway," Lilli began to segue, "about Christmas…"

"Dad and I are looking forward to seeing you. We have a huge turkey and your favorite—"

"Mom."

"Oh, I don't like the sound of that. You've changed your mind about coming home."

She stopped unwrapping the dishes and heaved in a big breath. "I'm sorry, Mom. I want to, but it's only two days away. With the move and all," Lilli scanned her new apartment, gesturing with a sweep of her hand, even though no one was there to see it except her and her cat, "there's just too much to do."

She moved the phone to her other ear and wiped a stray tear from her cheek.

"Are you crying, dear?"

"God, Mom, how do you do that? It was one tear. I didn't even make a peep. Not even a sniffle."

"A mother just knows these things, Lilli. You'll understand someday."

"Not at this rate, Mom."

"You'll get through this. You always do. Dad and I are very proud of you."

She snatched a tissue out of the box on the counter. "Why?"

"Because. You stood up for yourself. It's hard to walk away from someone you love, especially when they say they need you. You did the right thing."

"Thanks, Mom. I love you."

"I love you too, Lilli. And don't worry about Christmas. We'll see you after the new year, once you're all settled."

"Okay."

"Now, stop unpacking for a few minutes, blow your nose, quit thinking about Bradley, and make yourself a cup of tea. That always makes you feel better."

"No, Mom, having *you* make it for me after a nightmare, that's what made me feel better."

"Well, just pretend I am making it for you. After all, in a way, you did just wake up from a bad dream, didn't you? Make yourself a cup."

"I will. Thanks for listening. Again."

"That's what mothers are for."

"Give everyone a hug for me, and yourself too. I'll call you on Christmas morning. I'll miss you."

"Me too. Good-bye, dear."

"Bye, Mom."

Lilli hung up the phone and thought back to when she was a little girl. If she closed her eyes, she could vividly imagine sitting at the table after a nightmare, a cup of honey-infused chamomile tea steaming in front of her. She could almost reach out and touch the butter-yellow walls of her mother's kitchen, feel the worn oak cabinets, picture the white cotton curtains, peppered with some kind of small blossom that Lilli could not name—maybe Black-eyed Susans. She could almost smell the lingering aroma of roast beef and potatoes.

Lilli wrapped her arms around herself as the memories tugged at her heart. Then, smiling, she filled the kettle and plugged it in, making her way to the storage room to get another box to unpack. A waft of dustiness reached out to her as she twisted the cold metal handle of the storage room door. She bent down to pick up a box marked *Kitchen-Pots & Pans-Lilli*.

Seeing her name written in black Sharpie marker gave new life to her sadness. She thought about the last week and a half. It had been difficult, being around Brad, waiting for this apartment to open up. Packing and labeling her things, separating them from Brad's stuff. Life really could change in the blink of an eye.

All she'd been planning that night was to go upstairs to get ready for bed, maybe watch a movie and snuggle on the sofa with Brad. But when she went into the room, there it was, sitting on the floor, right in front of the bedroom door, a beacon, taunting her. Brad's precious little secret.

Every time she'd seen him take that damn black case into the washroom Lilli's insides had twisted with uninvited comprehension. Seeing it there that night, the suspense was more than she could handle. Lilli hadn't wanted to know the truth, but she'd needed to know. She'd forced herself to open it.

Even though, on some level, she'd suspected he was using steroids, she'd still been shocked and disgusted to see the vials and needles, read the labels. Horse testosterone. Lilli had stormed down the stairs, tightly clutching the case, and, when she'd had Brad in her line of vision, she'd hurtled it directly at his head. *Thwack.*

Brad had recoiled from the blow, staring at her, a dumbfounded expression on his face, as Lilli had launched the full force of her anger and betrayal.

Now, as she stood in the storage room, staring at how her life had been reduced to cardboard and black marker, she replayed the night.

They'd talked until it was almost sunrise. Took turns crying and yelling. Brad had promised he would stop using. She'd told him she loved him, but couldn't handle the dishonesty. That was the worst part. He'd lied. To her face. Repeatedly.

What she'd needed was time to think, so she'd decided to move out. He'd begged her to help him. She'd said she would, from a distance, as friends only. She had started looking for a place the next day. So had he.

She gazed through the storage room door into the living area. She'd been lucky to find this place.

The Madison Gate apartment was bigger than she needed, two bedrooms and two bathrooms, but they allowed her to keep her cat, and it was a ground-floor apartment, with a little yard—maybe she'd plant a container garden in the spring. It would be nice to be minutes away from work in downtown Seattle. Plus, she would be close to Capitol Hill, with easy access to I-5 and I-90, and not far from CenturyLink Field—her boss Chuck had season tickets and Lilli loved football.

Too big or not, this was a good thing. Rent was a little more than she would have liked to pay by herself, but it was worth it. Who knew, if Brad had a chance to get his act together, maybe…

She shook her head. She had to stop thinking that way. Lilli groaned and kicked the box, regretting it immediately, as her big toe began to throb. What was it her mother was saying about beating herself up?

She could not spend her life waiting for Brad to live up to some mythical *potential.* What a ridiculous concept that was. He was damaged goods, and Lilli had to believe she was not responsible for fixing him. She would be his friend, help him—if that was what he truly wanted—but as far as more, she had to move on, get ahead. Simple as that.

Simple. Yeah right.

"Get ahead? I'm so far behind I think I'm in the lead," she mumbled the words to one of her father's favorite sayings, let out a single mirthless laugh, and that was it.

She felt the solidness as her back hit the storage room wall. In what seemed like ridiculous slow motion, Lilli's limbs went weak, her muscles and bones turned to rubber, and she slid down the narrow patch of bare wall until she hit the floor with a dull, hollow thud.

Then, *they* came. The tears spilled over like a waterfall.

She knocked the back of her head into the wall, two times, and then once more for good measure. Then, she took the stiff palms of both her hands and forced the tears from her cheeks, thrusting them out to the sides.

Toughen up already. Geez.

Lilli knew she didn't really need to toughen up. If anything, she was probably too strong already. Too independent. She refused to ask for help, even when she needed it. *I can do it myself* was her childhood mantra. And she always did. No matter what. Her family often reminded her how stubborn she was. Determined, she thought, but whatever. Same result.

WHEEEE! The sharp whistle of the kettle beckoned and she scurried to the kitchen as simmering water began to erupt from the spout.

Stumbling over an empty box, then cursing, Lilli quickly unplugged the kettle, a little spark issuing from the wall outlet. She rummaged for the perfect cup—the big green one with *Niles the Angry Kitten* on it. She gave it a quick rinse and then hunted for her tea.

She plopped one in, holding the cup as she poured the water, watching as the lonely teabag bobbed aimlessly inside the over-sized mug. Searing heat pelted her skin and Lilli yanked her hand away. Mesmerized by the dancing teabag, the boiling water had cascaded over the side of the mug and onto her hand.

Dashing to the sink to run her scalded hand under cold water, she almost tripped on the box again, only this time it was no longer empty. Her cat, Toby, had conquered it, taken it as his fort, his yellow eyes glittering in victory.

As she ran her hand under the tap, she regarded him. "Sorry to ruin your adventure, kitty, but I have to move your fortress into the other room. God knows I don't need an excuse to trip over my own two feet."

He mewed as she tried to carry it with one hand, with him still inside. She balanced it on her hip and wrist as she supported it with her non-injured hand, walking with purpose to the spare bedroom.

As she placed it inside the door, he leapt out anyway.

She turned around, feeling the sharp stinging in her left hand, and realized the cold water was speeding pointlessly down the drain. She trudged back into the kitchen and depressed the lever. Using one of the dishtowels she'd used to pack her coffee mugs, she mopped up the spilled kettle water, then folded it in thirds and hung it on the oven door.

She pulled her hand inside her sleeve as insulation and, hugging her teacup, she plopped into her favorite chair, taking a break as her mother had instructed. It had been a long day, and she'd done most of the work herself, borrowing Chuck's larger SUV to haul the big stuff. Finding willing bodies to help move was a challenge at the best of times. Make it snowy and two days before Christmas—good luck with that. Her girlfriends could only carry so much.

Lilli sat for a moment before taking a deep breath and blowing gently on the steaming hot tea. She took a tentative sip at first then, in spite of the heat, she took a longer, deeper draw. Maybe the fragrant chamomile beverage would chase away the monsters in her closet. Just like when she was a little girl.

She smiled at the memory again as she caressed the cup with her sleeve-covered hand.

Maintaining her tea-tradition helped Lilli cope with the distance that moving to Seattle had put between her and her family when she'd left home at nineteen. She couldn't explain it. It was just something she'd had to do. After spending most of her life feeling as though something was missing, her heart had told her to try finding it in Seattle.

She was still looking.

Her legs curled up beside her, she nestled cozily underneath the tattered but colorful patchwork quilt her grandmother had made for her tenth birthday—the first birthday she really remembered. Periwinkle blue, bright apple green, two shades of pink, violet, and even orange—she loved all the colors and she felt at ease. She could finally relax.

Lilli turned on the TV and flipped through the channels, happy when she found her favorite movie just starting. *It's a Wonderful Life.*

Yes it was. This was a good omen. It was exactly what she needed. Lilli loved Jimmy Stewart—she loved George Bailey—but doubted that men like that existed outside of old Hollywood's grainy black-and-white world.

The last time she'd watched it was with Brad, last Christmas Eve. They'd been so happy together. What happened?

She sighed. Brad was no George Bailey, but he was handsome enough to be a leading man, yet somehow he'd been so insecure that he had to inject himself with horse testosterone. Then the mood swings, the rage, watching the man she loved turn into a monster at the drop of a dime.

Oh yeah, right. That's what happened.

Finishing the last drop of tea, she *plunked* her empty mug on the side table as Toby hopped up and began to purr. Lilli pulled the quilt up to her chin and snuggled in. George Bailey was just about to be slapped in his bad ear by Old Man Gower. It was the first point in the movie that Lilli always cried, relished it, and if anyone distracted her before she'd submerged herself in the emotion of it, she hit rewind and started over.

AT SOME POINT Lilli had drifted off because George Baily was now a grown man. He and Mary were walking back from the dance as Lilli opened sleepy eyes and made a blurry attempt to focus on the screen.

George was asking Mary if she wanted the moon. "Just say the word," he said, "and I'll throw a lasso around it and pull it down for you."

Lilli smiled at the couple on the screen. She didn't know if life had ever really been like the movie portrayed, but the purity of it made her heart sing with joy.

"Hey! That's a pretty good idea!" George proclaimed. "I'll give you the moon, Mary."

Then Mary spoke as Lilli echoed her words. "I'll take it. Then what?"

Yes, if given the opportunity Lilli would take that *Wonderful Life* in a heartbeat—problems and all. What she had taken away from the movie, and what she strived to incorporate into her guiding principles, was how everything intersects. Connects. We are all one thing. Energy. Pure interconnected energy. Every single thing, every person and their choices, mattered. And it all had a reason.

She yawned, then burrowed deeper in the quilt, her eyes darting to the empty teacup. Lilli imagined her mother whispering goodnight. On the wings of a waking dream she felt her mother tucking the blanket all around her, followed by a wisp of a kiss on each cheek, the nose, and the forehead.

Sweet angel dreams.

Then and now, Lilli was cozy and warm, safe under her patchwork quilt.

Her lids drifted open and closed, the weight of exhaustion—and stress—tugging them toward sleep. Then, just as George Bailey was getting his own dose of bad news, Lilli finally succumbed, allowing her dry, aching eyes to remain dormant. Sweet, blissful sleep.

CHAPTER TWO

TOBY'S LOUD PURRING in Lilli's ear nudged at her awareness. She peeked open a single eye and gave him a pet. "You're such a noisy kitty, Toby. And yes, I'll feed you soon."

She rubbed the sleep from her eyes, stretched, and then padded to her bedroom window. The first deep orange traces of a new day had already begun to tickle the Seattle skyline and a warm glow was beginning to color the morning, reflecting off the light dusting of freshly fallen snow.

Christmas had come and gone rather uneventfully. She'd spent most of her time settling in to her new apartment, but had taken a few hours off on Christmas day to go over to Cassie's, which was just three blocks away. Being the unattached half of their foursome of friends, they'd enjoyed what Cassie had referred to as "a single girl's Christmas feast." It had consisted of a large oven-baked turkey breast, some instant mashed potatoes, and a tossed salad. And don't forget the vino. White for Cassie. Red for Lilli.

The two friends had exchanged gifts—nothing over twenty dollars. Cassie had cheated. Lilli had too. Amid smiles and crinkling tissue paper they'd tore into the gift bags, breaking into a fit of giggles when each had pulled out a silk scarf. Green for Lilli. Pink for Cassie. Then, when the evening had grown dark, Lilli had gone home to resume hanging pictures and adjusting furniture placement.

While away, she'd been gifted with a voice message from Bradley, thankfully only one, in which he'd mentioned that he'd found a place and would be moving soon. It had sounded as if he'd gone home to be with his family for Christmas. He'd said he missed her, wished her a merry Christmas, and told her he still loved her. Simple, yet not so.

Toby mewed at Lilli's feet and she pulled herself away from the view to follow him into the kitchen, where she poured him some kibble and inserted a coffee pod in the machine.

As it gurgled and sputtered, filling the room with the enticing scent of coffee and the dash of cinnamon she'd added to the cup, Lilli appraised the view inside. "This place is shaping up pretty good, wouldn't you say, Toby?"

He meowed. Clearly the feline agreed.

As soon as the Keurig machine finished brewing, Lilli took her coffee to the sofa and turned on the TV—a local morning news program. The female anchor rattled off a recipe for savory turkey stew, touting the many great ways to use up all of your leftover turkey.

It wasn't until sports came on and they started talking about Sunday's games that Lilli took real interest. She turned up the volume and listened to the preppy-looking sportscaster.

"With Seahawks starting QB on the injured list as of last week's game against the Arizona Cardinals, it looks like rookie Jake Edwards is going to get his shot. The last match of the regular season and a heck of an opportunity for Edwards to show us what he's got."

"You know, I went to college with Jake Edwards," the female cohost spoke off camera.

"Did you go to the games?" Preppy asked.

"Well, not too many, Todd, I have to admit, but I did hear good things."

The sportscaster picked up his network-logo mug and took an exaggerated sip, nodding in the direction of the off-camera cohost. "Let's hope those good things prove true this weekend. With the Seahawks at ten and five going into week seventeen, a lot of folks are waiting to see if Jake Edwards will live up to his college reputation." A wide flash of gleaming white teeth, then, "Back to you, Cara."

"Thanks, Todd. And in other news—"

Lilli muted the TV and contemplated how she could convince her boss to give her at least one of the company tickets for Sunday's home game. She would like to see Jake Edwards get his first NFL start.

She didn't know him that well—Brad had introduced them in the spring. Since then, Jake had been hitting on Lilli whenever they'd crossed paths—behind Brad's back of course. She'd always turned him down, but still, it would be fun to see him play. Brad had known him in high school and had told her all the stories when they'd heard Jake had been drafted by the Seahawks.

She was about to dial Chuck's cell when she remembered he was in Cancun. Even if he hadn't given the tickets away already, there was likely no way to get her hands on them. She wasn't about to bother him on vacation.

Resigned to watching the game on TV, she finished her coffee and made some scrambled eggs on toast.

As she ate breakfast, a commercial came on for Bucky's Boxing Gym, which was nearby. With the New Year approaching, all the gyms were competing for the resolution crowd—the fitness industry's bread and butter. Promises made on January first were forgotten before February fourteenth. That signed, unused, three-year contract was money in the bank.

Boxing was something Lilli had always wanted to try. She loved watching the sport and had heard it was not only a great workout, but great self-defense prep too. No time like the present. She finished eating, slung her gym bag over her shoulder, and set out to walk the short distance to the gym.

TURNED OUT THAT Bucky's was closed until after New Year's, but Lilli made a promise to go back and sign up for the boxing fitness class. As she'd wandered home, Lilli made a spontaneous diversion to the local Starbucks. Might as well get a feel for the vibe of her new neighborhood.

The barista handed Lilli her latte and she took it to the high counter that faced the street. She settled onto a stool and slid her tablet computer out of her handbag. She'd downloaded an eBook and was eager to pick up where she'd left off before the move.

Barely a chapter in, a girl approached her. "Can I sit beside you?"

Lilli glanced up to see a rather plain, young-looking girl with mousy brown hair and absolutely no sense of fashion. Gray sweatpants tucked into knee-high, stripe-topped gym socks, and those horrifically ubiquitous Uggs boots. Interesting choice.

Although she couldn't gauge what this apparent street urchin wanted, Lilli being Lilli, she smiled and gestured to the empty stool.

The girl kicked the stool out with her foot and extended her mitten-covered hand. "Hi. I'm Donna. You're new to the neighborhood."

"I am. But how did you—"

"I would remember if I'd seen you around before. You're really pretty." The girl shrugged out of her down-filled parka and sat.

"Thanks?" That had come out sounding more like a question than gratitude. Lilli couldn't help but study this girl closer.

Donna seemed to recognize Lilli's discomfort, and she giggled. "I'm not a crazy person. I noticed you outside Bucky's a while ago, on my way to work—and no, I didn't follow you. I was coming here too."

"Oh. Yes," Lilli said, "I went there to sign up for a fitness class, but they're closed for the holidays." She reached for her latte. "My name is Lilli."

"Nice to meet you." Donna chewed on a hangnail as she spoke.

And it's interesting to meet you...

"So, do you work at Bucky's?"

"I help out sometimes. We're sort of related." Donna shrugged as she continued to gnaw at her fingernail like a ravenous badger.

"That's cool. He must have a lot of interesting stories to share."

More starving badger.

Lilli worked at a sincere smile, but she felt awkward. What should she say now? She'd expected the comment to elicit at least a short burst of conversation. The air around them was uncomfortably silent, and Lilli's gaze was enticed down to her tablet. She wanted to keep reading but wasn't sure how to achieve that without being rude.

Donna's eyes had followed Lilli's path to her eBook. "I'm such an idiot. You want to keep reading, don't you?" The girl scrutinized her fingertips and then chose a new target for demolition.

"You know what..." Lilli turned off the device. "No. It's fine. I'm just taking a break from settling in to my new apartment."

Donna's face lit up with a smile. "You moved in this week—I mean, if you're still settling in and all, you must have." She unzipped the hoodie she wore and rotated on the stool to face Lilli straight on. "This is cool. We can chat for a bit. I've got time to kill, you know, before my shift."

"Your shift?"

"Yeah, I work here."

That was a relief. She hadn't had a clue that this girl had a purpose here, outside of perplexing Lilli. None of the other employees had greeted her when she'd entered. She bobbed her head toward the counter. "Did you want to grab yourself a coffee, Donna?"

She scrunched her face. "*Blech.* No. I don't touch the stuff. Well, I *touch* it, I just don't drink it."

At least she'd stopped devouring her fingernails—for now.

Lilli forced a smile, and forced her thoughts away from her own needs, sat back, and listened as Donna rambled on.

CHAPTER THREE

NEW YEAR'S EVE and Lilli just arrived at Charlie's apartment with Cassie in tow. "You two are gorgeous," Charlie exclaimed as the girls stepped out of the taxi.

"You too." Lilli motioned for Charlie to spin around. She did, and Lilli leaned back to appraise. "That little black dress fits you like a dream."

"Why thank you. I could say the same of yours." Charlie whistled.

With her blond hair swept into a tousled up-do, bejeweled in a sequined, silk chiffon halter dress that landed mid-thigh, Lilli sparkled under the lights outside Charlie's apartment building.

"Let me guess," Cassie inserted, "SWAG?"

"No, but highly discounted." Lilli grinned. "Carmen Marc Valvo."

"Oh. I love his stuff," Cassie enthused. "Let me know when you're ready to hand it down."

"Of course." Lilli swept her arm toward the waiting taxi. "Ladies, our carriage awaits."

The three friends hopped in, scrunching together in the back seat, and headed off to the ballroom at the Four Seasons for the flashy party that Willow's Modelling Agency put on every New Year's Eve. It would be a blast. Chuck Willows knew how to get his party on.

The cab dropped them right in front, and the girls tipped him generously, then sashayed inside, drawing gazes from all sides.

"LILLI!" Chuck breezed over, decked out in a tux. He took both her hands and leaned in for a kiss on her cheek. Only one. Chuck wasn't into dual cheek kissing—too mainstream. "Hey, hey, sexy girl. You look *ah*mazing." Chuck's darting finger flashed between her friends. "Are you going to introduce me to Charlie's other two angels?"

Smiling, she indicated each in turn. "Angel number one is Cassie Roth, and angel number two is, well, Charlie—Charlene—Lafontaine."

Chuck broke into a wider smile—if that was possible. "Thanks for coming, ladies." He gestured to the bar. "Drinks are on me. It's almost midnight, top up those champagne flutes. Now, if you'll excuse me, I have to find my own angel." He jacked a thumb toward Lilli. "Since this one keeps turning me down." He kissed the back of Lilli's hand, then bristled off in search of whatever arm-candy he'd brought to the party.

Cassie and Charlie watched him flitting from guest to guest, gracing each with a brief burst of animated energy before moving to the next group. When they both turned to Lilli, she offered a shrug and a smile. "That's my boss."

"I can see now why he's Seattle's party king," Charlie said.

"What do you mean?" Lilli downed the last sip of her Dom Pérignon.

Charlie waved her arm. "Look at him—he's a party waiting to happen. Too much energy for one person."

"A person can never have too much energy." Cassie raised her glass and toasted before tossing back the last swallow.

Lilli and Charlie exchanged a glance and then burst into giggles.

"What?" Cassie looked completely baffled. "Why are you giggling?"

"You," Lilli said. "You are the queen of too much energy."

Cassie shrugged it off as Charlie finished her champagne too. "Perfect timing." Cassie snatched the flute from Charlie's hand and set it on the table behind her. "We need more champagne, ladies."

"Agreed." Lilli linked arms with her two friends and they all turned to head over to the bar for fresh bubbly.

"Whoa!" Lilli halted as quickly as her stiletto heels would allow, narrowly missing a collision. The server was carrying a tray of glasses at shoulder level, blocking her vision.

"Oh my. I'm so sorry. I didn't see you through all these bubbles." The server lowered the tray. "Wait—Lilli?"

"Donna?"

"Oh, that's right. You work for Willows Modelling, don't you?"

"I do, but what are you doing here?"

"I got the gig through one of my coworkers at Starbucks. Poor thing slipped at work yesterday. Sprained ankle." Donna extended the tray toward them. "It's almost midnight. Have some more champagne. Here." She handed a glass to Lilli and let Cassie and Charlie take theirs off the tray. "Cheers," she said and then set out toward a group of boisterous partiers.

"She's interesting." Charlie raised her brows. "How do you know *her*?"

"Yeah," Cassie agreed. "She's kind of an odd one."

"The Starbucks near the new apartment. She's a barista." She turned to Cassie directly. "Don't you recognize her?"

"Nope," Cassie said. "But then again, in the morning I usually take my instant cappuccino in a travel mug from home."

FULL AND EFFERVESCING glasses in hand, the three friends went to stand by the floor-to-ceiling windows. The lights danced and sparkled across the water as they got ready to ring in twenty-thirteen.

"Well, girls," Lilli began, "twenty-twelve ended on a rough note for me. Breaking up with Brad was hard." Her throat caught against the lump of emotion whelming there. Charlie rested a hand on Lilli's shoulder, and she reached up, placing hers on top. "I guess it's still hard," she continued. "More than two years of my life, but you know what? I've got you guys, and there's no one else I'd rather start this next year with." She lifted her glass. "Who needs a man when they have great friends?"

Both Cassie and Charlie cast their gazes over Lilli's shoulder, their expressions indecipherable. She narrowed her eyes. "What?"

"You may have spoken too soon, Lilli."

"Huh?"

"Look." Cassie prodded with a head bop. "Behind you."

Lilli spun around and found herself standing so close to Jake Edwards that she was bathed in his scent—a combination of heated pheromones and musky cologne. It ignited a little spark within her, causing her voice to become wedged somewhere on the way to her lips, along with her breath.

Just then, the room erupted in a count down. "Ten. Nine…"

Lilli swallowed and cleared her throat, finding a single word to utter. "Jake."

The crowd continued. "Eight. Seven…"

Jake bobbed his head once, then shifted his observation. "Where's the boyfriend?"

"Six…"

Torn between the ache in her heart and this new ache deeper down, she pushed her gaze toward the floor. "We broke up."

"That's too bad."

Her vision traced back up, over his full height, lingering on the expanse of his muscular chest, before coming to rest on his intense hazel eyes. "Is it?"

"Three. Two. One." Cheers rang out and glasses were raised amid shouts and whoops, but at this moment, it was mere background flutter.

"Nope." Jake held her stare and then bent down low, leaning in to kiss her.

Lilli closed her eyes, her heart flickering wildly against her ribcage, but instead of feeling the soft warmth of his lips on hers, she felt the cold sting of a slap to the face.

"Bitch."

Lilli's eyes shot open just as the girl grabbed Jake by the arm, attempting to drag him away.

"Let's go dance, Jake. Now."

He backed away from Lilli, quirking his eyebrow and rolling his eyes. He mouthed the word *oops* as he was tugged away into the throng of cheering partygoers.

Lilli turned to Cassie and Charlie now. They were both looking as flabbergasted as she felt. "Was that—"

"Yup," Charlie answered.

"And did she just—"

Cassie's face melted into a grin now. "Uh-huh."

Lilli rubbed her cheek and clicked her jaw from side to side. "I was bitch-slapped by Jessica Moreno."

Charlie lifted her champagne. "Happy New Year!"

AFTER THE MIDNIGHT cheers died down, the crowd at the party had thinned out, but Jake was still around. He had two things to celebrate—New Year's Eve and his team's win the night before—so she didn't envision him leaving early. Lilli watched covertly as Jake and the young local-girl-turned-Hollywood-actress danced and made conversation around the room. From time to time, paparazzi approached and they would pose for a photograph, Jake looking tough and Jessica beaming like a cover girl.

It seemed that Lilli's momentary connection with Seattle's new golden boy had been lost, or rather, stolen, when Jessica had interrupted. She decided it was probably for the best. The last thing she wanted was to get a jealous girlfriend after her—especially the kind that came with an entourage, a publicist, and a throng of paparazzi.

Her phone rang and she slipped it from her purse. It was Annie. "Happy New Year."

"Same to you," Annie replied. "Are you and the girls having fun?"

Lilli sent a final look toward the crowd in search of Jake. He was nowhere to be found. "We are. Miss you though. I'll fill you in when I see you."

Cassie gestured for Lilli to hand her the phone.

"Hang on, Annie, I think Cassie is dying to give you all the details right now. Listen, I'll talk to you soon. Give Bill a big hug for me."

"Will do. Love ya."

"Me too." She handed her cell phone over and whispered to Charlie that she was going to use the bathroom.

Really, she just needed to escape for a moment. Maybe a part of her was still hoping to see Jake around somewhere, as if she wanted proof that the blazing burst of intensity between them had been real. But, as she made her way out of the ballroom and toward the restroom, he was still very much MIA.

CHAPTER FOUR

LILLI HEAVED OPEN the heavy washroom door and scooted inside, craving solitude. The booming music diminished to a dull thud as the door swooshed shut.

She stood at the mirror and touched up her makeup before secluding herself inside one of the stalls. After closing the lid to the toilet, Lilli sat down and breathed a deep sigh. She hadn't realized how lonely she'd been feeling until her nerve endings had ignited with the electricity that had surged between her and Jake as she was poised for their almost-kiss.

Some things just weren't meant to be, and a romance with Jake Edwards seemed to top that list. Before, her relationship with Bradley had prevented the fruition of Jake's flirtations, and tonight, Jessica Moreno's right hand served as a stinging deterrent.

Lonely or not, Lilli would be fine. She could handle this. She didn't need a man to make her whole. She had great friends, a rewarding career, and a garden to plant in the spring, not to mention Toby. "Oh, God," Lilli groaned. "I'm already starting to sound like a cat lady."

The heavy restroom door scraped open then shut. Lilli listened for the click of high heels on the tile floor but none came. Instead she heard a shuffling, like rubber-soled shoes. Immediately, Lilli's attention lasered in. Was there a man in the ladies washroom? Before she could formulate a guess, the lights went out, plunging her into a void of darkness.

That couldn't be good.

A dim light beamed outside the stall and she eased her feet up so they couldn't be seen under the door. Lilli held her breath as she waited to determine what this person was going to do.

A stall door farther down the row squeaked opened and banged closed. Shortly after she heard the sound of someone using the toilet.

Lilli breathed a sigh of relief. It was just someone coming in to use the facilities. The extinguished lights were only a coincidence. She lowered her feet and moved to open the latch, feeling around in search of the metal slider. Just as the bolt glided sideways, a loud crash reverberated off the walls.

She sucked in her breath and froze to her spot.

"Hello?" Hopefully another woman, equally scared in the dark, would answer back.

There was nothing, but she could hear breathing. And scuffling.

Rifling through her bag, realization dawned—she'd left her cell phone outside with Cassie. *Crap*. What now?

"Hello?" she said again.

Still no response.

Was someone messing with her or was she being paranoid? She would make one more appeal, and if met with silence, then Plan B it was. She swallowed her fear and called out. "Hello? Is someone in here?"

Damn it. Nothing. Except the rasp of breathing and the rustle of footsteps.

Lilli eased the stall door open a smidge and leaned her ear close, listening to determine which direction the sounds were coming from. They were coming from the left. If she timed it right...

As the rasping and rustling appeared to be nearing, Lilli pulled in a breath and centered herself, silently counting off beats. Three, two, one. With all the power she could muster, she thrust the stall open, making direct contact with something solid. Feeling the weight against the door give way and crash to the floor, Lilli pushed out, and scurried, arms extended, in the direction she hoped to find the door.

She slowed as she noticed a thin sliver of light along the floor. She'd made it. Without so much as a fleeting glance behind her she yanked on the handle and rushed out, into the hallway toward the ballroom.

Pausing only briefly to try to catch her breath, Lilli spun on her heel to look for Charlie and Cassie. She took one step and ran smack into Jake Edwards' chest.

SHE REACHED OUT to stabilize herself as he placed his large hands on her shoulders. "Whoa. Where you going in such a hurry?"

"I…someone…the lights…" Breathless, the few words Lilli could mutter added up to virtual nonsense.

Jake led her to a bench adjacent to the elevators, sat her down, and took the space beside her. Right beside her. Then he dropped his arm around her and pulled her close.

Damn it. There was that smell again, accompanied by a fresh whisper of shivers dancing across her skin. She scanned the area, wary of another slap from Jessica Moreno. The girl was small but she packed a wallop.

"She's gone."

Jake spoke the words directly into her ear, and the deep, husky vibration sent further tremors along Lilli's back. She snaked a hand up, rubbing her neck in an effort to calm the goose bumps. "I hope it wasn't because of what happened before." That wasn't completely true. Lilli actually kind of hoped it was.

Jake raised his wide shoulders in a shrug. He didn't seem too concerned. "She wasn't feeling well, something she ate or drank probably. When I didn't swoop her into my arms and carry her out of here, she summoned her *people* and left, giving me a one-finger salute."

"Oh." It was all Lilli could manage while keeping her face from breaking into a wide grin.

"So, what has you all worked up?" he asked.

"I'm probably being silly, but the lights went out in the washroom after someone came in and I thought maybe they—oh shit!"

"Well, it is a restroom, Lilli."

"Ha ha, but no. I meant, I think I may have hurt someone. Whoever it was. They wouldn't answer me, so I slammed them with the stall door. Then I ran out. Into you. What if I killed them?"

The adrenaline surged again and Lilli fidgeted, restless. Jake pulled her closer and wrapped his other arm around her too. He gave her a squeeze and then released her.

Painfully aware of the energy pulsing between them, Lilli shifted uncomfortably, but resisted the urge to pull him back, instead matching eyes with him. "Someone should go in there."

Jake raised his hand to signal someone in the distance, but made no attempt to increase her personal space.

When one of the bartenders arrived, Jake told him what Lilli had said, and the man nodded, then went into the ladies room with his cell phone set on flashlight. He came out moments later. "One of our servers," he jacked a thumb toward the door, "a new one. Temp. She's out cold." He walked away to call for an ambulance.

"God, I'm such a twit." Lilli felt her cheeks heat up and she turned her face away from Jake. "Thinking someone was after me. I mean, why would someone stalk *me* into the washroom? Jessica Moreno, perhaps, but Lilli Brooks? What if I really hurt her, Jake?"

Somehow, even with the existing lack of space between them, Jake found a way to move closer. Dragging Lilli practically into his lap, he dipped a finger under her chin and forced her to meet his eyes. "Listen, you did what you had to do. I, for one, am proud of you. You're hard core. I better make a note to stay on your good side."

He was smiling at her and she began to relax, until a flurry of hotel employees rushed up and into the ladies room, the paramedics trailing behind.

Jake stood and held out his hand to her. "Come on, let's go back into the party. Let these guys do their work."

Lilli's teeth sank into her bottom lip. She was still worried about the waitress she'd knocked unconscious. Part of her wanted to stay to find out who it was. Maybe she could do something nice for her. Make it up to her somehow.

"Don't worry about whoever is in there. I'm sure she'll be okay."

Was Jake a mind reader? She looked into his face, and he pierced right through her with his hazel-eyed stare. She once again became aware of how the air around them seemed to vibrate with a high-voltage current. Still, she took his outstretched hand and followed him into the ballroom.

HE LED HER to the windows overlooking the bay. Off in the distance, fireworks were still shooting into the sky above Seattle, erupting into the air, reflecting a torrent of colors onto the inky black surface of the water.

As they stood, holding hands and watching the pyrotechnic display, Lilli was acutely aware of every sensation, every tingling nerve ending, yet she could barely tell where the exploding rockets stopped and the wild beating of her heart began.

As if sensing her need, or maybe his own, Jake turned her to face him, speaking not a single word but communicating everything that needed to be said. She took another deep inhale of his masculine aura and blew out the breath with force. Maybe it would clear her head. All the champagne she'd consumed was definitely clouding her better judgment because she found herself leaning into, rather than stepping away from, Mr. Jake Edwards.

She dragged her bottom lip through her teeth, then swallowed to mollify the tension that was building. "So, some game last night, huh?"

The green flecks in Jake's eyes seemed to intensify with heat as he made a move toward her. Lilli made a move back. He advanced, and she retreated until she felt the cool glass grazing her bare shoulders. An intense shiver flitted though her. There was nowhere else to go. She was effectively trapped against the window overlooking the bay.

This time no amount of swallowing could relax the tightness in her throat. Her heart began to palpate in a rapid staccato, and her breathing came shallow and swift as anticipation built.

Jake caged her in, extending an arm on either side of her, his hands flat on the glass, then he wasted no time taking the kiss he had almost taken a short while ago.

Lilli gave in, feeling the heat from his lips surge throughout her entire body, all the way to her tiptoes, as she raised herself to meet his kiss. Her heart pounded frenetically in her chest as they stood there, Lilli's arms at her sides, Jake's still firmly planted on the window behind her, the only thing touching were their lips, and that was more than enough. The passion rushed to a peak, causing Lilli to feel lightheaded.

She placed her hands on either side of Jake's face, feeling the grit of his whatever-o'clock-shadowed cheeks. She had meant to break the kiss, but Jake had taken it as encouragement. Instead of stepping back, he tangled his strong hand in her hair and held her captive to his lips, using his other arm to pull her body so tight it almost merged with his.

Lilli moaned softly into his mouth as he pressed himself against her, oblivious—or uncaring—of their surroundings, his teeth catching her bottom lip, tugging gently.

Just as she felt as though she might succumb to the heady combination of lust and champagne, a voice bellowed from behind them.

"Hey! Edwards. Get a room."

The heated kiss froze on their lips as they both clearly recognized the slurring command. "Oh shit," Lilli mumbled.

Chuckling, he reached out and tugged at Jake, drawing him backward. "Come on, Edwards, give Jessica some room to breathe for fuck's sake. Helluva game last night though." The laughing halted. "What the fu—Lilli? What the fuck?"

"Leave her alone, Brad." Both Cassie's and Charlie's voices rang out in warning from behind him.

"Me leave her alone? You shittin' me? This asshole is the one shoving his tongue down her throat."

"Back off, Vanderson." Jake placed a hand on Bradley's chest, straight-arming him as though he were breaking a tackle. "Just leave it alone, man. Just walk away."

"Walk away? Me walk away?" Brad swooped his hand underneath Jake's, dislodging the impediment. He shoved with both hands now, but the mountain that was Jake Edwards didn't budge.

Something menacing flashed across Jake's face, but he took a deep breath, pinching his lips together. Still, his squinting eyes glimmered with ferocious intensity. One more deep breath and the popping of his knuckles reverberated with an implicit threat as he took a single step toward Brad.

Just then Chuck marched up and tugged on Bradley's sleeve. "Come on. Party's over. I knew it was a bad idea to let you in here, Vanderson. Let's go."

Brad jerked away from Chuck's grip. "I'm not done here."

"Yes, Brad, you are." Chuck snapped his fingers and waved two of the bartenders over.

They both latched on to one of Brad's arms, dragging him out of the room.

"This ain't over, Edwards." Brad struggled against the two men as hotel security took over at the doors to the ballroom.

Chuck placed a hand on Lilli's shoulder. "Sorry, girl, I thought you had gone home when Brad showed up. I figured it would be okay to let him in."

Lilli shook her head. "No. I was in the bathroom. There was someone—"

"That was you? Remind me never to piss you off." Chuck was grinning, but Lilli was not ready to find amusement in what she had done.

He patted Jake on the shoulder. "Good game last night." Then he led Lilli over to a bench by the entryway. "Hey, don't worry. That Starbucks barista is going to be okay. She has a mild concussion I think. They're keeping her overnight for observation, but I'm sure she'll be released tomorrow."

"Barista? Was her name Donna?"

"Donna. Debbie. Something like that." Chuck stood. "Listen, girl, I gotta wrap some things up here, sign a few checks."

She placed a smile on her face and watched her boss breeze off as Charlie and Cassie approached the bench and sat beside her.

"So, some night, huh?" Charlie flashed her trademark smile and rubbed Lilli's back.

Lilli shook her head and bowed down, dropping her face, briefly, into her hands.

"Some kiss," Cassie added.

Charlie gave her a playful slap on the arm.

"Well it was."

Lilli's face spread into a smile now. "Yup. Felt that one all the way down to my toes."

"That's not where I felt it." Jake sauntered over, his hands thrust deep into his pockets and a Cheshire-cat grin filling his face.

"That's our cue." Charlie pulled a reluctant Cassie by the arm. "We'll be waiting over by those two hunky bartenders," Charlie added, towing a now-willing Cassie behind her.

Jake sat down beside Lilli, placing his hands flat on the bench on either side of him. "Down to your toes, eh?"

Lilli felt the heat rise to her cheeks and she dragged the edge of her lip between her teeth, bobbing her head in agreement. "Mm-hmm."

"Definitely had to work for that one tonight."

Lilli nodded again. "Yup."

"What now?"

CHAPTER FIVE

A SHIVERING CHILL DANCED across Lilli's skin as she climbed out of the warm bathtub. The scent of spring-fresh fabric softener wafted up as she pulled a big fluffy towel off the shelf. She caressed the droplets of water from her skin before folding the towel into thirds, placing it over the smooth, chrome towel bar.

Her hand reached over to the hook on the back of the bathroom door but came up empty. She must've left her pink bathrobe in her bedroom. Lilli shivered again, darting a rueful glance at the perfectly folded towel. With a groan, she scampered, buck-naked, to her bedroom, stopping only to turn the heat up on the thermostat.

As the radiator clanked to life, sending warmth emanating toward her, she retrieved her favorite perfumed lotion from the basket on her dresser, stood near the heat and began smoothing it over her body, following the same practiced route she'd used when drying herself. She inhaled deeply, enjoying the clean scent of lotus, rose, and lily flowers. When she was done, she slipped into her black-silk pajamas.

She flounced onto the bed and gave Toby's furry tummy a rub. "Well, kitty, it's a brand new year. And big things are going to happen for me—I can feel it."

He peeked open a single eye as he rolled on his back and extended his paws straight out before resuming his curled position at the foot of her bed.

"Fine. Sleep." Lilli pinched her lips together, then the corners of her mouth lifted in a smile of remembrance. "You may not know this, Toby, but tonight I was kissed by a boy—no, check that—tonight I was kissed by a man. A great-smelling, sexy man. I think I should celebrate with a glass of wine."

Lilli reached back and released her long, blond hair, shaking it out until it cascaded down her back in damp waves. "You go ahead and be aloof, Toby. Nothing can ruin this night for me." She rose from the bed, flicked off the light, and headed toward the kitchen, the only sound, a distant purring and the soft padding of her feet.

As Lilli opened the fridge to grab the sparkling wine she had put there to chill, her desire to luxuriate in the memory of that fabulous kiss competed for attention with the growling noises emanating from her stomach.

Her eyes darted to the clock on the microwave. Three thirty-three AM. Having not eaten since dinner at the Four Seasons, Lilli was famished. She grumbled, hummed and hawed, and then grudgingly decided to eat.

Although normally passionate about cooking, she had no interest right now in pinches of this and dashes of that. Instead, Lilli pulled out some leftover Chinese takeout and popped it into the microwave, poured herself a glass of wine, then grabbed a pair of chopsticks from the cutlery drawer.

She attempted to distract herself with a recent copy of *Vogue*, but her mind could not focus on anything except Jake Edwards, or, more specifically, his lips. Suddenly voracious, she ate with purpose, finishing everything on her plate.

After downing her wine, she went to set her plate and glass on the kitchen counter. As she turned to leave, she released a long sigh and spun back around. Then, she opened the dishwasher and placed her dishes where they belonged.

She glanced at the glowing blue digital display on the microwave. It was almost four now. A yawn pushed its way across her face and Lilli arched her back in a stretch. Now all she wanted was to crawl between her crisp cotton sheets and let her dreams rapture her back into Jake's powerful embrace.

After a quick cleaning of her teeth, she turned out all the lights, except for her bedside lamp, and nestled herself in bed, next to Toby. He didn't even blink a sleepy eye her way. However, the volume of his purring increased slightly, letting her know he approved of her warmth beside him.

As Lilli was reaching over to extinguish the lamp, her phone vibrated on the dresser where she'd left it. Groaning, she climbed out of bed and retrieved it. Seeing the name on the display, she rolled her eyes. "You've got to be kidding me."

Should she answer it? Lilli tapped a quick beat on the nightstand. No. She would let it go to voicemail. Brad was the last person she wanted to speak with right now. She pressed the power button to decline the call and then silenced the ringer completely. Then, in an afterthought, she scurried to the dining room to turn off the home phone as well, just as it started to ring. "Not tonight, Brad."

Scooting back under the covers, Lilli rolled over and pulled the extra pillow down, bunching it in her arms. As she pushed thoughts of Brad away, she allowed her senses to drift back to the New Year's Eve party, replaying the highlight reel in full Technicolor glory, she sighed and drifted off.

IN HER DREAMS, Lilli found herself strolling through the spectacular Kubota Japanese Garden, wandering over its hills and valleys, mesmerized by the sound of the running water from the nearby streams. The breeze whisped her hair from her face, and she took in a full breath, inhaling the sense of peace and freedom she felt.

She was wearing a flowing sundress and leaning down to smell the wonderful blossoms surrounding her, when she was suddenly trapped inside a wooden crate. She began pounding her fists on the walls of her timber prison, furiously. Shouting.

"Hey! I'm here. It's me. Lilli! Open up. Come on!"

The pounding kept getting louder, building in a crescendo, until her eyes flew open and Lilli realized she was in her bed. But the hammering wouldn't stop.

"Come on. Lilli! It's me. I came all the way here. Open up."

Brad? Really?

Lilli stiffened and remained still, listening, waiting for him to give up and go away. "What nerve. Who the hell does he think he is, Toby?" She tousled the cat's long fur, causing him to raise his head and nudge himself a little closer. "Don't worry, kitty, he'll leave when he realizes I'm not coming to the door."

It was silent for a few minutes, and Lilli allowed herself to relax, sinking back into the pillows, releasing a deep sigh. "There. See. Told ya."

Toby purred his reply and she could feel his tension release too.

Lilli nearly leapt out of her skin when the banging resumed, this time alternating between her bedroom window and the french doors to her little yard.

"Listen, maybe you won't let me in, but I want to talk. I want to say I'm sorry. What I did was stupid—okay, beyond stupid. I was stupid. I saw he was kissing you and I lost it, okay. You don't know Jake like I do."

He sounded breathless and agitated. His voice faded in and out, as if he were pacing between the two windows. "Why did you have to let him kiss you like…like…aw shit…like you two should just get a room or some—"

The furious thrashing on the window resumed. How long would the windowpane hold up to such battering abuse?

"Oh fuck! You don't need to get a room, do you? Is Edwards in there? Lilli. Answer me. He is. Fuck! Why won't you answer me?"

Bam!

With that, a deafening crash sliced the air, and Lilli heard the unmistakable explosion of shattering glass.

CHAPTER SIX

LILLI SAT ON THE sofa with Toby curled up nearby. The world was spinning around her and she needed to make it stop. Her fingers fidgeted with a tangle on Toby's hindquarters in an effort to rein in her anxiety. It wasn't working.

Muted voices from outside drifted in through the broken window—thankfully only one of the small panes in the french door—along with a cold pitch of night air and a few errant snowflakes. She shivered and pulled on her cardigan, shrouding herself in a tighter cocoon.

Toby cast a longing look and she resumed petting him, but her agitation at not being able to hear what was going on outside caused her to absentmindedly resume tugging at the cat's matted fur.

What the hell was Brad thinking? What was he on? This mood swing seemed like something more than steroids. He'd sounded crazy.

What might have happened if one of her neighbors hadn't called the police when they had?

Lilli didn't want to know. She hated that they'd had to, didn't want to be known as the weak girl with the crazy ex-boyfriend. She hoped to settle down in her new building, make friends there. Why the hell did Brad have to line up and take a swan leap off the deep end? Why did he have to show up at the party and find her lip-locked with Jake Edwards?

"No. This is not my fault, Toby. I will not blame myself for this." Her fingers worked aggressively on the densely packed tangle of fur, and Toby gently pushed his back paw on her hand, his claws ever-so-slightly grazing her skin.

"Sorry. I'll stop."

"He's all yours, Montgomery." Just then, one of the officers rapped his knuckles on the glass and she let him in. "Officer Brian Harris. Are you hurt, ma'am?"

"No. Not physically anyway." Fear and confusion started to climb back to the surface. She swallowed it down. "Is he gone?"

"He's out in the squad car with my partner, having a little one-on-one. He's pulling the innocent act. But don't worry, tonight she's playing the role of Bad Cop."

"That makes you Good Cop."

"I guess so." He grinned. "How am I doing?"

"So far so good."

He closed the distance between them and flipped open a notepad he'd pulled from a breast pocket. "Can I ask you a few questions?"

"Sure."

The house was still dark, only a subtle glow cast inside from the streetlights reflecting off the snow. "Do you mind if I turn on a light?"

"No. Go ahead," she said. "Behind you, on the wall."

The cop pivoted and flicked up the switch for the ceiling light.

Lilli's pupils contracted severely as the room flooded with bright light. Toby released a sharp mewl in protest, and Lilli's eyes squinted shut.

From the darkness into the light.

God. How had they ended up here? She'd tried so hard to help Brad, to be there for him—to forgive him.

"Ma'am?" Quiet, soft and distant, it almost didn't register. "Ms. Brooks?"

Lilli shook her head. "Sorry. I guess I went somewhere. What did you say, Officer?"

"I asked you if you have someone you could call—anyone who can come and stay with you." His soothing demeanor was an almost tangible commodity, drawing Lilli back to the present.

Her eyes raised to the ceiling, running over the list of her friends. Charlie and Cassie were likely out of it after celebrating the New Year. Annie was likely sound asleep at her new boyfriend's downtown condo. There wasn't anyone that Lilli wanted to bother.

"I'll be all right by myself."

The cop nodded once. "You sure you want to be alone after a scare like this?"

Lilli's heartbeat intensified again, thudding against her ribcage like a frightened little Tweetie Bird. She curled her bottom lip between her teeth, panic creeping to the surface once again. Brad had scared the hell out of her tonight, but she refused to let it get the best of her. She refused to succumb.

She closed her eyes, took a breath, and allowed anger to fortify her attitude. "I hope that doesn't mean that you're going to let him off the hook. He didn't seem to want to be alone tonight and I think he could benefit from making a few new friends, cellmates as it were, maybe someone named Bubba, Big Stanley, or some such."

There. That's better. Feisty, not panicky.

For a moment, she felt confidence rise up, starting in the pit of her stomach, ascending through her entire being, filling her*self* with strength, her lungs with air, and her heart with calm. She let the air out, breathed it in again, and tried to let go, but there was the lingering matter of the truth—making jokes was her coping mechanism, a way of trying to convince everyone, herself included, that everything was hunky-freakin'-dory.

The cop's deadpan *just-the-facts-ma'am* expression changed a little. It was subtle, hardly noticeable, but she was sure the corners of his mouth had quirked up into a smile.

"Don't worry, Ms. Brooks. We're headed downtown, and your ex will be riding with us." He nodded, as if coaxing her agreement. "My partner will see to that. She's ambitious, goal oriented. Fancies herself a future FBI agent."

Lilli offered a smile, but it felt weak.

He gave her one in return, but his was strong and sympathetic. "I know it seems like a lot to process right now," he slanted an appraising look her way, "but I'm a pretty good judge of character, and I think you have a bit of the bamboo in you."

"Bamboo?" Lilli repeated the word, thinking how odd it seemed coming from him.

He offered that crooked grin again. "There's a Japanese proverb that says the bamboo that bends is stronger than the oak that resists. I think you're like the bamboo—resilient."

Lilli scanned his hulking stature top to bottom. His complexion was lightly tanned, but with his blue-gray eyes, and sandy-blond hair she was pretty sure he wasn't Japanese. He didn't look much like a Buddhist monk either—more like a buff surfer boy.

He chuckled and shrugged. "What? Big guys can be Zen too."

"I never meant—"

"It's unexpected, I know. My dad is one hundred percent beat cop and my mom is a tarot-card-reading Reiki master who moved to Hawaii in the sixties to align herself with Mother Earth. A cliché, I'm not."

"Fair enough. Now it makes perfect sense. I guess I'm just used to dealing with a different kind." She nodded her head toward the parking lot, where Brad sat, likely still trying to convince the other cop that this was all just a misunderstanding.

Toby seemed to relax beside her now, or he sensed she needed to, and he snaked his purring self around her ankles. She responded by bending down and giving him a little scratch under his chin. Then she regarded the cop. "I hope you're not too Zen to toss Brad into a cell with the aforementioned Big Stanley."

"Might be Bubba tonight. I think they released Big Stanley last week." The officer gave a quiet chuckle that turned to focused resolve. "Don't worry, Ms. Brooks. I'll channel the five generations of Irish cops from my dad's side of the family on this one."

She smiled now too, and it was genuine this time. It felt good.

"Thank you, Officer—sorry, I forgot your name."

"Harris," he replied. "Here, take this. In case you need anything, have questions."

She accepted his card, glancing down at it before slipping it into her sweater pocket. "Thanks."

"Not to worry, just—"

"If you say just doing my job, ma'am, you may have to take back the bit about not being cliché."

His warm laughter caused Toby to glance up and narrow his yellow eyes in scrutiny.

"Tough crowd. I was going to say just give me a minute to go grab something from the car to cover up the hole in this window." He jacked a thumb toward the parking lot.

"Oh. That's good too." Lilli smiled. "It's cold out there and Toby and I would really appreciate that."

"Just doing my job, ma'am." He tipped his chin in a small nod and the serious expression he wore melted into a grin as he turned to leave.

As she watched him disappear into the darkness, a tiny clawing at her foot earned her attention. She looked down to see Toby blinking up at her. "Yes, he is cute, Toby. And funny. But I think I have to go with bachelor number one." She bent and picked him up, then filled her lungs with the chilly air, thinking of Jake and the kiss that started all this mess. "Assuming he still wants me after he finds out how far Brad is willing to go to try to stop us from being together."

Officer Harris stepped through the door with some thick plastic wrap and a roll of tape. Lilli watched as he quickly sealed out the Seattle night air.

"Tomorrow, you should give the property manager a call. If he gives you any grief about fixing the door, pass him my number."

She nodded.

"And get him to install a better lock while he's here replacing the glass. A single woman living on the ground floor—seems justified."

"I will. Thanks again."

A small reminder of their earlier interaction came through in the smile he offered before he turned to leave, his parting words trailing behind him as he stepped through the open french door. "Be the bamboo."

She gave him a thumbs-up and watched him stride out to the car. Lilli latched the door, resisting the urge to peek out at Brad for fear he was looking at her.

What a night it had been—the glamorous excitement of celebrating New Year's Eve with Cassie and Charlie at the Four Seasons, the memorable experience of being slapped in the face by a famous actress with a jealous streak, the horrible encounter in the ladies room, and the toe tickling from that tantalizing kiss. All of this punctuated with the exclamation point that was Brad's slip into insanity.

She didn't want to believe that Brad was capable of hurting her, but the way he'd acted was more than a mood swing from steroids. Something was going on with him—but what?

"It's not my job to figure that out, Toby. I really need to stop trying to fix everything." Lilli groaned and then placed a kiss on Toby's head, pulling him with her as she sunk back onto the sofa, running her hand down his silky back. He meowed his protest as her fingers tugged on his tangled fur again. She released the twisted patch and rubbed him softly on the head. "I'm sorry. I didn't mean to take it out on you."

As he jumped to the floor, Lilli's eye was drawn down to a rock, about the size of a baseball, which had come to rest under the coffee table, an irrefutable tribute to Brad's instability.

Toby noticed it too and slunk over, stalking it as if it were prey. After a couple of sniffs he apparently decided it wasn't worthy of his regard and he padded toward the hall, heading to the bedrooms. He stopped only long enough to cast a questioning glance her way.

"All right, kitty, let's go to bed."

She stood and stepped over to the table, bending down to pick up the rock, setting it on the shelf beside the TV. There were no words. She flipped the lights off and followed Toby to bed.

CHAPTER SEVEN

OFFICER HARRIS STRODE out to the car, shaking his head. She was a pretty girl. Seemed smart too. Here he was—a good catch if his mother did say so herself—and he was very single, and yet idiots like this numbskull sitting in the back of his cruiser were getting women like Lilli Brooks and then treating them like shit. Made no sense. How a guy could win the girlfriend lottery and then totally blow his good fortune making dumbass choices was beyond him. But Brian was fine with that. He'd rather be a good guy, spending too many nights alone, than a badass fool on his way to lockdown.

He slowed his pace as he neared the door. He could see Montgomery turned around in her seat, a wash of determination dulling the glow that usually radiated from her. After three years as partners he knew to hang back and let her work her angle. It was funny though, how different they appeared. Physically he was the burly, stoic-looking one—six foot two, blond hair, blue-gray eyes. Her features, on the other hand, were an ambiguous mix of her mother's Hawaiian ancestry and her father's Scottish one. Dark skin, light eyes, gorgeous enough to be a runway model in spite of her efforts to downplay that beauty while on the job.

She'd spent the first five years of her life on the islands, moving to New York city with her parents in time to start grade one. So, while he had taken on his mother's spiritual philosophies, Monty was a New York girl through and through. They were polar opposites emotionally. He was out taking yoga classes to unwind, and she was on the firing range equal times per week, perfecting her aim and blowing off steam.

But mentally, that's where they clicked. They might use different techniques to read people and situations, but they usually came to the same conclusions.

And right now, she was working her magic with the guy in the back seat. Brian was making his own assessments from outside the vehicle, reading Vanderson's face and body, gauging his energy. The guy was insecure. That was obvious. He might look like he fell off the pages of GQ, but inside this guy was something else. The type that knew how to get the girl but had no idea how he'd done it, and then sabotaged himself at every turn until he managed to convince her that he was as worthless as he believed himself to be.

Montgomery's eyes shot up to make contact, and Brian took that as his cue. He opened the driver's door and leaned in, toward Vanderson. "So, has Officer Montgomery convinced you of the error of your ways?"

He turned to Brian, his eyes narrowing as if he were trying to determine the meaning. Then he pinched his lips into a straight line and leaned back with a crossed-arm shrug, offering a mumble that sounded like *I don't know*, but without any consonants, only vowels.

Brian slid into the seat and secured his seatbelt, turning to his partner. "He that talkative with you?"

She turned forward, snapping her seatbelt into place. "More."

CHAPTER EIGHT

MORNING HAD COME too soon for Lilli. It would have arrived much sooner though, if she hadn't muted both her telephones the night before. As she erased Brad's last message—he'd left three, two from a number she didn't recognize and one from his cell—she set the phone down, and sat in shock as her morning coffee churned in her stomach.

She placed a hand on her belly and rubbed, trying to coax the feeling away.

In his messages, he hadn't sounded like the crazed maniac who'd scared the hell out of her the night before. He'd sounded like a sad, lost little boy.

She thought about his words.

He was sorry. He loved her. He'd overreacted. His mind was racing and he couldn't make it stop. No he wasn't back on the juice, but he was scared and he wanted her help.

What was she supposed to do? Hadn't she just sworn to Toby that it wasn't her job to fix Bradley?

She threaded her fingers into her hair and pushed it off her face before sighing and slumping down on her folded arms on the dining table. "Why am I feeling like the bad guy? What is wrong with me?"

She looked to Toby for reassurance, but her questions went unanswered, except for a soft mew.

"Well, you're no help, Toby." She stared at her phone and began to dial. The call was answered after three rings. She sucked in the deepest breath she could, then spoke. "Hi, it's me. Can you come over?"

"THOUGHT YOU'D WANT THIS."

They were pulling an early shift after a late one. His partner sauntered in with two venti Starbucks and took a sip of one as she handed him the other. "Crap." Monty scrunched up her face, then reached out. "Gimme that. This one's yours. I don't know how you can drink that stuff when there are perfectly good espresso-based beverages available."

Brian extended the cup and took the other one with a grin. "Green tea is good for you. You should try it sometime, Beatrice."

She scowled over the rim of her cup.

"Okay, okay." He raised his hands, insinuating it was an innocent mistake. "What I meant to say is you should try it sometime, Montgomery."

"Now you're going all formal on me again. The list of allowable names may be small, but you know it well—Bea, Montgomery, Monty is always good, but never Beatrice. It makes me sound matronly."

He chuckled. "Matronly you ain't." Brian raised his cup in salutation before taking a big gulp.

She nodded her agreement then licked a dollop of whipped cream from her macchiato. "God, that's good." She scraped a chair across the floor and positioned herself in front from him. "So, you looked deep in thought when I came in. What's up?"

He leaned back and laced his hands behind his head. "Do you ever have those days where you wonder why you became a cop?"

"Yeah, Bri, we all do."

"Well, what do you do about it? You ever want to quit? Just give up and go meditate at the summit of Haleakalā?"

"Um, no. Dude, I'm not into climbing volcanoes—Hawaii or not. That's dangerous."

"Then enlighten me. What is the Montgomery Plan B?"

"Come on. You know. I wanna join the feds."

"'Cause that's not dangerous." He scoffed and rolled his eyes as he took a swig of his tea.

"You've got your thing. I've got mine. Now," she tapped her finger on the desk, "tell me what brought this on today? I mean, besides having to fill in for Tucker and McElroy?"

"THANKS FOR COMING BY." Lilli moved aside as Annie stepped through the door into the apartment.

Annie acknowledged the comment with a hug. "Always. You know that." She set her purse on the floor then slung her coat over the hook beside the door.

The two women made their way into the living room and settled on the sofa while Toby perched on the floor and stared at Annie.

"I don't think your cat likes me, Lilli."

"Nonsense, Annie. He just senses you're more of a dog person."

"Call it what you will. At best, he tolerates me. Remember that time you went to your folks' place and I came by to water your plants?"

"He was being a guard cat."

"He almost ate me." She giggled.

"Now you're exaggerating."

Annie pinched her fingers close together and grinned. "Maybe a little, but next time you go away you're going to have to put cat duties on one of the other girls. Now, tell me everything."

Lilli picked up Toby and held him on her lap, stroking his fur as she told her friend everything that had happened the night before. Annie said she was shocked but not surprised, then asked Lilli what she was going to do.

"I don't know, Annie. Why do I have this nagging cloud of self-doubt hanging over me?"

"It's not your fault, Lilli."

"Maybe it is, Annie. All my life I've been like a magnet. Stray cats and dogs were always following me home. Sometimes they even showed up right at my door. Maybe I've just graduated to stray humans."

Annie grinned. "Your words, not mine. But he's only one stray human, so it's not a pattern. Yet."

Lilli let her eyes wander around the room. "What if I told you there was more than one?"

"More than one stray human?" Annie grinned again.

"I'm going later to see this Starbucks barista that I knocked out at the Four Seasons last night."

Annie's eyes went wide. "You did what now?"

"Long story. It was a misunderstanding. Anyway, they took her to the hospital, and I'm going to visit her."

The phone rang and Lilli glanced at the call display. It was a number she did not recognize, so she answered with hesitation.

"Ms. Brooks?"

"Yes, speaking." She darted a quick glance to Annie.

"Ms. Brooks, this is Officer Brian Harris, Seattle PD. How are you today?"

Looking at Annie she mouthed the word *police*, then replied into the phone, "I'm all right. Still shaken up, I suppose. He left me three voice messages—Brad did."

Did she just hear Officer Harris sigh?

"There's no easy way to tell you this."

There was that sigh again.

"He was released sometime between the end of last night's shift and the start of this one. I heard through the grapevine that his father has some contacts at the DA's office. I'm not too pleased about it either."

"I can't believe he got bail so quickly."

"He didn't."

"But you said he's out of jail, and one of his calls was from his cell so—"

"Not bail. They dropped all charges."

"What?"

"I'm sorry. If he threatened you in those messages—"

"Actually, it was the opposite. He apologized. Said he loves me."

"I can't tell you what to do, Ms. Brooks, but I will suggest you don't rush into anything."

"I won't."

"If it's any consolation, I don't think he will try B&E again. He may not have been locked up long, but Bubba or no Bubba, I don't think he wants to repeat the experience anytime soon."

LILLI SANK BACK into the sofa, setting the phone down beside her.

Annie gestured toward it. "He's out isn't he? I got that much from your side." She flopped back, laced her arms across her chest and her ankles on the coffee table, shooting a glare toward Lilli. "I know what you're thinking and you can't do it."

"Do I have a big sign painted across my forehead or something?"

"No." Annie smiled. "It's just a little sign, but I can read it clearly and you're not going to get caught up with Brad again."

"But, Annie—"

"What? He needs you? No one else can fix him? Uh-uh. New year. New you, Lilli. He's unstable and you have to get away."

"Easier said than done."

"I know how to change that."

"Enlighten me."

"You need a new man. Or, better yet, an existing man. Mr. Epic Kiss."

"Jake?" Lilli thought about that for a moment. "I don't even know if he'll speak to me after he finds out how crazy Brad is."

"You won't know if you don't try."

Lilli glanced around the room. While there were no longer any signs of Brad's attempted B&E—at least the manager had seen quickly to the broken windowpane—the feeling of it remained.

Annie followed Lilli's eyes. "You need to think of your safety too, Lil. You may think you know Brad, but we can never truly know what someone is capable of. And, since the building won't let you get a Rottweiler, how about the human equivalent?"

"Are you referring to 'the pit-bull'—Jake's college nickname?"

"Rottweiler, pit-bull…same thing. It all adds up to two hundred and whatever pounds of Brad repellant."

"Maybe you're right. Why don't we go out tonight?"

"Can't. Bill has, finally, offered to cook for me."

"Took him long enough. How many weeks in?"

"Too many. Maybe he was secretly taking cooking classes."

"At least you know the new man can cook."

"*Claims* he can cook." Annie laughed. "If I don't end up with food poisoning, he's definitely a keeper. You should call him."

"Bill?"

"No. Jake, silly."

ANNIE LEFT TO GET ready for her date with Bill, but only after she'd made Lilli promise to call Jake—even though she'd doubted that Lilli would follow through. And she'd been right.

In spite of her affirmation to the contrary, Lilli knew she would chicken out too. She had called Cassie and Charlie to see what they were doing, hoping to get in to a private party at Trinity nightclub. It was being hosted by one of the agency's top clients and Lilli had the idea she might cross paths with Jake—easier than having to call him—but they'd both been busy.

Lilli plopped down on the sofa and sighed. Toby meowed, and, in Lilli's mind, he was judging her for giving up so easy.

She contemplated him and the situation. "Listen, Toby, it's not that simple. You know that. I don't like those types of challenges, okay."

He looked away, disinterested now, and began grooming himself.

About to open her laptop to check her email, Lilli snatched up her cell just as it chirped Annie's ringtone. "What did you forget? Or did you change your mind about going out with me?"

"Look out your window."

"What? Why?"

"Just do it, Lilli."

At the patio door, her eyes skimmed the rows of parked cars, searching for Annie. There she was, standing beside her Toyota. Lilli did a double-take, flashing to the other side of the lot. "Is that—"

"In the flesh."

"Shut the f—"

"Front door," Annie supplied. "And the back door too. Then lock it."

"Tell me I'm seeing things, Annie."

"Well, you are seeing things, but the thing you're seeing is Brad—with a truckload of moving boxes."

"Maybe he's helping a friend."

"He's alone, Lil. I'm sure of it. That's what took me so long to call. I watched for a few minutes to make sure."

Lilli stepped backward, away from the window, and sank onto the sofa. "What am I going to do?"

"Call Jake, that's what."

"Right. Call Jake."

"Listen, I gotta go, Lil."

"Go. I'm fine."

"Yeah right. But hey, I wasn't entirely joking before when I said to lock the doors."

"Don't worry. I will. I did."

"You sure you're okay?"

"Yes, Annie. Go enjoy your date with Bill."

They said their good-byes and Lilli went to draw her curtains. Peering out through a small opening, she studied Brad, hoisting a box up and out of the moving truck. Now what? What would stop him from harassing her every day if he wanted? Jake would, Lilli supposed, but still, she wasn't ready to cold-call him. Her options were limited.

Brad had made this decision. So, Lilli made the next.

She caught sight of him plodding toward the main entrance to the building next door and she ducked back behind the curtain, tugging them all the way closed, before he saw her too. She snatched up her purse, deciding to sneak out and go to the hospital to see Donna. At least that would clear one thing off her cluttered mind.

CHAPTER NINE

SHE ARRIVED AT the hospital with flowers and fashion magazines in hand. Lilli approached the main reception desk and inquired about Donna, realizing she didn't even know her last name. She went with honesty and told the nurse what had happened and that she was there to apologize.

The woman looked sympathetic as she scanned the computer for women named Donna fitting the time of admission and injury type that Lilli had described.

After a few moments she gazed back to Lilli. "I'm sorry, miss. It seems she was released first thing this morning."

Lilli regarded the flowers in her hand and was about to hand them to the nurse when she remembered that Bucky was "sort of related" to Donna. She knew where to find him, and maybe she could convince him to tell her where to find Donna.

LILLI NEARED THE gym and pulled into an empty lot. Empty except for a single weary-looking minivan, parked near the back. Right. The gym was closed until after the holidays. As she turned around to head home, she caught sight of a man in her rearview mirror. He was loading things from out of the van.

New year. New Lilli.

She took the chance, did a reverse one-eighty, and now faced the gym's back door. She approached a mid-twenties, fit-looking fellow, whose left eye was almost as black as his hair. He stopped what he was doing and studied her. She hesitated, briefly, as she rolled her window down, wondering if he was safe. An older version, minus the black eye, stepped out the door, heading toward the van. He too stopped and stared at Lilli.

Through the open window she asked if Bucky was around.

On his way inside, the young version jacked his head toward the older version, whose face lit into a smile, his cheeks balling into rosy globes.

"If someone else is lookin' then Bucky ain't around, but if it's a pretty thing like you doin' the askin'...well, you just found him." He set the boxes down, dusted his hands together, and then extended one toward her. "Bucky Burks. Nice to meet you."

She met his handshake, firmly as her father had taught her, unable to resist smiling back at him. "Lilli Brooks. Nice to meet you too."

Grinning, Bucky pulled back his hand, shaking it as if she had crushed it. "Strong handshake you got there. Ever do any boxing?"

"The only boxing I've done is packing and unpacking them." He chuckled at that, and Lilli continued. "Although, in a roundabout way, I'm looking for you today because I was interested in taking some classes."

Bucky raised an eyebrow urging her to give more information.

"I came by here the other day looking to sign up, only to realize you were closed for the holidays. So, I did the next best thing—I grabbed a latte at Starbucks."

"Best coffee there is," Bucky said.

"Agreed."

"Now, explain to me how that led you here today?"

"Oh, well, I ran into your—I'm not sure what she is exactly but she said you were related. Her name's Donna."

Bucky scratched his chin. "Oh, you mean the Parker girl."

The Parker girl?

"I suppose she's sort of like family, all right. Knew her father, trained him back in the day. Shame about that whole situation." Bucky lowered his shaking head a moment. "Years later she started hanging around here. Wanted to learn to box. The girl looked like a puppy that had been left out in the rain—couldn't turn her away. I traded boxing lessons for her help around the gym. Haven't seen that much of her lately though, come to think of it. Course she's come and gone a few times over the years. Didn't think much of it."

"She..." Lilli pushed herself through the hesitation, "Donna was admitted to the hospital last night."

"Which one? I suppose I should go see her."

"Actually," Lilli began, "they sent her home this morning. I went to visit but she was gone. I was hoping you could tell me where she lives." Lilli reached over and lifted the flowers off the passenger seat. "I was hoping to bring her these. It's my fault she was in there."

The former boxer stepped back, assessing her.

"I didn't mean to, but I knocked her out cold."

He jabbed his finger toward her. "See, I knew I recognized a boxer under all that blond hair." Bucky gazed at the backs of her hands. "No bruises on the knuckles. You're not wearing enough makeup to cover up a black eye."

"It wasn't a boxing match, Mr. Burks. It was a door, a bathroom stall door, to be precise. And it was not intentional. I feel horrible."

"I believe that you do. I can read any face. Learned it in the ring. All right. I'll point you in the right direction. I'm sure the girl could use a friend. If she has any problem with it you can send her to me."

He disappeared inside the gym and returned moments later with Donna's address scribbled on a scrap of paper. "I'm not sure which apartment it is, but her name is likely on the buzzer."

"Thanks again, Mr. Burks."

"Bucky'll do. Mr. Burks was my dad."

"Thanks, Bucky." She set the paper on top of her purse, then began to roll up the window, stopping when he leaned in.

"You make sure to come back and schedule those lessons soon. Ask for me and I'll give you a fair price."

LILLI TURNED OFF the engine and checked the address Bucky had given her. She sent her gaze to the building number and affirmed she was in the right place. She inhaled deeply and blew the breath out with a puff. While it was true she hated putting herself out there in situations like this, it was more true that she couldn't shirk anything that she felt responsibility for. This left her with one choice. Lilli opened the Jeep and climbed out, tugging down on her jacket and then reaching for the flowers and magazines.

She ascended the stairs and ran her finger along the rows of names looking for Donna's. She found it but did not immediately press the buzzer located beside D Parker. "If only she was still in the hospital," she mumbled, then shook her head. That didn't come out right. She didn't wish more injury on the girl. She only wished not to have to deal with being a disembodied voice speaking through an apartment intercom system.

Lilli silently rehearsed what she would say—not that she hadn't already played it through her mind three dozen times or more on the drive over. *Hey, Donna, it's Lilli Brooks. You know, the nut-job that knocked you out when you went for a pee.* She chuckled a little at that version. At least that one felt honest. After a big sigh, Lilli lifted her hand toward the buzzer, just as someone breezed past her. And there was her answer—a young guy in full Seattle-grunge apparel holding the door wide open.

Perfect. At least her guardian angel was on duty today. Now she could make her way to the apartment and knock, not having to worry about identifying herself without the visual aid of being live and in person.

She smiled and thanked the fellow, and then planted a foot in front of the door while she feigned fussing with the items she carried in order to shoot a quick glance at the name panel again to make sure she had the right apartment number.

He held the elevator door for her, but she shook her head, saying she would take the stairs. She needed more time, and a little space, to psyche herself up for this. About halfway up, she began to regret her choice. She could have let him go and then waited for the elevator to come back down. Now she was out of breath and beginning to perspire in her heavy winter jacket.

Lilli sat down on one of the stairs, taking a big lungful of air, wondering why she always seemed to complicate things for herself. She undid the top few buttons on her coat and loosened her scarf. That was better. Lilli played a silent mantra inside her head. She could handle this. Besides, her other choice was to go home and deal with the fact that Brad was moving in next door.

That thought caused her to let out a groan and shake her head. But after a few more gulps of air she began to relax. Just as she stood to recommence her stair climbing she heard the dull thud of a door a couple of floors above. For a moment her heart skipped, feeling trapped in the stairwell, but then she talked herself into the fact that it was just some random person who likely lived in the building but probably wouldn't recognize that she didn't.

She began climbing, ready to smile and acknowledge the person as if they were just two neighbors passing in the stairwell. Whoever it was had more momentum heading down than she did going up and they were making faster progress. Lilli stilled herself as she heard the footfalls stop one flight up.

Lilli held her breath, waiting. After a brief vibrating sound she heard a voice and Lilli cocked her head, focusing on listening. It was a woman's voice, muffled but Lilli could tell she had answered her phone.

Now what? She felt frozen to her spot. She didn't want to linger there, eavesdropping, as the person would eventually keep descending and would see her there, knowing she'd been listening. On the other hand, she didn't want to turn around and head back down or keep going forward.

As she debated with herself, the voice above grew louder with a tone of agitation. Lilli was drawn back into the conversation.

"I said I can't talk right now. A bunch of stupid stuff has set me back. My plans are ruined. Never mind what plans. Just leave me alone. You don't understand." The conversation ended abruptly and footfalls set to a brisk jog began reverberating off the walls.

Lilli quickly adjusted her things and tried to appear as if she had just arrived on the landing. She looked down, only briefly, to make sure she didn't trip, and she slammed straight into the girl who had been on the phone.

The magazines and flowers flew from her arms, and Lilli twisted her ankle, then reached out to grasp the railing.

"Crap."

"Ouch!"

"Lilli?"

"Donna?"

AFTER AN EXPLANATION about how she'd come to apologize, and then an apology for coming to apologize—or, at least, for taking the coward's way out, sneaking in rather than just using the intercom, Lilli finally allowed herself to breathe.

Donna set a glass of iced tea down on the table in front of Lilli. "I'd offer you coffee, but—"

"You don't drink it. I remember. This is fine." She picked it up and took a sip, smiling politely. "It's more than I deserve after assaulting you twice in as many days." She looked around the apartment. It was, at once, both not what she expected and yet not a surprise. On the one hand it looked as if Donna had attempted to decorate and organize, some of her things reminding Lilli of her own possessions, which she hadn't expected. But on the other, the place was a mess, which didn't surprise her. Not after the way Donna had looked on the day they'd met—while not unkempt per se, she'd been, at best, a little rough around the edges.

"I like your bookshelves," Lilli said.

"Thanks. They're new." Donna smiled and gazed around the room. "Actually, most of this stuff is. I went shopping at IKEA the other day."

Lilli nodded her agreement. "I have a lot of the same things in my place too. I almost always leave IKEA with an armful of stuff I don't need but desperately want." She laughed. "I'm pretty sure that's why they have it set up like a maze. The longer you spend in there, the more you fall under their evil Swedish spell."

Donna got up from her spot on the sofa and went to adjust some knick-knacks on the bookshelf, turning two wooden human figures to face each other. "So," she started, "do you have plans tonight?"

How should she answer that? While she did want to go out—and hopefully run into Jake—she didn't know this girl very well. The thought of them going out together felt awkward. She couldn't picture Donna fitting in at Trinity. Maybe if Lilli did her makeup...

Oh, what the hell. She didn't want to go home and deal with Brad. How bad could it be hanging out with Donna for one night?

Lilli mentioned the party at Trinity, and Donna's face lit up like the harbor had on New Year's Eve, reflecting all the fireworks.

"Count me in!"

"Are you sure you should be going out after just getting released from the hospital?" Lilli asked.

"Yes. It's exactly what I need."

She couldn't argue with that. "How about nine?"

"Nine's good, but I can be ready sooner."

Lilli raised a hand. "Maybe you can be ready sooner, but I can't. I need the works. It's Trinity. I want to look my best."

"How hard can that be?" Donna chuckled. "Have you seen you?"

"Good genetics."

"As if you don't know the effect you have on people, Lilli. I've seen them looking at you—at Starbucks. Men want to have you and women want to hurt you."

"An illusion. Remember? I'm a makeup artist."

"You wake up perfect—I mean, you must. Like right now, you're really not wearing that much makeup, and look at you. If you weren't my new best friend, I might hate you too."

Donna laughed at her comment, but there was a tinge of something in her voice that made Lilli feel uncomfortable. She didn't know how to reply.

There were a few awkward seconds of silence before Donna spoke again. "Teasing, of course. I could never hate you. There's something special about you, Lilli. I sensed it when I first saw you. And when you showed up today, I knew it was true. Not many people would go out of their way like this."

EVERYTHING HAD WORKED out after all. Lilli had managed to apologize to Donna as well as find an excuse to go out looking for Jake. And, as she stood there now, she didn't just have butterflies in her stomach, she had a swarm of angry wasps buzzing around.

Tonight Trinity was hosting a special event—a client's private party. She had to believe Jake would be there. Everything was falling into place.

She glanced away from the mirror toward the windows, wondering what Brad was up to. No. She refused to give him any more power over her life. It was time to move on. Maybe everything with Donna was meant to be. If it weren't for what happened then she would not be going out with her tonight. "You see, Toby, everything happens for a reason. Tonight I will find out my reason."

The closest thing she got to a reply was a single outstretched paw, followed by a twitch of whiskers.

She resumed her stance at the mirror, fussing until her makeup was perfect. She twisted her blond mane into a tousled up-do, regarded her reflection, then pulled out the hair pins and shook her hair loose. Too formal. She wanted to appear carefree, easy-going. She gently teased the top and back with her fingers then sprayed it into place, appraising her image once again.

"That'll do."

Lilli wandered to her closet and rifled through the clothes. She needed the perfect outfit too. The one that would make Jake's jaw drop. The churning anticipation tangled her up in memories of their kiss, her thoughts wrapping her in tingly remembrance as she sampled various outfits.

The melodic jingle coming from her phone beckoned Lilli back to the real world, real time. She shot a glance at the clock. It was nine seventeen. She was late. Donna was likely already pacing.

She skipped over and snatched her cell phone off the dresser, pressing the *Talk* button reflexively just as she realized it was Brad. She could hang up without saying hello but he'd probably just call back, so she sucked it up, groaning loudly. "What do you want?"

"I've got a surprise for you."

He hadn't seemed to register the impatience in her greeting, and she wasn't about to let on that she knew about his move. "I don't have time right now, Brad."

"Guess who just moved in next door?" Brad chuckled as if he were the only one in on the joke of the year.

"Charles Manson?"

His laughing subsided. "That's a dark place, Lilli, real dark."

"The point."

"Prince Charming moved in, that's who. Look out the window and wave, baby."

"At Prince Charming? I don't believe in fairytales, Brad."

"At me, Lilli. Look out the window and wave at me. I'm your new neighbor."

Lilli responded with silence. What could she say?

"Nothing? What gives?"

"That's what I was wondering."

"Huh?"

"Nothing." Lilli *pfff'd* at an errant strand of hair that had fallen over her eye. "Fine. Welcome to the neighborhood. I'm fresh out of house warming gifts, though, so…"

"I guess I won't ask you to help me unpack then. You know, since you have no time."

"Thanks." Lilli regarded the black leather skirt she'd earlier discarded for being impractical, based on weather conditions. On second thought, it would actually do just fine. All she needed was the right pair of boots. "Speaking of which…"

"If I didn't know better, I'd think you were trying to get rid of me tonight."

"I can honestly say I am not trying to get rid of you *tonight*."

Lilli disconnected the call without waiting for a good-bye. What she'd said was true. She was actually trying to get rid of him for much longer than one night. She snatched her leather skirt off the bed and shimmied into it, then groaned as she surveyed her bedroom. She had tried on almost everything in her closet and now the space resembled the backstage area after a fashion show. Clothes were strewn about everywhere—and so were shoes, handbags, dresses, jackets, and pretty much all the new secrets she'd purchased from Victoria after her other ones had vanished without a trace of lace. No time to deal with that now.

She slipped a turquoise crocheted sweater over a black Lycra tank top and stepped back to gauge the effect in the mirror. It caressed her curves with a lover's touch. Perfect.

Now, where had her black leather over-the-knee Jimmy Choo boots landed?

She spied one peeking out from under a mountain of clothes. She pulled on the heel, shaking it free from the pile, then slid it on and zipped it up. Toby eyed her with curiosity as she hobbled across the room to get the other from under the bed.

After she added a handmade turquoise necklace and silver hoop earrings, Lilli took one last look in the full-length mirror. She nodded her affirmation, grabbed her purse and tossed her phone, lipstick, and wallet inside, then snapped off the bedroom light.

Lilli would text Donna from the Jeep to say she was on her way. Why give Brad extra time to complicate things? She grabbed her keys, said farewell to Toby, and zipped out the door.

SCANNING THE COURTYARD and parking lot, Brad was nowhere to be seen. Her heels ticking along the pavement, she scurried to her Jeep, pressing the key fob as she went. She grabbed the door handle with force, but her hand slipped back, catching the french tip of her nail. She shook off the slicing nerve pain and pushed the unlock button again. Hearing the chirp, she tried the door once more, this time, thrusting it wide and tossing her purse onto the passenger seat.

Just about to step up, she heard the low whistle coming from behind. Her shoulders dropped in silent defeat. Had he been hiding in the bushes waiting to pounce?

"Looking good, babe." Brad was right behind her now, wrapping his arms around her waist, pulling her close, pressing his considerable appreciation into her backside. "Pretty dolled-up tonight."

Annoyed, she jerked her hips back, shoving him away, then she spun to face him. "Hands off, Brad."

He chuckled. "News flash, princess—that wasn't my hands."

"Well, you shouldn't be touching me with *that* either. Friends, Brad. No benefits."

"My friendship comes with plenty of benefits, all of which you are very well acquainted with, I might add." He jacked his brows up and down, a gleam reflecting off his steel-blue eyes as his gaze wandered from the top of her blond locks to the tip of her Jimmy Choos.

She resisted grumbling, instead giving him a brief dissertation on how she was running late, friends were waiting, yadda, yadda, yadda.

Finally taking his cue, he stepped back, palms raised, gesturing he would be hands off.

Lilli seized her opportunity and hopped into the Jeep, taking the word multitasking to a new level as she turned the key while simultaneously snapping her seatbelt into place with her left hand. Then, as if accentuating her resolve, she gave it a little too much gas, spitting a deluge of gravel as she spun off.

She shot a glance into the rearview. Seeing Brad's arm raised, shielding his face, she felt guilty—she hadn't meant to gun the engine like that. Her heart twisted as she looked at him, standing there, hand to his chest, as if mortally wounded.

She sighed and placated him with a counterfeit smile and a genuine wave.

CHAPTER TEN

THE STIFF SUSPENSION of the Jeep lumbered over the speed bumps as Lilli pulled up to Donna's building for the second time that day. Relieved to see the girl waiting in front, Lilli honked twice to get her attention.

Donna breezed up, her face painted with a mixture of angst and excitement. She gave Lilli a once-over through the open door, her face melting into full-on angst. "I thought I looked okay." She appraised herself. "Considering I'm not exactly an experienced makeup wearer, but now that I see you...you look amazing, Lilli. I feel like the Ugly Duckling."

Lilli studied Donna and her outfit. "The dress is nice," she said of the simple black tank dress that Donna wore, which earned a half-smile. "The hair looks good too. Simple." Three-quarter smile. She raised her eyes to look at Donna's makeup. "I suppose I could help you with the makeup."

Full smile, excitement radiating unabated. "Would you? Oh, Lilli, that would be awesome. Should we go inside?"

"No. I can do it here. It's bright enough with the inside lights and you can flip down the visor. There's an illuminated mirror there."

Donna did that, and Lilli fished in her gym bag behind the seat. She had a travel case of spare cosmetics for after her workouts. She slid back into the driver's seat and unzipped the bag.

Donna had removed her glasses and turned to Lilli, eyes closed and ready to begin. Her eagerness flowed out of her as she held her position, allowing Lilli to dust shadow onto her eyelids, blush onto her cheeks. After a bit of charcoal eyeliner, a swipe of mascara, and a deep-plum lip color, Lilli announced she was finished.

"Can I look?" Donna asked.

"Of course." Lilli smiled at Donna's childlike wonder. She supposed makeup was rather foreign to the girl, and imagined herself at nine when her mother had allowed her to wear colored lip-gloss for the first time. "Our little secret," her mother had whispered, meaning *don't tell your father I let you do this because he already thinks you are growing up too fast.*

"One, two, three," Donna counted, then shot her eyes open and turned to the mirror on the visor. She studied her face for a full minute before speaking. "Wow. I don't recognize myself, Lilli." She turned this way and that, never taking her eyes off her reflection. "I just can't believe it. I actually look pretty."

Trying not to smile, Lilli had to admit she had done a good job. The old Donna was practically unrecognizable underneath the color pallet on her face now. This was what Lilli loved most about being a makeup artist—the reveal. It never ceased to excite her when someone was this impressed with her efforts. Working with models she seldom received this kind of reward. They all knew they were pretty and expected nothing less than stunning when she was through. But this, this felt good. It felt as if she'd actually done something significant, changed someone's life for the better.

"Thanks." Donna stole her eyes away from the mirror long enough to glance at Lilli. Her face broke into a smile that balled her cheeks into rosy globes and danced right into her eyes. "I mean it, Lilli. Thank you so much. I never ever dreamed I could look like this. I mean—" the grin faltered and her eyes dimmed, "well, I'll never be as beautiful as you are, but…"

"Nonsense. True beauty is on the inside, Donna." Lilli buckled up, then shifted into gear. "Ready?"

Donna snapped her belt on too and settled back, not flipping the visor up. "I'm a whole lifetime of ready."

"All right then, let's go." Lilli flashed a look over her shoulder then began pulling out and navigating her way into traffic. "It's going to be a great night. I can feel it."

"I hear the DJ at the club is awesome," Donna said. "His name is Jeff something-or-other. I saw his picture on the website. He's cute. Maybe I'll even try flirting with him tonight."

"He is." Lilli reached into the console between the seats. "And I happen to have a mix-CD. Here. Put it in the stereo."

"Oh. I didn't realize—you've met him already. Did you two…you know, date or something?"

Lilli slanted a glance at her, feeling as though she should have kept her trap shut. Time to backtrack. "Date? No, not at all. I ran into him at the mall last week. I think he just happened to have a bunch of discs in his car, so he gave me one. No biggie." Smiling, she moved the CD case closer to Donna. "Go ahead. Put it in. I think you'll like it."

Donna's eyes were locked on Lilli's profile—she could feel them piercing the space between them. She reached out, hesitating as she took the CD, then turned her shoulders, and her gaze, toward the window.

Lilli wasn't quite sure how she should deal with this, what she should say, but she was saved—if you could call it that—from having to decide as Donna twisted back toward her.

"Well, there's another guy that won't choose me over you." She darted her eyes at her reflection and then snapped the visor up with a flick of her wrist.

"Come on, Donna, it's not—"

She tossed the disc on the dash and laced her arms across her chest. "Yes it is, Lilli. You're perfect. Once a guy has set his eyes on you, no one else exists. You don't know what it's like to be second best," she looked down, assessing herself, "what it's like to be me." A huff of air rushed out as Donna sank back against the seat, her arms winding around herself. "Never mind. Thanks for trying. I know you mean well. It's not your fault you're flawless."

"I'm not—" Lilli applied the brakes and shifted into neutral as she rolled to a stop at the red light. In tandem, she suppressed the sigh that was pushing at the base of her throat, working on her own neutrality and allowing the breath to escape in a slow deliberate pace.

She looked to Donna to gauge where her mood had shifted to now. She seemed somewhat placated. Lilli breathed her relief and then spoke. "There's a cute bartender. He broke up with his girlfriend last month. He's still pining."

Donna quirked an eyebrow and grinned mischievously. "I guess we'll have to see what we can do about that—and by we, I mean the new me, of course."

WHEN THEY ARRIVED downtown, they drove past Lilli's favorite Pike Place Market and found a spot at Washington & Occidental Parking Lot. They strolled a short distance along Madison, then up Second to Yessler, to the hip and happening Trinity Nightclub.

The two-level, multi-room nightclub was deep in the heart of Seattle's storied first historical neighborhood. Lilli loved the building's architecture, plus, it was surrounded by an eclectic assortment of galleries, shops, eateries, and quirky boutiques.

This was one of Lilli's favorite areas to explore, shop, or just kickback with her friends. Being just a short stroll from CenturyLink Field made it an almost sure thing as far as Jake showing up. Plus, with her favorite coffee shop on, literally, almost every corner, how could she go wrong.

The nightclub itself had something for everyone with three individual, uniquely themed club rooms, plus the VIP Room. Tonight's destination was the Main Room, which Lilli felt was the best place to see Jake.

They stopped in front of the Pioneer Building and eyed the long lineup, which snaked to the corner and around the block. It was even longer today than it was on most Saturday nights. There were a lot of lonely people in Seattle on New Year's Day Lilli supposed.

Donna's face fell to the curb and she gave Lilli a disappointed look. "We'll never get in. Look at how many people are ahead of us."

Lilli grinned and gestured for Donna to follow her as she stepped up to the outside bouncer, an enormous fellow, shaved bald, who everyone affectionately referred to as Bullet Head.

After a brief chat, Bullet Head beamed like a lovesick schoolboy and unhooked the red velvet rope, gesturing the two women into the busy nightclub.

As they sauntered in, he turned to the grumbling crowd and raised his meaty pointer finger to his lips in a shushing motion. No surprise, but the chorus of protests stopped immediately. They all recognized that their collective fate—whether or not they got their party on tonight—was in his hands.

Donna appeared suitably impressed. "That was pretty cool."

"It's all about having the right people on your side."

"I'm glad you're on my side then." Donna turned and looked back at the waiting pack of nightclub dogs as they drooled and begged for their chance to get in. Her face split into a wide smile. "Bet those guys would do almost anything to be in my shoes right now."

Lilli laughed and pulled her friend by the arm, through all the dirty looks, as the pretty red-haired girl at the reception counter took their jackets and waved them through with a smile. Lilli dropped some money into her tip jar, and then her eyes surveyed the massive room. It wasn't even eleven but the celebration was going strong already. The pulsing music filled the air, and the dance floor—one of the largest on the west coast—was packed with the rhythmic twisting of sweaty bodies engaged in the hypnotic ritual of dance.

She didn't bother to look for Jake yet. It was too early. Instead the two women started toward the bar, but a familiar voice behind them stopped Lilli midway.

"If it isn't my favorite flower. Miss Lilli, you do look good enough to—" It was Dante, the tall, dark, super-sexy, and extremely flirtatious front-door attendant, and he left his intention hanging in the air like a promise. He draped his arm around Lilli and pulled her into a hug.

"Hey, Dante." Hesitant, Lilli glanced toward Donna to see how she was reacting. She was gazing all around, as if her eyes wanted to drink in every detail and assimilate it into herself, so Lilli relaxed, allowing Dante to drop a single kiss on her cheek.

He leaned in close and whispered in her ear with his deep, sexy Barry White voice. "You better watch yourself tonight, girl."

A tickling shudder ran the length of her spine as his voice reverberated through her. Her shoulders crept toward her ears and she reached up to rub the shiver from her neck, then she pushed him away playfully.

He snatched her hand, yanking her back, then, biting his bottom lip, he released her to resume his post at the front door.

Lilli tapped Donna on the shoulder. "Come on. Let's get a drink."

"That doorman was kind of like, all over you, Lilli. Doesn't that bother you?"

She waved her hand, dismissing the comment. "Dante's just a flirt. It was nothing."

"It didn't look like nothing. I saw your reaction." She quirked an eyebrow and tilted her head, scrutinizing Lilli a little too closely.

Lilli couldn't really put her finger on the pulse of it. Donna seemed to be a walking ball of confusion. She appeared both unconventional and ordinary, all at once. Lilli took her to be socially inept and attributed her quirks to that.

Donna admired the ornate crystal chandelier hanging over the bar, then her eyes drifted down, a smile returning to her face. "Who is that?"

"That's Joey—the bartender I told you about. The one that just moved here from New York. The one who is recently single."

"Yum." Donna grabbed Lilli's hand and pulled her toward the bar.

Lilli stumbled slightly with the unexpected momentum of Donna's tugging grasp, but quickly fell in stride alongside her. Before they even made it to the counter, Joey was grinning and tossing the cocktail shaker—Lilli's martini, no doubt.

With a flourish of presentation, he handed her the glass—no olive, with a dash of cranberry juice—and turned to Donna. "What'll you have, sexy?"

Donna blushed at the nickname and leaned over the counter to place her order, most assuredly giving Joey a full view of her cleavage.

Joey did what any red-blooded male would do in the same circumstance—he ogled. Then, he produced a vodka cooler, setting it in front of Donna, flipping off the cap with an exaggerated flick. "On the house, ladies."

"Oh my God," Donna stressed each syllable, "he is so hot."

"That he is," Lilli agreed. Then, noticing a thin veil slice across Donna's features, Lilli quickly added, "but he's not my type. He's all yours."

DONNA AND LILLI worked their way to a spot near the base of the elevated DJ booth. As the contagious beats flowed around them, they sipped their drinks and enjoyed people-watching, making observations on what select individuals were, or were not, wearing, fully aware that somewhere on the other side there were probably two other women making observations about them.

After they finished their drinks they fused with the amorphous sway of bodies on the dance floor, chatting above the din. Donna flirted unabashedly with every nearby male, while Lilli kept her eyes open for Jake to saunter in. Late as expected, at eleven fifty-five, he strolled through the back door, flanked by his entourage.

Lilli positioned herself so Jake would notice her immediately, but so she could appear as if she had not seen him. There was nothing wrong with being a little hard to get. Jake seemed as if he was accustomed to having things come to him easily, including—or especially—women. She wanted to be different, more than the next fling.

After making his circuit through the crowded bar, shaking hands, patting backs, allowing everyone to take notice that the great Jake Edwards—Seattle's newest golden boy—was in the house, he came to a halt in front of Lilli.

With hands in pockets and a single upward nod of his head, he offered one word. "Hey."

"Hey back," Lilli replied in her own attempt to conceal the butterflies flitting about in her stomach.

He turned to his friends. "Go get us some drinks." Then a glance at Lilli. "What are you drinking?"

"Martini, with a shot of cran."

Back to his friends. "Get two of those, a couple Stellas, a round of Cuervo, and whatever you guys and the girl want. Tell them it's for me, they'll put it on my tab."

The guys nodded in unison as Donna tugged on Lilli's sleeve. "He was at the party. Isn't he the new quarterback from the Seahawks? You *know* him?"

"Kinda," Lilli whispered, working at aborting the smile that was pulling at her lips. Then, wanting to be alone with Jake she bobbed her head in the direction that Jake's posse was headed. "Two of them plus the bartender…makes for good odds."

Donna picked up Lilli's meaning, her face lighting up as she scurried off to catch up with them.

"So, how are your toes tonight?" Jake said.

"My toes?"

Jake leaned in closer. "Yeah, are they still tingling?"

Lilli's face felt hot with the remembrance of their kiss. She looked down at the tip of her boot as she wiggled her toes inside. How was she going to respond to such a heavily loaded question?

Jake's gaze had followed hers downward. "Nice choice in footwear." He grinned and a mischievous glint played across his features as he leaned back and raked his eyes over her body with the intense deliberation of a hungry lover. "The whole combo really. You got the bad-girl thing going on with the skirt and boots. Then there's the sweater, which hints at a good-girl side, but we can see through it to the top underneath, so the good girl is really more of a suggestion than a statement."

Lilli was both surprised and impressed with his assessment. She'd never known a man to have such detailed observation skills. "That's quite a comprehensive review," she said. "Most men don't pay that much attention."

"Most men don't have someone like you to pay attention to. I mean, how could I ever, willingly, take my eyes off of you?" He broke into a wide smile. "That and the fact that whenever my sister visited she only watched the fashion channel."

"Visited?"

"I guess you don't know. We try to keep it private. She spent time in an institution. She was—I guess I'm supposed to call it *mentally challenged*." He shrugged. "Long story."

"I had no idea."

"Yeah. I kinda took the brunt of my father's stress. I could never please him. But I was big. I was tough. Better me than my mom or my handicapped sister, I guess."

The clouds of emotion that had dusted Jake's face cleared away now, revealing an innocence that endeared him to Lilli even more. She reached out and grazed his fingertips with her own and he smiled at her, just as their friends arrived at the table, followed by a waitress with a huge tray of drinks.

Before she could begin to set the glasses on the table, Jake reached over and snatched a shot glass from the waitress's tray and downed the hit of tequila.

The waitress started to protest, telling Jake he was lucky he hadn't upended the entire tray by messing with the balance, but she stopped abruptly as he tossed a hundred-dollar bill on the tray and gave her a placating smile.

"I guess she's the lucky one tonight," Lilli said.

"No. It's still me." Jake took a long swig of his Stella Artois and then mitigated Lilli's confusion. "Because I have you." He scooted his Nikes close and played footsy with her for a moment before downing the rest of his beer. "Drink up," he said, indicating the shots of tequila.

The guys all grabbed a shot without hesitation while Donna shook her head. "God. That stuff even smells awful. I'll pass."

"More for me." Jake tossed back the shot and handed the last one to Lilli.

She eyed it, shrugged, declined the offer of salt and lime from Jake, then threw the tequila back without flinching.

"Well, all right then." He grinned and grabbed her hand, hauling her onto the dance floor. "Let's dance."

SHE WENT WILLINGLY, although, she dashed a glance at Donna as Jake spirited her away, and her friend didn't appear too impressed with the situation. She felt bad, or, thought she should feel bad, but she was having trouble connecting with that emotion right now. She was far too caught up in the warmth radiating through her that she could only partially attribute to the tequila.

As Lilli danced with Jake she let her eyes wander toward Donna a few times, watching as she took turns talking to each of Jake's buddies. Finally she hit on a winner and Vincenzo followed Donna onto the dance floor.

Good. Now Lilli could relax and enjoy the rush of being this close to Jake, knowing the passion he could stir within her. She watched him move to the music, not really dancing, more like shunting side to side with what could be considered an acceptable amount of rhythm for a man of his size. It made her smile.

Jake shot a glance to the guys at the table, then his hazel eyes settled back on Lilli. "They're keeping an eye on our drinks for us. If you want I can get them to bring them out to us." Then, without waiting for her reply, Jake gestured in a circular motion and his friend Craig scurried over with two drinks and then melted away just as quickly.

He handed Lilli her martini and she took a grateful sip. It was getting warm out there and had it been water she would have guzzled it down.

They slowed the pace of their dancing as they held onto their drinks. Twice Lilli almost ended up wearing hers after being bumped by a couple of gyrating females looking as though they were starving for attention the way they played at sexual innuendo. She decided to gulp it down just to save her designer boots.

Without prompting, Jake did the same and, somehow, Craig showed up and took their empties away as if he'd been on call.

One of her favorite songs came on and Lilli laced her fingers in her hair, moving seductively, as she closed her eyes for a moment, feeling the pulsing beat, and the after burn from the vodka and vermouth, as it moved through her. When she opened them again, it seemed as if all eyes were on them.

Jake pulled her to him and leaned in close to speak into Lilli's ear. "Normally I would say they were staring at me, but, ah," he angled back to study her, "I'm pretty sure it's those sexy moves of yours that has them in awe this time."

The intoxicating combination of alcohol in her veins and pheromones that seemed to be radiating from every pore in Jake's skin had Lilli feeling rebellious. She flashed a wide smile and began to sway her hips to the sultry R&B song. If her goal had been to tempt Jake, he confirmed she'd succeeded when he wrapped one strong arm around her waist and thrust her body to his.

Lilli sucked in a quick breath, gasping, as Jake pushed himself against her, pulling her so close she wasn't sure anyone would be able to see daylight between them.

"That's what you get," his voice whispered into her ear, thick with desire, causing goose bumps to shiver across her skin, "for dancing like that."

"You don't scare me," she murmured back, snaking her hands around his neck, clasping her fingers loosely, allowing their bodies to fuse. The attention of the crowd drifted into the backdrop as their bodies melded together, moving in sensual unison through three more songs before Lilli was drawn back by the wolf-calls coming from the edge of the dance floor.

Jake's friends were whistling and hooting like frat boys at a strip club, while poor Donna looked like a lost and timid rabbit, trying to fit in with the pack of wolves that, at the moment, seemed oblivious to her presence.

"Get a room," Vin hollered, his hands cupped like a bullhorn in front of his mouth.

Those words in particular—the very same ones Brad had uttered the night before—brought Lilli straight back to reality. "Maybe we should get off the dance floor and join them." She tossed her head toward their friends.

Jake leaned down, his beard stubble rasping her neck as he spoke, his voice still heavy with raw sexuality. "Maybe we should get outta here. I got a few rooms we could get into back at my place." He let his palm drift down her spine until it settled on her backside, which he used to hold her in place as he pushed his considerable temptation into the soft flesh of her abdomen.

She brought a hand down from where it had been draped around his neck, using it to fan herself. "Getting hot in here, huh?"

He quirked the corner of his lips into a sly grin, but didn't confirm or deny her observation, instead allowing her to squirm a little longer under his heated gaze.

Her skin moist with perspiration, Lilli ran her fingertips along her forehead to soften the sweat to a dull glow—and to buy time as she recovered from the effects of Jake's brazen hunger.

After not one, but three, deep breaths, she peered up at him. In that moment, something flashed across his eyes, and Lilli could only guess what he was thinking. She swallowed against the thickness in her throat. "As tempting as that offer is, Jake, I, uh…I shouldn't abandon Donna."

His face was blank. "Donna?"

It was at that moment that Lilli realized she had not even introduced Jake officially. Guilt washed over her, pulling her gaze toward her new friend. "I can't believe it. I—shoot—I never introduced you. That's Donna over there. The girl I'm here with. She's the one from last night. The one from the bathroom."

"The one you pulled a Mike Tyson on?"

Lilli groaned at the reference to her knocking Donna out cold. "The very same. I felt bad and I went to check on her today. She seemed to be feeling all right and she wanted to go out tonight. I couldn't argue with that."

Jake raised an eyebrow in question.

"You never know who you might run into at Trinity." Lilli focused her gaze on the floor. When she looked back at Jake he was grinning. "So I better take a rain check on your offer."

"I'll hold you to that." He forced her body tighter against his, causing her to emit a sudden gasp. "The rain check, that is." Still grinning, he released his predatory grip.

Lilli finally exhaled and then smoothed her skirt down, leading him toward their friends. By now Craig had wandered off, and Donna had succeeded in taking some of Vin's attention away from his testosterone-filled scrutiny of Lilli and Jake.

AS THEY ARRIVED at the table, Craig stepped up, followed by a waitress setting another round of drinks in front of them. Without hesitation Jake snatched up a beer and took a long pull while sliding a new martini toward Lilli. She did hesitate, though, contemplating if she should stop drinking so she could drive home safely.

As if sensing she needed convincing, Jake sipped his beer as he casually stroked his fingertips along her stocking-covered thigh at the bottom edge of her skirt.

A tingle tremored through her and she shuddered, then pinched her lips together in restraint, eyeing the cocktail glass. The colored lights from above the dance floor sparkled in the cranberry-tinged liquid and Lilli did not resist the urge, pulling the glass to her mouth, then draining the almost pure alcohol in a single, desperate gulp. She whooshed out a breath, then, with a single finger she wiped below her lips and set the glass back on the table with more gusto than she had intended.

Jake moved the beer bottle away from his mouth and wore a satisfied-looking expression. He'd gotten to her and he knew it. With nothing more than a nod of his head and a dart of his eyes toward Lilli's empty glass, he spurred Craig into motion in the direction of the bar.

"I'm not going to drink that you know." Lilli crossed her arms playfully and leaned back against the wall of the DJ booth. "I need to be able to drive home."

"Or," he began, "Vin can drop us at my place and we can get your car in the morning."

Since Craig had headed off, Donna was finally smiling again. She seized her opportunity to drag Vin onto the dance floor, winking at Lilli as she went.

Lilli wagged her finger at Jake. "I told you, rain check. You think you can charm me that easily? Stop misbehaving, Mr. Edwards."

He faced her, leaning in and placing his hands on either side, whisking her back to New Year's Eve when he'd had her pinned against the cold window. He sniffed along her earlobe, inhaling deeply, the sibilant sound, once again, sending shivers along her spine. Having had barely a few minutes to reclaim her composure, Jake's closeness accelerated Lilli's breathing again—along with her heart rate and her imagination.

"That wasn't misbehaving." His breath felt heated enough to singe the hair on the back of her neck as he leaned in close to her ear. "But this is." Pressed unyielding against her, Jake's desire lingered. "So, what is it gonna take for me to get your number so I can collect on that rain check?"

Her mind a tangle of firing neurons, Lilli worked at articulating her thoughts, but failed miserably when all she could come up with was a bit of stammering gibberish.

Jake captured her against him and it summoned a chill that tickled her spine, causing her words to catch in her throat, rendering her mute.

He flashed a cocky grin, leaning in until they shared each panting breath. But he didn't speak, didn't so much as touch her lips, a prolonged moment of sublime torture until neither could resist the close proximity any longer. Their mouths met in a swift, hungry kiss. Two starving beasts both darting for the kill at the same moment.

Then, if the prelude had been drawn out, the kiss itself seemed fleeting.

Lilli shuddered and sucked in some air as she raised her eyes to meet his. With that one single look, he sent a deep, penetrating hunger piercing into her. She felt as though she needed to gaze away or she wouldn't recover her sanity.

After a quick surveillance of her Jimmy Choos, she finally spoke. "That."

He quirked a brow. "Come again?"

"What? No. Oh…repeat myself. Yes." Lilli's cheeks heated. "I said *that*. You asked what it would take, and *that* is what it took."

Confusion lingered on Jake's face now, and then a grin slowly spread from one side of his square jaw to the other as the lightbulb clicked on. All pretense of machismo faded to the back and Jake wore an expression of astonishment as he bobbed his head.

She reached into her purse and then took his left hand, turning it palm up. She gently stroked Jake's fingers back, making a flat surface, then began to write, deliberately slowly. She angled a brief glance upward, just her eyes, and watched as his jaw clenched and his Adam's apple wavered up and down as he swallowed hard. The rhythm of his breathing quickened, his chest puffing in and out.

After she wrote two phone numbers there and circled them with a heart, she curled his fingers up, as though she had placed something precious in his grasp, then she clicked the end of the pen on the bar and slipped it back in her bag.

He looked at his hand but made no attempt to open it yet.

"That way," Lilli smiled, "you can't lose it."

"Never would." He swallowed again and cleared his throat but offered no more words as he looked at the blue ink on his hand. He then nodded his approval while slipping his other hand in his pocket, making an awkward adjustment.

He looked suddenly conscious as his friends approached, and he resumed his male posturing while Lilli tried to read the look on Donna's face. She should go over and talk to her. So, as a grinning Vincenzo sidled up to Jake and slugged him in the arm, Lilli moved toward Donna.

"ARE YOU HAVING FUN?" Lilli asked.

"I wasn't at first. I felt a little out of place, but then Craig wandered off and Vincenzo and I were able to get to know each other a bit. He said he's between jobs right now, but I don't really care about that. I think he likes me."

"That's good," Lilli said, although, she wasn't giving Donna her full attention. She heard Jake say her name and then her ears tuned in to the conversation taking place beside them.

"Earth to Lilli." Donna waved in front of Lilli's face. "I asked if you think so too."

With reluctance Lilli pulled her attention back to her friend. "Yeah. Sure. Of course."

Donna slipped closer to Lilli, pulling on her arm, trying to get her to move off to the side. "Let's move a little so we can talk better."

Lilli held back. "In a sec. I wanna try to hear what they're saying."

Donna made a small huffing sound and then took a step away.

Lilli held her breath and listened intently, wanting to know what Jake was saying about her to Vin. Based on her two most recent encounters with Jake, it looked as though her emotions might catch fire rather quickly. Cassie would advise her to make sure he was serious about dating her before she ignited that flame. Thankfully for Lilli, although the music was loud, the conversation was louder.

Vin was chuckling. "Looks like you're gonna score a touchdown tonight, dude."

"Maybe. Maybe not. I don't mind waiting for this one."

"Jake Edwards wait? That's a new concept."

"I think it'll be worth it." Jake again adjusted himself.

"Let's go to the bar and do a shot," Vincenzo coaxed. "Or are you having trouble walking?"

Jake laughed and shoved his friend toward the bar. "Wouldn't you be?"

"I've got eyes don't I?"

"So you get my point."

"Most def," Vincenzo patted Jake on the back as he turned toward Lilli.

She quickly diverted her attention toward where Donna had been, but she was gone. So much for her cover—and her plan to make things up to Donna for ignoring her all night. She pretended to be focused on the crowd as Jake approached her.

"Hey. You wanna join us for a shot?"

"No. I need to find Donna. I've been a terrible friend tonight."

"Why? Because you thought about yourself for a while?"

Lilli stood on her toes and scanned the nightclub. "No. Yes. Well, sort of, but more that I didn't think of anyone but myself." She gave up on her search, turning her attention to Jake. "And you, of course."

"Relax," Jake said. "She's probably just in the washroom. You females seem to spend a lot of time in there."

He was right. She didn't think that Donna would leave without saying anything. There was probably just a long line up for the bathroom.

"Come on, man," Vin prompted from the sidelines. "The more I drink, the prettier her friend looks."

"Go," Lilli said, pretending she didn't hear Vin's comment.

Jake shrugged his massive shoulders and fell into step beside Vin, heading to the bar.

She watched as they made their way through the crowd, then as they reached the bar, Jake swung his hand in a circle and the female bartender set down three glasses and poured—likely more Cuervo Gold. Vincenzo sprinkled some salt on his hand, confirming Lilli's thoughts, then Jake and Vin lifted their glasses. Jake nodded toward the bartender and she picked up the third, smiling flirtatiously as they downed the shots.

LILLI WAS ABOUT to head to the washroom to look for Donna when a guy stepped up and began hitting on her. Jake had only been gone for a few minutes—the guy either had not seen her with Jake or he was awfully brave.

She was not good in situations like this. She felt confronted and awkward. The guy wasn't bad looking, and he seemed nice enough, but she was not interested and hated being direct. Luck was on her side because Jake arrived before she had to brush the guy off.

He pushed his sizable form between Lilli and her would-be suitor, asserting his territory. He gave the much smaller fellow a deliberate once-over. "'Scuse me, son. Can I help you with something?"

"Shit. Number Eleven. You're even bigger in person than you look on TV." The guy moved back a bit. "Listen, I wasn't trying to step on anyone's toes. My buddies," he darted a glance to the other side of the club, "they bet me I couldn't talk to your girl while you were at the bar."

Jake's face softened. Maybe he saw this guy in a new light now. "How much?" he asked.

"A hundred."

"A hundred bucks, huh? And what were you supposed to get for a hundred bucks? A phone number? A date? Get her to leave with you?"

"No way, man. Nothing like that. Just talk to her. I swear." He looked at the floor. "A dance woulda got me an extra fifty."

Jake seemed to ponder things for a moment, and Lilli wondered if there would be a fight. She watched as the guy shunted foot to foot. She imagined he wanted to run right about now.

"I'm a big fan, dude. That pass you made to Segretti was off the chain."

That seemed to be enough for Jake. "All right, I'm not gonna punish you for this. It took balls to do what you did."

"Thank you. Thanks," the guy said, bobbing his head. "Can I, uh, can I go now?"

"Not so fast." Jake leaned in, speaking quietly in the guy's ear.

He nodded and then dashed away to his friends.

Jake spun back to Lilli, a wide grin on his face. He raised his beer bottle to his lips and took a long, satisfied drink.

"What did you say to him?" Lilli asked.

Jake shrugged. "I told him to go drop that hundred onto my tab…in exchange for me letting him live." He chuckled and took another sip of his beer.

"Oh," she said. At least, she reasoned, it was better than him pounding the guy into oblivion. She slipped her purse over her shoulder. "I'll be right back, Jake. I want to go look for Donna in the washroom. Maybe she wasn't feeling as better as she thought after her concussion last night. I should make sure she's okay."

CHAPTER ELEVEN

LILLI WANDERED BACK into the throng of people, still glancing around for Donna. When she arrived at their table Jake too was nowhere to be found. Was everyone deserting her or something?

She slumped into the empty chair and tapped out a beat on the table, her eyes straining to find at least one of the people she'd been with. She spotted Craig not far away and waved him over. Maybe he would know where everyone was.

He took his time lumbering toward her, and, in the meantime, Jake sprinted up to the table, sweaty and out of breath.

"I was worried about you," Lilli said. "Is everything okay?"

"Yeah." He dragged up a chair and sat beside her. "I just had to step outside and take care of a little business."

Business? That was rather vague sounding. But Lilli did not want to push for an explanation and have him think she was clingy or insecure, so she let it go at that. "Okay. Have you seen Vincenzo? I'm wondering if he knows what happened to Donna. I still haven't found her."

"I left him outside. She was talking to Bullet Head when we came back in. He didn't remember her and wasn't going to let her in the club. I vouched for her, and now she's hanging out somewhere with Vin."

Donna had been outside? Lilli found that to be a little strange, but her thoughts were pulled back to the present when the DJ stopped the music and made an announcement.

"Last call for alcohol. Drink up, folks. You don't have to go home, but you can't stay here."

"Last call. You want something?" Jake asked. "Anything you like."

"I'm fine. I have water here." Lilli had sobered up enough to drive home and she didn't want to complicate things by having another drink now.

Vin came up to Jake and leaned in close to say something Lilli couldn't hear. Jake grinned at his friend, slapping him on the back with a loud clap.

Donna approached Lilli then too, her cheeks red and bunched up in a smile. "I'm going home with Vincenzo," she announced. "You okay to drive, right?"

"Yeah. I stopped drinking a while ago." Lilli wanted to add that she'd stopped when Donna had gone MIA, but she kept it to herself. "Listen, Donna, I wanted to ta—"

Donna dashed off, giggling on Vincenzo's arm, before Lilli could finish telling her she wanted to talk.

"Call me tomorrow." Donna waved and they disappeared into the crowd that was filtering out of the club.

The nightclub staff was winding things down and Craig had disappeared again, leaving Jake and Lilli alone at the table.

"So," Jake reached over and stroked Lilli's hand, "Vin was kind of my ride..."

Lilli was now in the position of offering to drive Jake home. She pulled her keys from her purse and jangled them in the air. "Come on."

He grinned, and the two of them headed toward the coat check. After they slipped into their jackets, Bullet Head held the door wide and made a sweeping gesture, pulling it back up for a small salute. "Have a good night, you two."

Lilli was glad she had sobered up. Aside from driving, she wanted to keep her wits about her, not rush into anything with Jake. She had no intention of going inside his place when they arrived there, but she felt he had every intention of trying. Something about the gleam in his eye when Vincenzo told him he was taking Donna home. It was more than a good-for-you-man kind of gleam, seemed more personal.

THE NIGHT AIR brought a chill that almost had Lilli regretting her decision to wear the short skirt, but Jake left his jacket open and pulled her close enough to wrap her inside his coat with him. They strolled the short distance to Washington & Occidental, snuggled up so close they could have passed for conjoined twins. Lilli felt a stillness inside that matched that of the chilly Seattle air. They spoke very few words as she melted into the heat of his body, watching as their breath escaped in tiny puffs of clouds.

"This is me." Lilli pointed as they approached the near-empty lot, where her green Jeep sat, a solitary soldier testifying to the lateness of the hour. Lilli pressed the key fob to unlock the doors, but something aside from the quick double-beep caught her attention. "Shit."

"What is it?" Jake asked, releasing her from his jacket-embrace.

She glanced down and barely resisted kicking the tire. "It's flat," she said.

Without hesitation Jake pushed up his sleeves and instructed her to unlock the back. "Where's your jack and your lug wrench?"

She showed him, and he began the task of changing the tire. Once he had the old one off he leaned it against the Jeep and wandered back to release the spare.

Lilli came up behind him and placed a kiss on his cheek. "Thanks for helping me," she whispered into his ear.

Jake winked at her. "You're my ride home. What choice did I have?"

She popped him on the shoulder. "There's always a choice, Jake. But you made the right one, at least as far as I am concerned." She stepped back as he reached up to loosen the spare.

"Uh, Lilli?"

She slid back up to his side. "Yes?"

"The spare…it's flat too."

"What?"

"I didn't want to say anything before because I wasn't sure, but…"

"But what?"

"It looks like maybe someone cut your tire on purpose."

"You're kidding?"

"Nope."

"Who would do something like that?"

"Can't say, but, whoever it was, they were thorough. I mean, they thought ahead enough to make sure your spare was useless too."

Lilli paced around the Jeep. "God that makes me angry. Where's the fun in vandalism anyway? Do these idiots lurk nearby so they can get a laugh when the person shows up and sees what they did? I mean, seriously." She spun around the parking lot, scanning the nearby area.

"If you're out there," she spoke to the empty night, "ha ha—I guess you win this round. Yay you." Then she collapsed onto a concrete parking barrier, folding her arms and groaning in defeat.

Jake walked over to her, sat down, and placed his arm across her shoulder. "For what it's worth, I'm sorry this happened. You were right about one thing—people are idiots. They see someone who has what they don't and they just react out of spite."

"But this didn't come easy to me, you know? I have to work to pay for everything I have. I earned my own way in life. No one gave me a free ride. And I'll have to pay for two new tires now too. It's not worth an insurance claim. Just like this." She stood and walked around to the driver's side, pointing to a twelve inch scrape along the door. "See this? I found it after I came out of a movie theater a couple months ago. Haven't had the money to get it fixed yet."

He took her hand and pulled her back to the barricade, tugging her down onto his lap as he sat. "I know a guy," he said. "I'll hook you up."

"That's sweet, Jake, but you don't have to. It's not your responsibility. I can't ask you to do that for me."

"I know, and you didn't ask. I offered."

She stroked a finger along the ridge of his brow. Jake was a good man. She placed a gentle kiss there.

He gazed at her, then looked away. "I know it might seem like things come easy to me, Lilli, but I've had to work hard too, so I understand. My old man...let's just say he wasn't exactly father of the year. I mean, he was a hands-on kind of guy, but not in the way a kid wants."

"Jake, I—"

He raised a hand. "Don't. It's okay. I'm over it, and honestly it's what made me tough. What made me, me."

She tried her best to conceal the pity-face she knew she was inclined to display in situations such as these, as she rose from his lap. "So, what now? If I leave my vehicle overnight it'll probably get towed."

Jake whipped out his cell and began to dial. "Yeah, Jerry? Hey, Jake Edwards." He raised his eyes to her. "Thanks. Happy New Year to you too, man. Sorry to call so late, but my—uh, my date tonight, got her tires slashed and we need a pickup at Washington & Occidental before morning." He gave Lilli a thumbs-up and then relayed the details to the man on the phone.

He disconnected the call and went over to her. "So, we're all set. He said to leave the keys in the left tire well, inside."

"Is that safe?"

"Yeah. It'll be okay. Jerry isn't far and he said he'll leave right away. He's a man of his word. Besides, no one can drive it anywhere."

"All right." Lilli took his hand in hers. "But now how are we going to get home?"

Jake pumped his eyebrows. "Your place or mine?"

"Nice try." Lilli smiled at him. "But it's too soon for that."

"Can't blame a guy."

The silly grin that spread across his face almost convinced her of his innocence. Almost.

"Okay," he said, "honestly, I have a confession to make. My place is not that far."

"So, you really needed a ride home, huh?"

He raised a finger to his lips. "Shhh. Count your blessings that I'm a truth bender. Otherwise you'd be stranded out here all alone."

"You have a point."

"So, we can take a taxi, or walk, and I can let you borrow my old Honda."

"Jake, I couldn't."

"Sure you can. It's not that special anyway. Like I said, it's my old car. I'm driving a little incentive from management right now, so I don't really need the Honda. Does that make it simpler for you?"

She leaned her head against his chest, and he wrapped her into the warmth of his jacket, holding her shivering body close. It felt good. And when he bent his head down and sniffed her hair, she just smiled and sighed, allowing herself to melt into his embrace.

The moment was pulled away as Jake let out a sharp whistle and began waving his arm around. She raised her head to see who he was waving to, as a taxi rolled to a stop beside them.

"You need a taxi?" the driver called through the open passenger window.

"Yeah," Jake replied. "Can you take us just up the street a ways? To the Wave?"

"Sure. Get in."

Jake held the door for Lilli and then climbed in the back seat beside her. She studied him intently, deciding that his truth bending, as he'd called it, was harmless enough. He'd only wanted to spend more time with her. And he was right. She would have been there all alone with two flat tires and no "Jerry" of her own to call. "Okay. I forgive you," she said.

"Good. That's good."

He let his hand rest beside him on the seat, their fingers almost touching, and Lilli smiled. In some ways, he had this boyish charm, and Lilli had to admit, it was growing on her. Fast.

CHAPTER TWELVE

IT TOOK LESS than five minutes to arrive at Jake's building. He paid the cab driver while Lilli stood on the street and gazed up, admiring the view. The way each level of the massive glass-and-metal structure seemed to be in juxtaposition to the next gave the building a wavelike appearance. Lilli had admired the recently developed building and had wondered what it looked like inside. She'd even read that you could see the Seahawks games from the rooftop patio. One thing was true, Seattleites had been in almost unanimous agreement that the buildings at Stadium Place would be an economic and social win for the Pioneer Square area.

Jake sidled over and slipped his arm around her.

She looked up at him. "I can't believe you live here. Can you really see the field from the rooftop?"

"Yup. It's an awesome view. I can show you, you know, some *other* time."

"I'd like that."

"I do have to go up and get the car key though. No strings. I promise." Jake held his hands up, palms out, to punctuate his oath.

Lilli worked at reaching a decision. Should she go up with him or wait downstairs? It might be uncomfortable waiting alone in the lobby, but she might allow herself to get sidetracked if she went up with him.

He lowered his hands and gradually closed the distance between them, his breath rising from his nostrils in puffs of vapor, like a slowly advancing bull ready to charge full force at any moment. Near enough now to brush some hair off her forehead, he leaned in, sniffing her neck then running his fingers through her hair. Before she knew it, he was caressing her left cheek and turning her face so he could kiss her.

Lilli did not resist. She wasn't sure she could have if she'd tried. With his strong arms around her, she forgot about the cold. She forgot they were standing under radiant pools of illumination created by the tall floodlights in the parking lot. She thought of nothing outside of the feelings, heard nothing except their coupled breathing and the pulsing beat of her heart. Lilli did more than simply surrender her lips to his—she passionately returned his ardor, kiss for kiss and touch for touch, the heat between them softening the assault of the frozen night air.

"Let's take this inside," Jake suggested through heavy breath.

Although her body was sending mixed messages to confound her mind, Lilli knew she didn't want this to be a fling, a rebound, or even just an escape from Bradley. She wanted to do things right. She had a good feeling. Her heart was telling her that much.

"I can't," Lilli panted the words without breaking the kiss, "it's too soon."

"I promise I won't let it go too far." Jake tangled his hands in her hair and pulled her closer, kissing her hard and deep, thrusting his tongue inside, begging her with actions now, instead of words. "C'mon," he urged through hungry lips, "I have amazing self-control."

She kissed him hard, gently biting his bottom lip before pushing herself away. "I don't." She ran a finger along her lips, tracing the tingling sensation that still lingered there.

Jake reached out toward Lilli, but she raised a hand and halted his progress, trying to ignore the thick, muscled armor of his chest. She inhaled deeply then released her frustration in an animalistic groan. She wanted him. But she knew if she went inside, if she let it go any further, she may very likely let her desire take the lead. "Not tonight," she said. "Soon. But not tonight."

He must have sensed he was not going to win this battle because Jake became a reluctant gentleman. "Well then, I should, uh, go get the keys I suppose. You can wait in the lobby. It's safe there."

A car pulled into the parking lot just then, piercing the still night air with the grinding from the small amount of gravel under the tires. They both turned toward the sound, and Lilli squinted as the brief sweep of headlights blinded them with its halogen-white beam. Then, just as fast as it had arrived, it sped off, out of the parking lot and down Occidental Avenue.

"I wonder what that was about," Lilli said.

Jake shrugged it off as unimportant, reaching for her hand and leading her to the lobby.

As they stepped through the doors, Lilli could have sworn that Jake was walking with a little more swagger than he had before. She supposed that her less-than-hard-to-get behavior of a moment ago had qualified for a tick in Jake's win column. She didn't care if he knew how much he got to her on a physical level. It was equally clear what effect she had on him, when, just as she faced him again, he made a crotch-directed adjustment.

He cleared his throat as he slanted a glance at her, catching her looking. He pressed the UP button, then pulled her in for another kiss, not letting go of her until they heard the *ding* of the arriving elevator.

"I'll be right back. Promise."

She smiled and let the sweet feelings linger inside her as he stepped onto the waiting elevator and the doors swooshed closed. "Jake," she whispered his name, tasting the way it sounded on her just-kissed lips.

As the sensations leveled off and Lilli felt her pulse rate slow, she relaxed against the wall across from the elevator, watching the lighted numbers to see when he was heading back down.

A rush of cold air blew past her and Lilli heard the front door close with a deep thud. When she heard no footsteps and no one approached the elevator, she began to feel a little nervous, wanting to spin around and look, yet afraid to do so. Another chill washed over her but this time it didn't feel like a breeze. She shook her head. She was being silly. Obviously a tenant had come in and had decided to take the stairs. As to why she hadn't heard the stairwell door open or close, well, Lilli decided she just must have missed it.

The *ping* startled her and she looked up to see Jake's broad shoulders filling the open elevator doors. Relieved, she stepped forward and sidled up to him. "Hey, you."

"Good to see you survived without me for a few minutes." He reached for her hand and swallowed it up with his own. "Doesn't look like you missed me too much."

"I managed."

THEY STOOD NEXT TO Jake's silver Honda as he placed the keys in Lilli's hand.

"Thanks, Jake. I really appreciate all you did to help me tonight."

"I do what I can." He kicked at a small rock near the tire and it skittled across the concrete.

She glanced at the keys in her hand. "I guess I should start it."

"Probably should."

She pressed the key fob and unlocked the door, and Jake reached over and opened it for her. She leaned in and tossed her purse on the passenger side, then climbed in, adjusting the seat all the way forward.

After Lilli fired up the engine, Jake lowered the driver's side window then shut the door. He stood with his hands in his pockets as she made adjustments to the mirrors and snapped her seatbelt in place.

He placed his hands on the edge of the open window and leaned all the way in, making intense eye contact with her before brushing some hair off her forehead, then kissing her, soft and quick.

"So..." she said.

"So..." he countered.

"I guess I should go."

He nodded. "If you don't, I might rip your clothes off and take you in the parking garage."

Lilli looked deep into his eyes, feeling conflicted. "You're still here," she said.

"You're still here." With a look of reluctance, Jake stepped back and let her reverse out of the spot. "Text me when you get home so I know you made it safely."

"I can't."

Jake looked confused, then seemed to clue in, walking around to the passenger side then opening the storage compartment. He scribbled on a piece of paper then handed it to her.

"Now I can." She smiled and slipped his number inside her purse.

He stepped away from the car, slowly walking backward and wearing a look of longing. Lilli's stomach flip-flopped as he brought two fingers up to his lips and blew her a kiss in a very sexy way. Her skin seemed to vibrate as she pulled out of the garage, her breasts rising and falling as she sighed and thought about the abandoned-puppy face he'd given her just before she drove off.

CHAPTER THIRTEEN

LILLI DROVE HOME feeling exhilarated. The car carried a faint Jake-like scent, and the sense of safety his embrace had given her lingered there with it. The drive home flew by in a blur of whirling thoughts and emotions. Before she knew it, Lilli was pulling into her building's lot, setting the parking brake. She opened the door but hesitated, reluctant to abandon Jake's car too swiftly.

However, in the very next moment, Brad was in her face, rocketing her back to reality.

"Do you have any idea what time it is?" The appraisal he passed over his watch was ripe with drama. He ran his hand along the vehicle then double-tapped the roof. "Where's the Jeep?" He angled back and inspected the car. "This car looks kinda familiar. Now, who do I know that drives a silver Honda Civic?" He tapped a finger on his chin as though he were actually cogitating about it. "Oh yeah, that's right. Jake fucking Edwards."

And just that fast Lilli's bubble of euphoria burst wide open, carried away on the clouds of breath expelled with Brad's judgmental words. She watched it dissipate in the frosty night air, offering no response.

And so, he pushed.

"How, *exactly*, did you come to be driving a car belonging to Seattle's golden boy?" He eyeballed his watch again. "At almost three AM?" His shoulders heaved an exaggerated shrug. "Just curious." He crossed his arms and widened his stance, steely blue stare unwavering.

How was she going to get out of this one? She had no reasonable explanation, at least not that Brad would accept. Avoidance. And there was only one way to achieve that. Lilli snatched her purse off the seat and slammed the car door, pushing hard against the unrelenting wall of Brad until she was free. She began striding toward the entrance, raising the car remote and aiming it backward over her shoulder, locking the car as her boots tapped a hasty beat.

He galloped after her, his mouth surpassing the pace of his feet. "No wait. Don't answer that. Let me guess. I think I can paint a decent Van Gogh on this one. Step one, Jake shoved his tongue down your throat on New Year's Eve. Step two, you say, 'Hey, I kinda liked that.' Step three—and this is the cherry on top—you think, 'Fuck Brad, I'm gonna date his friend.' Does that about sum it up, Lilli? But the *why* of the car, that's another story."

"Brad, if you must know—"

"Wait. I got this too. After a night of tarnishing every available surface in Jake's apartment, he's done with you, so you commence the walk of shame to where your Jeep should be, but lo and behold, it's not there. Towed away because in your haste to get upstairs and spread your legs, you accidentally parked in a tow-away zone."

"You're sick, Brad." She quickened her stride, readying her key as she clipped along. "And you're way off. I went out with a new friend tonight, and when I left the club my tires were flat. And Jake—who happens to be a real gentleman, by the way—offered to let me borrow his car. I never even went inside his apartment."

She struggled to place the keys in the front lock, Brad's breath hot on the back of her neck. She shook the door handle in frustration and it popped open without her keys. She thrust it as wide as his close proximity would allow, then squeezed through and stormed down the hall.

Brad pushed his way into the building and stayed on her heels, leaving little space between them as he shadowed her path. "Ha! Edwards? A gentleman?" He sniggered. "Yeah right. In what universe? You have no idea. He's a psycho stalker who gets off on terrorizing chicks when they finally come to their senses and ditch him. I dare you to ask any of the cheerleaders he dated in high school."

"Fuck off, Brad." They were at her apartment door, but she was hesitant to unlock it, fearing he would force his way inside there too. Then she'd be screwed. At least in the hall she could scream to alert a neighbor.

"Well?"

Lilli tapped her foot, restless and apprehensive. "Well what, Bradley?"

"Unlock the damn door" He reached beyond her and jiggled the knob. It gave way and swung open. "Never mind."

He pushed inside there too, leaving a speechless Lilli standing in the doorway, her jaw slack. How she could have been so stupid as to leave her apartment unlocked all night?

Oh yeah. She'd been trying to escape from Bradley. That worked out well, didn't it.

Brad stood on the other side of the threshold mirroring her stance. "You coming?"

Her forward progress was deliberate and hesitant.

He stared her down. "What? You don't trust me now? I make one little mistake and I'm the bad guy?"

"It was a *big* mistake." Lilli quirked her fingers to make air quotes, wanting to drive home her point.

"Not *locking* your door was a *big mistake.*" Brad made a matching gesture, mocking her, as he exhaled an audible rush of air. "You see? It's a good thing I'm here. What if some creep got in and was lurking in your closet?"

Standing on the other side of her door now, she considered his words. Maybe she should let him make sure she was safe from creeps in closets. But would she be safe from him? Anxiously, she weighed her options. Brad was a known unknown. A stranger in her apartment was a total ambiguity.

Lilli crossed her arms in one more attempt at defiance. "Maybe I didn't leave it unlocked. Maybe you came back and finished what you started the other night. Maybe you broke in here."

"Are you kidding? You can't seriously think I would—" Brad advanced toward her. "Lilli, you have to know I would never hurt you. I was jealous when I…I'm not the bad guy here. Sure I'm a little messed up sometimes, but I'm not the one you need to worry about." He grabbed both sides of her head as though he would kiss her, then released her so suddenly she stumbled backward.

He raised a hand to her. "Stay there."

As Brad navigated the apartment, opening doors and looking behind and under everything, Lilli slipped Jake's number and her cell from her purse, tucking them in the waistband of her skirt. When he came back out and announced it was all clear, she excused herself to use the washroom.

Brad shrugged and wandered into her kitchen, the sound of the fridge door opening matched that of the bathroom door closing. Lilli locked it behind her and put her cell on mute. She then began to text Jake. He responded right away, and she smiled to herself as she wrote that she'd had a great time with him, thanking him again for his car. She added a smiley face but left out the part about Brad and the unlocked door. Jake replied with a goodnight, see you tomorrow, and a kissing emoticon, at which point Lilli flushed and ran the water for good measure, then left the bathroom.

SEEING BRAD STILL snooping through her fridge, a wave of powerlessness swooped through her. She stomped into the kitchen and pushed the refrigerator door shut, forcing him out of the way. "You're not going to find what you want in there."

His expression flared with something Lilli couldn't decipher. It was as though his eyes glowed with jungle-cat hunger and ferocity. "You're absolutely right. I won't find it there." Brad stalked the short distance between them, closing it in a flash. He the predator, she the prey.

Lilli had retreated as far as she could, when Brad's right arm darted out, coming to rest with his palm splayed against the kitchen wall behind her. Lilli shrunk back as much as she could, but he was still close enough she could feel his hot, whiskey-drenched breath on her skin. Why was it that drunks so often chose such a vile spirit as whiskey? She faced away from the stench. "You've been drinking."

He didn't move. Didn't so much as flinch. "A little. I was bored. Tom Petty had it right, you know."

"What's that supposed to mean?"

"The waiting really is the hardest part." He chuckled, thinking himself clever, no doubt.

The next thing she knew, he was leaning in to kiss her, but Lilli saw it coming and ducked left to avoid him. His left arm shot out too, blocking her escape and almost knocking down the small gold-framed print of a quaint Parisian café.

She pushed her chin up in defiance and her hands against his chest. "C'mon, Brad. It's late and I'm tired. Please."

Brad withdrew slightly, giving her some much-needed breathing space. Lilli exhaled and dropped her shoulders, easing away from the wall.

"I only wanted to talk, Lilli. That's all." He sunk back against the fridge door. "Talk."

"I don't have the energy, Brad. Go home and sleep it off."

He scrubbed his hands over his face and through his hair. "But I don't have anybody else, Lilli." His words slurred out, and with them the drunken odor of his breath wafted toward her.

"You're drunk, Brad."

HE FOLLOWED HER as she strode to the living room and found a spot on the sofa beside Toby. "I have a reason, Lilli. A good one."

She narrowed her eyes and studied him. Something did seem off. She took the bait. "Okay, Brad, what's your reason for sucking back a fifth of whiskey? And don't give me that tired speech about nature versus nurture and how you have both strikes against you."

He flopped onto the sofa beside her, stirring Toby, who opened a single eye and glared before closing it and drifting back to sleep. Brad tossed his head back and shoved his hair from his face, expelling a groan. "Okay. Fine. I'll leave my dad out of it. You know how I went home over Christmas, right?"

Lilli nodded.

"Okay, so my mom gets all up in my face over dinner because I gambled and mentioned my sister. She was all like, 'How dare you bring that up, and at Christmas of all times.' And she starts to cry, and then I feel...I feel like a total shit, you know?" His words were coming so fast they began to swirl together, then, he stopped and looked around, pulling at his shirt collar. "Got any water? I could really use some water."

She sighed and padded to the kitchen to get him some from the fridge. "Can you accelerate to the point, Brad?" Lilli handed him the bottle and sat back down.

"Okay. I am. I will." He cracked the seal and downed almost the entire bottle without stopping to breathe, then he swiped the back of his hand across his mouth.

She was tired and her patience was thinner and more fragile than damp tissue paper. She wanted to be back in her euphoric bubble, thinking of Jake. Lilli tapped out a beat on her leg, fighting the urge to find some way, *any* way, to get him to leave.

She saturated her gaze with a flare of urging as she focused on him, desperate to speed up his process.

It seemed to work too well as his steel-blue eyes glistened with tears and he began to breathe in a rapid, uneven staccato. Then, just as he took a deep, rasping breath, Brad began to sob. "I can't do it, Lil. I just can't. I'm scared shitless and—I mean, what if it's true? Then what? And I haven't been sleeping. I don't think I've slept in three days. What am I gonna do? I just can't—"

What the hell was he referring to? Drunks only made sense to other drunks, and Lilli clearly had not imbibed sufficiently to interpret. Still, whatever Brad was feeling, it was real. She reached out to him, her hand caressing the saline from his cheek. "Brad?"

He connected with her eyes.

"Brad, honey, you're not making any sense. You need to calm down."

In a swift, desperate motion he grabbed onto her and pulled her to him, his tears soaking through to her skin. "You're so good, Lilli." He mumbled the words into her shoulder then sat straight, his bloodshot eyes boring into hers. "I never told you this before, but my dad…he was bipolar, and—oh shit—Lilli, my mom thinks I am too." He dropped his head in his hands and continued to sob. "I should have never mentioned my sister."

Okay. That was unexpected. If his mother's suspicions were true though, nature might win this round.

"Brad, just because your dad—"

"That's not the only reason she thinks that. She says I'm acting like him. I wanted to blame my mood swings on using steroids, you know," he swiped at his cheeks and shook his head, "but I couldn't. I couldn't tell her."

"You *are* using or *was*—never mind, look at the bright side, Bradley. Maybe that's all it is. Maybe if you stay off them you'll feel better."

"No." He lowered his shaking head. "I'm going to see a doctor next week. A specialist. My mom says I have to. You don't understand what it was like, living with my father. He'd take his meds and he'd be this zombie-dad, but then he'd stop—and we all knew he had, because he'd act crazy, manic, out of control. Start drinking. It was fucked up, Lilli. Real fucked up. I can't live that life. I can't be him."

Lilli was feeling guilty because she'd wanted to kick him out. This was news with a capital *N*. How could she send him home, alone, like this? Although no words could fix this, she turned toward him, she would at least try. "Brad, I—"

Slumped over, his head still balanced on his hands but wobbling side to side now. He had fallen asleep, or passed out, but either way, he was now her overnight guest.

She made a shushing motion toward Toby, and then dragged the blanket from the back of the sofa, placing it over Brad. She eased his legs up and his body down, tucking him up to his chin. She then picked up her cat, locked the apartment door, and flipped out the light on her way to her room.

Beyond the point of exhaustion, she slipped out of her clothes, put on a pair of lounge pants and a t-shirt, and shoved all the discarded clothing from earlier into a giant heap on the floor. Lilli tugged back the covers and was about to crawl between the crisp sheets, but hesitated, turning back and engaging the privacy lock on her bedroom door. Then, feeling a bit guilty for thinking she needed to lock Brad out, Lilli finally slipped into bed. Following her lead, Toby hopped up, fit himself behind her bent knees, and purred, lulling her into a deep sleep.

CHAPTER FOURTEEN

PEOPLE SOMETIMES SAY things like "It scared the piss out of me." You ever heard that? Well, it's true. That can happen. I've never admitted this to anybody before, but on some of those occasions when *Daddy Dearest* became the daddy I fear most—I can't believe I'm going to say this but I used to wet myself. And I'm not talking about a dribble here and there. No. I used to soak myself like a pathetic little baby. And it really messed me up too. I couldn't have friends over. I mean, aside from worrying that my father might trip into insanity, freak out and go berserk, let's face it, my room always smelled like piss. How do you explain that to a friend?

I soaked the rug in my bedroom closet so many times that one day I snuck out and stole a bottle of Formula 409. When I got caught by the store clerk I broke into tears and sobbed so hard she gave me the damn cleaner. Must've figured an eight-year-old kid would have to have a pretty good reason for stealing spray cleaner instead of candy.

It promised to get the stink out. It didn't. Maybe that was my fault for pissing so fucking much. Maybe it was my dad's for using his hands to beat on me rather than pat me on the back. I don't know. Either way, it was another let down in a world of dropped promises. As a sidebar, I got better at stealing. Never got caught again.

But I digress.

Right now I have more important things to think about. Big plans to work on. You pinkie-sweared that we'd be together forever, but everything's changed. I saw a future for us, Tabitha. Before. But not now. Not anymore. At least, not that way. And it's not because I don't still want that. I do. But everything's changed.

Wait. Did I already say that? It doesn't matter. What matters is that tonight did not go according to plan, you know? What about me? What about my needs? All I wanted was to spend a little time with her, but no, she had other ideas, other plans. Better things to do. How could she just leave me hanging like that? What type of a person does that to someone?

I'll tell you the type. One who thinks they are better than everyone else and they can do whatever they please as long as they smile at you while you're dying inside.

Trust me. I know. I'm an expert on that type of person. Hell, I've never known any other type. But I really wanted Lilli to be different.

She's not.

Sure, she may look different than my father. She may have a prettier face and a softer voice, but deep down she's really just the same. You watch. The next time I see her she'll act all sweet and nice, but it's just a front.

There is one difference, though. She's young enough to learn. And I'm going to be the one to teach her. Somebody has to. That's why I found her after all these years.

My dad did what he did and he got away with it for a long time. Too fucking long if you ask me. Karma has a way of catching up, though.

All my life the people I cared about underestimated me. My father did. I didn't think Tabitha did…

And now she is.

But that's the beauty of it. Karma is a sneaky bitch. No one ever sees her coming.

CHAPTER FIFTEEN

LILLI'S CAT STOOD on her chest, purring loudly and tapping lightly at her cheek with his paw. "Really, Toby?" Lilli blinked open her sleep-filled eyes and gazed wearily into his innocent little face. He batted his feline eyes at her. The LED display on the clock went in and out of focus. Lilli rubbed her eyes. "Kitty, it's only nine fifteen. Can't you wait to eat?"

He stepped off her and hopped onto the floor, landing with a soft thud, reminding her that a skipped meal wouldn't hurt him any. He paused at the doorway, a look of urging on his face. He took another step forward then regarded her again.

"All right, all right. I'm coming." She grudgingly rose from bed. "You're lucky that you're so darn cute." Lilli tied her bathrobe around her waist and the two of them shuffled toward the kitchen.

She darted a glance to the sofa, expecting to see Brad there, but he was not. She looked to the door. His shoes were gone. There was a yellow Post-it note attached above the peephole. It read: *Thanks for listening. I'll be okay. You have my reluctant blessing...I guess.*

His blessing? Did he mean her and Jake?

Stuck between relief and worry, she shrugged and then went to open the cupboard to give Toby a scoop of kibble.

After the pellets jangled into the bowl, the cat regarded his food, then his mistress.

"Only one scoop right now, chubby kitty, you need to cut back."

He voiced his dissatisfaction, waited for a pet on the head, and then began to crunch his kibble, purring all the while. "Silly cat." No matter how hungry he was, Toby always waited for her to pet him on top of his head before he would begin eating.

Lilli filled his water bowl, then made herself a coffee and turned on the news. There was a story about Jake and Sunday's wildcard matchup. Something about it being the second time that both teams had rookie quarterbacks starting in a playoff game. Her cell was flashing blue. She checked it to see a missed call from Jake and a text from Donna. The decision was a no-brainer. She smiled, muted the TV, and dialed Jake's number.

She hesitated for a second after he answered. Hearing his voice sent a shot of guilt pulsing to her chest—about Brad. "Hi, Jake. Sorry, it's early isn't it? It's me. Lilli. I hope I didn't wake you."

"Naw. I got practice today." Jake cleared his throat a couple times. "I am tired though. Didn't sleep well. Too much thinking and planning. How are you?"

"A little tired too. Listen, Jake, I need to tell you something."

"Okay."

"After I got home last night, Brad showed up. He pushed his way inside."

"Did he—"

"No. Nothing happened. He was drunk. Needed someone to talk to. He's worried about something. Anyway, I just wanted you to know. I don't want us to have any secrets."

Jake didn't say anything but cleared his throat again, so Lilli continued. "I'm sorry. I didn't feel right about it, but we just talked."

"I see."

"Jake?"

"Uh-huh."

"There's nothing going on between me and Brad."

"Okay."

"Not anymore. I just want you to know."

"Listen, Lilli, don't take this the wrong way, but if you're only with me to make him jealous..."

"No. It's not like that. I promise. I like you for you." Jake remained quiet, so Lilli attempted to change the focus. "I had a really good time with you at the club last night, and...you know...after too."

"You sure? What about Brad?"

"Yes. It's true."

"Go on."

"Fine. I'll confess."

"Confess?"

"Okay, wrong choice of words. What I meant was, I'll admit that I was hoping to run into you, specifically, last night." So much for playing hard to get. "Do you believe me?"

"Starting to. I have to admit something myself."

"Okay." Lilli held her breath.

"I didn't really know what to think, you know? The way you kissed me when we were together...it was weird to hear you spent time with Brad after that."

"So, you feel better now?"

"Yeah."

Lilli relaxed, exhaled. "I'm glad."

"I gotta hit practice. See you later?"

"I think we can arrange something."

"You think?" Jake paused a beat. "I'm not planning to take no for an answer, by the way—even if I have to kidnap you and shackle you to my bed."

"I guess I have no choice then. I'm at your mercy." Lilli giggled. "Be gentle with me."

Jake chuckled. "The cuffs are fur lined."

LILLI WAS STRETCHED out on her unmade bed, reliving her conversation with Jake. There was no work again today, but Jake would be tied up in practice. She'd decided to allow herself a lazy afternoon in bed, daydreaming and napping until she needed to get ready for their date.

She'd languished there for an indeterminate amount of time, dozing on and off, until eventually, her stomach had protested and she'd wandered out to forage for food.

With peanut-butter toast, sliced banana, and a glass of milk, she shuffled to the living room and turned on the TV, not bothering to change the channel. There was a program on sharks and Toby seemed enthralled. He crouched on the floor, directly in front of the television, wide eyes staring, little head bobbing side to side, as the large predators stocked and devoured their prey.

He paused his study just long enough to send her an apprehensive glance.

"Don't worry, kitty," Lilli said. "There aren't any sharks here. We're perfectly safe."

When the show was over and she had finished eating Lilli clicked off the television and took her dishes to the kitchen, rinsing them before placing them in the dishwasher.

As she dropped another scoop of kibble in Toby's bowl her phone began to vibrate on the nightstand. She darted over to answer, hoping it was Jake. It was Donna. She didn't really feel like talking to her—she'd rather take her time getting ready—but obligation was a strict mistress. Lilli pressed *Talk* and forced a smile into her voice as she answered.

"Hey, Donna. I was going to call you." It wasn't a complete lie. She was going to do it, just not today.

IN SPITE OF spending more than ninety minutes on the phone with Donna, Lilli had managed a quick trip to the gym to sign up for her boxing class, and was now made-up to perfection, lightly scented with Issey Myake perfume, and dressed to kill.

She spun in front of the mirror, checking all angles, then dabbed a bit of gloss on her lips and exited the bedroom. The thought of Brad fleeted across her mind, but only briefly. She was moving on. She had his blessing. Sort of. But it was sufficient.

Lilli poured herself a glass of red to help quell the nerves in her empty stomach as she waited for Jake to arrive. Would he run into Brad outside? What if he did?

Standing in the kitchen, she downed the wine in three gulps, which, along with the anticipation, left her with a sense of buoyancy. And, why not? She was about to have dinner with Jake Edwards. Their first official date, yes, but still, maybe after...

CHAPTER SIXTEEN

LILLI POURED MORE WINE—half a glass—and paced the small kitchen in her black Manolo Blahnik stilettos, which were SWAG from an ad campaign she'd worked on. Jake was thirty-five minutes late and hadn't called. She wasn't quite ready to start worrying, but she was getting close to being annoyed. It was their first real date. He could have at least sent a text.

Jake must have sensed her, telepathically, because just then the phone did ring.

"Hello," she answered.

"Okay, don't be mad at me," Jake begged. "I'm late and I know it. I'm a schmuck, and I know that too. I can't believe I kept a beautiful girl like you waiting."

Relieved that he was finally calling, she decided not to overanalyze. "Are you late? I hadn't noticed," she lied. "Is everything okay?"

"Yeah. I ran out of gas, if you can believe it. I guess my mind was on other things."

"I guess I can forgive that."

"Anyway, GPS says I'm almost there."

"Perfect. I'll meet you outside."

No sense giving Brad any extra time to cross paths with Jake tonight. Blessing or not.

Besides. Lilly had her doubts about that anyway.

She tossed down the wine, grabbed her jacket from the back of the dining room chair and did a quick check in the hall mirror. She wore a black pencil skirt that fit her like a second skin, a red cashmere sweater, and those fabulous shoes—not practical, but they were definitely perfect. She reached for her small leopard-print purse and cell phone, draped her jacket over her arm, and locked the door behind her.

Stale smells, cooking odors and trash from the open garbage chute, met her in the hallway. The random buzzing of televisions and stereos mixed with the sound of the couple in 127 arguing. Again. The usual.

Yet, something was off.

Lilli felt a tingle on the back of her neck and a little shiver dashed down her spine. With a sudden jerking motion, she spun her head around, looking behind her and down the hall. There was no one there. She shook her head. She was starting to get paranoid. Still, she quickened her pace and scurried to the front entrance, where she figured she had less chance of running into Brad.

Jake was standing right outside the door as Lilli hurried through, almost crashing into him. He reached out and caught her in his arms. "This is becoming a pattern," he teased. "You been taking lessons from Clay Matthews? I know I'm late, but that's no reason to sack the quarterback."

Lilli relaxed in his arms and caught her breath. When she inhaled she smelled his musky scent and melted further into his chest.

"You all right?" he asked.

"I am now," she answered, feeling safer.

"Something happen?"

"No. I'm just being paranoid." She stood up on her tippy-toes and kissed him on the cheek. "Let's go."

He released her and went around, opening the door and offering her a hand up into the black Land Rover. Lilli hopped in, feeling thankful that she had directed Jake to the front. Brad could probably see the back lot from his window. She hadn't heard from him all day but she wasn't taking any chances. She didn't like not knowing what he was thinking.

She gave her head a shake. No Bradley tonight. She gazed at Jake. He was looking at her.

"By the way," he said with eyes wide, *"wow."*

"You approve?" There was a serious bite in the night air and she slipped on her jacket to ward it off.

"Wow," he repeated, then swallowed hard.

"Thanks." She adjusted her seatbelt and got comfortable. "You clean up pretty good yourself."

He was wearing tan slacks paired with a navy button-down Tommy Hilfiger dress shirt that, beneath his open leather blazer, draped nicely across the muscled expanse of his chest. He put the key in the ignition but hesitated, staring at her for a moment. While she appreciated his adoring gaze, a part of her wanted to tell him to hurry up, but since she'd vowed that Brad would not be an issue tonight, she only smiled.

Jake admired his prize for a moment longer, then the powerful engine roared to life, and he sped out of the parking lot. He adeptly wound his way through a few side streets and found a shortcut onto the freeway.

As they merged into the traffic heading toward downtown, Lilli finally relaxed.

Jake reached over and stroked her arm. "Where do you want to go for dinner?"

"Surprise me."

"Ah, I see, the lady is going to challenge me. That's fair. That's fair. Jake Edwards can handle any challenge." The light turned green and he made his turn and headed into the core.

THEY MADE SMALL talk and drove until Jake pulled up in front of the Cobb Building at Fourth and University, where a valet dashed to attention and opened Lilli's door.

Jake had already circled the vehicle and reached out for her hand, helping her step down out of the truck. He slipped the keys, and likely a twenty-spot, into the valet's open palm, then led her into The Capital Grille.

He glanced down at her, perhaps to see if she approved. She did. She'd never eaten there before but had heard good things about it. Good steaks. Even better seafood. And an award-winning, very extensive, wine list. She had read somewhere that the American Culinary Federation had given them an award for excellence, so it seemed like Jake had indeed made a good choice.

A pretty blond hostess wearing a sleek, black, off-the-shoulder dress approached them immediately. She recognized Jake instantly and fumbled nervously with the menus. "One moment, Mr. Edwards, I just need to check if your table is ready." The girl scurried off to speak to a nearby busboy. Moments later, she returned and led the couple to a private dining room. She gestured inside with a wide sweep of her arm.

Lilli walked slowly, taking in all the details as she did. *The Board Room* was elegantly appointed in rich mahogany wood paneling and trim, with a large round table set with white linen and crystal. With ten black leather and mahogany chairs it could seat a small group, but tonight they had only two place settings on the table, side by side, facing the double wine cabinets that were flanking a replica of a sailboat.

"May I take your jackets?" the hostess asked.

Lilli removed hers and handed it over as Jake did the same, then he pulled out a chair for Lilli. She smoothed her skirt as she sat, then scooted closer to the table as Jake reached into a pocket then turned to the hostess, placing something—likely another tip—into her hand. "Thank you."

She smiled. "My name's Chantal, and you're welcome. Otis will be with you shortly. He's one of our best." The hostess moved to the doors and began pulling them closed. "Enjoy your evening," she said and then Lilli and Jake were alone.

Jake sat beside her and moved his chair closer. He stroked his thumb across the back of her hand and leaned in, planting a soft kiss on her cheek, then he pulled his gaze away and scanned the room. "Well?"

Lilli admired the décor and nodded her approval. "Great choice. I wasn't expecting a private dining room. And on such short notice too."

"Okay, I confess." He grinned and it radiated all the way up, igniting the flecks of gold in his hazel eyes. "I made reservations here first thing this morning. Needed to have one of the owners pull a couple strings actually. I had to promise him three TDs in the wildcard game on Sunday." Still holding her hand, Jake's face softened, his gaze appearing to reach out for her too. "Totally worth it."

A rush of endorphins brought Lilli a feeling of bliss. There was nowhere else she would rather be. "Worth it, huh?"

"Totally."

"What would you have done if I'd suggested a different restaurant?"

Jake's face split into a grin as a reddish hue swept over his cheeks, giving his features a visage that Lilli could only describe as boyish charm.

"You were counting on me letting you take charge tonight, weren't you?"

"Little bit." Grin got wider. Cheeks got redder.

Lilli's heart beat faster. "Well, score one for number eleven then."

"Six," he said. "Score six. Plus an extra point—maybe two—if I convert." Eyebrows dodging up and down.

Lilli understood Jake's football-speak. He'd scored a touchdown with the restaurant, the extra points, he was hoping, would come after. The way Lilli was feeling right now, they just might.

The little butterflies were stirring up her insides, creating a fluttering heat that was rising to the surface. Jake might be worthy of a little rule-breaking. Something about him felt so right. And it wasn't just the fact that he was the epitome of tall, dark, and handsome—with a whole bunch of big and strong thrown in for good measure. No. It was more than that. She sensed a deeper connection. A strong pull of destiny, leading her into...*something*. Not sure what. But something.

Otis arrived, breezing through the double doors and positioning himself at their table, in between them. He introduced himself as he poured water into their glasses and then stood, arms behind his back, like an obedient servant at their disposal. "Can I start you off with something from our wine collection? Have you had a chance to peruse the menu?"

Jake sent his eyes toward the wine list, and the hundreds of choices, and then settled his gaze on the waiter. "Otis, my good man, I am going to let you do the honors. The lady prefers red?" He darted a glance at Lilli and she nodded confirmation. "Red it is. The best."

Otis bobbed his head and slipped from the private room, the doors swooshing shut behind him.

Lilli picked up the wine menu and flipped through it. "You are aware that some of these bottles are," her eyes went wide as she looked at the descriptions—and the prices, "shall we say, rare?"

He didn't verbalize his response, but offered a look that told her she was still totally worth it.

A moment later the doors opened again, only it wasn't Otis that had returned with their wine. A smiling man in a chocolate-brown suit approached the table, grasping a bottle of red wine as if it were a treasured and rare artifact. Maybe it was. He introduced himself and informed them he was The Capital Grille's Master Sommelier.

Impressive.

He displayed the bottle for Jake to approve. "It is a twenty-eleven Domaine Jean-Louis Chave Hermitage. Dark and brooding, with bitter cherry and cassis characteristics and robust back-end power."

Jake's face went momentarily blank. "I can't even pronounce all that, but with a description like that it has to be good. I'll take your word for it."

"You'll be glad you did, sir." He waved toward the doors, where Otis appeared with a white cloth draped over his arm, ready to uncork and pour.

"Enjoy," the sommelier said, then he bowed his head and left the room.

Otis expertly opened the bottle, pouring a small amount and handing it to Jake, who raised his palm toward the extended glass. "Again, not my department." He gestured to Lilli.

She slipped the stem between her fingers and cupped the deep bowl in her palm as she swirled the dark purple Syrah, inhaled then took a sip, letting it dwell on her tongue. She was no master sommelier, but Lilli recognized the peppery fruit flavor, tannic qualities, and balanced taste. She nodded to Otis, who filled both their glasses then took their dinner order.

Jake asked for fresh oysters on the half shell as an appetizer, while Lilli chose prosciutto-wrapped mozzarella with vine-ripe tomatoes. Then, as they waited for the entrées to arrive, they engaged each other in a playful Q&A session.

SHE SIPPED HER wine and focused on Jake. "I'm having a really good time," she said while toying with the stem on her wineglass. There were still plenty of first-date jitters, but she was beginning to relax. She took another long pull from the glass.

"Me too." Jake picked up the bottle and topped up her wine. "I should be planning and preparing mentally for Sunday, but I don't think I could have concentrated on football anyway."

"Why do you say that?"

"You. Kissing you. Staring at you. Kissing you."

"You said that part already."

"Sometimes I digress, and some things rate mentioning twice."

The kissing was good. Lilli could not argue with him on that count.

His expression turned serious, and he reached over and swallowed her hand in his. "I've never felt this kind of connection to a woman before."

Her heart escalated its rhythm. She felt it too. It was so soon, but she was definitely falling for this guy. Lilli shoved a piece of tomato and mozzarella in her mouth in order to keep from blurting that out.

Time seemed to cease its linear progression as the evening lingered on. Somehow they managed to eat their meals, feed each other a truly decadent dessert and drain a second bottle of wine.

Lilli was right where she belonged. Maybe it was the effects of rich food and even richer wine, but Lilli knew deep in her soul...Jake Edwards would change everything.

CHAPTER SEVENTEEN

"THE LAST FEW days have been crazy." Lilli had the phone cradled between her shoulder and ear as she scanned contact sheets with a magnifier. She was talking with her friend Charlie. "I got absolutely no rest last night. I can't believe I made it to work."

"I'm surprised you had any time to sleep," Charlie joked.

"Who said I slept?" Lilli giggled.

"What happened to your *rules?*"

"Totally not like me, I know. What can I say? He makes me feel so—and I just—I think I might—" An audible breath hissed into the phone, followed by a groan. "What if I wake up and this is all a dream?"

"It's not a dream, Lil. I was there on New Year's Eve. Remember? The heat between you two was palpable."

"I know, Char, but it seems too good to be true. Even Bradley's been leaving me alone, in spite of his moving in next door."

"That's good though, right? Don't waste your time thinking of him. He's not worth it."

"I'm not. It's just that…"

"That what? That you're still punishing yourself? That you still won't allow yourself to be happy? Come on, Lilli, not everything in life is meant for you, and you alone, to fix."

"But what if I can?"

The deep sigh that filtered through the telephone didn't surprise her. Her friend knew her well enough to know how Lilli's mind worked. She steeled herself for Charlie's traditional point-blank response.

"Oh. My. God." Another sigh. "Are you kidding me? Lilli, Brad is a grown-ass man and he is not your boyfriend anymore. If he has this disease then it's his problem. His family will help him. You don't have to—even if you can. You are an extremely bright and capable woman, Lilli, but having the *ability* to do everything does not inherently compel you to actually do it."

Charlie was right. However, while the ability might not compel her to take action, Lilli's *self* often did. If she fought that urge, the one that had her putting everyone else first, she usually wound up with such guilt that she did twice as much to make up for it. It wasn't something she liked about herself, but that in itself led her to diminish her own intrinsic value. Now it was her turn to sigh.

"I recognize that tone," Charlie began. "You know I'm right and you hate that you know I'm right. Too bad. Suck it up, princess. Life goes on. And yours is going on without Brad. Do not let him hold you back. Besides, for all you know he is faking this disorder to be passive-aggressive."

Lilli cleared her throat in an exaggerated attempt to switch gears. "Anyway…"

Charlie allowed it. "So, it's been—what?—three days now, and you and Jake seem to be almost inseparable. What's next on your whirlwind dating schedule?"

"It has felt like a whirlwind," Lilli agreed. "I don't know. Jake wants me to cook for him tonight. At my place."

"And you're worried about Brad."

"Yeah."

"You said he's been leaving you alone, right?"

"Uh-huh."

"Well then, expect that to continue, invite Prince Charming over and cook the hell outta something for him."

"That simple, huh?"

"That simple."

"Fine." Lilli stacked the photo sheets into a pile and tapped them on her desk before placing them on the top left corner. "I'm going to do it. Jake is playing out of town this weekend. I know he's been spending time with me when he should be getting ready for the game, so this may be our last chance to see each other before he gets back."

"Good girl."

She could practically see Charlie's satisfied grin through the phone, but Lilli wouldn't let her friend off that easy. "Yeah, yeah. Whatever."

"So cynical for such a young woman. Anyway, why don't you head to DC too?"

"I want to, but…"

"But what?"

"I've got a photo shoot for this huge magazine layout on Saturday." Jake had begged her to go with him, to cancel the shoot, but she couldn't, it was an incredible opportunity for her.

"So head up on Sunday and surprise him." Charlie paused a beat. "Yes. That simple."

"Not so simple," Lilli argued. "I don't like to fly alone, it's last minute, and you know how I feel about new situations, and—"

In true Charlie fashion she emitted a loud scoff over the phone line. "You really do like to complicate things, don't you?" Then, without waiting for an answer, which was best since they both knew what it would be, Charlie continued. "I'm sure one of the other player's wives or girlfriends must be going. See? Simple."

Charlie almost always succeeded at pushing Lilli out of her comfort zone. This time was no exception. "Fine."

"You keep saying that." Charlie giggled.

"But how would I—"

"I'm one step ahead of you—as usual."

Lilli waited as she heard the sound of Charlie rustling through papers. This ought to be good. How was her friend going to solve this one?

"Got it."

What Charlie had, Lilli braced herself to find out.

"Okay, you got a pen? Ready?"

She scanned the surface of the desk, then snatched a blue ballpoint from the caddy. "I've got a pen, but I'm not sure I'm ready."

Charlie rattled off a quick seven digits and Lilli scribbled them down.

"That, my friend, happens to be the number of a guy I met on New Year's Eve, who happens to have a sister, who happens to be a junior publicist at the company that does PR for the Seahawks. Easy-peasy."

Lilli was silent.

"An in, Lilli. An in. Now, I know all about your telephoning-strangers phobia, but suck it up and call this guy. He was really sweet. I would have told you but you've been kind of, you know, busy."

"You're sticking your tongue out at me aren't you? I can feel it."

"No." Charlie laughed. "Okay, a little. Call him. Maybe he can help. Maybe he can't. Just try. This is not a dress rehearsal. It's your life, Lilli. Live it. Gotta go."

And that was that. Charlie hung up the phone, effectively giving Lilli no choice.

CHAPTER EIGHTEEN

LILLI HEFTED THE plastic grocery bags out of her Jeep and looped her wrist through the handles. She'd bought all the ingredients for beef stir-fry. She'd started with a shopping basket full with everything to make lasagna, but had put it all back. That had been the first meal she'd made Bradley when they'd started dating, and the moment she'd had that thought she was compelled to come up with a new plan. So, stir-fry it was. That and a pricey cab-merlot blend.

As she lifted her knee to edge the Jeep's rear door closed, she felt a hand on her shoulder and let out a small scream.

She whirled around to face him. "God. You startled me."

"You startle easy. Let me help you with those." Brad extended his hand and reached for the bags that were lined up like soldiers on her left arm.

She yanked them away, but he countered her motion and slipped his arm through the handles before she could stop him, effectively cuffing their arms together. He grinned and raised his other hand in mock surrender. "All it will cost you is a few minutes of talk. Then I'll go. Scout's honor."

Although she was disinclined to do so, she was also uncomfortable with the physical contact between them, so Lilli eased her arm out of the bags and permitted Brad to take them. "I don't believe you were ever a boy scout, Brad."

"I coulda been a boy scout."

Lilli ground out the word "Fine" and allowed Brad to follow her inside.

He kicked off his shoes but left his jacket on. At least he wasn't getting too comfortable.

Lilli began to put the groceries away, periodically glancing over to see if he was watching her. He seemed perfectly content, arms and legs crossed, propped against the small patch of wall at the entrance to the kitchen. Another good sign.

"So," he began, "I've been doing some research on this thing."

"What thi—oh, the bipolar thing."

"Yeah. That."

"And?"

"It's kinda scary, Lil. Mood-altering drugs. Emotional ups and downs. What if it's too much to handle?"

He couldn't possibly be that obtuse, could he? Lilli released the carton of milk she was retrieving and stood to face him. "Okay, first thing, Brad, you have been injecting yourself with mood-altering substances for—well, I don't really know how long, but long enough—and the mood swings? Don't even get me started. So, from my point of view, there is nothing new here. Nothing you haven't been putting yourself, and me, through for quite a while already."

"But what if I can't do it?"

"Do what, Brad?"

He uncrossed his arms and raked the fingers of both hands through his shaggy hair, scratched his head, then dragged his palms down his face. After unleashing a deep guttural growl he commenced a lively session of pacing outside the small kitchen.

His amped-up agitation level was beginning to saturate the air with a foul aura that engaged Lilli's fight-or-flight receptors. She decided to grab the bag with her hair products and head toward the bathroom. Anything to not be cornered in that kitchen again.

"Where you going?" Brad's voice surged with desperation.

"Relax. I'm just taking these things to the bathroom to put them away." Everything in her wanted to scurry away, down the hall, but she resisted the deepening urge and forced herself to tread at a gentler tempo.

The tactic seemed effective. She heard Brad exhale loudly and his pacing footsteps ceased.

Good.

"You can keep talking," she called out as she opened the cupboards under the sink. But he didn't. Instead, there was an elongated moment of soundlessness so salient that Lilli swore she could hear his brain ticking like a clock. Or a bomb.

She held her breath, which only served to crank the volume of the silence. Then, just as she was about to close and lock the bathroom door, in the guise of having to use the facilities, she heard it. Something small and quiet coming from the kitchen.

She dropped her outstretched arm and took tentative steps, inching her way closer, but still vigilant. As she rounded the corner to the kitchen, first she saw Brad's feet, then his legs, bent and swaddled within the protective mantle of his arms. His head had fallen forward onto his knees and his shoulders were rising and falling in subtle yet rapid heaves as he sat on the floor.

She knew the stance. Had adopted it herself on many occasions. His sobs, although practically inaudible, were profoundly tangible. It dragged Lilli's emotions to the surface like a fish succumbing to the lure of the fisherman. Propelled her forward and onto her own knees beside him.

Her arms snaked around his pitching shoulders and pulled him close. A silence enveloped his body as their energies mingled together. "Shhh," she murmured. "Shhh."

Lilli released her hold, wiped a tear from her own cheek and extended her hand to pull him up.

He angled his gaze upward. The whites of his eyes, no longer pristine but tinged with red, sent the blue of his irises as arrows piercing the space between them. It wrenched her heart into a tight, mangled mass inside her chest. She swallowed against the weight of it pressing up into her throat.

Mutely, he rose, and she led him with the same stillness toward the sofa, where both sunk down onto the cushions, remaining entangled as he rested his head on her shoulder. He continued to cry, but Lilli only knew this because the fabric of her top began to feel wet against her skin. Still, she made no move to disturb him. Poor, poor Brad. Really, this would complicate his life so much. She supposed it already had. Perhaps instead of a marker delineating the tragic road ahead, the unconfirmed diagnosis of bipolar disorder was indicative of the road already traveled.

Lilli sighed quietly, ran her fingers through Brad's hair, and held tight to this man who had once meant so much to her. Obviously still did, at least on some level. But Jake…what about him?

CHAPTER NINETEEN

SHE CLOSED THE DOOR behind him and leaned against it, releasing all the pent-up emotion in one huge breath. At least Brad had left on a high note. She'd actually done nothing more than hold him, quietly sending calming energy to his tormented soul. But it had worked. Finally he'd raised his gaze to meet hers, kissed her on the forehead, then stood, making his way to the door.

She'd joined him at the entryway, her heart still pulsing powerfully against her chest. Her throat still constricted with emotion.

Brad had reached out and pulled her so tight to his body that he'd almost siphoned the breath from her lungs. He'd leaned down then and inhaled her hair, placing a soft kiss upon her head, whispering, "I love you." Then, placing a finger under her chin, he'd raised her face, the desire for a kiss struggling painfully in his eyes. Instead he'd merely sighed, then turned to leave, the single word "Thanks" left hanging in the air.

At her feet, Toby meowed, bringing her back to here, back to now. Bringing her, also, to the realization that Jake would be arriving any minute and she hadn't even started cooking. With the big game looming around the corner, his time was limited. She wanted to make the most of every second they had together.

Lilli followed Toby into the kitchen and noticed the carton of milk still in a bag on the floor. It probably was beginning to spoil after sitting there for so long. She picked it up, felt the coldness of it and placed it inside the fridge. However, after dropping some kibble into Toby's dish, she opened the fridge, brought the milk back out, and poured it down the drain.

She spotted her purse and went to it, opening it to retrieve her cell so she could check for messages. There was a single call from Jake's number with no voicemail left. No text. As she began one to him, two decisive strikes resounded against the front door, while simultaneously her cell began to vibrate in her hand. She glanced down to see Brad's name and number on the display. That must mean Jake was at the door. Thankfully Brad had left several minutes before. Lilli breathed a sigh of relief and sent the call to voicemail.

She ruffled her fingers through her hair and slapped at her cheeks to bring some color to her face. She didn't want Jake to suspect anything was wrong. A wide smile, deep breath, and she flung the door open.

Sure enough, Jake filled the doorframe, one arm extended up and leaning against the jamb. The other was resting at his side.

Lilli made way for him to enter, a true smile filling her face at the sight of this man. "Come on in. Dinner's not ready yet, sorry, but it won't take—"

Jake strode toward her, a fierceness in his eyes as he kicked the door shut. He eliminated the remaining distance in a single step, captured Lilli around the waist, and pinned their bodies together. Her pulse flared and she gasped for air as his lips swallowed hers with unsated lust.

Passion surged, electrifying the air, causing Lilli to feel about as steady as a freshly set bowl of Jell-O. Depleted of her strength, Jake stole all control and, with a single powerful arm, lowered Lilli onto the thick pile carpet in the entryway.

Towering above her, the flames of desire licked across his features as he discarded his jacket in a heap, kicked off his shoes, and compelled her with a single word. "Now."

In one swift motion, he was on top of her. Bracing himself with one hand on the floor, he used the other to release his belt. His zipper. Himself. That hand now yanked Lilli's skirt to her waist and eradicated the final impediment, tugging sheer lace aside, as Jake satisfied the promise that burned in his eyes.

Lilli was breathless. Her excitement tantamount to nothing she'd experienced before. The world around her faded away, and she barely registered the hardness of the floor beneath her as he took—and she gave—both her body and her soul. A single word escaping her mouth now, acknowledging her acquiescence. "Yes."

ONE WORD EXHALED on a breath articulated one thousand unspoken thoughts.

"Wow." Lilli pushed the tousled hair off her face and glanced to her bedside table, searching for her water bottle. She snatched it up and drained the remainder in a single effort, gasping for oxygen when she finished.

In the bed beside her, Jake expelled a low moan of consensus and pulled her into his arms, sweeping her in for a kiss.

Lilli responded, then placed two fingers over his lips, breaking the contact. "Not. Again. Jake." She giggled and attempted to sit up, but he wouldn't relinquish custody.

"Not again," he agreed, flashing a sleepy grin as he spoke. "At least, not right now. I think we're out of protection. Besides, even a supreme beast like me needs recovery time."

She popped him on the arm in a playful reprimand, then made another move to sit up.

He still wasn't having any of it. "Where do you think you're going, woman? No one gave you permission to get out of bed. What makes you think I'll give up that easy?"

Lilli leaned in and tapped her lips to his cheek. "I'm coming right back, silly. I just need more water."

He held fast, feigning sleep with a series of quiet snores. She busted him, however, when he peeked one eye open, resulting in direct eye contact with her. "But I don't wanna."

"I promise."

"Five minutes. If you're not back in this bed—correction, back in my arms—within the allotted time, I will come after you. Got it?" She ruffled his hair and kissed his forehead. "Got it."

He released his grip gradually, letting her drift out of his embrace as though she were fine silk floating through his fingers on a breeze.

Lilli made no attempt to rush her departure either, choosing to savor the emotion swelling inside her chest. It was crazy, she knew, but she was quite convinced she was already head-over-heels and beyond hope.

She dragged his t-shirt over her head as she padded to the kitchen. As she stood in the dark, Lilli inhaled deeply, feeling more at peace, more at home, than she had in a long time.

She pulled out two bottles of water and swung her hips to shut the fridge door. As she twisted one open, she practiced the words on a whisper, trying them on to see how they sounded. "I love you, Jake Edwards." Lilli breathed a deep, contented sigh.

They sounded good. True.

Felt exquisite dancing across her lips.

Now, if only she could bring herself to say them to Jake. She'd never been the first one in a relationship to say it. Certainly not this early. Of course, she'd never indulged physically this soon either. But could she even bring herself to utter the words? What if he didn't say it back? How awful would that be?

She practiced it one more time. "I love you, Jake Edwards."

Then, just as Lilli was raising the water to quench her thirst, two strong arms grabbed her from behind and spun her around, knocking the bottle from her hands, cascading water as it went. She gasped as he pulled her, forcing any space between them to vanish in an instant.

As his lips pressed down on hers, he spoke two hungry words into her mouth. "I lied."

The force behind his kiss rendered Lilli mute. Only a mouse-sized whimper of consent escaped her lips as Jake hoisted her onto the countertop. She wrapped herself around him, and he spun her to the side, backing her against the wall.

This time it was fast and fervent. Jake released himself into her, leaving her gasping for breath—sated yet hungry for more.

He leaned her back and she snatched the other water bottle from the counter where she'd set it, then he began to carry her to the bedroom.

"Wait," she said. "The water on the floor?"

He circled back, grabbed two towels that were draped over the handle of the oven door, and tossed them onto the puddle at his feet. He murmured into her ear, "Happy now?"

She looked down to see Toby, crouched and lapping at the water, and her face gave birth to the smile bubbling inside her heart. "Ecstatic," her whispered reply as he navigated through the darkened hallway with her still snaked around his waist.

Jake dropped her onto the bed and took his position, poised above her, his focused gaze sizzling into hers. There was something intense there. A penetrating resolve that he seemed to be struggling with. He studied her face, his eyes, two hazel-colored lenses mentally photographing the minutia of her features.

Beneath him, Lilli mirrored his intent, searching for her own answers, recording her own memories. What was he thinking? Then, just as she was about to break the pregnant silence, Jake's eyes took on a glassy appearance as his pupils dilated, seeming to fill his irises.

He opened his mouth to speak, and, although she couldn't say why, Lilli held her breath.

"I love you too."

He what now?

She almost choked on the air that was imprisoned in her lungs. "You love me? Too?" That confirmed it. He had heard her in the kitchen, whispering sweet nothings to her bottle of spring water. *Oh. My. God.*

Emotion whelmed up in her throat and a tear floated out of the corner of her eye. Her heart pounding, Lilli threw her arms around his neck, pulling him down to her. His name came out, partially submerged within her next breath, but spoken nonetheless.

In the next moment, in one fluid motion, he took up residence beside her, brushing a strand of hair from her forehead, leaving a whisper of a kiss in its place. Then, as their breathing became unified and her mind wandered the terra of pre-sleep dreaminess, a thought occurred to her in that singular moment before consciousness slipped fully away…

They hadn't used a condom.

CHAPTER TWENTY

SIX-OH-NINE AM. The sky is a muted shade of inky charcoal. A few clouds drifted in overnight. I watched them arrive. But only briefly.

In passing.

There were other things—more important things—to do. Like watching her sleep.

Right now the city is waking up. Soon, she will be too. But me, I could use forty winks. Or two hundred.

It's hard work you know—what I do. It isn't easy. My "extracurricular" activities do not lend themselves to a standard schedule. It's not nine-to-five when you have to answer a serendipitous calling. Destiny is an uncompromising commander.

I can hear you now, threatening to call a *wah*-mbulance for me, just like my dad used to when he said I was whining like a crybaby. But I'm not complaining. No. I love what I do.

Okay. Yeah, sure. After the rush wears off there's a bit of trepidation. Self-loathing. Regret. But, rest assured, that sweet rush always comes back.

Because, you see, I have her right where I have always wanted her. No more waiting for her to complete me. I am intact. Whole. Unbroken.

I know New Year's Eve had a couple—let's call them mishaps—but somehow it all turned out perfect. No. No. No. Not perfect. Sublime. Yes, that's exactly what it is—sublime.

CHAPTER TWENTY-ONE

"NO. NO. NO." She mumbled the repeated word into the pillow.

Lilli was face down, her hair blanketing all sides of her head, suffocating her attempts to draw oxygen. She pulled her arm out from underneath her body and slammed it on the bedside table, with absolutely no results. The damn phone alarm still had the audacity to keep playing that cheerful little birdsong tune. Those early birds were too early. They might as well be shouting, "Hey, Lilli, get your ass out of bed."

She raised her head and turned it to the side, huffing out a breath to dislodge the veil of hair. She could have sworn she'd heard an audible creak coming from her neck when she'd moved it. She was stiff from sleeping on her stomach, and her phone was nowhere to be found.

She twisted, shooting her gaze in the other direction. Apparently Jake was also MIA.

This was sufficient motive for her to force herself to sitting, and, hell, while she was there, she might as well hunt for the phone. Oh. There it was. On the floor. Several feet away from the bed.

How did it—ah, yes, that's how it got there. That summoned forth a smile.

It had flown there. Last night. While she and Jake…

Wow.

And he'd said he loved her.

Double wow.

But where had he disappeared to? She scanned the room for any sign of his clothes. Nope. Nada. She could have sworn she had felt his presence in bed with her just moments before she'd become aware of her six-fifteen alarm.

Now the birdsong was accompanied by a lilting piano melody. How cheerful. Pretty. But if she didn't reach the phone before the harps joined in, she was going to scream. With utmost reluctance, she crawled from the cozy confines of her down duvet with one mission— to silence the chirping and search for the man she loved.

The man she loved.

Those words gave full resonance to the smile on her lips, and a silly little sigh slipped out in the process.

As her feet greeted the cold floor, Toby joined her in the room, pawing lightly at her phone, his face reflecting curiosity rather than the annoyance that Lilli felt. Boredom set in and Toby turned his attention to his mistress instead. Now his expression matched her annoyance. Most likely with her. He was not accustomed to being kicked out of bed at night, and last night, he was forcibly expelled from it.

"Want some kibble?" she asked.

His ears perked up and he scurried toward the kitchen.

Lilli tugged her robe on and followed suit, snatching up her cell phone and silencing the alarm as she went.

She'd thought she might find Jake in the bathroom or the kitchen, but there was no sign of him. His shoes and jacket were missing too. He likely had a very early practice, with the big game just a couple days away, and he hadn't wanted to disturb her when he left.

Unless he'd remembered his confession of love and regretted saying it? Got up and got the hell out of Dodge, as it were.

No. Lilli gave her head a shake. This was not too good to be true. It was true, and it was better than good. It was sublime.

A loud meow from below.

"Okay. It's coming." She reached into the cupboard and pulled Toby's cat food bin out, dumping an extra full scoop in the bowl to make up for his being exiled to the spare room last night—the kitty equivalent to Siberia.

"Happy now?" She leaned over and gave him his pat on the head so he would commence with breakfast.

Lilli recalled Jake's words from the night before—*I love you too*— and she glanced down to where the water had spilled. The sopping wet remains of the incident rested there on the floor, the bottle having rolled into the corner by the fridge.

A smile lit her face as she bent down to finish the cleanup. "Yes, Jake, I am happy now," she murmured.

Then, Lilli busied herself preparing her morning coffee and checked her phone for a message from Jake. It was six twenty now, and, yes, there was a message waiting. At five fifty-five he'd texted her that he'd had to leave. Early practice. She'd looked so peaceful as she slept, he'd said, that he hadn't wanted to wake her. Oh, and she'd proven herself to be a wild animal that needed taming. He was the guy for the job.

There were also seven missed calls. Those turned out to be from Brad.

She tapped out a quick response to Jake, ignored the guilt biting at her to return Brad's calls, then danced her way to the shower, phone clasped against her chest, coffee in her other hand. Smile firmly planted on her face.

CHAPTER TWENTY-TWO

AS FAR AWAY as she'd had to park just to run into Starbucks to grab a latte, Lilli might as well have left her car at home and walked over. Still, nothing was going to bring her down. Not today. Her lack of sleep the night before may have forced her out of her way to get a pick-me-up before braving traffic on the I-5 Express, but that very same lack of sleep was the reason for the smile on her face this morning too.

She glanced around looking for Donna, but she didn't appear to be there. Lilli had thought she would be back at work after the holidays—and after their little mishap in the ladies washroom on New Year's Eve. She closed her eyes and fought the urge to grimace. She still felt mortified about that. And now she had to add guilt over ignoring her at Trinity in order to hook up with Jake again.

At least the line was moving fast. Lilli was next and she stepped up to the counter.

"Are you having the usual today?" the brunet barista asked.

She'd barely lived in the neighborhood for a couple weeks now and she already had a "usual" at this location. She pulled out her gold Starbucks card, further confirming her caffeine addiction. "I think I'll try the peppermint mocha today. Extra hot. Half sweet peppermint."

"Good choice. Anything else?"

"No, that's all. Thanks, Sara."

The barista scribbled on Lilli's cup and handed back her card.

Lilli smiled and stepped aside to wait as Sara called the next person in line.

She leaned against the cool windowpane and watched the busy coffee baristas steaming and frothing. Lilli pulled out her phone and tapped the screen, bringing up her work email. After a quick scan she determined she could delete seven of them and the rest she could deal with later. The one she had hoped to find—from Coco, one of the models scheduled for the big shoot this weekend—hadn't come through yet.

"Venti extra-hot, peppermint mocha, half-sweet peppermint," the blond-haired barista called out as she set the steaming cup on the counter.

Lilli stepped forward, lifting the cup carefully so as not to spill. As she navigated her way to the service area to pick up a lid and some napkins, she leaned down to lick a dollop of whip cream and chocolate sprinkles from the top. Yum. That was the best part. She really didn't get the concept of low-fat. Life was short. Why not indulge a little?

With her lid in one hand and her coffee in the other, Lilli exited the café. The brisk morning air was biting hard this morning, but Lilli's full hands didn't allow her to fish in her coat pockets for her gloves.

"Here, let me help you."

"Donna. Hi. Perfect timing." Lilli passed her the cup. "Thanks."

Donna smiled and reached out for the plastic lid that Lilli held in her other hand. As she fixed it onto the cup, Lilli dug into her pockets and pulled out her gloves, quickly tugging them on.

"I was going to ask about you in there, but they seemed really busy." She buttoned the extra top button on her coat and took the cup from Donna's extended hand. "How are you?"

"Good," Donna placed her hands on her cheeks as if warming them with the leftover heat from Lilli's coffee. "Tired though. I was up all night, studying. I wasn't supposed to be in today, but they called me saying they were short staffed, blah, blah, blah. So here I am."

"Studying? Do you have exams coming up or something?"

"Not exactly. Although it's sort of a test I suppose. But it's a subject I enjoy so I don't mind pulling an all-nighter."

"Still, that was nice of you to come in on your day off."

"Meh." Donna shrugged. "I got Sunday off now. Maybe I'll watch that silly football game on TV."

"Silly? Football is not silly, Donna—oh. You're teasing me aren't you?"

The grin on the girl's face confirmed it. Meanwhile, the proverbial lightbulb went off in Lilli's head.

"You have Sunday off you say?"

She nodded.

"What if we *went* to the game? Together."

"But isn't it in the other Washington? As in DC?"

"Yes, but suppose we could use my frequent-flyer miles to get a last-minute flight? And I have a discount coupon for car rental. We can drive straight to the stadium from—"

"Count me in."

CHAPTER TWENTY-THREE

BY THE TIME Lilli had arrived at work that morning, her venti cup had been effectively drained of caffeine and her body had been exponentially filled with tremors, both from the aforementioned caffeine and the bumper-to-bumper action that had turned her fifteen-minute commute into forty-five—at least.

The light snow that had fallen overnight had wreaked havoc with the traffic lights, and it seemed drivers had forgotten the rules of the four-way stop. Sure, Seattle PD had some poor schmucks standing in the eye of the traffic storm, blowing whistles and waving motorists through, but with Lilli's saturated schedule, her well of patience had been conversely dry.

The moment she'd arrived at the agency, she'd had to hit the ground running. Her day had consisted of coffee, and then more coffee, eating a single scone—consumed without breathing, she was sure—and then, more coffee. All while gracefully disentangling a snarled string of disasters. Or, to be more succinct, the modelling industry's equivalent of such. Meaning high-strung photographers who were fed up with higher-strung models. Starving waifs showing up for a shoot but fainting from low blood sugar. Advice: eat a Snickers bar already. Teary teens sure that an overnight pimple eruption would end their career. Advice: ditch the Snickers and reach for more water. Oh, and thank God for Bobby Brown—problem solved.

Yes, life was rough in the glamorous world of *Pretty*.

More disconcerting to Lilli were the series of hang-up calls she'd received. Had they been from Jake? A wrong number? She'd had no time to dwell.

So, needless to say, when she'd arrived home from work, worn out and disappointed that she hadn't spoken to Jake all day, the last thing Lilli wanted was to realize all her gear was at the agency. She needed it for the big shoot the following day, and if she wanted to make the red-eye to DC, she wouldn't have time to waste in the morning. The sooner she started with Treye on Saturday—she'd never get used to calling him that, and how he distilled the name Treye from Terrence, she had no clue—the sooner she would be able to get home and pack.

Now, it was eight thirty, exactly twenty minutes after she'd pulled into the parking lot at home—without getting out, mind you—and the Jeep idled at the entrance to the underground parking structure as Lilli rifled through her purse. Where was her security pass?

Her stress level rising, Lilli coerced a deep breath from her lungs. Then one more. And another. After a methodical dissection of her handbag, Lilli found the pass. Open window, swiped card. Nope. As usual, she'd misjudged the distance. Lilli pulled the parking break, shifted to neutral, removed her seatbelt, opened the door, and achieved her purpose.

Swiped card. Check. Houston, we have entry. The overhead door screeched and rattled its way up, taking twice as long as it normally did, just to piss her off.

She put the Jeep in gear, tried to advance, groaned and released the parking brake, then pulled forward. Victory was hers.

Jake and the team were probably settled at their hotel by now. She wasn't sure how things went for the team on away games, but she was certain how it was going for her. She missed Jake.

She shot a glance to the passenger seat and her cell phone, perched beside her handbag, the reigning king atop the mountain of hastily removed items. The red light was blinking, taunting her. *Tsk, tsk, tsk, you forgetful twit. I'm going to die soon and you could have saved me, but no—you left my charger at home. Tsk, tsk, tsk. Blink, blink, blink.*

"Shut up," she muttered, but the phone would not comply any better than her overactive, self-chastising imagination would.

She circled around until she reached the level marked *Willows Agency*. She found a spot with ease. No surprise. It was late, at least for a holiday Friday, and the lot was virtually empty, aside from cars belonging to diehard workaholics. Those vehicles were as much a fixture as the noisy fans and overhead fluorescents.

Lilli disembarked, set the alarm, and headed for the stairs. A shiver *zinged* down her spine. Maybe from the cold. Maybe from the eerie quiet that had captured her within its mute tendrils, affirming its silence with each reverberating *click, clack, click* of her high-heeled boots.

She counted her steps. *One, two, three, four, five, six, seven, eight...*

A fan hammered to life above her head, sending a jolt through her frazzled nerves. At least it diluted the purity of the stillness. Lilli slowed her pace. Her concentration and hearing converged to hone in on a new sound. Muted. Heavy. Slower. *Thump...thomp...thump,* paradoxically juxtaposed to her *click, clack, click.*

Someone else's footfalls? She hadn't heard the heavy garage door open again. Hadn't heard another vehicle. She quickened her pace, *adagio* to *allegro.* The thumping became a resonating bass, matching her tempo. Fear began to pound its own percussive drumbeat in her ears. She accelerated her stride. Her heels struck the pavement, swift and unwavering. *Click, clack. Click, clack.*

Thump, thomp. Thump, thomp. The heavier footfalls punched back, blow for blow, keeping time.

She compelled the air to cycle in and out of her lungs.

Breathe and relax, Lilli. You can handle this.

It was probably the security guard making his rounds.

Click, clack.

Thump, thomp.

No. Lilli couldn't relax. Couldn't shake the uneasy feeling simmering in her solar plexus. She maintained her pace.

So did the steps behind her.

She reached the stairwell entry. The elevator would be too risky, too slow. Her security pass was biting into her clenched hand, but she was glad for the pain. She swiped it. Fast. Dragged the door open. Then, holding her breath, she heaved her weight against the heavy door until it appeased her with a satisfying thud-click.

Now she could breathe. If someone had snuck under the door when she'd driven in, they couldn't follow her anymore. Not without a security pass.

A lungful of oxygen—or as close to it as this recirculated air came—and she commenced the twenty-six-flight expedition to the agency, with one quick and furtive glance over her shoulder.

Scaredy-cat.

Lilli had trudged almost two flights when she heard the weighty thud of the door again. The lights flickered in the corridor. Motivated by adrenaline, she began taking the stairs two at a time. The heavy footsteps behind her also quickened. She didn't slow to turn around.

Scaredy-cat or not, the nerve endings tingling along the back of her neck told her someone was closing in on her. She squeezed her eyes closed for a flash, then looked up, blinking rapidly. Think, think, think. What had she heard on the radio news this morning? Someone was attacked around the construction area of the First Hill Streetcar Line. A woman. A rape maybe? Or a mugging? Teenagers? She didn't know. She should've listened to that story. Shouldn't have turned it off.

Driven by apprehension-filled uncertainty, she surged forward. *Click, clack. Click, clack.* She was in good shape, but still, Lilli's legs were beginning to feel as sturdy as limp spaghetti.

Huff. Puff.

She could handle this.

The landing of the next level arrived. A brief respite from the stairs, but no time to slow down. No time to rest.

She could hear—*feel*—someone's breathing. Right behind her.

A heavy paw seized her shoulder, and the resulting scream sliced the air.

Propelled by another surge of adrenaline, she sucked in a breath, whirled around, pushed, then kicked her assailant. The kick did it.

He grunted and flailed his arms as he fell backward.

Lilli watched in rapt horror—a comedic yet disturbing image—as her attacker stumbled down several stairs before latching onto the handrail, halting his descent. She stared at the shadowy form, squinting to focus in the dimly lit stairwell.

"Back off, asshole." She shouted the words with more bravado than she truly felt. "I know karate." She assumed, what she hoped to be, a sturdy martial-arts stance.

"Bullshit," the man challenged.

"Brad?"

Yes. It was Brad.

And she wasn't sure if she was relieved or not.

He regained his balance and bent over, clutching the rail and his stomach, grunting and gasping. "You got a sniper's kick though. I'll give you that."

They stood in silence, staring each other down with combative gazes fixed—two wild animals sizing each other up.

Lilli spoke first. "You scared the hell out of me."

"I scared you? You just about killed me!" He rose to his full height and rubbed his stomach. "Shit."

"What do you expect? I didn't know it was you. You could have said something. There's some sort of rapist or maniac out there, you know, attacking women on the streetcar line." Lilli let out an exasperated groan. "Why are you here? Better yet, how did you get in?"

"I still have my passkey. Not women. One woman. And it's not a rapist, just your everyday, run-of-the-mill maniac." His words came out matter-of-fact without a single breath of pause in between.

"Explain the difference. And how do you know so much about it?" She threw her arms up in resignation. "Never mind. Why are you here?"

"I was waiting for you at home—well, at your home—and when you pulled in and then drove off I decided to catch up to you. You're not easy to follow you know. You were driving like a lunatic. You ran two yellows and a red. That's not like you. So I had to run three reds—one so red that I barely made it through without getting t-boned. Man that guy was pissed! Anyway, I need to talk to you. It's important."

His words continued to blast so rapidly from his mouth that Lilli felt as though she were at Daytona, watching a NASCAR event. She honed in on the last thing he'd said—needing to speak with her. "You have heard of the telephone, right? It's a new invention, Alexander Graham Bell and all that."

"Funny stuff, Lil. Listen, I did try calling you. If you didn't hang up on people maybe they wouldn't have to stalk you through the streets of Seattle." He raised his brows and tapped the side of his head, as if telling her to think about it.

"That was you? I'll have you know, you hung up on me. Seven times."

"Seven? I only called twice, and you hung up. Whatever. Anyway, I was just trying to catch up to you. I'm sorry."

"I'm busy, Brad, and, believe it or not, I actually don't want to be here. Get to the point."

"I was worried this might be my only chance to talk to you for a while. Your *boyfriend* will be back in a couple of days, and he seems a little insecure around me. Don't know why. Anyway, he threatened me yesterday you know. After I left your place. He was lurking outside and he jumped me. Shoved me against the building. Offered to rearrange my pretty face—his words, not mine—although I am rather good looking I suppose. I got the bruises to prove it."

"I don't believe you." Crossing her arms, she studied his face, expelling her annoyance through a rhythmic toe-tapping on the concrete landing. The blue-eyed puppy-dog stare he was working did nothing to put her at ease.

"He didn't touch the handsome bits. Yet." Brad unzipped his coat and began to lift his t-shirt, his sculpted six-pack already visible above the low waist of his faded jeans.

She raised a hand. "Whoa, whoa, whoa. That's far enough. This isn't Chippendales and I'm fresh out of singles."

He pointed to a patch of angry red-and-purple fist-sized proof. "But I—"

Lilli stopped him again, causing him to chuckle. She was no longer frightened. Just irritated. "The point, Brad. Assuming there is one."

"I'm worried about you, Lil. Jake—he's not stable. You think I did steroids? Who do you think convinced me to try 'em? Yeah, that's right. Your hunky monkey, Jakey-poo." He laughed at his self-perceived cleverness.

"You're full of shit, Brad."

"Am I? Can you be so sure of that?" He sniffed the air in a melodramatic display. "Someone is full of shit though." He sniffed again. "Smells like Jakey-poo, poo." Now a full-on fit of giggles. "Like what I did there? I brought it back around."

Lilli rolled her eyes.

"See, I'm funny too." When she didn't bite, he swiped a hand down his face and came back looking serious. "Fine. If you don't believe me, ask his ex-girlfriend from college. Her name's Ashley."

"What the hell are you talking about?"

"After they broke up, he stalked her, made her life hell. She had to get a restraining order. Anyway, after he went all psycho-fuck on me yesterday, and then you wouldn't answer my calls…I needed to make sure you were unharmed."

Unharmed? God, he was laying it on thick. He could try to sell her manure, claiming it would help her flowers grow, but no matter what he called it, a load of shit was still a load of shit.

Lilli called what she saw. "The only one I see stalking me is you, Brad."

"You and Jake are so close these days." He crossed his fingers. "Inseparable. Two peas and all that. I'm surprised he hasn't told you. You and all your honesty mumbo-jumbo."

"Mumbo-jumbo? Honesty is not—*argh*." She fisted her hands at her sides. "So some broken-hearted bimbo sees Jake hit the big league and she makes up a bunch of lies. Wouldn't be the first time some chick tried to capitalize on a guy's fame. Jake would never do that. He's sweet and gentle, and—"

Brad opened his mouth, stuck his finger in the gaping hole, and made gagging sounds.

"Real mature." She spun around and her heels resumed their tempo toward the next flight of stairs.

His words echoed behind her. "You really don't know."

Her foot hovered above the first step, but she set it back on the landing and turned around. "Don't. Know. What."

Brad ignored the implication behind her singularly enunciated syllables. In fact, he seemed more than happy to enlighten her. "I ran into Craig at the gym the other day. He told me everything. For one of Jake's BFFs he sure doesn't take loyalty very seriously. It's all true."

"Shut up."

"Wouldn't stop calling. Following. Lurking. It's all in some cops flippy little notepad, I promise you. She had to file a report. That kind of stuff is breaking the law, you know."

"Breaking-the-law stuff, Bradley? Like chasing her through red lights? Stalking her through parking garages? Breaking into her apartment? What a crime! What kind of man would do such things?" Lilli's voice boomed off the concrete walls. She tried to lower her pitch, but her escalating blood pressure deterred the attempt. "You're a liar and a hypocrite, Bradley. You are the jealous one. You want me to break up with Jake and you think if I do you'll get me back. Not gonna happen. We're in love."

On the last word, she whirled around, ready to storm off, but he reached out to stop her.

She glared at him and shook his hand away. "Don't touch me. Ever. Even if this shit was true—which it's not—and even if I broke up with Jake—which I won't, guess what? I wouldn't go back to you. In fact—and here's another newsflash you might want to jot down in your own flippy notepad—I started dating Jake to get rid of you."

"Get rid of me?" He spat the words at her as though firing splintered glass.

Lilli volleyed her own shards back. "Yeah. Get *rid* of you. You screwed up one too many times. I'm done with you. D.O.N.E. Done." Lilli dusted her hands together in an exaggerated gesture meant to punctuate her intent.

She wanted to leave, but Brad wasn't finished. He latched on to her sleeve. "See? He's already changed you, Lilli. You're acting like an ungrateful little—"

Lilli jerked out of his grasp, but he captured the bottom of her jacket instead. She crossed her arms in defiance. "Go ahead, Brad. Say it. An ungrateful what?"

His lips pressed tight as his eyes fired daggers, but he remained mute.

Her stance resolute, she began tapping her foot, her own eyes stretching wide, daring him to continue. "Well?"

The thin outline of his mouth began to undulate with subtle waves of reluctance. Lilli was certain she could fill in the blank he'd left hanging in the air between them, but she wondered if Brad had the *cajones* to do it, now that she'd forced an intermission.

Oh, what the hell. She had emotions to set free too, so why not push him to expel his own demons. "Come on, Brad. Don't have the balls to say it? I'm what? An ungrateful…" she prompted, rolling her hand to further encourage.

The wavering lip line morphed into a full sneer as the dam broke wide open. The word surged forth, potent and unrevised. "Bitch!"

It was nothing she hadn't expected, but Brad was all-in now, so he might as well continue. His voice rose in tempo and pitch, belligerence no longer threatened but guaranteed.

"You're acting like an ungrateful bitch, Lilli. And you're going to regret it when there's no one to protect you."

Her own limits breached, it was Lilli's turn to vent. "I hate you! I hope I never lay eyes on you again."

"Careful what you wish for. There's more than one way that could happen."

Angry beyond words now, her hands fisted in tight balls at her sides, Lilli's jaw clenched so fiercely that the tendons in her neck were cording. She released a low, rumbling growl, barely containing what wanted to become a primal scream.

She forced three words through her teeth. "Leave. Me. Alone."

Brad's eyes glistened with ferocity as he wagged a finger at her. "Watch your back, Lilli." His mouth contorted into a bitter sneer, then he opened it to speak again. "And watch your front too. Jake's been known to attack from all sides. He hates to lose."

He released his grip on her jacket and she made another move to leave, this time following through.

"You'll see," he shouted to her back as she stalked away. "He can't keep up his Mister-Nice-Guy act forever. I have nothing to prove. I'm the good guy here. You'll see." The words trailed behind her as if clinging to her shadow. "Just looking out for a friend is all. When you're ready to come crying back to me, you know where to find me."

Heavy footfalls resounded behind her as he stormed down the stairs.

Once they were far enough away, Lilli groaned and sat down on the upper flight to regain her composure. She pictured Brad getting into his Mustang, revving the engine, and speeding up the ramp into the street, fishtailing on the slick pavement as he raced home to plan his next stupid move.

Maybe his aggressive driving would slam him into a pole. Lilli shook her head. That was no way to think. Not even about Brad. She would never wish harm upon anyone. She raised her eyes to the ceiling and whispered, "I take it back."

CHAPTER TWENTY-FOUR

SHE NEEDED TO FOCUS on tomorrow's shoot, but Brad's antics, and his warnings, played out in Lilli's mind. She found herself silently dissecting every word, every nuance. Each one drifting back to her consciousness, jabbing her brain like a resolute woodpecker. But she was equally tenacious, pushing back, shoving the thoughts aside. She'd think nice things. About Jake.

This strategy finally worked, and Lilli managed to accomplish everything she'd set out to do, including getting her mind off Brad's ludicrous accusations. Loaded up with supplies, she trudged back to reception to call security for a walk-down.

She was relieved when Tom answered—she liked him. He usually worked during the day though, and they had a new guy on nightshift. Hired not long ago. He gave her the willies. He had these piercing eyes that lingered too long and made her shudder just to think of them. Surely they had to pass some sort of clearance to work security.

She gave Tom a brief rundown on Brad still having a functioning security card, at which point he grumbled something about the new guy not showing up—again. Dropping the ball—again. Said he would rectify both. Cancel the pass and deal with Jason next shift change. *If* he bothered to show up for work.

She doubted that she would see Jason, or his creepy-eyed stare, again. Probably wouldn't have a job to come back to after Tom was done with him. She felt bad for the guy. He was probably harmless.

Five minutes later Tom was outside the agency holding the elevator door for Lilli. Thankfully, there was no Brad lurking in the shadows of the parking garage.

She thanked Tom and waved good-bye as she rolled through the lot, finally exiting onto the street, pausing to check for pedestrians. And Brad. He didn't appear to be lurking there either.

SHE JOURNEYED HOME, the silence proving to be too much. Her mind began to tingle with apprehension. She couldn't shake the feeling that she was being followed, couldn't rip her eyes away from repeated checks of the rearview mirror. Finally, she rolled down the window a little to let the crisp night air wake her other senses. It had been a hectic day.

She longed to talk to Jake, so, when she stopped at a light, she pulled out her cell. Two percent charge remaining. She pressed the message envelope to see if she'd missed a text from Jake and that single act used the last of the battery, plunging the screen to black.

The light changed and Lilli flipped the radio on. The final bars of a song faded away as the news came on. Lilli reached out to snap it off but hesitated. Maybe she should listen to it. If some rapist—or run-of-the-mill maniac—was stalking the women of Seattle, she probably should know more about it.

The DJ mentioned a few traffic mishaps that had occurred earlier in the day, but no word about the attack along the streetcar line. Lilli was relieved. No news, good news, and all that.

Another playlist began, interspersed with commercials, and before long Lilli was home. Brad's car was outside his building and Lilli felt silly for thinking that he'd been following her. She was just on edge, probably from the lack of sleep since she'd hooked up with Jake.

She moved quickly as she carried her gear inside, darting constant glances around her. After two trips, she was relieved to be inside her apartment without Brad. Lilli locked the door, her shoulders relaxing, a giant yawn stretching her face. God, she was exhausted.

As much as she wanted to go straight to bed, Lilli snatched up the home phone instead. It was late, but she wanted to see if she could reach Jake. When the hotel clerk finally answered, he sounded frazzled. Other lines were ringing in the background. The big game. Hotels must be at capacity.

Hesitant but determined, she asked for Jake, by name and room number so the clerk wouldn't think she was just a random football groupie.

He seemed reluctant, but the nonstop ringing in the background must have swayed his decision and he put her through without further questions. It rang twice. When Jake didn't answer immediately, she felt so much guilt about possibly waking him that she hung up. She would plug in her cell and shoot him a quick text message instead.

A headache began erecting skyscrapers of pain behind her eyes, so, as Lilli searched the apartment for the power cord, she detoured by the medicine cabinet to grab a couple painkillers. She downed them with water from the bathroom faucet, then shuddered at the taste of the chlorine.

Toby arrived at her feet, crouched and licking his paw before wiping at his face. His dinner devoured, his contented purr resonated a quiet backdrop to his self-cleaning routine.

Maybe he'd found her phone charger and taken the cord as a plaything. She went to her bedroom, which was the last place she remembered charging her cell, and lowered to hands and knees to spy underneath everything. All she saw were a few dust bunnies, a discarded sock, a Hershey Bar wrapper, and a Lisa Gardner novel under her bed. No power cord.

She narrowed her gaze, intense scrutiny aimed at her cat, then massaged her temples and pinched her eyes closed as another pain-structure graced the skyline inside her head. What she needed was sleep. No doubt there.

As she rose to standing, a wave of dizziness sent her stumbling. Lilli dropped onto her bed, then collapsed to a prone position, one arm draped over her eyes. She should drink some water. And eat something. What had she eaten today besides the scone? Nothing she could recall.

Her both-ends-of-the-candle life had finally burned wicks to the middle. Work. Jake. No regrets. But without external distractions her body quickly seized its opportunity. One lingering moment with eyes shut was all it took. Lilli was gone.

CHAPTER TWENTY-FIVE

FIFTEEN MINUTES. She was late. But it could have been worse. At least she'd woken up in time to shower. With her cell phone DOA and waiting to be charged, she'd had no alarm, aside from Toby, who, thankfully, was in a perpetual state of hunger and had pawed her face until he'd roused her.

She'd had less than no time to even considering calling Jake on her home phone, barely enough to scoot out to the Jeep, her equipment in tow.

Laden with cosmetics, Lilli arrived at the photo shoot amid the typical chaos and confusion. Serge, the stylist, just finished coifing the last girl and the flare of hairspray was threatening to reacquaint Lilli with last night's headache. She popped a couple Advil.

Nothing like a twittering group of eighteen-year-old girls to make her want to crawl back into her cave. She'd take hollering football fans any day of the week. The girls were flittering about, their voices blending into an amorphous cacophony, creating a palpable energy as Lilli laid her brushes and cosmetics out on the counter.

Scanning the faces in the room, her concern grew. Her star model was not among them. "Hey," she raised her voice above the din, only to regret the loudness in her own ears, "has anyone heard from Coco?"

The collective response was a series of shaking heads followed by a resurrection of chatter, the models self-absorbed and unaffected by the news. Lilli checked the time and, once again, was grateful that Saturday morning traffic had been light.

She went into the hall to find some quiet. A few minutes to spare and she used it to prowl for someone with the same phone model so she could, hopefully, charge her cell. Besides wanting to hear from Jake, she hoped maybe there was a message from Coco.

No luck. Everyone had an iPhone. The charger was completely different.

As the models filled the wardrobe area, waiting to find out the order of the garments they would be wearing, Lilli sought refuge in the makeup room. She grabbed a stool and ran through a string of models in her mind. Who could she use to replace Coco on such short notice? She was about to phone her boss, Chuck, when Terrence, flew into the room.

"Lilli Brooks!" He said her name as if it were a cheer and then proceeded to give her a hug and air-kiss both cheeks, saying, "Muah, muah." He stepped back. "Darling, where is our blond bombshell? I have seen everyone *but* Coco." He cupped his hand and leaned in conspiratorially. "And between you and me, she's the only one I care about." His gaze flitted about the room, even though it was clearly empty aside from the two of them. "Olly olly oxen free!"

Lilli picked up a powder brush and began dusting it on a tissue, finding a reason to avoid making contact with his lens-enhanced ice-blue eyes. "It's not hide and seek, Terrence."

"Treye," he corrected her.

"Right." A bob of her head and a reminder scribbled across her brain. "I'd tell you to sit down for this, *Treye*, but it looks like you couldn't if you tried." Now she fidgeted with the silver chain around her neck.

"You're right about that. Damn Starbucks." He raised his hand in a dismissive gesture. "Love 'em. Hate 'em. What can I say? I'm addicted."

"Me too. Coffee shouldn't taste that good, but I'm glad it does." Her laughter teased at the edges of her burgeoning headache. The Advil should kick in soon. Hopefully.

He jutted a hip and set his hand on it, the other flourishing a sweep through the air. "All right, just spill the coffee beans, darling. What is going on with the venerable Coco now?"

"I haven't heard from her since before Christmas," Lilli confessed, washed with guilt. She'd been so caught up in breaking up with Brad, Brad breaking in, and breaking her take-it-slow rule with Jake that she'd let this slip. She should have touched base with Chuck about it days ago. Lilli bit down on the french tip of her pinky nail. "Coco was supposed to wrap up in Milan and be back on Thursday."

"Two weeks is a lifetime in this business, Lilli. Names have been made and forgotten in that amount of time."

"I know, Terr—Treye. I had her word."

"Coco's word, darling. Coco's. You cannot print that and spend it at Macy's."

"I know that too."

Terrence—*Treye*—brought one hand up to his pursed lips, thinking. "Hmmm." He tapped a beat with his index finger on his upper lip, shunting his eyes side to side for dramatic effect.

"I was just about to call Chuck," Lilli raised her cell, "but my phone's dead. I think Chloe is free. Maybe Brit."

He took her outstretched hand and yanked Lilli off the stool, then spun her around. "Uh-uh-uh. We simply do not have time for that." He sized her up, and his face sparked with light, then gave birth to what Lilli could only term a wicked, evil grin. "We're going to improvise."

"Improvise?"

"Yes." He dragged her from the room and into the hall.

She opened her mouth to protest, but he hushed her before she'd even gotten a word out.

"Chop, chop." He clapped his hands together, placed them both on her back, and shoved her into the fitting room.

"Kate." He snapped his fingers loudly, and the wardrobe girl turned to look, straight pins bit between her teeth. "Darling, where are Coco's outfits?"

"Over here," Kate replied, although it came out sounding garbled through her pressed-tight lips. She added a head bob for clarification, gesturing to the center rack.

"Perfect. Hand them over to Lilli—she's taking Coco's place."

"I'm what now?" Lilli was sure her mouth was as wide as the Grand Canyon at that moment. "But I—"

"No buts, my dear—except yours in that Versace over there. You're perfect. You've got the body, the bone structure—Kate has a mouth full of straight pins and wardrobe has six-inch platform heels. Voilà." He did another flourish and twirled around to leave. His mind was made up.

Lilli gaped from Kate, to the models—who had now found a reason to be quiet—back to Kate, and then to Terrence—*Treye, Treye, Treye*—who was lingering outside the door. "But I still need to do makeup on all of them."

"We'll shoot you last. You'll have time to work your magic on this scraggly bunch." He tossed a hand gesture toward the models. "Kate can help, and trust me, darling, you will be fabulous." He sashayed down the hall in full-on Treye mode, leaving Lilli at a loss for words.

Kate shrugged and handed her an armful of clothes with cursory directions on what goes with what. "I'll stop by after to do a fitting."

Lilli felt overwhelmed, and the emotion must have tagged her face like graffiti because Kate patted her shoulder and offered a sympathetic look. "I'll help with makeup. I know I don't wear any, but I do know how to apply it." She offered a warm, sincere smile that *almost* put Lilli at ease. "Don't worry, hun. You'll do great. All you have to do is stand there and look pretty." Kate scanned Lilli from toe to head. "And trust me, you got that covered."

Lilli mumbled the word "Thanks" as she slunk out of the room, her arms burdened with thirty pounds of designer fashions.

As she stood in the hallway, she tried to get her mind around what just happened. Then, gathering her resolve, Lilli took a deep breath and gestured toward the door. "All right then, ladies, let's go." The models followed her like dutiful sheep into the makeup room.

"Who's first?" She looked at the schedule. "Mackenzie, you're up."

The model whispered something to the girl beside her, who giggled a response, and then she hopped up on the stool and twisted her hair back while the others waited their turn.

Lilli attempted to ignore their mindless chattering as she began her work. Kate did the foundations, while Lilli did the painting. In a flurry of brush strokes and powder puffs, one by one, the transformations were completed, and, one by one, the models went into the studio for their shots. She could hear the music pumping in the background, and Terrence/Treye barking directions. It was not until she finished the last model and turned the brushes on herself that she fully considered the ramifications of what had transpired earlier.

She was excited at the opportunity she supposed, but anxious about the extra time it would take. She still hadn't spoken to Jake since before he'd left, and her only solace came in knowing that, between practice drills and studying the Redskins game film, he was likely as busy as she was.

THE DAY HAD flown by already and she still had to do this model thing, then haul her supplies home and try to get to bed early. Oh, and pack. Sheesh. Lilli blew at a whisp of hair that had fallen across her left eye. Then, right on cue, Serge bustled in, muttering something about having a full schedule and having to come back.

When he saw it was Lilli he needed to coif, he softened his tone from bitter to sullen, then began spraying and backcombing her mane until she thought she resembled a wild jungle cat. Thankfully, between the two of them, it didn't take long to transform her into the sexy glamour look that Treye had commanded.

Kate was about to start with Lilli's wardrobe when Treye flounced in, lifting the camera from around his neck. "Honey, I *have* to eat or I'm positively going to *die*. Running to the deli while you're getting wardrobed. Want anything?"

Her body was craving some real food too. All she'd had was coffee, M&Ms, and Coca-Cola. "Sure." Lilli reached into her purse and pulled out a twenty.

He waved it away, edging into the hall. "On me. I'll bring you something delish," he sang on his way out.

Lilli followed Kate into the wardrobe area and began trying on all the garments so that Kate could make any needed alterations. Half an hour later, she was finished. Kate went home and Treye still wasn't back from the deli.

She began to pace, feeling very much like the caged beast she had thought she resembled. She eyed her darkened cell phone screen. Maybe she could will it to have life. Or, she could track down an actual landline. About to prowl for one, Treye bustled in, looking flustered.

"What happened?"

"Nothing to worry about, darling." He smoothed his shirt, then his hair. "I had a little run-in with my ex-boyfriend." He raised his hand dismissively. "Apparently they'll let anyone work in the service industry these days."

"You sure you're okay?"

"Okay? Darling, I'm fabulous."

Terrence had recovered his usual flare, but the shadow in his eyes made Lilli want to comfort him. Still, she really wanted to get done here. Lucky for her he seized the moment.

"Let's eat—and no, Dean did *not* prepare our food. Then…we have magic to make."

Lilli unwrapped her sandwich and devoured it, barely chewing, causing her stomach to rumble noisily. Then, she couldn't help it, she looked up at the clock on the wall. Again.

"Worrying causes wrinkles, darling."

Lilli diverted her gaze back to him, her cheeks full of turkey and rye. Unable to respond in words, she just mumbled.

"You're thinking maybe you should have blown this off and that you didn't sign up for this much commitment. Or attention." He folded his sandwich wrapper and walked over to the garbage can. "But, girlfriend, let me assure you, whatever you are giving up to stay here late will be more than worth it." He took a sip of soda and wagged a finger. "In fact, I wouldn't be a bit surprised if you become a hot commodity when this issue hits."

After six wardrobe changes and an equal amount of film rolls, Treye finally announced the end. "That's a wrap. Lilli Brooks, you are a natural."

"Thanks, Treye," Lilli replied, the nickname beginning to flow from her lips with more ease, as she scooted behind the screen to change into her own clothes.

"The camera adores you, Lilli. If I was anybody else I might blush at the way it makes unabashed love to you, right in front of me."

"I'm glad it worked out. After all, if I hadn't screwed up—"

"Guilt causes wrinkles too, darling." He snapped off his spotlights. "I don't believe in it, and neither should you. Now go." He nudged her toward the door. "We both want to blow this churro stand."

CHAPTER TWENTY-SIX

LILLI COULDN'T GET home fast enough. Still, she caught herself checking the rearview a couple times, admonishing herself for creating a new bad habit.

Finally she was unlocking her apartment door, beyond glad to be home. She had barely turned the deadbolt and the telephone was already ringing. Lilli flung the door open, dropped her purse, and kicked off her shoes, avoiding Toby as she scurried over. "Hello?" Clutching the phone to her ear she crossed back and shut the door, securing the locks in succession. "Is anyone there? Jake?"

After a brief delay, he spoke. "You're finally home."

"Jake, I'm so happy to hear your voice," Lilli said as Toby circled her ankles. "I've missed you."

"Where you been?"

"The photo shoot. Remember? And my phone died—last night—couldn't find my charger, and you wouldn't believe the crazy couple days I've had."

"Right."

Was that sarcasm?

"I thought you'd be home a long time ago." He paused. "Did you go out after?"

"No. I tried to call you at the hotel, and—gosh, this day has been so hectic. The most unexpected thing happened, Jake. You won't believe it."

"Unexpected?"

"You won't believe it," she repeated. "I barely believe it and I was there."

"Tell me."

"The feature model bailed on the shoot—Coco, of course—but guess who took her place?" Lilli didn't wait for his reply. "Me. Can you believe it? That's why I'm so late." Lilli wandered around the apartment as she spoke, feeding Toby, tidying up a little. "They shot me last. Anyway, I'm glad to be home, happy to hear your voice. Finally. How are things going there?"

"Hmmm," Jake responded. "Practice went okay, I guess, nothing special. Just been waiting to talk to you."

"Sorry. I wanted to talk to you too—so much. Stupid cell."

"I was getting worried about you. All alone. Without protection."

"Were you thinking about the streetcar attack victim?"

"What? No. I was thinking about you."

"That's sweet, Jake. Me too."

"I don't know how I'm gonna play without my lucky charm tomorrow." The hesitation in Jake's voice crackled across the line. He hadn't struck her as superstitious, but he must have forgotten some sort of trinket at home.

"Did you forget your four-leaf clover?" Lilli made an attempt to lighten his mood. "Or was it a lucky rabbit's foot?"

"Neither."

"Something from when you were little?"

"According to my mother, I was never little, but no. My lucky charm is something new. It's you, Lilli. You're my lucky charm."

See. She was right. Jake could never have done all those things Brad said he did.

"Just imagine I'm there, Jake." She pictured the look on his face when she made it to DC after all. A part of her was aching to tell him she'd booked a flight, but no, the surprise would be worth it.

"I'll try." Jake said the words, but it sounded as though he'd put only half his heart in them. "Listen, Lilli, I don't want to, but I have to go. I'm supposed to be getting to bed early."

"Okay." Lilli held back her desire to pout. Saying good-bye was for the best. She wanted to get to the airport early so they could make it through security with plenty of time to spare. Plus, she still needed to pack, shower, get ready, and go pick up Donna. She'd sleep on the flight. "I guess I'm pretty tired too."

"You're going to watch me play tomorrow, right?"

"Of course," she said. "I'll have front row seats—in front of the sports channel. In fact, I've planned my whole day around the game."

"Yeah. All right."

Again, she wanted to tell him her secret—he sounded really down—but she held back. "I'll be thinking about you all night." Lilli waited for a response from Jake, but he offered only silence. "Jake? You there?"

"Yeah."

"You okay?"

"Lilli?"

"Yes?"

"You said you'd be thinking of me all night."

"I did."

"I want you to know something. I think about you every night. Every day. All the time, Lil. I never stop. Even—"

She waited for him to finish his thought, but he let it die on the next breath. The energy coming off him was tangible. It carried a brooding texture, even across the miles of telephone line. "Jake?"

"I gotta go."

"Jake?" she tried again, breathing in a huge lungful of air, preparing herself for the next words she wanted to say. "I..." Another intake of oxygen. Just because she'd said it before—sort of—didn't make it any easier now. It was still foreign territory.

Her chest seemed to shrink five sizes, causing an almost painful twinge in her heart. She inhaled deeply and cleared her throat, then chose to spit out the words in rapid succession before she could change her mind. "I love you." There. She did it. That wasn't so hard now, was it?

"Oh God." He unleashed his own loud rush of breath. "I love you too."

CHAPTER TWENTY-SEVEN

BRIAN LIFTED HIS mug off the desk and cradled it in his hands as he shifted to the windows. He needed a break from thinking. From overthinking. The recent attack in the construction zone of the streetcar line was niggling at him. Monty had said there was something familiar about it, but she wasn't sure what.

She was probably right. Usually was when she made those calls. His partner was an FBI junkie. Her idea of downtime was lurking on the Fed's most-wanted site, studying the faces and names, hoping, waiting really, for her chance to spot one of these guys in a crowd of faceless people.

Beatrice Montgomery. But don't ever call her Beatrice, at least not to her face. She hated it. Call her Montgomery, Monty, Bea—that she could handle. Beatrice never went over well. He was pretty sure she didn't know his middle name, even after three years on the beat together, but still, he only ever pushed the name game on rare occasions, like when she had her hands full and couldn't get him in a headlock or pin his arms behind his back.

Not that he couldn't hold his own with a girl. He just chose not to. His mama raised him right. Although, his partner was anything but a girly-girl. A lithe beauty of mixed descent, she owned every one of her five feet eleven inches worth of sinewy muscle. And yeah, she'd arm wrestled a few of her brothers in blue, and won.

Brian couldn't say whether or not some of them had *let* her win, but speaking for himself, he'd worked for every single victory. Yeah, she was that tough. And she ate, slept, and breathed those three little letters. Was determined to join the feds one day. She wanted to exercise some of those Psych credits she'd earned in college.

Then, as though his thought digression had been her segue, his partner strode into their shared work area, both hands brandishing Starbucks cups. He glanced at his ceramic mug, half filled with what they delightfully referred to in the bullpen as *Mississippi mud*—green tea was not going to cut it tonight. That was enough motivation for him to greet her in the fashion she desired. "Monty!"

She scrunched her face into a scowl, then allowed a smile to beam through. "You're only saying that because I have these." She raised the cups, then extended one toward him.

He reached for it and she yanked it back, her smile morphing into a mischievous grin. "Admit it, Harris. Admit you were thinking about calling me by my great-grandmother's name, and I'll replace your mud with this sweet, black nectar."

"We're still talking about the Starbucks, right?"

She rolled her eyes, looked at the coffee in her hands, and handed him one. Then, she proceeded to slug him in the shoulder. "I'm more of a cinnamon brown, and trust me, I'm not that sweet."

He elevated his in toast then rubbed his arm in mock suffering. "Might leave a mark. Still, totally worth it." He reigned in his smirk and brought the cup to his lips, savoring the first sip. "Yup. Sweet and black—just like my partner."

Monty growled at him. Actually growled. Snarl and all. Then she made a "bring it on" gesture with her fingertips. "You want another? I won't go easy this time." She set her cup down and cracked her knuckles. "You're gonna cry like a little girl, Harris."

He lifted his cup to cover his chuckle, took a sip, then raised his hand in surrender. "No. No more. You win."

"That's what I thought."

Oh, did he mention Monty *hated* to lose?

She folded herself and perched on the edge of his desk, then she slid his chair backward with her foot and motioned for him to sit.

Without preamble, she launched right into the reason for her intense visage, stopping only to breathe occasionally and sip her coffee. By the time she was done, she'd enlightened Brian to the cause of the familiar feeling regarding the recent attack. She'd read about it as an unsolved crime in another state.

"Now, here's the really interesting part." She rose from his desk, her fingertips thrumming a quick pulse on the surface as she stared down at him.

He waited patiently beneath her fixed gaze. A suspect—guilty or not—would certainly cave under her intimidating stance, but Brian knew her well enough to know she'd hit her point shortly. Which she did in the next beat.

"In two separate states, within the last eight years, there have been similar situations. First, a young blonde was found beaten in an alley in New Orleans. She recovered from her injuries but never had an accurate description of her attacker. But," she waved a pointer finger in the air, "several weeks later, another woman, with similar features and hair, went missing from her college dorm. *She* has never been found."

"Okay," he said, "but how does this tie in with our—"

"I'll tell you how, but wait. So, part two of our little story. About three years after that, in Illinois this time, another pretty young blonde is attacked, her face disfigured, permanent brain damage. Vegetative."

"Let me guess," Brian started, "a couple months after that another flaxen-haired beauty goes missing, never to be seen again."

She snapped her fingers then pointed. "Close." She lifted her Starbucks cup, shook it and realized it was empty, then set it back on the desk.

He counted a beat of ten in his head. The point was coming…

"This time it was only three weeks later. Less than a month after the original attack outside a diner in an older part of town. Similar, though not exact, MOs. But close enough to chalk it up to an evolving criminal mind." She reached in front of him and snatched a carrot stick out of the plastic container on his desk, then snapped off a bite. She thrust the remainder toward him as she spoke. "So, what do you think?"

"I can see the correlation between those two, but so far, ours could just be a random attack."

"Could be. But I don't think so." She popped the last bite of carrot into her mouth. "Guess what color our vic's hair was?"

"Blond?"

"Blond." She breezed to her own desk and flopped into her chair, spinning it around to face him.

He followed her lead and picked up a piece of broccoli. "If this is the same guy attacking our girl here in Seattle, then it stands to reason that another blonde is about to vanish."

She nodded.

"But we have nothing to go on."

"I know. That's the crappy part. We need more on our end if the feds are gonna get involved."

"So, we wait?"

"We wait."

CHAPTER TWENTY-EIGHT

LILLI HAD MANAGED to get everything done and be out of her apartment by midnight. Although she was sure she'd noticed Brad lurking in the shadows, watching her load the Jeep, he'd said nothing and had not approached her. She put a mental tick in the win column on that one.

Her luck had continued when she'd arrived to find Donna ready to go as well. "You look great, Lilli." Donna tossed her large duffle in the back and climbed in. "Your hair looks...*different*."

She eyed herself in the rearview. Her hair was still wild and she had on more makeup than usual. "This is from the shoot today. I skipped my shower, but at least I'm on time." She turned her gaze to Donna, searching for something she could compliment her on too. "That's a cute hat," she said.

"Thanks. I skipped the shower too, so I thought I'd hide under the beanie. Good job booking the flights, by the way."

"I know. I was so relieved. Surprised, but relieved. I don't even mind the short layover in Phoenix, under the circumstances." Lilli shifted gears. She couldn't wait to get to the airport, obtain her boarding pass so she knew it was official, and then get through security. Their flight didn't leave until four twenty AM, but there was something to be said for the early bird with all the airport hoops one had to jump through these days.

"What time do we arrive at Dulles?" Donna asked.

"We're cutting it close. We're supposed to arrive at three-oh-one—DC time—but it should be quick getting through. That's why I made sure we only brought our carry-on luggage. No time for the carousel. Then after we get the rental it's about a forty-five-minute drive to FedExField. Kickoff is at four thirty."

"You really are cutting it close."

"I know. It was the only flight that had room for two. But if we miss kickoff that's okay. It'll be easier finding our spots after everyone is seated."

Donna opened her mouth in a gaping yawn, raising her hand to cover it. "Sorry. I've had to pull some nightshifts lately."

"Nightshifts? At Starbucks?"

"Oh, yeah. We have to get the baked goods ready and stuff." She leaned back in the seat and stretched her arms above her head. "So, you never did tell me how you managed tickets to the game too."

"That's where 'who you know' comes into play. My boss, Chuck. He always has tickets for everything. Likes to be ready to wine, dine, and entertain clients at a moment's notice. Of course, I had to promise him an as-yet-unnamed favor in return."

"I'm definitely impressed with your skills." She pulled her hood up and over her eyes, and leaned toward the window. "Let me know when we're close to the airport. I'm going to take a little nap, if you don't mind."

"Sure. Go right ahead. I'll wake you before we get there." Lilli was actually thankful. All she really wanted right then was quiet. As much as she took a positive stance, in truth, she was a little worried about the close timing and needed to calm her nerves before getting on the plane. So, as Donna rested beside her, Lilli did some deep breathing and listened to an ambient CD.

THEY'D MADE IT through security, had their boarding passes, and had located their departure gate. Lilli spied a row of seats with three available spots at the end. She sat down and rested her bag, alongside Donna's, on the extra seats, while Donna headed off in search of a quick bite to eat.

Lilli rotated her head and neck, then stretched her back before slouching down on the seat. When she could no longer see her friend wandering down the long corridor, she reached into her purse and pulled out her boarding pass. She had made it. She was actually going to the game. Maybe late, but at least she'd be there. Jake would be so happy to see her.

Although she was dead tired, she didn't think she could relax. She was too excited. As much as she'd worried, everything seemed to be coming together effortlessly.

"I hope you like stir-fry."

Lilli glanced up to see Donna with two Styrofoam containers on a tray. "It'll do. Thanks. What do I owe you?"

"Nothing. Just smile and say thank you. It's my treat. You made my life, taking me on this trip with you."

"Your life?"

"Okay, maybe my month." Donna stood holding the food, studying Lilli with expectancy in her eyes.

"Thank you," Lilli tried, then offered a smile.

That was the magic word. Donna handed her a container and a fork, then she plopped down where Lilli had cleared their bags from. "Month, life, whatever. In case you hadn't noticed, I don't have many friends." Donna shoved a forkful of food into her mouth.

Lilli didn't know what to say to that, so she followed suit and did the same, shoving a bite between her lips. She was starving. Hadn't eaten much since the sandwich at the shoot. But after a couple mouthfuls, she detected a bitter taste to the chicken. She sent a peripheral glance toward Donna to see if she seemed to notice the same thing. She was still busy devouring her meal, so Lilli figured it must just be her imagination. She ate several more bites, focusing more on the rice and veggies than the chicken though.

She caught sight of a few passengers with children lining up near the gate. "They're about to call for boarding," Lilli said.

Donna nodded and shoveled the last of her food into her mouth, then rose and snatched up her duffle. "That was delicious." She tossed her empty container into a nearby trash can then reached for Lilli's.

She handed it over.

"You barely touched yours," Donna mumbled through her mouthful of food.

Lilli shrugged. "I guess I was so hungry that I lost my appetite."

"Waste not, want not." Donna flashed a glare at the leftover food as if Lilli had committed a crime. "You wanna take it with?"

She shook her head. "Thanks for the suggestion, but I really won't eat it and then it'll just be garbage anyway. I can pay you back for it."

Donna thrust the container in the trash, a few grains of rice falling to the floor as she did. Then, she turned to Lilli with a wide smile—

one that didn't quite seem to reach her eyes. "Wouldn't hear of it. I know you're grateful. Even if you didn't finish your supper." She linked her arm through Lilli's. "Let's go."

THE ALMOST THREE-HOUR journey dragged on. Donna seemed content to drowse off while Lilli flipped through the inflight movies, not able to settle her mind on one. Every now and then she gazed across Donna and stared out at the dark sky, straining to see the twinkling cityscapes below.

The time seemed to pass excruciatingly slow. There was a baby seated a row or two behind them, and every now and then it would start to cry. Lilli wondered what would happen when the plane was landing in Phoenix. The poor baby's ears were going to start to hurt.

It wasn't long before she got her answer. As the plane began its descent, the baby began to howl and scream. The mother, who sounded quite young herself, hushed and cooed in a frantic voice, trying to calm the infant. Finally, an older-sounding woman, likely the grandmother she supposed, took the baby and, within moments, all was quiet again.

That was a relief. A vile headache was already threatening to attack the temple region of Lilli's head. She didn't want to be grumpy when she got to the game, but she had already stowed her handbag under the seat, and the flight attendants would chastise her if she took it out to fish around for painkillers right now. Lilli bit the bullet instead.

THE LAYOVER IN Phoenix was brief. Barely enough time to grab a drink, use the bathroom, and then jaunt through the terminal to meet their connecting flight.

They shared few words as they scooted around other weary travelers, hustling to get to the gate and claim their seats. After lining up in the queue—and a quick survey by Lilli to see if the baby would be joining them on this flight too—they made their way on board, without the baby and her mother.

Donna grabbed Lilli's carry-on bag and stowed it with her duffle above their row, allowing Lilli to claim the window seat this time, while she took the aisle. Lilli wondered what Donna would do when the person who was sharing their row showed up and wanted the aisle seat.

She got her answer when a heavy-set man, who appeared to be in his forties, squeezed in between them after giving Donna a look that would have made Lilli change position if she had been in the aisle. Donna, however, didn't budge, letting the man fold his large frame into the center seat.

Great. Now Lilli could spend the next four hours and twelve minutes scooched up to the window in order to avoid making full body contact with the wheezing, smelly man beside her. At least Donna had room to lean away.

Lilli wondered, briefly, if Donna was holding a grudge because she hadn't finished the food she'd bought for her. But that was silly. No one would hold a grudge over something like that, and besides, there was no way Donna could have known an overweight man was going to share their row.

Her headache seemed to have smoothed out a little, but now her stomach was churning. Maybe she should've stopped eating after the first bite of that awful stir-fry. She wished she'd paid attention to the name on the napkins so she could make certain not to eat at that restaurant again.

She decided to shut the window cover and close her eyes. Hopefully time, and her queasy stomach, would pass quickly.

APPARENTLY LILLI had managed to fall asleep. She only became aware of this fact when the man beside her began to snore—loudly. Thankfully, the plane felt like it was beginning its descent, which meant they would soon touch down at Dulles.

She raised her seat and adjusted her seatbelt right before the announcement came on telling passengers to do just that. Donna sat up and rubbed at her eyes before doing the same, but the large man was still sawing logs. Lilli debated nudging him awake, but didn't want to engage him in conversation. The flight attendants would walk the aisle shortly and wake him up, so she let that one go. She reminded herself it was not her responsibility.

Lilli closed her eyes and took a deep breath. A small amount of turbulence, combined with the plane's declivity, caused a resurfacing of the nausea from earlier. If she had to use that little paper sack to throw up, Lilli would be mortified. Mind over matter. That's all she needed. She could handle this. Breathe in. Breathe out. Focus her attention. She would not vomit.

That was the moment the sleeping man in the middle decided to wake up. He lifted his arms to rub his eyes and the action wafted his sweaty stench toward Lilli. She wrinkled her nose and then held her breath. She could handle this. Mind over…

He opened his mouth in a gaping yawn and if his own body odor had had legs the smell of his breath would have sent it running. It was that bad.

Lilli's stomach clenched and heaved. A small amount of burning vomit rose into her throat. She forced herself to swallow it back. She could handle—

Nope. No she couldn't. She scrambled to yank the paper sack from in front of her. It was caught behind the inflight magazine. *Crap.*

Donna thrust a hand in front of Lilli's face. Lilli grabbed the bag from her, pulled it open, and regurgitated the contents of her stomach into it. Just in time.

One more heave and a panting Lilli darted sheepish eyes around her to see how many passengers had witnessed her little show. Four in total, aside from those in her own row. Two were giving her sympathetic smiles, one was staring, and the other was looking offended.

At this point, Lilli forced herself not to care. Instead she switched her focus to maintaining her current non-vomiting state. Then, as the wheels touched down on the Dulles tarmac, and several passengers applauded the landing, she breathed a sigh of relief. She'd made it. Well, almost. They still had to drive to Maryland, but it would be smooth sailing from here, and she couldn't wait to see Jake. Yes. Things were only going to get better. They couldn't get any worse.

CHAPTER TWENTY-NINE

WITH ONLY A LIGHT dusting of snow along the Capital Beltway, driving conditions were good on I-495 as Lilli swung past Jones Point Park, ready to cross the Potomac. Donna had her face turned toward the side window and Lilli couldn't tell if she was awake and watching the scenery go by or if she'd closed her eyes and drifted off. The slouch of her head gave Lilli the impression the latter was true.

Mostly, Lilli kept her eyes on the horizon, but every now and then, she allowed her gaze to appreciate the delicate beauty of the frost-covered trees along the Interstate. Soon, she reminded herself, they would be there soon.

The signs for their exit started appearing, getting closer with each passing mile marker, and a sense of relief swept over her. However, the nearer they got to their destination, the more the traffic seemed to become saturated. Probably a few other last-minute fans making their way to the game.

As she hung a left onto Arena Drive, her heart began to flutter in her chest. When she made a right onto Brightseat Road, the thumping rose to a crescendo in her ears. Lilli sat up a little straighter in the seat and dropped her shoulders from their hunched position.

Donna seemed to be stirring back to life in the seat beside her. She yawned and stretched, adjusting her hat, which had tipped askew on her head.

Lilli had been avoiding looking at the dashboard clock, not wanting to get stressed about time, but she was so close now. She broke down and slanted a glance at it. Could have been worse.

"Four forty-five," Donna said as if she were reading Lilli's mind. "Game's already started."

"Yeah." Lilli sighed, then caved in and turned the satellite radio on. "Might as well hear the score, I guess."

Donna scanned through the channels until she came to the NFL station that was airing the game.

Lilli reached down and turned up the volume, then tuned her ears to try to hear the announcers above the almost deafening clamor from the crowd.

"We've got a third-and-long situation here, Howie," the first commentator spoke.

"Third and long? That's one way of putting it, Jim." Howie chuckled. "That last penalty cost the Seahawks fifteen, and Edwards has no choice but to go to the passing game."

"Why not? The running game has been ineffective against this Redskins defense."

"Play clock winding down. Redskins are showing blitz."

Jim's voice was rising. "The crowd is so loud here at FedExField. Edwards appears to be struggling to hear through his earpiece."

"He's calling an audible."

"I sure hope this rookie knows what he's doing, Howie."

Lilli pulled over to the side of the road. The energy was too intense. She couldn't concentrate on driving. She listened as Jim called the play-by-play.

"Edwards in the pocket, looking downfield. The Redskins have got man-to-man on Garvin."

"Garvin was his intended target, Jim, I can tell you that, but with Jeremy Bell practically wearing Garvin as a suit, it's just not worth the risk."

"That's right, Howie. Wait. Edwards drops back. He's got Harper Traynor in the end zone."

"I love the way this guy can read the field."

"Edwards under pressure—oh!"

"Almost sacked by Clive Henderson, but Henderson seems to have lost his footing going in for the grab."

"The field conditions are definitely subpar, Jim. Henderson is not the first player that slipped here today."

The crowd roared even louder, and Lilli was biting her nails now.

"He's on the run. Edwards is determined to move the chains. Past the forty. Past the fifty. Into Redskins territory now. He's almost got the first dow—oh!"

Whistles blew and shouts rang out in the stadium. Then, the cheering gave way to a hush, and the energy seemed to change. Donna and Lilli faced each other. Something wasn't right. She couldn't make out what was going on, but a chill ran the length of Lilli's spine and the prickly sensation spread over her entire body. She held her breath.

"Edwards is down."

"Oh my God," Lilli murmured.

Donna reached over and placed her hand on top of Lilli's, which was clenched around the steering wheel of the Toyota Prius she'd rented. "I'm sure he'll be okay, Lilli."

There was a steady buzzing from the crowd. She could picture them all waiting for Jake to get up. Clearly he wasn't, or there would be cheering—even from those on the opposing team's side. This was one moment most fans suspended their rivalry, and that just wasn't happening.

Lilli forced herself to breathe. Closed her eyes and willed Jake to get up. *Come on, Jake. You can handle this. I'm almost there. Please.*

"Medics are on the field, Jim."

"They're surrounding him, talking, but it does not look like Edwards is responding, Howie."

"Here comes the ambulance. Looks like he may be going to Cheverly, Jim."

"This does not look good for Jake Edwards. Or the Seattle Seahawks."

Lilli turned the volume down a little and slumped back in her seat, staring straight ahead. This could not be happening. No. Jake was supposed to be playing the game of his lifetime, and she was supposed to arrive and surprise him. No. No. No.

"Maybe he'll come back," Donna said.

"No, Donna. That's not how it works. There are other options before an ambulance comes out. The player can get up and walk off the field. He can limp off with a guy on either side. Even hoisting him onto a stretcher and carting him off is better than an ambulance. Something is very wrong, Don—"

"Howie, we have just gotten word from the booth that Jake Edwards will not be returning to the game today."

Lilli fought to get air into her lungs, but sobbing overtook her body before she could.

Donna sat in silence beside her. Really, what could she say?

Suddenly weak, Lilli dropped her head forward onto the steering wheel. As she took in a shuddering breath, she whispered a single word. "Jake."

"ALMOST THERE?"

"Almost."

"Thanks for taking over at the wheel, Donna. I'm so worried about Jake. I don't think I could have driven, much less figured out what hospital to go to."

"That's what I'm here for." Donna reached over and squeezed Lilli's hand.

Lilli sighed deeply and flipped the visor down to check her makeup in the mirror. Her eyes were rimmed red and a little puffy. Thick black smudges ran underneath. She slid the pads of her fingers beneath both eyes and swept away the traces of mascara. She pinched her cheeks to give them some color, a trick her grandmother had taught her, then she closed her eyes for a moment, just to breathe.

When she opened them again, they were in front of Prince George's Hospital Center. The red-brick building loomed large and daunting. Donna stopped in front of the emergency entrance. "Are you okay to go in alone while I park the car?"

"Yes." Lilli got out and leaned in the open door, offering a smile of appreciation. "Thanks."

Donna mirrored the gesture and then scooted Lilli away.

Without looking back, she hurried into the hospital, her eyes darting in all directions. To her right, she noticed a group of EMTs rushing a gurney down the hall amid lots of chatter. Then, a blur of blue and green scrubs encircled it, effectively blocking her view. That had to be Jake.

Another surge of adrenaline shifted her into a higher gear, accelerating her pace. Desperate, she ran over and pushed her way into the cluster of interns. A feeling of horror whelmed in her at the sight she beheld. Jake's large form was lying on the gurney—with the sheet pulled over his face.

"Is he—" She swallowed hard against the immovable lump in her throat, but she couldn't bring herself to finish the sentence.

One of the scrub-wearing interns turned to face her. "I'm sorry, ma'am, are you related to the deceased?"

The deceased?

Lilli's head began to spin. The world was surely crumbling down all around her. Her vision skittered in and out of focus as her limbs lost all strength. The cacophony of voices around her began to blend together as she slipped into a void of darkness.

CHAPTER THIRTY

FLOATING, PITCH-BLACK obscurity had swallowed her whole. Lilli could hear a far-away beeping and distant voices, talking to her. About her. A *squeak-squeak-swoosh* and the din of clinking glass and metal rounded out the awkward symphony. Where was she? What was happening to her?

Lilli's nose twitched as the sulfurous aroma of brussels sprouts combined strongly with the unmistakable scent of chlorine bleach. Her eyes fluttered...once...twice.

Overwhelming white light reflected off stark white walls and her eyes drifted closed again. Cold institutional linoleum pressed into her back and she heard the echo of footsteps, running toward her, getting closer. Her eyes fluttered again, this time staying open. People staring down at her, faces she didn't recognize surrounding her. In the background, a Filipino woman pushing a food cart.

"She's coming out of it," someone shouted.

Then she saw Donna running toward her.

"Oh my gosh. Is she okay?" Donna had Lilli's purse and she dropped it to the floor then crouched down, breathless, beside Lilli. She sent questioning eyes up toward the group. "What on earth happened to her?"

"Fainted. Went down hard too." The response came from a lanky redheaded fellow in mismatched scrubs that looked to be at least two sizes too big for his slight frame.

"Why would she faint?"

The redheaded fellow dodged his scruffy chin toward the large sheet-covered figure on the gurney, and Lilli watched with uncertainty as Donna's eyes drifted in that direction.

Then, Lilli remembered why she'd fainted. She immediately tried to get up, but a hand pressed down, gently but firmly, on her shoulder.

"Not so quick. We need to check you out first."

"Do we have to? It's an emergency. I can't just lie here."

"Hospital policy, ma'am."

Lilli acquiesced, albeit reluctantly.

"I'm sorry. We need to make sure you didn't injure your neck or spine when you fell." The man felt along the back of her neck, gently manipulating the vertebrae. He then pulled a penlight from his pocket and attempted to check her pupil dilation.

Her eyes began to fill with tears though, complicating his further examination, so he paused. The light drifted to the side, and Lilli blinked, releasing the salty stream down her face, where it came to rest, pooled in her ears.

She wiped at the tears, then turned to Donna and began to shake uncontrollably. "He's dead, Donna. He's dead." Lilli sobbed as her friend looked with desperation toward the group.

One of them spoke to her. "You next of kin?"

She gave Lilli's hand a squeeze. "No." Donna stood to face him, jacking a thumb toward Lilli. "But she's his girlfriend."

"Uh, girlfriend?" The orderly was clearly puzzled. "Sorry if this sounds indelicate, miss, but this man was seventy-five years old. Are you sure you have the right person?"

"Jake Edwards? The football player?" Donna replied. "That's not him?"

"Jake Edwards?" The question came from a distance away.

Lilli remained on the floor, helpless and frustrated, until a handsome young doctor with golden-blond hair and a compassionate demeanor appeared above her.

"Yes. Jake Edwards," Donna answered. "Do you know something about him?"

"I do, but I'm afraid you can't see him."

"Why not?" Lilli tried to sit up once more, but the same hand stopped her again. She shrugged it off this time. "I'm fine. Now let me get up and go see Jake."

"She's feisty enough, and she doesn't seem injured." The doctor nodded his confirmation. "It's all right, Joshua. You have my permission to break with protocol."

He bobbed his head in response, released Lilli, and then helped her up.

Lilli turned to face the young doctor, searching his eyes for answers. "Is Jake okay? Can I see him? Doctor—"

"Sheldon Blake." He gestured to the nametag suspended from a lanyard around his neck, then, shook her hand.

"Lilli Brooks," she supplied.

"I was the ER doctor. I had first contact. Mr. Edwards is in the MAU—Medical Assessment Unit that is, we've assessed and treated his overt injuries. The neurologist is in with him now. Let the triage nurses know you're waiting and as soon as Doctor Reynolds has completed his exam you should be allowed in."

"Thank you, Doctor Blake."

He smiled and wished her luck before joining the group as they pushed the gurney onto the waiting elevator.

Lilli wandered over and found a seat by the wall. Donna joined her as they watched the gurney bump over the edge of the elevator doors. Lilli's eyes welled up again.

"It's not him," Donna affirmed as she gently placed her arm around Lilli's shoulders.

"I know, Donna, but what if—"

"No what if. It's a sad thing, Lilli, but it's not your sad thing." Donna held the eye contact, reaching for Lilli's hand. "Listen, I know you don't do passive very well, so I'm going to be a rebel on your behalf, and cross that yellow do-not-cross-this-line line and see what I can find out. You okay here for a minute?"

Lilli took in a lungful of recycled hospital air, smiled at her friend's attempt to lighten her mood and then replied, "Go get 'em, tiger."

Donna stood but hesitated.

"Seriously, go. I'm fine." Lilli wiped a rogue tear from her cheek and grabbed a magazine from a small, lacquered table. She waved it at Donna, who still hadn't moved. "Scat."

Then, the sound of Donna's steps faded into the backdrop as Lilli began to flip, uninterested, through the dusty, tattered pages of a fashion magazine full of trends that were no longer trendy.

Her mind began to wander. She contemplated death as the sounds of hospital life faded into the background too, turning into nothing but white noise. She thought about the poor man on the gurney. At least he had lived a fairly long life. Seventy-five wasn't ancient, but it was better than dying at twenty-something. James Dean may have been attributed with John Derek's famous line from the movie *Knock on Any Door*, but Lilli had to respectfully disagree—it was not better to "Live fast, die young, and have a good-looking corpse."

What would she have done if she'd been confronted with Jake's death? She didn't have much experience with the subject. Beloved pets "wandered away" according to her mother. Both her grandfathers passed away before Lilli even existed.

There was the faintest memory of when her maternal grandmother had died. Lilli had been quite young. Too young to remember really, so it was more a lingering sense of her mother's quiet suffering. A sense of being a good girl and trying to stay out of the way, reading her storybooks, wishing she could fix this thing she was too young to comprehend. A barely there whisp of something that must surely have contributed to her lifetime pattern of *if only* thoughts—if only she did this or, if only she said that…then everyone would be happy. Right?

Grandma Nettie, her father's mother, was the only grandparent she'd ever really known. That made her extra-special. She got four grandparents' worth of Lilli's love and devotion.

Lilli closed her eyes and pictured her grandmother. Her long, gray hair always perfectly twisted into a loose bun at the back of her head. The warm smile that appeared on her time-worn face always reaching up and crinkling the corners of her sparkling blue eyes when the family came for Sunday dinner.

Lilli vividly recalled everything about her grandma's little suite in The Evergreens. The worn maple dresser, covered with a crocheted doily and topped with ceramic figurines, kissing musical angels, and the plastic-framed, black-and-white wedding picture of Lilli's parents.

That photo and the angels held a position of esteem among the treasures on Lilli's own modern IKEA dresser now. A few years ago, Grandma had begun handing out her collections to her grandkids, not wanting to wait until she passed to have someone else do so.

Lilli had always loved going there to visit her, having lunch at her wooden kitchen table, eating farmer sausage and hermit cookies. It was the best place to go.

A long, drawn-out sigh. If only she could turn back time.

"Sweet and creamy." Donna returned with a reassuring look and a steaming cup of coffee, startling Lilli out of her reminiscence. She handed it to her. "It's not Starbucks, but hopefully it'll do."

"Thanks, Donna." Coffee was exactly what Lilli needed. Although her nerves were frazzled, the caffeine would help her stay attentive. And she wanted to be alert and prepared when she saw Jake and spoke with the doctor. "You've really become a good friend to me. I don't know what I would have done without you. Actually, that's not quite true."

The smile fell from Donna's face and she looked as though someone had just kicked her in the stomach. Hard.

Lilli was quick to reframe her statement. "I mean, I do know what I would have done without you because I already did it while you were out parking the car. I fainted like a little girl, that's what."

She removed the plastic lid and blew on her coffee before taking a slow draw. Donna was right, it wasn't Starbucks. It was sweet and it was creamy, even if the "cream" was a powdered substitute, but there was a slight bitterness that Lilli decided to ignore. The caffeine buzz was more important than the flavor at that moment. "Did they tell you anything while you were up there?"

"No, I couldn't get a darn thing out of the nurses except that they would have the doctor come over and talk to you when he's done."

"Thanks for trying."

Donna offered a sympathetic nod, and then the two women sat side by side, waiting. Seemingly cognizant of Lilli's need for stillness, Donna began to flip through Lilli's recently abandoned magazine.

Lilli leaned back in the chair and rested her head against the wall, closing her eyes for a moment before once again blowing the steam off her coffee. It may be bitter but at least it was hot. Then, pensive, Lilli studied the faces of the people around them. Most of them had been there when she'd arrived, and they now wore expressions of anguish and annoyance.

What a sad state of affairs. So many people suffering as they waited their turn. Where would Jake be if he didn't have money and fame?

CHAPTER THIRTY-ONE

"BROOKS."

The nurse's voice rang out from the business side of the yellow do-not-cross line. Lilli snapped to attention and regarded an older woman dressed in a fairly traditional uniform of white dress, cut to mid-calf, and sensible white shoes. Her ashen-colored hair was the most current thing about her and the only thing that separated this woman from being the head-nurse archetype—it was cut in a chin-length bob. Still, she stood out as a throwback among the younger nurses who sported colorful scrubs and matching Crocs.

"Lilli Brooks," her authoritative voice beckoned again.

"Yes, that's me." Lilli jumped up and quickly closed the distance between them. "Is there news about Jake?"

"Doctor Reynolds is in the consultation room waiting for you. He's a busy man. Follow me." All business, no bedside manner.

Lilli looked back at Donna, who waved her away while mouthing the words *I'll wait here.*

She nodded and followed the nurse down a long corridor and then through two wide swinging doors labeled Neurology Department.

Lilli was hustling to keep up to No-Nonsense Nurse, when, midway down the next corridor, the woman stopped abruptly, forcing Lilli to slam on the brakes to avoid a full-on collision.

The sign on the door to her left said Consultation Room. The nurse gestured her inside, nodded at the waiting doctor, and made rapid strides back down the hall. Places to go. People to poke with needles. Judging by the look of the emergency waiting room, Lilli supposed No-Nonsense Nurse did have things to do.

Lilli crossed the threshold to the bland little room and the palpable odor of grief and desperation encircled her. She shuddered and wrapped her arms around herself as if to ward off a deeply imbedded chill. Glancing at the dingy mint-green walls, she wondered if the paint had once been bright and cheery but had actually been faded by sorrow.

She moved toward him as the doctor stood up, unfolding his tall, athletic frame from the small wooden chair in the corner. He was a mature man, his hair mostly salt with a bit of pepper still remaining. His face wore the tanned visage of a man who enjoyed the outdoors, perhaps on a golf course. Of course, the latter was pure stereotypical conjecture on her part. She judged him to be in his late-fifties to mid-sixties, handsome in an aging George Clooney kind of way. Beneath his unbuttoned lab coat, he wore a yellow polo shirt and tan Dockers. Sneakers clad his feet rather than the anticipated black dress shoes.

Lilli considered the shabby-but-not-so-chic beige sofa along the wall and wondered why he had chosen the too-small chair.

As if sensing her query, his eyes made contact. "Too soft. I sink right down and I'll be damned if I can't get back up again." He indicated his height. "Six foot five, and it's a curse sometimes." He reached out and shook her hand. "Doctor Tim Reynolds, Chief of Neurology."

Beneath his anxious expression, Lilli could detect kindness in the set of his square jaw and the sparkle of his clear blue eyes. She reigned in her eagerness to skip the formalities and just get on with it already and took his hand, calmly introducing herself as well.

She fixed her gaze and leveled her voice. "What can you tell me about Jake?"

"Well, Lilli," the doctor began. "May I call you Lilli?"

"Of course," she answered, as she began to scrape at her cuticles.

He gestured for her to take a seat on the sofa. She eyed it surreptitiously, and then sat, not sinking nearly as low as she had feared. He dropped down, again, in the uncomfortable-looking wooden chair. Then, to Lilli's relief, he cut to the chase.

"Whiplash of course, goes without saying. He took a major blow to the head, both sides mind you. Helmet to helmet, as they call it. At the least, he has a mild to moderate TBI."

"TBI?"

"Traumatic brain injury—a concussion. Lately there has been mounting evidence supporting a high incidence of CTE—chronic traumatic encephalopathy—in former players. Unfortunately, a definitive diagnosis can only be made post-mortem. There are, however, an increasing number of former NFL players reporting symptoms of CTE."

She studied the doctor as he sat, leaning forward, elbows on knees, hands clasped between them. He appeared the antithesis of how she was feeling. The calmness to counter her anxieties. Her attempts to follow along were choppy at best—she'd have to Google this later.

Her face must have been painted in confusion, for Doctor Reynolds stopped talking and took a deep breath, almost as if he were willing her to follow. She did, and he resumed, but curbed the focus.

He steepled his pointers and gestured with his clasped hands. "Let's stick with the concussive issues. Normally, recovery on the mild types of these injuries is quick, however…"

Expectation rose up as he paused, a little longer than was comfortable for her, and Lilli found a hangnail, then tugged at it nervously.

"Well, Lilli, CTE aside, with repeated TBIs, such as we have here, we have to be concerned about the possible deleterious effects of multiple concussions on the brain."

"Meaning what, exactly, Doctor?"

"Data from a recent study confirms the occurrence of chronic brain damage as a result of multiple head injuries. Players with four or more concussions have a greater chance of personality change and fatigue, not to mention all the standard concussive symptoms."

"Which are?" Lilli stopped picking at her cuticles and clasped her hands tightly in her lap, clinging to the last threads of patience. She smiled stiffly and sensed it probably didn't appear genuine. She didn't care. She just wanted to hear Jake was okay. Would be okay.

"Well, the most common initial symptoms for concussions are headaches, dizziness, memory and various cognitive problems— somatic complaints…" Doctor Reynolds paused as if waiting to see if Lilli was going to ask another question.

Instead, she wrung her hands and chewed on her bottom lip.

He remained leaning forward, his face the perfect countenance of compassion, then continued. "On my initial examination, Jake showed signs of retrograde amnesia, difficulty with immediate recall, and overall difficulties with cognition and general memory."

Speechless, her mouth felt like desiccated cotton. Lilli raised her still-clasped hands in front of her in an unconscious prayer. Her breathing became tremulous and her eyes stared straight ahead, unblinking, still dry though, as she silently waited for the other shoe to drop.

Doctor Reynolds paused again, as if aware of her needing a moment to absorb the news. Then, in what appeared to be a much-practiced move, he leaned sideways and picked up a box of tissues from the table. He held it out to her just in time for her to catch the first tear as it betrayed her and made its way down her cheek.

"We still need to perform a CT scan and an MRI, but I have to say, Lilli, there is a very good chance I'll be recommending that Mr. Edwards take a break from football."

"Oh my God," Lilli gasped. Football was Jake's life. Distraught, she leaned back now and placed her fingers at her temples, rubbing in little circles, focusing her breathing.

The doctor leaned toward Lilli again and raised his hands from his knees to his chin as if drawing her eyes to make contact. "I'm still waiting for the results on several tests we've run," he supplied. "With any luck we'll have them within the hour. Unfortunately, right now, I can't tell you the degree of injury or the length of recovery." He broke the eye lock and gazed down. "Then, depending on what the tests reveal, we may need to do a lumbar puncture."

"What's that? I've never heard that term before."

"We also refer to this as a spinal tap—it's used to analyze the cerebrospinal fluid. This can tell us, for example, if there is any bleeding in the brain or spinal cord areas."

"This is all too much to absorb," she murmured, wringing her hands. She dabbed at her cheeks with the tissue and looked up at Doctor Reynolds. Then, placing a hand near her collarbone and inhaling deeply, she added, "When can I see him?"

As if sensing that she'd had enough he leaned back, breaking the intensity. "No more medical mumbo-jumbo." He stood and placed his hands on his hips. "Is right now good?"

She wanted to reply that an hour ago would have been awesome, or that hell, twenty minutes ago would have been good too, but instead she nodded and graciously took the doctor's outstretched hand, an offer to help her off the sagging old sofa.

He opened the door and led her, gratefully, out of the small, airless room and down a long white corridor. They made several turns, and then, as they neared the end of the final corridor, they came upon a huge cluster of reporters. She closed her eyes and wished to blend in and walk by them, but one of them recognized her, likely from a photo of her and Jake in the paper.

"That's her! That's the girlfriend! C'mon," the reporter shouted and then, suddenly, the throng moved as though a single unit. In an instant, their posture went from relaxed and chatty to ready, set, go.

In Lilli's overwhelmed state the voices fused into an unrecognizable clamor. She was immediately grateful for Doctor Reynolds' apparent expertise as he raised his left hand in dismissal and calmly stated, "No comment." Then he placed his right hand, barely touching the small of her back, and ushered her to the safety that existed on the other side of a door marked Authorized Personnel Only.

"Thank you," she offered with a smile, more genuine this time.

"Tut-tut, nothing of it—not my first hayride you know."

That made her smile as he led her into the Medical Assessment Unit. He stopped outside a door marked Occupied and then he spoke in hushed tones. "Don't let his appearance alarm you. He has bandages on his head, there's some bleeding, it looks much worse than it is."

Lilli nodded and stepped toward the door. "Don't stay too long and don't let him get worked up. He needs rest and plenty of it. Tell Mr. Edwards that I'll be in to see him shortly."

"Thank you, Doctor," Lilli said as she watched him walk away. She decided she liked Doctor Reynolds after all. He might have taken longer than she'd liked to get to the point, but in fairness, her agitated state had likely made time seem immovable.

LILLI TAPPED LIGHTLY on the door and then eased it open. Jake looked up, his eyes seeming to need a second to focus.

"Hey, you," she greeted him.

"Lilli's here. Hey. I missed you. How they got your number? You got here so fast too. Is that really you?" Jake sounded like he was on some good painkillers.

She edged toward his bed. "I came to watch you play. I wanted to surprise you." She worked a smile onto her face and raised her arms to the side in a motion of *ta-da*. "Surprise," she said.

"Really?" His eyes were glassy as he reflected her smile back to her. "I didn't see any Lilli there."

"Got here late. Heard the game on satellite as I was driving from Dulles. I came straight to the hospital." She caressed his forehead below the bandage, kissed him on the cheek.

"And I thought I was lucky charm-less." Jake reached for her hand. "C'mere." Injured and doped up as he was, he still had the strength to pull her onto the small bed. "I can't believe it's really you," he slurred. "I was *all alone*, Lilli. All. Alone."

"Not alone," she said. "I've been here the whole time, waiting for them to let me in."

His large hands clumsily caressed her face and hair. He looked like he was going to pull her in for a kiss, then paused at the back of her head. "You have a bump. Why do you have a bump?"

"It's nothing." Lilli felt silly for overreacting when she had arrived. Just like her to jump to conclusions.

He sat up with a sudden burst of energy. "Where's my jersey? My pads? My helmet?" Jake darted his eyes around the room. "I want you to see me play. My girl's here now. I can still win this game."

Lilli didn't know what to say. Clearly Jake had no idea how much time had passed or the extent of his injuries. She went with the obvious segue. "Have they told you anything yet?"

"Told me anything? Told me what?"

"Honey, the game's over." Lilli took Jake's hand and tried to get him to focus on her eyes, but the contact was splintered at best. "I don't think you'll be discharged today. We should wait for the doctor."

"No offense, Lil, but I don't do waiting. I mean, I waited for you—a long time for you—but the team needs me. And those Redskins need some payback." He placed his arms on either side and pushed himself to a straighter sitting position.

Lilli turned pensive. "I spoke with Doctor Reynolds before I came in here. He's the neurologist that treated you. He said you have whiplash and a concussion. He's waiting for some tests to come back."

"A concussion? No biggie. I've had plenty of those." His gaze settled on his gear in the corner and he slid his legs over the side of the bed. "I'm gonna get dressed. Hand me my gear, Lil."

"Jake," Lilli started, just as Doctor Reynolds walked in.

"I would like to speak with Mr. Edwards alone, if you don't mind, Ms. Brooks."

Ms. Brooks? No longer Lilli. She understood that Doctor Reynolds was not really asking her permission, so she reluctantly agreed. She kissed Jake and slipped out of the room.

CHAPTER THIRTY-TWO

LILLI HAD BEEN reluctant to leave Jake's side. After wandering part way down the corridor of the MAU, she stopped and debated with herself. There was only one thing to do. Lilli twirled around and headed back.

She peered through the window in Jake's door. Doctor Reynolds was still in with him. The look on the doctor's face told her that the conversation with his patient had been unproductive, while the expression Jake wore confirmed it. He was going home today and that was that.

She gently eased the door open just enough that she could hear what was being said.

"Look, Doc," Jake pushed, "I been through this before. I know the drill. Take it easy for a few days, yadda, yadda, yadda. Just write me a scrip and I'll be on my way. Since you told me we won today, that means I've got a big game coming up. NFC Divisional on the thirteenth."

"Mr. Edwards, it is simply…" the doctor appeared to struggle, "well, it's simply not that simple. Not this time. Because of your previous concussions, we need to observe you longer, run some more tests."

He paused, and Jake appeared to at least be listening to him.

"The damage can be cumulative in these situations, and while the initial tests show nothing, we need to do a CT and an MRI."

Lilli heard voices coming from down the next corridor and it sounded like Jake's parents. While she didn't know them, the tone of the conversation made it clear they were discussing Jake. She released the door and darted into an empty room across the hall.

Moments later she watched as the couple barged into Jake's room. She could hear Jake's father's voice clear as a bell. He wasn't a quiet man by any means.

"What are you doing lying down?" he shouted at Jake. More of a statement than a question. No hello, no how are you, just judgment. The futility of the situation would accelerate from difficult to impossible in sixty seconds flat, of that Lilli was certain. Jake had told her enough about his family, his father in particular, to anticipate that.

She slipped out of the room and tiptoed back across the hall, barely peeking through a corner of the window to see if she could get away with opening the door again.

Luckily she didn't have to. Jake's voice had risen to match his father's. "Hey, Dad," Jake said. "I was just trying to convince the doctor to let me get up."

"What's to convince? Get dressed. I'm double parked. We're taking you home." The senior Mr. Edwards' gruff demeanor left no room for discussion.

Still, Doctor Reynolds—the epitome of patience Lilli was sure—gave it one last try. "I appreciate you wanting your son at home, Mr. Edwards, however, it is in his best interest that he stays for observation, at least until tomorrow."

"Jake ain't no pussy, Doc," he jacked a thumb toward his wife, "even though his mother treats him like one. Babies him if you ask me. We can handle this at home. Throw some meds at the kid and let's go. He'll be fine."

Lilli watched surreptitiously as Jake's mother turned her lips into a smile that didn't reach her eyes. It made Lilli cringe inside. Truly, Jake had not been exaggerating when he'd told her that his dad was a jerk. He'd used other words, but Lilli didn't care to repeat them, even in her own thoughts.

Then in a rough attempt to "close the deal," Jake's father gave him a feeble pat on the arm. "Whatever doesn't kill you makes you stronger, right, Son?" Pat, pat.

Jake plastered a smile on his face and nodded his agreement, and then his father *suggested* that Doctor Reynolds go sign the release forms. They would wait.

The doctor, wearing an exasperated look of resignation, rose to his full height, almost matching the senior Mr. Edwards, who equaled

Jake in stature. The doctor had obviously done everything he could in this situation and accepted that he would not change the minds of either of these headstrong men, so he turned to leave.

She scooted back into the other room and counted a beat of twenty as Doctor Reynolds' footsteps receded down the corridor. As she crept back into the hall she heard Jake mention that she was there, had arrived before them and would be back any minute in fact, and he could travel home with her.

Jake, however, was no longer top dog—the Alpha had arrived and had his mind made up. "Your mother and I flew here and drove all the way from Dulles. You are going with us," he barked, then turned his attention to his wife. "Patricia, go start the car."

"Yes, John," she replied.

That was Lilli's cue to make another covert exit and across the hall she dashed. Then, she peeked through the gap in the door as Patricia Edwards left the room and strode down the hall.

Across the way, Lilli heard Jake speak her name. "What about Lilli? What should I tell her?"

"She can go back whatever way she came," Jake's father replied. "Tell her anything that you want, but make no mistake, you're going home with your mother and me."

"But, Dad—"

"Get dressed, Jake. If that doctor knows what's good for him, he'll be up with those goddamn release papers soon. Grow a spine, man up already. Tell the bimbo to fly home alone."

Bimbo? Of all the nerve. And what was with all the shouting? Did these two not know how to keep their voices down when they were together or did they just not care? Maybe that man wasn't used to a woman standing up for herself—clearly his wife never had—but Lilli had to work at not going in there to set him straight. She would never do that to Jake. It would make his trip home miserable.

"Who wears the pants in that relationship anyway, Jake? Maybe you are a pussy after all." One last twist of the verbal knife in Jake's back and his father left, muttering under his breath, and storming down the hall. Jake must be so embarrassed.

"Bastard," she heard Jake mumble as she opened the door and let herself into his room. He was pulling jeans and a t-shirt out of a plastic bag.

"Hi, Jake," Lilli said.

"Lilli. You're back." He yanked his hospital gown off and stood to pull his boxers up. "So they're springing me after all. Cool, huh."

"Yeah. That's great, Jake. Listen, I'll make this easy for you." She pulled in a deep breath and released it slowly, then wandered to the window. She watched Jake's reflection as he tugged on his jeans and dragged the t-shirt over his head. "I saw your father leave the room. He didn't see me, but I'm sure he didn't come all this way to watch you fly home with your girlfriend, so..."

"Thanks," Jake replied.

His eyes cast downward as she spun around to face him again. She wouldn't push the issue, and he was visibly relieved. She wouldn't mention how he was a grown man and how he should stand up to his father. She was right about him needing to, but maybe it was harder than she knew.

Standing up to his dad didn't seem like something Jake was good at. Give him a hundred and twenty yards of turf, though, and he could stand up to anything. Until today, anyway.

She went to him and stretched her arms up around his neck. He reciprocated, wrapping his around her waist, pulling her closer. He leaned down and she rose up on her toes, and they met in the middle for a kiss.

"Thanks for coming," Jake said.

She reached up and stroked her finger along the edge of the bandage, her eyes searching his face, his eyes, his heart. She believed he loved her. Believed he would rather go home with her than be trapped in a flying metal tube with his father for seven-plus hours. But she could tell he wasn't ready to say no to "the boss." Jake had clearly perfected the art of placating his father.

She wondered what it must have been like growing up with that man. Jake had told her the stories of how in the off-season, he still pulled shifts at his father's sporting goods store. He hated it. Always had. Had been slaving for his dad since he was twelve years old. Jake had spent his weekends and summers stuck in a dingy little store trying to sell soccer balls and skateboards to obnoxious teenagers. He felt that he was above this now. He was a football icon, a hero, and why should he belittle himself by schlepping sporting goods.

She watched him at the mirror, running his hands through the tufts of hair sticking out over the bandages. He tried to smooth them down but there was no way. It made her smile. One day she would convince him he could stand on his own feet. One day soon. He was the one who let them run his life, and he was the one that could put a stop to it.

He flashed a twisted grin at his reflection and shrugged.

She stood and went to the bed. "Come here." She patted the edge of the mattress. He did, and she made a few quick moves that had his hair tamed. Lilli rose and draped her handbag over her shoulder. "I suppose I should go then."

"Yeah, I guess. The doc should be here soon with my release papers."

"I know you wanted this, Jake, but I hope you're not making a big mistake," Lilli said.

"Don't worry. Remember who you're dealing with here." He patted his chest. "Jake Edwards and he's unstoppable."

Looking at his crooked grin and gleaming hazel eyes she wanted to believe him. Still, Doctor Reynolds had talked about complications. There were things that might be beyond even Jake's powerful grip. There were risks that he'd allowed, welcomed even, and couldn't take them back. Either he was in major denial, or he actually was invincible. Lilli prayed for the latter.

She gave him a kiss on the cheek. "I'll see you at home? You could come over after they drop you off? I'll come pick you up if you want me to."

He wrapped his arms around her, drawing her close. "Thanks for understanding, Lil. You're the best." He pressed his lips against hers. "Love you."

"Love you too."

He kissed her again, more fervently this time, as his hands traveled a familiar path down her back, gripping her with both, he pulled her so close she could feel his ardent appreciation.

"Easy there, gunslinger, I guess you must be glad to see me."

He leaned in and whispered in her ear, his breath warm on her cheek. "Very glad."

An involuntary shiver ran down her spine, he had definitely managed to distract her from being frustrated about the situation with his father. If there was one thing he was good at, it was getting her mind on other things. She tried to slip out of his strong embrace, halting this little scene before he got carried away or someone walked in on them. He released his grip slightly then he pulled her back forcefully.

Doctor Reynolds strolled in. "I'm sorry," he said, not in the least bit embarrassed at walking in on the couple. "I can come back," he added with a chuckle.

They stepped away from each other, Lilli, blushing a little, and Jake, looking proud of himself. She hitched her purse higher on her shoulder, told Jake she would see him soon, blew him a kiss, and turned to open the door.

"I'm a lucky man, Doc," she heard Jake say as she left the room.

"Indeed you are," he replied, "in more ways than one. Speaking of which, do you think I could convince you not to push that luck, maybe reconsider your decision to go home? One more day?"

Lilli lingered outside the door, waiting, hoping to see if Jake would reconsider.

"Can't do it, Doc," Jake replied as expected. "I can't keep a woman like that waiting too long. Know what I mean?"

Lilli smiled to herself and breezed down the corridor. Everything was going to be fine. Jake would be fine. He had to be. This was the happiest she had ever been. Besides, hearing him speak and seeing him just now…he was the same Jake she fell in love with just a few short days ago. No bump on the head was going to change that.

CHAPTER THIRTY-THREE

THEIR RETURN FLIGHT didn't leave Dulles until two PM Monday afternoon, but at least it was a nonstop and Lilli had arrived in Seattle by shortly after five. Sure she was a little jetlagged from losing three hours in the time-zone switch but it was worth it. No baggage claim and Donna had kindly offered to take a taxi home so Lilli could go straight to her apartment to wait for Jake.

And she had done just that. Waited.

After sending several text messages she'd tried to call his cell only to have it go to directly to voicemail. The battery must've died and he hadn't been able to charge it. She had no idea what flight he would have been on and wasn't really even sure that he was back in Seattle, but she assumed he must be. She couldn't see his father hanging around in DC waiting. He would have hired a charter jet if he couldn't pay his way onto the quickest flight available.

She'd left a message, but a fragment of her wanted to get in her Jeep and drive to his apartment. She didn't, but she'd had to convince herself.

Now it was almost eleven PM and Lilli lay awake in her bed wondering where he was and why he hadn't called, texted, or come over. She had to work in the morning and really should be asleep, but her mind simply would not shut down. Something didn't feel right, but she couldn't put her finger on it.

She was not angry with Jake. She was too worried for that. Maybe a glass of wine would help. She glanced at Toby, curled near her feet, and asked him to go pour her a glass. He offered a blank stare, adjusted his position, and resumed purring.

"Fine. I'll go. I think I left the lamp on in the living room anyway." She caressed him on the back of his head and slithered reluctantly out of the blankets. The nights were rather chilly, and she was clad in nothing but a snug-fitting pink tank top and a pair of Calvin Klein boxers, which, as it turned out, had not been stolen along with her other unmentionables. She'd bought them for Brad—too small—so she'd kept them for herself.

She slipped a light robe over her shoulders, scampered to the kitchen, then yanked the cork from a bottle of red she'd opened last week. Lilli sniffed the contents. Still good. She poured a full glass, took a huge gulp, snapped off the lamp in the living room, and then scurried back to her warm bed. As she crossed the threshold to her bedroom, a knock at the door caused her hopes to soar. Jake had made it after all.

She set her wineglass on the dining table and flung the door open. "You're here!" Crap. Should've checked first. When would she learn? Not Jake. Bradley. And he was clearly much happier to see her than she actually was to see him.

"That's a greeting and a half." He wore a huge grin. "More than I was expecting." He stepped into her apartment and wrapped his arms around her. "I missed you," he said, "but I didn't realize you missed me too."

Lilli pushed her hands against his chest to extricate herself from his solid embrace then cinched her robe around her waist. She shut the door and sighed. After the incident in the stairwell he'd proven that he was not going to leave until he'd said his piece.

"I'm still mad at you, Brad. I opened the door because I thought it would be Jake. He was supposed to come by after he got home," she told him. "I'm a little worried actually, after what happened yesterday."

"Yeah, I heard. Actually, I saw. I was down at Hugo's Pub watching on the big screen. What a hit. Edwards got jacked up! That'll definitely make the highlight reel for years to come."

"This isn't funny, Brad. If you don't play nice I *will* call Seattle PD." Lilli snatched her wine off the table and took a big swig. She didn't need more stress. "Jake had to go to the hospital, you know."

Brad took her cue and dialed it back a notch. "Sorry. I was worried about you. I noticed your light on and thought you might need someone to talk with."

"I couldn't sleep," she confessed. "I don't know if Jake even made it home yet or not. His cell is going straight to voicemail. I'm really worried."

"Wine?" He looked at her glass. "On a work night?"

"Like I said, I couldn't fall asleep."

"Red wine always had a way of relaxing you."

"That's what I thought, ergo…" She raised the glass.

Brad gestured with his empty hands. "Sorry. Can't toast."

As she downed the last of the wine, she wandered to the kitchen for just a little more. Brad showing up had given her a reason for another glass. Lilli watched him as she picked up the wine. Seeing him there gave her a little flashback, so she moved out of the confines of the kitchen and set the bottle and her glass on the dining table. After she poured some, she pulled out a chair and sat sideways on it as she studied him, wondering what his agenda was.

He pulled out a chair too and spun it around, straddling it backward. "So, talk. Tell Doctor Bradley everything."

"I don't think that is such a good idea, Brad."

"Listen, you need someone to talk to and I have ears. See." He grinned and wiggled his ears with his fingers. "You used to say they were the cutest ears you'd ever seen."

Maybe getting her feelings out would help her sleep. She narrowed her eyes in suspicion, considering.

"Ten minutes," he said. "Then I'll go."

"Ten minutes?"

"I swear."

She was still unconvinced.

Brad walked to the phone and brought it over. He pressed two keys and then set it down next to her. "There. I hit nine and one. If I misbehave you only need to hit another one and your friendly neighborhood Seattle PD is on the way."

"Fine."

"Fine?"

"Yes, Brad, fine. Ten minutes. But only because you owe me and because I need to get some sleep."

Sometimes Lilli had trouble talking about her feelings, so she took a few moments to breathe and gather her thoughts. It was not long before the warm rush of the Merlot began to relax her and she opened up and told Brad everything.

"So that's that," she said then picked up her glass and took a slow draw, savoring the pungent contents. It was a good label, good vintage, with a range of fresh flavors—plums, cherries, blueberries and blackberries mixed with black pepper tones. This was the most relaxed Lilli had felt in a while.

"Are you okay, Lilli?" Brad asked. His face appeared worried, but she couldn't imagine why.

"Of course I am. Wait. Why are you here again?"

Brad lifted the bottle of wine and eyed the remaining contents. "Did you drink all of this tonight?"

"No." She yanked it from his grip. "I've only had a little." Lilli picked up her glass and raised it to her lips, but Brad took it away from her and downed it, then poured the last few ounces from the bottle and drank those too.

"What are you doing?"

"I'm making sure you don't drink any more tonight." He stood and took the empty bottle and glass to the kitchen. "You're drunk, Lilli."

"Am not," Lilli said as she allowed her eyes to close—only for a moment. She hadn't had nearly enough wine to be considered drunk. A girl had to keep her wits about her around a Don Juan like Brad. "I just need a minute to rest here."

"I'll get you some water." Brad went back into the kitchen and pulled open the fridge. "Where's your bottled water?"

"In the bottles."

"Lilli—aw, forget it."

She heard clinking glasses and then the sound of the kitchen faucet. Then Brad returned with a large glass of water.

She wrinkled her nose. "That's tap water. I can smell the chlorine."

"Drink it," he said. "There is no bottled water and you need to drink some."

Her eyes went from the glass to his face, back to the glass. "Fine." She took it and raised it to her lips, taking a sip. "Yucky."

He placed his fingers under the bottom of the glass, tipping it toward her mouth. "More."

"Do I have—"

He crossed his arms and nodded. "All of it, Lilli."

"Fine." She drank as much as she could and then set the glass on the table. He didn't argue with her so she closed her eyes for a moment, just to rest them, but she began to feel herself nodding off. She opened them and stuck out her hand to Brad. "I think it's beddy-bye time. Help me up."

Brad took Lilli by the hand, pulled her to standing, and led her toward her bedroom.

They neared the door. "Nuh-uh," she said, wagging her finger at him. "Not you. Only me." Then she stumbled a little and fell into the wall. "Oops." She giggled. She sincerely actually giggled. Okay. Time to admit it. She must have consumed more wine than she had thought, or else she hadn't eaten enough, because Lilli was drunk. As a skunk.

"I'm only going to help you lie down." Brad's voice sounded convincing, and the bed looked awfully convincing too.

"I have to go potty first," Lilli declared.

Brad turned her back around and stopped in front of the bathroom door. Lilli stepped inside, then proceeded to pull down her shorts and pee. "Close the wall, Brad."

"You mean the door."

"That's what I said."

"No, it's—never mind." He pulled the door most of the way shut and told her to be quick.

When she stood to pull up her pants, a wave of dizziness swept over her, causing her to stumble into the wall. "Oopsies."

Brad pushed open the door and stepped inside. Lilli began to giggle again. Twice now, and in one night. That made her laugh more.

"Lilli?" Brad snapped his fingers at her. "Earth to Lilli…"

"That's funny, Brad." She looked down at her shorts around her ankles, then up at him. "I'm a little dizzy-ish. Can you help me?"

"You can't even pull up your own pants?" He was shaking his head. "Are you sure you only drank a little?"

She made a gesture with her thumb and forefinger, showing him just how tiny the amount was. "Only a smidge," she said.

He reached down and grabbed the waistband, then yanked them up. "Are these mine?"

"Not anymore." She wiggled her bottom. "They fit me better."

"I can't argue with that," he said and guided her out of the bathroom.

She dug in her heels and refused to walk. "My hands," she said, waving them in the air. "I need to wash my hands."

Brad groaned and took her to the sink, ran her hands under the water, and then wiped them on a towel. "Now bed."

"But," Lilli began.

"No buts." Brad bent down and placed an arm behind her knees and one at her back. He then proceeded to hoist her into the air.

She sniffed at his neck. "You smell good," she said, sniffing again.

"Stop it." Brad lifted his shoulder to his ear. "That tickles." He crossed into the bedroom and lost his footing, regaining it just before they fell forward onto the bed. He dropped her onto it and then raised his hand to his head. "Now I feel dizzy."

"Dizzy-ish," Lilli corrected.

"What the hell kind of wine was that anyway? Shit."

"The really, really good kind," Lilli said. She scooched herself up on the bed. "Tuck me in, Brad."

He leaned over her and dragged the duvet up to her chin, and she made a few quiet sounds as he tucked it around her. She sank into the bed and squirmed around a bit, trying to get comfortable.

"What's the matter now?"

"I'm too hot."

"Are you joking? It's freezing in here." Brad walked toward the hall. "Fine. I'll turn the heat down."

When he came back into the room she had already discarded her top and her shorts and was in the process of pulling the blankets back up. "Help me?"

He was shaking his head, looking at where she'd thrown her clothes. "God, Lilli, what are you trying to do to me here? If you think I'm some sort of saint, you can get over that idea right now." He closed the distance between himself and the bed, then stood there staring down at her. He picked up her tank top and brought it to his nose. "You smell good too, Lilli. Good enough to—"

Brad tossed the shirt beside the boxers on the end of the bed. "Not a saint, Lilli. Just a man."

All the thoughts that had plagued her mind just a short while ago were now a distant memory. Floating away, just like Lilli was. She was so tired. Couldn't keep her eyes open if her life depended on it. Then, as Brad tugged on the edge of the duvet, she felt her tensions give way to a deep sense of relaxation. A sense of familiarity. Comfort.

CHAPTER THIRTY-FOUR

FLUNITRAZEPAM. Roofie. Forget-me Pill. Rib. Roche. Rope. Roopie. Mexican Valium. Or, simply, Circles—even though, currently, they are olive green and more of an oblong shape. But lucky for me, I managed to score some of the old-school Circles. Good thing too, although, if you have a dark enough base to slip it into, the green dye doesn't show. Still, why take chances? Sure it cost me a little more than five bucks a pop, but she is *so* worth it. And, really, when you stop to consider what *I'm* getting out of it, well, it is a no-brainer.

Rohypnol.

Bless the goddamn pharmaceutical companies for making my life so much easier. And *viva!* Tijuana for making the supplies so plentiful in mainstream America.

What else could make someone fall to my will as though they were a mere puppet on my string? Add lowered inhibitions and a little anterograde amnesia to the mix and what you have, my friend, is a sublime cocktail. Oh, and did I mention it dissolves like magic? Nice, right? Tasteless. Odorless. A thing of beauty.

Think about it—if this had been available back then, everything, at least where my father was concerned, would have been so much better.

But, again, I digress. Bad habit. One of 'em anyway. Now, where was I? Oh yeah. Her...

You might think that slipping her a Roofie was a tad bit extreme, but it wasn't. It had to be done. Some things just have to be done, all right? Leave it at that. It is all part of the plan, and I do have this planned out. Down to a T.

The accident at the game...well, that wasn't part of the plan, but I adapt. That's what I do.

Did you hear me, Dad? I adapt. I learned that from you. Sometimes you just gotta roll with the punches. No pun intended.

So, I changed it up a bit and that's okay. And now, now I have her in the exact position I wanted her in. Face down and naked.

Did I mention bless the pharmaceutical companies?

CHAPTER THIRTY-FIVE

THE SUN WAS piercing through a small gap in the curtains and Lilli draped her arm across her eyes. It wasn't enough to block the light, so she reached over to grab the extra pillow in order to put it over her face. But it wouldn't budge. "Toby, get off the pillow."

"Whuh?"

That was Brad's slurring query. What the hell was he doing in her room first thing in the morning? Although, it couldn't be first thing though—the sun was far too bright for an early January morning.

Lilli squinted one eye open to gauge the time. What she received for her effort was a single-lens, fuzzy world that refused to come into focus. Beside her, Brad moaned and shifted position. Crap. Crap. Crappity crap.

How much did she drink last night? It couldn't have been that much. The wine had only been slightly more than half full when she'd gotten up to pour a glass. Since when did she get this hung-over from a couple glasses of Merlot? And since when would she have allowed Brad to spend the night?

As her senses began to creep back to the surface of rationality, she was hit with the stark realization that she was stark naked. Top to bottom, bare as the day she was born.

In spite of the heaviness in her head and the sinking in her stomach, she forced her eyes open. Whatever brief hope she'd that it was actually Jake's voice she'd heard a moment ago was short-lived, when she looked next to her to see that, yes, it was Brad. *Oh. My. God.*

She didn't want to wake him fully before she had the opportunity to determine what exactly had taken place last night. She again regarded her nakedness. She couldn't have. Wouldn't have.

She paused, holding her breath, as she attempted to access her memory. It was all so fuzzy. She recalled getting up for a glass of wine. She remembered the knock on the door and thinking it was Jake, but it had turned out to be Brad. She summoned up an image of a second glass of Merlot, but after that…nothing.

That was innocent enough. But where the hell were her clothes and why the hell was he in her bed? Lilli took a deep breath and gingerly lifted the duvet. She squinted her eyes shut. She couldn't look. What if Brad was naked too? She peered one eye open and there she had it. Her answer. Brad resembled the proverbial jay bird.

But none of it made any sense. She would never cheat on Jake. She would never let Brad get her clothes off. She would never get that drunk from a half bottle of wine. Yet she had. Obviously.

Lilli rested her buzzing head back on the pillow and stared at the ceiling, thinking. Remembering—or trying to anyway. Coffee. She needed coffee. And she needed to call work because she was obviously late.

She wiggled slowly sideways until she was out of the bed without disturbing the blankets, or Brad. She was definitely not ready to deal with him yet. She snatched her tank top and boxers off the end of the bed, almost feeling angry with them for having left her body, and she tiptoed to the bathroom to get dressed.

The entire apartment was tilting haphazardly as she attempted to walk. Had Brad secretly brought over a bottle of tequila? And had she downed the whole thing herself? Had she ever been this hung-over? Ever?

Lilli reached out to the wall to steady herself as the pounding in her brain increased in tempo and volume. With both hands she grasped her head, as though if she were to let go it might split wide open. But the pounding continued. *Bam, bam, bam.*

Please, God, make it stop.

Nope. Still pounding. Then, "Lilli! Open up. I know you're in there. Your Jeep is still in the lot, and they told me at the agency that you didn't come in. Or call. Lilli?"

Now it made more sense. The banging on the door was matching that in her head. She reflected on the image of Bradley asleep in her bed—naked as a jay bird she reminded herself. So she forced herself off the wall and to the door. She had to answer it before the knocking and shouting woke him up and, God forbid, he came out.

The chain rattled and the deadbolt clanked—both sounds resonating louder than she ever remembered. Lilli jerked the door open and then whirled on her heel and ran to the bathroom with her hand over her mouth.

She slammed the toilet open and proceeded to vomit. Somewhere, beyond the sound of her own retching, her name was being said in a masculine voice. No. A feminine one. No. Both, actually.

With more effort than she could even comprehend would be needed, Lilli raised her head away from the toilet bowl and wiped her mouth with a nearby cloth, turning toward the doorway.

So. Not. Cool.

Donna stood there, mouth agape, staring, although not at Lilli. She was ogling Brad, feet planted on the floor across from her, hands on hips, jay-bird style.

Oh Crap.

It was enough to make her retch again, only this time she had nothing left to sacrifice to the all-mighty porcelain gods. Instead her stomach clenched and heaved. Clenched and heaved. Now gagging. Oh fuck.

Please let her go back to sleep. Please let this be a dream.

Have. To. Fix. This.

She placed one hand on the edge of the seat. And the next. Now, push, Lilli, push. In a staggered motion she rose to standing, the smell of vomit wafting up with the flow of movement. No. Not that.

She held her breath and wiped at her face again. She raised a single finger, calling for a brief timeout and she moved to the sink, where she turned on the cold water and placed her cupped hand under the faucet. Swish, spit. More water. Swish, spit.

Oh, God, what was wrong with her?

Now when she focused her vision on the door, both Brad and Donna were studying her, both appearing hesitant to enter the bathroom.

She wanted to raise her hands in question. *What?* But she already knew the answer. A glance in the mirror confirmed it. She looked like hell. No. She looked like hell would look if it had consumed an entire winery's worth of vino, puked its guts out, and had an eternal-feeling hangover.

Donna and Brad exchanged a stare. Then Donna's gaze dropped to the money shot. She motioned for him to put his clothes on. He wandered off to oblige. Then Donna came over to Lilli and placed an arm around her shoulder.

"Lilli, you look like—"

She raised a palm. "I know, and trust me, I feel even worse."

"Can you sit?" Donna asked.

"Worth a try." Lilli swallowed and balked against the lingering taste of bile in her throat. "Water. Must have water."

Donna led her to the sofa and then handed her a Starbucks cup. "I'm not sure how hot it is. I walked it over and was knocking for a while too." She headed to the kitchen. "Water is coming up."

She returned a moment later with a full glass. "You seem to be out of bottled." She extended it toward Lilli, but Lilli refused it.

"I appreciate it, Donna, but the chlorine will make me gag again." She lifted her arm and pointed to the kitchen. "Think I have some apple juice in the cupboard. Would you check?"

Donna nodded and spun around, passing a fully clothed Brad on her way to the kitchen. They exchanged a silent glance, both skeptical of the other's motives it seemed.

As Donna was opening cupboards to look for the juice, Brad moved toward Lilli. Honestly, he looked as confused as Lilli felt. Didn't look quite as peaked, but still appeared as if he'd had a run-in with a Mack truck. He opened his mouth to speak, but she hushed him with a finger placed in front of her pursed lips.

"Not now. Later."

He nodded his agreement and went to the door to slip his runners on. A single glance back at her as she shook her head, and then he left with a quiet click of the door.

When she looked back, Donna was again standing in front of her, her hand outstretched with a glass of juice. She wanted to ask for ice, but instead she smiled and took the offered beverage.

Donna got a toehold on the footstool and dragged it over, then took a seat facing Lilli. She leaned forward, arms draped over her knees. "Something you want to talk about?" Her eyes darted briefly toward the door.

Lilli took a long, slow sip from her glass, swallowing it down with trepidation. When her stomach didn't roil, she took another sip. Okay. That one stayed down too. She eyed the coffee and then lifted her vision to Donna. "Thanks." The word came out as a razor-scraped whisper.

Toby finally showed his innocent little face, strolling by and rubbing against Lilli's legs. She wanted to reach down and give him a pet, but thought better of it. No sense agitating her stomach right then.

I bet you're hungry, aren't you, kitty?" Donna rose from sitting. "Come on, Toby. I'll feed you."

She strolled into the kitchen, but Toby refused to follow—until he heard the sound of kibble falling into his bowl. Then he scurried over fast as lightning.

"He needs a pat on the head before he'll eat," Lilli said.

Seconds later she could hear the soft crunching of Toby at his dish. Then, Donna returned and resumed her position in front of Lilli. "All right, so you didn't show up for work, and when I arrived here your ex was naked in your apartment and you were throwing up. Good thing I wasn't Jake. I can't imagine that going over well with him."

She was right, and Lilli was relieved it had been Donna at the door. Of course, she wouldn't have opened it if it had been Jake calling her name. She set the juice down and her hands went to her head. "I don't know, Donna."

"You don't know what?"

"Anything. I don't know what happened last night. I don't know why I'm so freakin' hung-over today, and I really don't know why Brad and I woke up naked together in my bed."

Donna's eyes became rather round and wide. "You woke up naked? With your exceedingly hot and sexy ex? And you don't know what happened? Lilli, that's sex-ed one-oh-one."

Lilli shook her head as if the action would negate the implication. "Drinking Merlot on an empty stomach…that I might do. Drinking too much…I don't remember doing it but clearly I did. But cheating on Jake…no. I wouldn't have sex with Brad, no matter how drunk I was."

The expression on her friend's face showed unconcealed doubt.

"I'm pretty sure…" Lilli added, just as much to convince herself of the fact. "Okay, this is what I do remember."

She began to relate the story, as Donna listened intently. Her revelations were brief, though, because not long after Brad had arrived was where her recollections began to a get little fuzzy. Or a lot fuzzy. Okay, they were as fuzzy as a baby chick on Easter morning.

She raised her hands in confusion. "And then I woke up. Naked. With Brad." Lilli once again eyed the Starbucks cup, sitting on the nearby table. She would try the coffee. It might help clear the cobwebs, maybe at least enough that she could shower.

Donna scooted the cup closer to Lilli, who picked it up, grateful it was still at least warmer than room temperature. As she removed the lid and took a sip, Lilli became conscious of the fact that she was only wearing the pink tank top and boxer shorts. "I'll be right back," she said.

As she rose to standing, Lilli paused in an attempt to steady the dizziness that threatened to overtake her. Regaining her balance, she scanned the room for a throw blanket, to no avail, so she eased her way to her bedroom to get her robe. She looked at the unmade bed. Whatever did happen last night, no matter what it was, sure as hell was not going to happen again.

Her head still spinning, she stopped in the bathroom on her way back. Maybe she would try showering. She placed her coffee on the counter and sat on the side of the tub while she adjusted the water temperature, setting it to a scarcely endurable level of cold, knowing that a hot shower would only serve to lull her back to sleep.

Lilli continued her desperate attempts to piece together the grainy bits of information she could recall, without much success, as she systematically went through her usual cleansing routine.

As she was lathering up the back of her golden locks, her hands lightly brushed the nape of her neck, flooding her brain with vivid imagery.

She could virtually feel the sensation of Brad's hands on her, the tactile sensuality of him softly kissing her neck. No. It was all in her mind. Had to be. She had been with Brad so many times in the past that her imagination was giving her a made-up version to fill in the blanks. However, the facts certainly seemed to point to such conduct, and the sinking feeling in the pit of her stomach rendered her almost unable to lather, rinse, and repeat.

If she thought for a second that Brad would tell her the truth, she would just ask him directly, but maybe she really did not want to know. As long as she was uncertain, she could stay in denial. Right?

A quick triple-rap on the door startled her out of her internal debate.

"Hey, Lilli, I'm going to let myself out. I have to get back to work. I kind of lied to get away to check on you and I've been gone too long."

She turned off the water and snagged a big towel off the rack. "Sure. I understand. Make sure you lock up—and, Donna?"

"Yeah?"

"This is just between you and me, right?"

"Of course."

Lilli heard the door slam shut, and she slipped out of the bathroom. All she wanted to do was drop into bed, but she needed to call work. It was unlike her to simply not show up. She picked up the phone and dialed.

LILLI HAD BARELY hung up the phone and there was a knock at her door. She wondered who it was going to be—Brad, Donna again, or Jake. Her money was on Brad. It would be just like him to lurk outside and wait for Donna to leave and then come back to gloat over her recent nakedness in his presence.

She raised up on her tiptoes and leaned her eye to the peephole. She would have lost her bet. It was Jake. She was, at once, relieved and terrified to see him. After three deep breaths she opened the door and splayed a giant smile across her face. "Jake!"

Instead of returning her smile he pushed past her into the apartment, his eyes snaking around with a suspicious glint. "So," he continued to dart his eyes as he wandered, "what's going on, Lil?" Without waiting for her answer he moved to the kitchen, then bathroom, then bedroom, appearing to be looking for something. Or someone.

She followed him into the bedroom where he was tossing her duvet back onto her bed. He lifted a pillow and then threw it back. Then the next, same thing.

"Jake?"

He spun around, his eyes flashing. "Yeah, Lilli? Something you want to say?"

"Jake, I—what's wrong?"

"I'll tell you what's wrong, Lilli." He crossed to her closet and pulled on the doors. He looked inside then left them open and marched over, stopping mere inches in front of her. His eyes bore into her. "After a fitful night of tossing and turning, in spite of all the damn pills I popped, I finally managed to get out of bed. Not so much because I was feeling ambitious, but because I smelled my mother's delicious pancakes wafting down from the kitchen. Did I mention my parents made me stay at their place? No? Well they did. But guess what?"

Lilli's neck was craned up to look at him as he spoke but the action was too much for her in her weakened and nauseous state. "Jake? Can we sit? This isn't very comf—"

He shoved her backward onto the bed. "You can't guess? Okay, I'll tell you. I didn't get to enjoy the damn pancakes because I got a random message telling me I better check on my fucking girlfriend. That was all. Just 'Jake, check on your girlfriend.' Oh, it was followed with an LOL and a winking smiley face."

He began to cradle one closed fist inside his other open one as he paced the length of the room. Back and forth. Back and forth. A caged beast ready to pounce. "So, tell me, *girlfriend*, why should I need to check on you?"

She opened her mouth to respond, but Jake silenced her with a glare.

"Never mind answering that. It was rhetorical. Let me tell you why."

A gleam washed over his face as though a marvelous idea had just struck him. He stopped pacing and released his fist, then closed the gap between them in one single step. Jake bent down and lifted the edge of her mattress, almost tossing her to the floor, and looked under the bed. He dropped it back down and grunted like a caveman.

"The why of it, Lilli, the why that I should be checking on my girlfriend about, has two names—Bradley and Vanderson."

Lilli remained silent. She had no idea what to say. All she knew was her head was not prepared to deal with this right now. Finally, she went with the only thing she could. Answer him with a question. At least then she could find out exactly what Jake knew. After all, she didn't even know what was going on. "What about Brad?"

He stormed back and forth in front of her again, his knuckles cracking as he pounded his fist into his hand. Then he stopped abruptly, stood in front of her and made grueling eye contact. She didn't dare look away.

"I don't fucking know. But I'm going to find out. I promise you that." Then he regarded her as if he were seeing her for the first time since he arrived. "You look like shit."

"Gee thanks, Jake. I love you too."

Okay, maybe she shouldn't have gone with sarcasm under the circumstances, but she felt like her life was spiraling out of control and she didn't know how to rein it in. She couldn't get her mind around anything that had happened in the last twelve or so hours.

"Fuck!" Jake spun around and blasted his fist through her bedroom wall. Then, his face unreadable, he glanced at her and then strode into the living room.

Should she follow him? A part of her actually wanted to lock the bedroom door and never let Jake in again. But another part of her understood what he was going through. She had no idea who would have sent him such a message—maybe Brad himself—but she could see where he was coming from. While her body didn't feel as though she'd had sex the night before, her heart was afraid she had. Not willingly though, that she was certain of.

Maybe Brad had slipped something into her wine and then he took advantage of her, or wanted her to think he had. That made some sense…except he'd had some wine too. And, while he didn't look as bad as she'd felt this morning, he also didn't appear to be without side effects.

Maybe Jake would calm down and maybe this would all blow over.

She tried his name. "Jake?"

She received a grunt from the living room.

"Can we talk?"

CHAPTER THIRTY-SIX

LILLI SAT AT HER desk staring at the other half of a plain bagel, toasted, with butter. She barely finished the first half and didn't think she could venture into second-half territory. Second half. It made her think of football. That made her think of Jake. That made her think of the last few days of her life.

She'd managed to get Jake to calm down, relax. It was as though seeing her, really seeing her, in the condition she'd been in, had flipped a switch in him, causing him to turn protective. When he'd seen how awful she was feeling he'd backed off, decided that someone must've been yanking his chain, as he put it. One of the guys on the team maybe. He'd been punked. He still didn't trust Brad any farther than he could throw him, but Lilli wouldn't have cheated on him—couldn't have. Not with the flu as bad as she had it.

He'd apologized for the hole in the wall. Had come over the next day to plaster over it. He was sorry he'd lost his temper. Didn't know what had taken him over, but he would never do it again She deserved better, he'd said.

She'd even managed to evade Brad. Although, it was kind of odd, it almost seemed as if he was avoiding her. Either way, she'd take it.

And here Lilli sat, still just as confused as she'd been two days ago, and still unable to finish her bagel. She hadn't thrown up again after that first morning, but she was so damn tired. Maybe it actually was the flu after all. She was grateful the office was quiet this morning, except that she was almost falling asleep at her desk. Not even Starbucks had managed to perk her up so far.

As she gave in to temptation and rested her head on the stack of contact sheets and portfolios piled on her desk, Clarisse, a tall, lithe former model, now head of placements at the agency, tapped lightly on the partially open door.

"Hey, girlfriend, did you get the license plate of the truck that hit you?" She glided into the room and flounced into the over-stuffed cowhide chair in the corner.

"Hey, Clarisse." Lilli didn't even try to mask her lack of enthusiasm.

"What's up with you, girl? No offence, but you look awful. Why don't you go home and sleep it off?"

Clarisse bore a striking resemblance to Halle Berry, although, she had recently allowed her hair to grow out into a soft natural afro. While her approach could sometimes use some polish, her appearance did not. Even in her forties—Lilli guessed, as Clarisse would never tell—she drew looks everywhere she went.

She lifted her head from the desk. "I probably should. I thought I was feeling better. I was hoping to clear my head by coming in here."

"Sounds serious. Wanna talk?"

"Maybe some other time, I think I'll take your advice and go home. Can you tell Chuck I'm still not feeling well?"

"Yes, *dahling*." Clarisse stretched languidly out of the chair, like a jungle cat stirring from a nap. "Be sure to get some rest. Call me." She waved and breezed through the door, the *clickity-click* of her Manolos trailing after her.

Resisting the temptation to lay her head back down on the desk, Lilli gathered her things and made her way down to the parking garage. She drove home in somewhat of a stupor—the events of the last several days had officially caused a mini-meltdown she was sure.

She had evolved from make-up artist to model on a photo shoot, planned a weekend to remember that turned into a weekend she'd rather forget. And she still didn't know what had happened with Brad.

LILLI PULLED INTO her parking stall at home and quickly grabbed her things, then sprinted inside. She shut and locked the apartment door behind her and sighed. She'd made it in without seeing Brad. Before she could even finish that thought, however, the telephone began ringing.

She didn't want to know. She could pretend that she didn't hear it beckoning and stay blissfully ignorant for at least a few minutes longer.

It rang two more times before voicemail picked up, and Lilli, resisting the urge to check to see who had called, walked right past the phone and straight into her room.

Opening the window a small crack to get some fresh air, she then stripped down and climbed into bed, hoping that sleep would come swiftly. It did but, regrettably, it was not as restful as she had hoped.

As she lay between the crisp white sheets attempting to drift off again, she could not help but summon up the memory of waking up with Brad beside her just few a short days ago. The guilt and confusion surrounding the circumstances were still weighing heavily on her. Her dreams overflowed with lustful images of Brad, followed by Jake on a jealous rampage.

Finally, Lilli gave up on the idea of a catnap and sat bolt upright in bed. "I can't stand it anymore!" She had to know.

She sat a moment longer, contemplating her limited options, and then realized there was no easy way out. She threw on a t-shirt and darted out to where the telephone sat—either a savior or a potential messenger of doom. She pressed speed dial two, took a deep breath, and waited for Brad to pick up.

"COME IN." Brad popped his head into the hall as if he were checking to see if she'd been followed. When he seemed satisfied that she hadn't, he closed the door and led her to the sofa.

"Do you want something to drink?" he asked.

She studied him, trying to decipher if he was being facetious or not. He seemed genuine, but still, she felt the need to clarify. "Nothing with alcohol," she said and tried to make herself comfortable while she waited for him to return.

She already regretted coming over. Why couldn't she just pretend nothing happened? What exactly did she hope to accomplish?

Just then, Brad entered the living room and handed Lilli a glass of iced tea. "Not the Long Island variety."

"Thanks, Brad." Lilli took an elongated sip, again avoiding the elephant in the room.

But not for long. "I'm glad you came over, Lilli. I wanted to talk to you about something."

"Yeah, me too, I guess." Lilli kept her eyes focused on the ice floating in her glass of tea.

"Me first." He took a sip of his own.

"Okay." Maybe Brad going first was a good thing. Maybe he would tell her something that would make her own worries fly away. Maybe.

CHAPTER THIRTY-SEVEN

THE SOUND WAS so faint at first that Lilli had to hush Brad, right as he was telling her how scared he was that his doctor confirmed he had bipolar. What was going on outside? Then it became louder and clearer.

"Lilli! Lilli!"

"Oh my God, that's Jake's voice," Lilli exclaimed. Then, completely overlooking the fact that she still did not know what happened with Brad, she hopped off the couch and ran to the door, pulling on her coat and boots as she moved. "I gotta go. Sorry, Brad, about the doctor stuff, and—I'll talk to you later." Without thinking, she dashed out of Brad's building and toward the sound of Jake's booming voice. He was outside her bedroom window.

"I know you're in there, Lilli. Your Jeep is in the lot. Lilli?"

As she neared where he was standing, she mentally crossed her fingers, hoping he hadn't seen her leave Brad's building. Damn. She worked on an excuse as quick as possible.

Jake spun his head and looked right at her, fire burning in his eyes. "What's going on? Were you with Brad?"

"It was going to be a surprise," she replied.

His shoulders dropped back and his chest heaved with air, as though he was about to go on the offensive. "What surprise?"

"I guess I can tell you, since he didn't have any anyway."

"Brad didn't have what?"

Jake clearly knew she was coming from Brad's place, so she might as well not try to lie about that.

"I wanted to make you some shortbread cookies and I didn't have enough butter. I only went over to see if Brad had any. He didn't. I'm sorry. I know they're your favorites."

Jake studied her intently.

She grabbed his hand. "Let's go inside. It's cold out."

Jake followed her into the building, but she could sense resistance in him.

"How are you feeling today, Jake?" she asked once they were inside.

"Okay, I suppose." He shrugged out of his coat and let it rest on the floor where it landed. Then he kicked off his shoes and assumed a sitting position at the dining table.

Lilli went to the fridge and pulled out some juice, then poured them each a glass. As she put the carton back she spied a full stick of butter, which she promptly buried under a bag of salad that was unopened but beyond resuscitation. At least now she could say she hadn't wasted it.

She gave Jake his juice, which he downed in a single gulp before wiping his mouth with the back of his hand. He ran his fingers through his hair, then palms down his face, leaving a humorless expression in its wake.

In the motion, Lilli's eye was drawn to Jake's craggy, unshaven jawline. That wasn't like him. Five o'clock stubble sure, but he had the full outline of a burgeoning beard shadowing his features.

He reached over and took her hands in his, then stared down at them.

"Jake? What is it?"

He released his breath in the form of a protracted, groaning sigh. "I don't know if I can take it, Lil. The waiting. The division playoff game is coming up and I haven't been cleared yet. No one's talking either. I can't get a damn word out of the coach, the other players aren't telling me jack."

He picked up his empty glass. "You got anything stronger?"

The mere thought made Lilli's stomach turn. Not to mention the fact that she knew he was on strong painkillers and drinking was the last thing he should be doing. She shook her head. "I can get you some more juice though?"

"Naw. I'm good. I've had enough." His eyes drifted toward the window. "I've had enough of a lot of things."

"What do you mean?"

"My folks. The first day or two were good. Mom was spoiling me. Dad was busy with the store. But he's already riding my ass like I'm a Venezuelan pack mule. He says if the team don't want me then I better get my lazy ass to the store and start counting inventory." Jake spoke the last bit using his version of his dad's voice, which was laden with gruffness and hostility. Then, "Fuck! I was supposed to be past that."

What a jerk his father was. And Jake's mother wasn't doing him any favors by treating him like a child either. Lilli had a feeling Jake would sit out the rest of this season. At least. If the Seahawks made it to the Super Bowl without him…she couldn't even imagine the devastation that would wreak on him. Football was his life. What if he could never return to it?

Lilli stood and moved behind him, then began massaging his shoulders. As he relaxed into her touch she rested her chin on the top of his head. "I can make an early supper, Jake. What would you like? I don't have much in the house but I can go out and pick some ingredients up. I'll make you whatever you—"

Jake's phone rang and he frowned when he looked at the caller ID. "It's my old man." He pressed talk and answered the phone. "What?"

Lilli could hear the loud-mouthed diatribe echoing through Jake's phone. Although she couldn't make out what his father was saying, she heard enough to tell he was angry. Mind you, when didn't he sound angry?

Jake flashed her a *here-we-go-again* look, and then he spoke, clearly placating the man. "Yeah, you're my father. That ain't no way to greet you. Respect. Uh-huh. I get it, Dad." Jake rolled his eyes and used his free hand to puppet a snapping motion—*natter, natter, natter.*

With an unexpected surge, he bolted upright in his chair. "They're what? When? Yeah, I'll be there. If they get there first, tell them to wait. Yeah, Dad. I'm on my way. Whatever. I said I am." Jake hung up and met with Lilli's gaze.

"They're coming to talk to me." Jake pulled her onto his lap and deep into a hug.

"Do you want me to come with you?" Lilli whispered into his ear.

"No. My Dad won't—that's not a good idea. I have no clue what they're going to tell me. I need to go alone."

She got off his lap, and he stood, then made his way to the door.

"I wish you could stay," she said.

"Me too. Supper sounded like a good plan."

"Maybe you can come back? Spend the night?"

"Maybe," he said. "We'll see." He leaned down to kiss her and then opened the door to go. "I'll call you."

"Okay, Jake. Drive safe."

He grinned. "Me? Drive safe? Never."

"Drive like a maniac then."

A huge grin, followed by, "Yeah. Now that's more like it."

She watched him walk down the hall toward the main doors, and she sighed. Why did life have to throw her another curveball? Hadn't she hit enough home runs to get a pass for once? Just when she had allowed herself to break the rules and fall hard and quick. Now her so-called Prince Charming was vacillating between Charming and Toad.

She locked the door and went to flop down on her bed. Dead tired she wanted to just relax until Jake called her with whatever news he got. But her brain wouldn't allow it, instead sending her through repetitive patterns of thinking, reliving and re-reliving every moment of the last several days.

It occurred to her that she had left Brad hanging in the middle of their conversation. A confirmed diagnosis of bipolar disorder was a big thing. Even though he'd suspected it would turn out that way, it still had to be hard. Lilli almost believed she was his only real friend. What if he had no one else to talk to?

"Stop it, Lilli," she told herself. "This is not your responsibility."

Again, her brain toyed with her rationale, taunting her—the breaking in, the stalking in stairwells, the rage, it wasn't Brad's fault. Caring about our fellow humans is everyone's duty, isn't it? Or should be. Compassion and the golden rule and all that.

But soon, thankfully, Lilli's eyes began to feel heavy. Maybe she would call him after a little nap.

CHAPTER THIRTY-EIGHT

MY HEAD'S POUNDING but I don't really give a flying fuck. I'll be honest. I just don't care about that. No pain, no gain, right?

But Lilli, I give a fuck about her, including the flying variety. I have a little competition. So what? That's not a problem. I'm going to win.

See, another thing my father taught me is this—the key to success is to want something so bad you can taste it. Really, actually, physically taste it. Savor the lingering spice of it on your tongue. Once you can do that, the rest is like eating pie. And I do have a predilection for pie. Got that from Mom. She made great pie.

I'll be the first to admit I have a few hurdles to get over. A few challenges to overcome. But I learned from my past attempts. I perfected my techniques. If you make a batch of cookies and they don't taste right, what do you do? Toss 'em out and start over. If that batch don't work, toss out the recipe. It ain't no damn good. Wasn't to begin with. Move on. Works with pie too. Ask Mom.

Just make sure to take the trash out back before Dad gets home and sees the evidence of wasted attempts. Learned that the hard way I did. Of course, most of my lessons came in that manner, but it makes for a solid education, that it does. Graduated with honors from HKU—Hard Knocks University.

But, again, I digress. I'm still working on that one.

Back to my current situation. I was so close. So. Fucking. Close. The trip to DC was supposed to turn out different. But I'll find a way to make it work to my advantage. Rolling with punches. Leaping over obstacles. Taking the hits.

A little more patience. A little more time.

Minutes. Hours. Days.

I got all the time in the world.

They say no news is good news. Maybe. But I've been dealing with bad news all my life, so, yeah, I can handle this. I have already gone through so much to get here. Been through the incendiary gates of hell.

And back.

More than once.

Through fire and brimstone *I* have taken the risks. I deserve to reap the reward. So bring on the news—good, bad, or otherwise. Just one more hurdle to clear. Easy-peasy. I will not let anyone ruin this for me. I will keep my eyes on the prize—in the words of dear old Dad. Gotta be in it to win it. And I am.

You see, the others before her, they *seemed* right at the time, but they turned out to be failed cookie batches. Toss 'em out. Hide the evidence. Move on. But the recipe? I'm not ready to discard that yet. A few tweaks here and there and it's better than ever. No burnt edges. No soggy centers. Just sweet golden bliss. I finally have the perfect cookie and I refuse to share.

My sister would tell you finders keepers, losers weepers. It's true. My so-called competition can commence with tear shedding. I'll call that *wah*-mbulance. Got the number on speed dial—1-800-cry-baby.

Lilli Brooks is mine to keep. I found her. Fair and square. I have earned her trust. I have earned *her*. If I believed I still had a soul, *she* would be its mate.

Can I be happy knowing I'm part of her world? No. I must *be* her world.

A lifetime of emptiness shall be sated soon. It is our destiny. We pinkie-sweared.

And I know how to take out the trash.

CHAPTER THIRTY-NINE

SHE'D SLEPT MUCH longer than she'd intended and Lilli awoke with a start, blinking in the unexpected pitch-dark obscurity surrounding her. She fumbled around for her cell phone and squinted her eyes against the light from the screen as she pressed the button to check for messages.

There was one from Jake. *Call me when you get this.* Two from Donna. *How are you doing and do you want to hang out again soon?*

But there were none from Bradley and something about that didn't feel right to her. Sometimes no news isn't good news.

Lilli scooted out of bed and battled the darkness on her way to the window, proud of herself for only tripping on one thing. No toe stubbing either. Brad's apartment was not at the perfect angle, but maybe if she tilted her head and pressed her face against the glass at the far edge of the pane she could at least tell if his light was on.

She gazed beyond the lampposts in the parking lot and narrowed her eyes. She couldn't get a fix on it. She thought she almost had it when a shadow darted by and behind a nearby tree, pulling her vision to follow it. Too big for a squirrel, and large dogs were not allowed in the complex. Only small ones and indoor cats.

A little shiver laced up her spine and Lilli dodged across the room and leapt into bed, yanking her feet off the floor, suddenly wary of having them near the underneath of the bed. Now she felt silly. Letting her imagination create monsters in the dark. Still, Lilli couldn't resist the urge to shine the light from her cell phone all around the room.

Toby glanced up, sleepy-eyed and annoyed. Even her cat thought she was losing it. He was probably right. She dropped her head on the pillow and worked to stop the running loop of her most recent worries. But the random sounds teasing her from outside were doing absolutely nothing to quench her fears.

One time, when she opened her eyes at a scraping noise outside her window she could have sworn she saw a Jake-sized shadow move past the curtains. Memories of Brad's warnings in the stairwell at the agency came flooding back to her. Had Jake really stalked his ex-girlfriend? She had refused to believe it then, but after his outburst the other day, and the warnings from the doctor about mood swings and personality changes...it all added up to a sleepless night in Seattle.

That thought almost made her get up and pop in the DVD. Meg Ryan and Tom Hanks were both good for sufficient entertainment to encourage her mind toward better pursuits, but she couldn't shake the apprehension that pressed down on her belly. The thought of surrounding herself in the blue halo of luminescence that would emanate from the TV, or even her laptop, made her feel like a deer on the highway. Frozen and unable to see beyond the threat of oncoming traffic—traffic that could see her just fine.

She succumbed to the alternative, spending the rest of the night tangled among her blankets, caught in the stubborn vortex between sleep and sanity.

WHEN THE MORNING sunshine finally did greet her, she was ready to call the long night over and get started with her day. Easier said than done. Lying awake most of the night had extorted what remained of her depleted energy reserves.

Still, she rose from bed and showered for work. She'd never missed this much before. Adding in the days off over the holidays and then to go to the game last Sunday...if Chuck Willows wasn't such an awesome boss, her paycheck would have been almost nil. Instead, he'd not only paid her in full but had tacked on a jaw-dropping holiday bonus. Thank goodness—and Chuck—for that.

Going forward, she had to do better. Had to fulfill her obligations, and heck, she might as well take better care of herself from now on too. Heeding that, she threw a few things together for her lunch at work and, for breakfast, she cracked two eggs beside the three slices of bacon sizzling on the frying pan. As she gave two twists of the salt grinder, a triple tap vibrated the glass at her patio doors. Who would knock there? Ever since the cold snap, the front door had been sticking open and it seemed no one had to wait to be buzzed into the building anymore. Maybe the manager had finally fixed it. She peeked her head around the corner. Wrapped only in her bathrobe she made sure to show caution before coming into full view of the doors.

The curtains were drawn. Of course they were. But the silhouette behind gave the impression of Jake. She pulled back the drapes to reveal the image of a man who appeared to be freezing to death. Jake's breath was coming out in ragged gusts of vapor and he was rubbing his bare hands together fast enough to start a fire.

She hustled to release the locks and the new security bar, and thrust the doors wide, allowing him solace inside the warm apartment.

He reached for her, but she evaded the frosty embrace by walling her hands between them. "Uh-uh. You're like the abominable snowman, if you hug me I'll turn to ice."

He took a step toward the entryway door.

She glanced at his feet. "Shoes off." She pointed at the floor where they were standing. "Here. Please."

He grimaced, used the tip of one foot to anchor the heel of the other, and then bent down with a groan to pick up his shoes.

As he wandered to the entryway to deposit his dripping footwear, he began sniffing the air. "Something smells good."

"The eggs!" Lilli dashed into the kitchen and turned off the element, sliding the frying pan to a cold one. She grabbed the spatula, broke the yolks, and flipped them over. The pan was still hot enough to cook the other side.

"Now this," Jake arrived at the threshold to the kitchen, bobbing his head, arms stretched out and braced against the entry, "this, I like. The smell of bacon-y breakfast promise. The sight of my gorgeous woman in front of the stove, scantily dressed, I might add." His brows hitched as his eyes wandered like a river of molasses, flowing over her, top to toe. "That's another kind of promise—I assume you *are* naked under that robe."

He closed the distance between them, spun her to face him, and tugged at the tie to her robe, letting it fall open and tumble off her shoulders. His eyes twinkled with hazel-colored mischief and the accompanying grin quirked his lips as he reached out to pull her to him.

Lilli shrieked and swatted at his cold hands on her backside. "Get those ice mitts off me," she teased. "Why are you so cold anyway?" She shivered and belted her robe again. "And why are you here so early? Traffic from your parents' house must have been rush-hour crazy at this time of day."

He shrugged, then folded his arms across his chest. Lilli studied the movement. He was shaking. She slipped her hands into the fold of his arms and pulled on his, holding them stretched out.

"Jake, you're trembling." Actually, his entire body was shaking.

After doing a double-take to ensure she had turned off the stove, she led him to the sofa, and placed a blanket around his shoulders. "You feel cold to the bone, Jake. What did you do? Spend the night in a snowbank?"

CHAPTER FORTY

TWO WEEKS HAD passed since *The Brad Incident*. Lilli was finally feeling like her normal self again—more or less, aside from brief periods of recurring nausea and being ridiculously tired. She was trying to get the hang of this taking-care-of-herself thing. Really she was.

She still had no idea what had actually transpired between them that night though. They never did get back to their conversation. He'd been MIA since their last encounter, therefore, she found it easier to pack up the memory and lock it securely in the back of her mind.

And then there was the issue of Jake. He had taken her on a rollercoaster ride this past week and a half.

They'd released him from the team, citing the injuries and the doctor's bleak prognosis. Jake was no longer golden. He was a liability. And if that weren't enough, the trembling she'd noticed that morning he'd come through her patio, in from the cold, wasn't strictly from the frigid temperatures. It turned out he was having seizures, so they added anti-seizure medicine to his pharmaceutical repertoire, most of which, Lilli was convinced, he wasn't taking regularly anyway. The pain pills, sure, he was likely on top of that one, but as far as the others, probably not so much.

No, these days Lilli was in such turmoil she couldn't care less about what had happened with Brad. She'd convinced herself he was okay and dealing with his bipolar issues just fine. On the other hand, she was almost positive Jake had been following her home from work, maybe even sleeping in his car outside her apartment.

She wasn't sure because he'd had to go back to driving his silver Honda—the lease on the Land Rover was too expensive—and silver sedans were a dime a dozen on the streets of Seattle. Still, Lilli was becoming hyper-vigilant, leading to one conclusion. Wherever she went and whenever she went there, a ubiquitous silver car would be there too.

Jake's sense of self-identity seemed to have washed up alongside the industrial contaminants on the shores of Elliott Bay, right beside his career. The drive that he'd put into football for so long had nowhere to go now. He'd refused to watch the division championship game against the Atlanta Falcons—until the fourth quarter when a friend had texted him news that the Falcons had pulled off a legendary comeback, after an equally legendary meltdown, when their QB completed two long passes and then they kicked a forty-nine-yard field goal with only eight seconds remaining in regulation.

Jake had flipped the game on in record time to catch the replays. The Seahawks' strategy to call time-out seconds before the ball was snapped for the kick had carried the intention of breaking the flow, but ended up working against them. They'd shot themselves in the collective foot. The Falcons shanked the first attempt—as per Seattle's plan—but didn't waste their second chance. Straight up the middle, sailing through the uprights to give them a 30-28 lead to win the division title.

That he'd celebrated.

Jake had commented that maybe now the Seahawks understood how it felt to want something so bad you could taste it, only to have it snatched away. They would have won if he'd been there, he'd said. He'd deserved to be there. Had earned it.

Apparently, any loyalty he'd had to the team had flown out the window when they'd released him from his contract. He'd gone out the day after the game and purchased a Falcons jersey, wore it all week, but took it off yesterday after San Fran kicked Atlanta out of the running.

So, now, as Lilli drove to work, she didn't even mind the bumper-to-bumper action. She was alone. She could finally exhale. Finally think.

Jake had called her his good-luck charm, and she hadn't believed, but now she was considering that he might be her bad-luck charm. Their relationship had started out with such promise, yet here they were, a few weeks in, and life had never been more complicated for Lilli.

Her heart kept reaching out to Jake, wanting to help him. Wanting to prove she wasn't the type to get lost when the going got tough. But he was making that harder by the day. She watched her back everywhere she went, and now she had two patched walls in her apartment—both courtesy of Jake's "mean right." He was mad. He was sad. He was up. He was down. He was spinning through a vortex of disturbing behaviors that made the rest of Lilli's body want to run like hell, regardless of what her heart was saying.

Her friends, it seemed, concurred with the latter, telling her to cut her losses. After all, she'd only been dating him a few weeks and, therefore, did not owe him a damn thing. And she hadn't ever even told them what Brad had said about Jake's proclivity for violence and stalking.

Her mother had called a couple times to see how Jake was doing. Lilli answered what she could be truthful about, but couldn't bring herself to mention the problems. Her mother would have told her the same thing as her friends—time to pack up and get the hell outta Dodge.

One thing was certain, Lilli didn't feel like she could go on like this much longer. The state of anxiety she was living in was doing a number on her. Her magazine cover had come out last week and she hadn't even realized until people started approaching her on the street, asking if that was her on the front of this month's *Fashionista Magazine*. Then, every store in the neighborhood had been sold out. She hadn't even held a copy of her own until yesterday when one arrived by mail.

Add to that, her birthday was coming up on February third— Super Bowl Sunday, no less.

She had hoped that once Jake felt better physically his mental state would improve, but in the meantime, she watched him suffer from dizzy spells, memory loss, irritability, headaches, hostility, and honestly, he didn't seem to be thinking very clearly either. Still, Lilli felt that she could help him through it. But should she? That was the raging internal debate.

She was having doubts—about him and about her own ability to read people. She was not ready to give up though. Not yet. She was waiting for a sign from the universe.

"WE NEED TO TALK." Chuck was at reception when Lilli walked into the agency. His expression was solemn, his demeanor restless. His lack of "Hey, gorgeous, how's it going?" told her there was something he needed to say, and she was about to hear it. "My place in five." He tapped a beat on the counter and headed to the swank corner office that, for Chuck, was more home than his lavish penthouse condo.

She showcased her pearly whites, hoping it came off as a smile. "Sure. I'll drop off my things and be right there."

It was time for Lilli's new daily ritual. The receptionist handed her a stack of four-by-five pink Post-it hell. Mandy's smile appeared more genuine than Lilli's had been, but spoke to sympathetic reluctance rather than cheer. That said it all. No words could weaken the wallop packed inside a ginormous wad of call-back slips.

Lilli strode to her office, the crumpled messages weighing like lead in her hand. Something needed to change. She'd had to resort to turning off her cell phone, or screening, often sending Jake's calls directly to voicemail.

It didn't matter where she was these days or what she was doing, if she dared to glance up, sideways, out her window, or in her rearview, there was Jake, lurking in the shadows. Sometimes she acknowledged him, forcing him out of hiding, while he grinned with the awkward guilt of a kid caught stealing a twenty out of his mother's purse. His behavior had become controlling, suspicious, and passive-aggressive.

If only she had seen it coming.

Bah.

She *should* have seen it. Brad did.

A couple of weeks had passed since Jake's injury, yet it had felt like months to Lilli. She'd tried to take it in stride—he'd been through so much, was still going through it—but it wasn't improving. It was getting worse. Exponentially.

Day by day, he was more and more riddled with anxiety. Day by day, he lost more and more self-control. Witnessing Lilli perpetually surrounded by male models definitely wasn't helping. Now Jake was jealous of Brad plus every other red-blooded male in Seattle.

How much more of this could she take? Where would it end? It did have to end, didn't it? One way or another. She couldn't let her emotions stop her from leaving if the situation didn't improve. Soon. She'd learned that lesson with Bradley.

Lilli dropped her bags on the floor and spoke her constant mantra—today would be different. But it never was. Her confirmation was right in front of her when she flipped through the stack of messages. No surprise, all but two were from Jake.

A forceful rush of air from her lungs did little to mitigate her self-torment. Chuck was waiting. Time to deal. Lilli removed the non-Jake messages and stabbed the remainder onto the overloaded metal spike on her desk. Felt kind of good. Cathartic.

She rolled her shoulders and rotated her neck, shrugging out of her coat. Lilli inhaled several deep intakes, then headed toward her boss's office, wishing, again, for a sign. All she wanted was one crummy little waving flag proclaiming: Do this, Lilli. That wasn't too much to ask, was it?

"WHY IS THAT RED flag draped over your table?" She'd noticed it the moment she entered Chuck's domain. It was out of place there. His office was decorated in a sophisticated style that Lilli would term World Chic.

He eyeballed it with a glint of amusement. "Client *SWAG.*" He used air quotes when he said SWAG. It was an acronym for Stuff We All Get—in other words, corporate incentives—and was usually something desirable. This thing was an eyesore. "You want it?" He man-giggled and flashed a row of gleaming veneers.

"Um…no. But thanks for thinking of me." Lilli couldn't resist. She snatched it up, unfurled it, and read the tagline. "Get out of your old ride and get the asterisk, pound sign, ampersand, exclamation mark *into* Dodge."

Chuck broke into another round of giggles. "The ad company told them it was a bad marketing idea to say hell so they went old-school and omitted it with symbols, *à la* Fred Flintstone uttering stone-age cuss words."

"So, instead of the Wild West slogan advising us to get the hell *out* of Dodge, they're saying we should trade in our old car and get the expletive-deleted *into* a Dodge. Okay. Cheesy. Bad. But I get it. Not sure it motivates me to trade in my Jeep, but I get it."

"Listen, Lilli…" Chuck made strides toward her, the gleaming white Chiclets no longer evident, his face, once again, somber. "I can't pretend anymore that I don't notice what's happening with you."

Here it comes. He's going to fire me.

Lilli fortified herself, tucking her thumbs inside her fists and wiggling her toes in what little space her pumps would allow.

Chuck swept the flag aside and pulled out a chair, gestured for her to sit. He parked on the edge of the table, hands clasped in front.

"I was leaving the agency the other day and I noticed Jake Edwards *attempting* to hide behind a payphone in the lobby. I say attempting because, let's face it, he's huge."

Compared to Chuck, yes, Jake was definitely huge. While Chuck's personality and power in the business arena made his aura immense, his actual physical presence took up much less real estate.

He leaned across the table, reaching out for her hands, which were now clutched tightly in front of her. "I figured it was nothing and let it go, but I've seen him two more times, and Clarisse said she's seen him too. Mandy told me how many messages he's been leaving. Lilli, we're worried about you."

"NO MORE GAMES, JAKE. I'm tired of it," Lilli shouted over the phone. "You have to stop calling me so much. Especially at work."

"I'm sorry, Lilli. I'll cut back on the calls."

"No, Jake. You have to cut *out* the calls. Chuck *invited* me into his office when I arrived. You know I don't like surprise conversations. I thought he was going to fire me."

"I never intended—"

"This has nothing to do with your *intentions*, Jake. It has to do with the results of your intentions. I know things have been rough for you, but—"

"You don't know what it's like, living in his house, under communist regime. Aside from you, Lilli, my life pretty much sucks."

Compassion tugged for purchase on Lilli's solar plexus. None of this was Jake's fault. His father had taken a perfectly good little boy and had ruined him. How could Jake have turned out any other way, growing up in that house? She almost felt as though she *was* all he had, but how long could she go on this way? Would Jake ever change back, or change *into*, the sweet man she'd thought him to be when they'd started dating? Did it even matter if he did?

She decided it did matter, at least for now. "Listen, Jake, I do love you, and I want to help, but you have to stand up to him. Tell him you're moving in with me and that is that. Let me take care of you. Let me help you get over this injury."

Lilli stopped talking and listened for a response, but the line was quiet on the other end. Not a sound besides Jake's breathing. "Jake?"

"He made me go into the store and help with inventory the other day. Fuck! These two guys came up to me and—I don't know how to do anything else, Lilli. Except for football that stupid store was my life growing up. I hate it. Hated it since I was like twelve. I want to, Lilli, I do, but…"

"I can't live like this, Jake."

One loud groan and then Jake's rough breathing again. She pictured him raking his hands down his face in frustration, could almost hear the rasp of his rough palms over unshaven whiskers. "I'm stuck, Lilli. Let's face it, my career is over. If my own team turned on me after all I did for them—they wouldn't have cinched that wildcard position if it hadn't been for me."

She would try another tack. "You're stronger than you think, Jake. Move in with me. Get another job. On your own. Your father would have no say in your life."

"I guess." Jake heaved a breath. "But besides football and my dad's store, I don't know how to do anything else."

"Of course you do," Lilli insisted. "You are strong and smart. There's got to be something you've always wanted to do, what is it?"

"Football, Lilli. And you."

It was time to stop pushing him. At least for now. Lilli redirected the sigh that was nudging the back of her throat. "Will I see you tonight?"

"I don't—hang on."

His father was shouting in the background. "You're such a putz. You're on the phone with her aren't you? When are you gonna learn? Don't put all your eggs in one goddamn basket. Guy like you can get a fresh piece of ass on every street corner—for free. Why pay so much for one damn woman? Must be good in bed."

Nice bit of work, Jake's dad was. The guy took uncouth and tactless to a whole new level.

Jake came back on the line. His voice was quiet, but she could hear the seething bubbling beneath the single whispered word. "Fuck."

CHAPTER FORTY-ONE

SITTING AT HER desk, Lilli pondered the situation with Jake. To her it seemed like a no-brainer—Jake should move in with her and tell his father to screw off. At least then they might have a fighting chance. Yet, for some reason, he seemed hesitant to do that.

Maybe she'd rushed into a relationship with him. Scratch that. There was no *maybe* about it. After Brad, she'd set out with deliberate intent. The goal—moving on, gaining a buffer zone between her and Brad. But perhaps she could have taken things slower, or dated someone else as a rebound. Though, if she were being honest with herself, she really hadn't had much say in the speed with which the whirlwind passion had escalated. A single kiss on New Year's Eve had sealed her destiny, and she'd proceeded to allow her heart to drive her further into the epicenter of the tornado—an unprecedented move that had rapidly spiraled, taking on a life of its own. Only now that life was threatening to choke hers into oblivion.

Should she stay and keep working at things with Jake, or should she cut her losses before it was too late? Maybe it already was. In the absence of a guiding light, it was not an easy decision. Despite the few short weeks they'd been together, Lilli loved Jake, deeply. Inside this big angry man was a broken little boy. If only he would stand up to his dad.

The rumbling in her stomach growled its annoyance. It was mid-afternoon and she'd missed lunch. She'd keep her better-care self-promise if she hit the deli downstairs. She could handle that.

Lilli slung her purse over her shoulder and breezed through her office door, decelerating but not stopping, to inform Mandy she'd be back shortly. Outside the main doors, she popped the down button for the elevator, not relishing the forced slowing of her momentum. She struggled between the competing forces of hunger and stress, alternating between gazing toward the stairs, tapping a rhythm on her leg, and pacing a small circle in front of the doors.

The *ping* of the arriving elevator brought a sigh of relief as the doors slid wide and several of her coworkers trickled out. Their symphony of chatter turned to smiles of greeting, and she wondered how many of them knew what she was going through with Jake.

She tapped her toe, impatient for the elevator to shut. It was taking forever. Right before the doors made sweet contact, promising her at least one floor of solitude, a hand darted between them and they bounced apart.

Crap.

Suppressing the urge to groan, she plastered on a pleasant façade and glanced up. At the other end of the extended arm was one of the agency's newest, and hottest, acquisitions. Trevor Dahl.

Double crap.

"Going down?" he asked.

Did somebody turn up the heat?

Smile and nod. Ignore well-placed innuendo. Lilli cleared her throat and resisted wiping her palms on her skirt. She hit the button for first, even though it was already lit, and poised her finger to see what floor he wanted. "How far down?"

A dangerous grin followed by, "As far as you'll let me."

She'd made that one easy hadn't she? Her cheeks began to warm and Lilli found herself performing an intense analysis of her feet— black leather pumps, patent, Steve Madden.

Chuck had found Trevor waiting tables at a *TGI Fridays* and had convinced him to relocate to Seattle to sign with Willows. Smart move. Her boss always did have an eye for talent. It's what set him apart from his competition when he'd started the agency against his father's advice. His dad had told him he couldn't compete with the big guns in the industry, but compete he had. Chuck was responsible for signing some of the most famous—and infamous—faces in today's marketplace. He'd earned the respect of his peers as well as enough capital to expand Willows to New York, Miami, and Toronto.

Then, he'd started a movie production company. Had a few films out there with his name attached. Good films. Had the statues on his mantle to prove it. She'd seen them. Held them. And, yes, they really are heavier than they look on TV.

So, when he'd had Lilli add Trevor's name to her class roster, declaring him as The Next Big Thing, Lilli chose to believe. In fact, Trevor hadn't even completed his training yet and the only thing standing between him and a nationwide Calvin Klein ad campaign was—you guessed it—his Calvins.

According to Chuck it was a done deal. The wheels at CK were tapping pencils, waiting to see shirtless pics so they could judge if Trevor's twenty-one-year-old six-pack was billboard worthy. The way that tight black t-shirt hugged his torso right now, and the manner in which those fitted Diesel jeans *fit*, Lilli was certain the deal would be put to bed quickly.

Trevor was a rare commodity. Jet-black hair, brooding gray eyes, tanned, fit, sexy with a capital *S*. And did she mention he had more animal magnetism than an entire pride of jungle cats? It had been evident from moment one when he'd arrived late to his first class, sauntering in amid audible reactions from the females in the room. Something about him stirred them up. Her too. Sweaty hands, nervous stuttering. The works. Yup. He would do the CK campaign proud. No doubt about that. If only half his charisma came across in his pics, that boy would sell underwear. A lot of underwear.

And what was with all the suggestive banter? Was he flirting with her specifically, or could he simply not deny the urge to entice? Maybe the universe was testing her. It had a way of doing that when she was on the cusp of a big decision. Maybe that's all Jake had been. A test. If so, she could stamp that page with an *F* and circle it in red.

Lilli pushed her gaze up. She'd probably been staring. Drooling too. She focused on the numbers and away from the mirrored doors, which only threatened to fire Trevor's penetrating gray eyes back to her as though they were a sniper's rifle with the safety disengaged.

She forced a deep breath, swallowed hard, attempted to untie her tongue, and then cleared her throat. She would dig deep for some sort of response that wouldn't have her seeming like a blathering idiot, but Lilli was certain that moment had passed. No. The smart thing to do was remain silent.

But a watched elevator display moves slower than a watched kettle boils, so Lilli attempted to target her vision straight ahead without ogling Trevor's reflection, however, studying her own image served to inflate her self-consciousness, and she allowed his image to draw her gaze.

He stood closer to her than was strictly necessary considering they were only two in a twenty-person elevator. He tucked an envelope under his arm and thrust his hands in the front pockets of his jeans, clearly unfazed by her lack of response to his mischievous innuendo.

Then, Trevor resumed his torment, the impish grin never leaving his face. Not even for a second. "Do you think you might look at the pictures from my test shoot? Tell me if you like what you see? Chuck says a large part of Calvin Klein's buying demographic is female, you know, shopping for their boyfriends."

Right. A stack of eight-by-ten glossies featuring the sexy man-beast beside her. In his undies. She could handle that. An awkward smile followed by, "Sure."

"Thanks."

"My pleasure." Her pleasure? See, blathering. Damage control time. She needed to yank the focus off her utter stupidity. "You can drop them in my office after class."

Titanium heat glinted in his eyes and mingled with a substantial measure of capital-T-trouble as it reached his words. "No time like the present. I've got everything you need. Let's just do it." Bang, bang, and he fired another round, close range. "You are on break, right? I could use a bite—or two. Let me treat you to something delicious." Wicked evil grin. "At the deli."

She was stuck between a rock and a very hard place, wasn't she? One more deep breath. A shrug. "Bites. Yes. I was wanting to go down right now." Blather, blather, blather. Head shake. "To the deli. I was wanting to go to the deli. To eat. Lunch." Suppressed groan. "Yes, Trevor, we can do it now—the photos. We can look at the photos." Shut up, shut up, shut up! "But I'm going to pay for it. My lunch. Deal?" She extended her arm in a handshake gesture, not really expecting him to reciprocate with his hands tucked into his pockets, but he did.

As he yanked them out, the envelope flapped to the elevator floor and several of the eight-by-tens slipped out. Lilli bent down to help gather them and got an eyeful of Trevor in all his glory. Close-up, glistening torso, dark gray, fitted cotton boxers, white waistband contrasting with his tanned skin, drawing her eyes dangerously close to the money shot. In fact, if those undies dropped any lower the rating on those pics would jump ahead in the alphabet from PG to XXX.

Yup. The Calvin Klein people were going to rush to sign on the dotted once they saw those abs.

Trevor slid the photo onto the pile he'd been arranging, which alerted Lilli to the fact that her eyes had been—let's say—riveted on the image. The same motion assaulted her olfactory senses with a wash of his masculine aura, bathing her in green apple, sage, and patchouli, mingled with a heavy dose of pheromones, she was certain.

Lilli stirred uncomfortably, quickly collecting the remaining pictures into a stack, before reaching for the envelope. At the same exact moment Trevor did. His hand grazed the top of hers and she yanked hers away as though scorched by lava, then felt silly for doing so, and wondered if he'd noticed. She raised her gaze to his face to make the determination, and Lilli found herself locked in a visual maelstrom, the spark of titanium storming within his eyes holding her captive.

Lilli giggled nervously as she slid the envelope toward him. "Here. I'll let you—"

"You'll let him what?"

She shot to standing, almost losing her balance, when a large Jake-shaped shadow darkened the space between the open elevator doors and the lobby.

Oh. Crap.

THIS MOMENT MADE your run-of-the-mill bad timing look like awesome good fortune, that's how bad it was by comparison. Well played, universe, well played.

"How's it going, Lilli?" Jake locked her in fierce visual contact, his voice dripping with sarcasm and jealousy. "Sorry to interrupt. Why don't you two kids just go back to whatever it was you were doing." He broke his gaze long enough to look down at the spilled photos. Intensity blazed across his eyes in a brilliant pyrotechnic display as he met hers again. "Don't mind me." He ignited an equal torch toward Trevor. "I'll just wait for my *girlfriend* over here." He jutted his chin toward a leather club chair near the entrance.

Trevor picked up the photos and stood, almost matching Jake in height, but not bulk. Lilli squeezed her eyes shut, hoping that he had enough sense not to hand her the envelope at this moment, let alone mention lunch. Or bites of any kind.

On second thought, she couldn't chance this to faith.

"I'll come with you, Jake. We're done here, right, Trevor?" She resisted the urge to plead with her eyes, knowing that Jake's own scrutiny would be unwavering.

Jake held his foot against the elevator door as Lilli stepped out, releasing it before Trevor could make it all the way across the threshold into the lobby.

The doors rebounded off Trevor's shoulders as a gunmetal glint flicked across his eyes. He stepped over without so much as registering the impact, then he did the unthinkable. He placed one hand on Lilli's arm and handed her the photos with the other. Thankfully, that was the extent of his assertion.

No it wasn't.

He stepped backward into the elevator, but as group of suits swallowed the empty space around him, he fired a look at Jake and smiled. "Your girlfriend is a *really* great teacher."

Not cool.

Lilli wandered toward the sitting area rather than heading toward the deli. Jake's sudden appearance had dampened any desire she'd had to eat. A few paces ahead, she sensed rather than heard Jake following behind her. He was shooting daggers into her back she was quite sure. Some things you can just feel.

Without turning around, she plopped into a chair and tucked the incriminating photos beside her, praying that Jake would let it go.

He perched on the table directly in front of her, leaning his elbows on his knees so that his face was less than a foot from hers. "So, *teach*, who's your little friend?"

Lilli resisted the urge to press her spine as far as she could into the plush club chair. She held her position and met Jake's visual invitation, narrowing her eyes as she formulated a response. Honesty. That was always the best approach. Besides, she had nothing to hide. She'd done nothing wrong. Had no intention of doing anything wrong. Period.

"He's Chuck's new project." There. That was vague, but honest. Maybe he'd drop it.

Or maybe not.

Jake grunted his acknowledgement, but she could see the wheels spinning in his head. "Project, eh. He's in your class. You're a *really* good teacher. Is he a good student, Lilli?" He didn't wait for a reply. "Never mind. I'm sure he is. And there are rules about fraternizing with your students, of course."

She pretended not to notice his facetiousness, choosing to sit back and cross her arms, preferring to have him come to his own conclusion that she was not going to play along.

Bad move.

She couldn't do anything to stop him. Jake's hand lunged forward and snatched the envelope from where it sat beside her. Then, before she could even formulate what his reaction might be, he tore into the package and began flipping through the photos, discarding each on her lap as he made a running commentary.

Lilli kept her vision targeted on Jake, refusing to look at the pictures raining down on her lap. She would wait this out.

She didn't have to wait long, though, as he opened his mouth to speak, not taking his glare off the last remaining photo grasped in his hand. He flicked the corner of it as he met her gaze. "So, is Mr. GQ applying to be the star of his own Calvin Klein underwear box or something?" He chuckled, as if he was jesting, but the truth flickered as a glint in his eyes.

"Well, actually—" How else could she answer that?

He leaned back, tucking the photo under his arm, and then rubbed his hands along his thighs. "Makes me wanna invest in Fruit of the Loom."

She was tiring of his game of cat and mouse. "Is there a point?"

"A point?"

She was beginning to feel trapped, regretting sitting there, having not anticipated needing an escape. Clutching the photos, she stood, unable to extricate herself further though, based on Jake's huddled position in front of her. "I'm hungry, Jake. I haven't eaten and I don't feel well. I need a sandwich."

The words seemed to register, but Jake was not in any hurry to move, doing so with painful slowness, finally leaning back to allow her egress.

She took two steps, shoved the pictures in her handbag, and then turned to him. "Are you coming or not?"

He stretched up from the table, and it made a creaking sound as he did so. It likely wasn't designed to withhold two hundred and sixty-five pounds of jealousy.

Lilli strode toward the deli and got in line, only gazing back once she had done so. "Do you want anything?" Ignoring the elephant in the room. That always worked, right?

"I want a lot of things, Lilli."

That was it. That's all he said. And weren't those words loaded with a million insinuations. She held her response, instead grabbing an egg salad sandwich and a Coke, then a chocolate chip muffin for him. Maybe his blood sugar was low. Feeding the beast couldn't hurt at any rate.

THEY MANAGED TO get through a quick meal without revisiting the whole Trevor issue. Lilli was grateful for that, but in so doing, Jake had pocketed the last photo. She decided to let it slide. Hopefully it wouldn't be missed. Perhaps he was going to tack it onto a dartboard and get his feelings out. Either way, Lilli just wanted to move on.

She decided to avoid the elevator altogether, choosing to take the stairs in order to not stir up Jake's memory. She made the first few flights in relative ease but began to slow around the fifth-floor landing, finally stopping at the sixth.

Jake arrived a moment later, huffing and puffing from the exertion too. He shoved past her and sat on the bottom stair of the next flight.

She'd had enough. Lilli spun on her heel and faced him. "Jake, what are we doing?" She didn't wait for an answer. "I mean, seriously. Shit happens to all of us. You're stronger than this, Jake. Move on. Get over it."

He was silent for so long Lilli could've sworn crickets had started chirping in the background. She wanted to forge ahead and resume her climb, but Jake had other ideas. Instead of letting her pass, he stood and grabbed her arms, a little too roughly, and pulled her to him. He kissed her lips hard before moving to her neck, kissing over-zealously there as well.

Lilli tried to push him away, attempting to make the move seem playful, yet he held her strong. "Jake. What are you doing?"

"Getting over it." He shoved her against the wall and pressed his entire body to hers, swallowing her mouth in another fervent kiss.

Although she pushed his chest with her hands, she was caged within his unyielding grip. The hard surface of the stairwell wall dug into the back of her head as she fought to turn her face away from his. Finally doing so, she shouted his name. When his hunger against her flesh seemed undeterred, she repeated it, louder this time. "Jake! Stop it! You're hurting me."

"What's the matter?" He lunged for her neck again, a starving vampire in search of fresh blood. "I thought you liked it rough."

"Not like this." She created sufficient distance between them to punch him in the chest. Not hard enough to do any harm, but it served to get his attention. "What's your problem?"

His eyes met hers and the fire dissipated, turning to an unreadable emotion. Sorrow maybe? Regret?

He allowed her escape, and she fumed past him and started up the stairs, stopping halfway up. "Are you coming or what?"

He didn't answer. Didn't make a move to follow.

She gritted her teeth, removed her pumps, and stomped up the next few stairs, halting briefly to assess his position. She shook her head. He was off in his own little world. Welcome to Jakeville—population one miserable soul.

"Whatever. Why bother anymore." She muttered the words and then turned, taking the stairs at a more comfortable pace this time.

"Are you mad at me?" he shouted from below.

Is she what now?

Jake had such an innocent tone to his voice Lilli had to stop and stare. Dumbfounded by such a blatantly absurd question, Lilli lingered a moment, unsure of her response. She was too irritated to be diplomatic. "Where the hell were you a few minutes ago?"

"What do you mean?"

Was he really that obtuse? "What do you mean what do I mean? You attacked me."

"I was trying to be affectionate."

"Are you kidding me? You call that affection?"

She studied him.

He offered no remorse, no awareness, no response.

"Fine. Whatever. I'm going back to work and then I'm going home. We need to talk, Jake. Either come over later or don't. Right now I couldn't care less what you choose."

Lilli trudged up to the next landing and went through the door, deciding to take the elevator the rest of the way. She hadn't heard Jake following, so she assumed he was sulking in the stairwell. Probably good. She had nothing nice to say to him at that moment. Wasn't sure she would have anything nice to say later either.

Her decision was becoming easier to make.

CHAPTER FORTY-TWO

AT LEAST JAKE had been smart enough not to follow her up to the agency after what had happened in the stairwell earlier. Lilli was grateful for that. She'd been planning to text him before she'd left work, reaffirming they needed to talk, but had decided against it, choosing to leave it to fate. If he showed up, they'd talk. If he didn't? Well, she'd cross that bridge when she came to it.

A heavy fog had settled over the city and the sun had already gone down by the time she was heading out. As she navigated through the murky streets, her eyes and brain were on high alert. As dense as the fog was, she could barely see ten feet in front of her Jeep. Behind her, a single set of halogen beams competed for her attention as it sent occasional flashes of light dancing across her rearview mirror.

Lilli repeatedly tugged her focus back to the small patch of illuminated street in front of her. If that car wouldn't pass her—and it likely wouldn't in this weather—then the best thing she could do was keep her own eyes on the road.

On the positive side, her driving focus was too intense to luxuriate in brooding, but on the negative, her knuckles were white from their tight grip on the steering wheel, and, by the time she arrived home, her nerves were completely frazzled. A large glass of Merlot was definitely high on her priority list. She felt ready enough to get back on that horse after The Brad Incident. Her current level of stress would make her ready.

After setting her things in the entryway, she went, to Toby's chagrin, directly to her bedroom to change into yoga pants, a tank top, and her favorite hoodie. Then, although the comfort of the bed called out to her, the unopened bottle of red in the kitchen shouted louder. Toby mewed at her feet, completely indignant that she had tended to her own needs before his.

She dropped some food into his bowl, refreshed his water, patted his head, and then proceeded to pour a glass of wine, which she took to the sofa, where she curled up to watch something mindless on TV.

As Toby hopped up beside her and began his post-mealtime washing ritual, she inhaled and then let out a deep soul-satisfying sigh.

She quietly sipped her wine and flipped through a few channels before settling on a Seinfeld rerun. Soon she was laughing and allowing her shoulders to drop back down to a reasonable level.

Just as the credits were rolling and Lilli was deciding that she might as well have a nice warm bubble bath, since it didn't appear Jake was going to stop by, there was a loud banging on the front door.

"Lilli! Hey. Let me in." There was another knock, louder than the last. "Lilli. It's me. Jake."

Yeah, she knew that.

The sigh she expelled this time was one of frustration and not relief. She'd already switched gears, ready to submerge herself in hot water and ponder what she would do about Jake.

"I'm coming," she hollered so he would stop banging his fist against the door. She crossed to the entry, relieved that he had to wait for her to open it. Since he hadn't bothered to move any of his things in, she hadn't bothered to give him a key. Seemed fair. The one morning she'd had to leave before him, she had made him slide the extra keys under the door after locking the deadbolt.

Lilli threw the door open but offered no words of greeting, instead, she turned around and headed back to her place on the couch, half-hoping he would disappear. She flipped the TV off and swallowed the last gulp of her wine.

The sound of the slamming door confirmed he had not, in fact, vanished. She raised her gaze to where he stood, hands thrust in his pockets, a dejected expression on his face. A brief flash of sadness prickled at her heart. It was time to see what fate had in store for her. "Take your shoes off before you come in." It was invitation enough.

Jake pulled his feet out of his shoes without bending down, then kicked them to the side. He shuffled into the living room and stood in front of her for a moment. His eyes communicated that he wanted her to scoot over to make room for him. She didn't want to budge, but she did anyway, and he perched on the edge of the sofa cushion beside her.

His face was pensive, but she wasn't going to make this easy for him. Why should she?

Finally his eyes sparked. "You hungry?"

She was.

"Wanna go out for dinner?"

"I don't know, Jake." Lilli tugged on her green pullover hoodie. "I'm kind of already settled in for the evening."

Now the crooked grin took over one side of his mouth. "Even dressed like that you'll still be the most beautiful woman, no matter where we go."

"Don't think you can charm your way out of this, Jake."

"I won't. I don't." He reached over and traced a path all the way down her arm, lacing his fingers with hers. With his free hand he lifted her chin, initiating contact with his pleading eyes. "You said you were hungry, right?"

Damn it. He was softening her up. "I could eat."

"Well? I want to take my beautiful girlfriend out for a nice dinner. C'mon. It's only a meal. Let's go. Anywhere you like."

Realizing that he was not going to let it go, she resigned herself, sort of. Lilli rose up from the sofa. "Fine. But I'm not going out. I'll cook something."

"Or..." He stood and crossed to her, taking both her hands in his. "How about I go grab a pizza?"

That could work. It would buy Lilli a few minutes to gather her thoughts and get a feel for where this relationship should be heading. "Okay. Deal. I'll make a salad while you're out."

Jake shook her hand. "Deal."

AS LILLI TORE apart and washed a head of romaine, she played and replayed the last few weeks. She'd been right, thinking of it as a rollercoaster. It had been that. But people paid good money and waited in long lines for a chance to get on those things, right? Maybe rollercoaster rides were not so bad. And maybe things would smooth over once Jake accepted his injuries. Right now he was not in a good place psychologically, but surely it had to improve.

Things were far from ideal, but he did seem to be trying. Maybe what they needed was a fresh start. A do-over. A nice dinner for two, a relaxing evening, and let Sister Fate dictate the rest. Yes. That was the answer.

Lilli tossed the salad, threw in some focaccia croutons, sprinkled parmesan, and spread plastic wrap over it before she placed the bowl in the fridge. She might even go change after all. Put on something a little nicer.

She popped in a jazz CD, poured a second glass of wine—the first hadn't argued with her—and Lilli scurried to her bedroom to change. It felt right. Things with her and Jake might not be perfect, but he'd been through a lot. It wasn't his fault. He was trying and that had to count for something.

CHAPTER FORTY-THREE

IMPATIENT AND READY to begin pacing, Lilli instead headed to the kitchen for a third glass of wine. She looked at the clock. It was almost ten PM, and Jake had been gone for much longer than it should take to grab a pizza. Had he flown to Italy?

Before she could pour, a loud hammering resounded through her entryway. *Finally.* Lilli shuffled to the door, but something inside urged her to check the peephole, even though Jake was the only one she was expecting.

"What the hell?" Lilli gave her head a shake. A hard one. Good thing she hadn't poured yet—a third glass of wine suddenly seemed to be a bad idea.

She stood on her toes and peeked again, to confirm she wasn't seeing things. A well-timed knock shot right through her ear, which was against the door as she peered out into the hallway. She lowered back onto the balls of her feet and rubbed a hand over her ear.

They must have the wrong apartment. Lilli had a couple unpaid parking tickets, but who didn't? It certainly did not justify a home visit from Seattle's finest.

"Open up! Seattle PD. We have a warrant."

She risked a third glance through the peephole, this time not allowing the side of her head to make contact. Sure enough the man on the other side was holding up his badge and a piece of paper. Behind him was a hallway full of men dressed head to toe in commando black.

Lilli eased the door open a couple inches, still convinced they'd made a mistake. "Can I help you, Officer?"

He mumbled that his name was *Detective* something-or-other, and handed her the paper, which was, indeed, a warrant to search the premises. Her premises. "This has my address on it." Lilli opened the door all the way.

"Yes, ma'am."

The detective waved his hand to the rest of the men in the hallway. The group pushed past her, the acronym SWAT emblazoned on the vests they wore. Why would they need Kevlar vests? What did they think was going to happen here? Without further ado, the Special Weapons and Tactics Team spread through the apartment and began sorting through her belongings.

She was stunned. This couldn't be happening. "Excuse me, sir." Lilli spoke to the detective who had given her the search warrant.

He halted his forward momentum and turned to her, his face stoic and unwavering. He said nothing.

"I'm confused." Lilli shot glances at the dozen or so cops rooting through her life. "Are you sure you have the right place?"

He pointed to the warrant in her hand, and she glanced at it.

"Yes. I see it has my name…but why? I haven't done anything wrong. I don't understand." Emotion began to whelm up in Lilli's throat and she choked on a sob. "I don't understand," she repeated.

"Does Jake Edwards reside here?"

"No. I mean, he's here sometimes, when he's not on the road—that is, he used to be on the road, he got cut from the—" She was blathering. Lilli harnessed the enormity of the situation to rein in her nervousness, even if momentarily. "Jake is my boyfriend, but he doesn't live with me. He lives with his parents now."

"He listed this address as a shipping destination for an item he bought on EBay last week." The detective surveyed the immediate area. "Have you received any packages addressed to Mr. Edwards?"

"No. I mean, I haven't checked the mail yet today, but…"

The detective brushed by her, moving farther into the apartment, leaving puddles of dirty snow in his wake. In fact, every single one of them had left their boots on, tracking a series of muddy prints throughout. She supposed that wiping their feet before violating a young woman's space was not part of their "special tactics."

He turned back and snatched her keys from the hook by the door. After flipping through them he held one up. "This the mail key?"

She nodded. "Yes, but what has Jake done wrong?"

"Bertram," the detective called to one of the SWAT members, who looked up from the bookshelf where he was dissecting her paperbacks, DVDs, and *tchotchkes*. "Check the mail." He tossed the keys and the man caught them.

"We have an eyewitness report that he may have been involved in the recent attack on a young woman."

Just when she'd thought the detective was ignoring her question, he answered it. In retrospect, Lilli almost wished she hadn't asked. Or he hadn't answered. A witness reported that Jake attacked the girl on the streetcar line? Brad's warnings rushed at her with potent and dizzying force. She felt as though she was going to be sick, and her head began swimming with vertigo.

The detective led her by the elbow, guiding her toward the dining table. "Ma'am, have a seat. It'll go a lot faster if you stay out of our way. I have some questions for you too."

Lilli fumbled with the chair as it dragged along the carpet. She sank onto it, allowing her eyes to swallow every detail of what was going on around her.

The detective strode to the kitchen and filled a small glass with water from the sink. He set it in front of her and then tugged a chair out from the end of the table. Reaching into his jacket he brought out a small notepad, which he flipped open, poised to write.

"Ma'am, how well do you know Mr. Edwards?" That was blunt. So much for easing into things. He hadn't even told her to drink the offered water, simply plunked it on the table in front.

Staring at the glass, watching the oxygen bubbles dissipate, Lilli's emotions seemed to take on the expelled cloudiness, filling her with dread and dissociation. A room full of heavily armed strangers touching her things—her life—was more than she could fathom. Someone had to wake her up. Now would be good.

"Ma'am?"

"I…that is, we…" Her mouth was so dry she could barely speak. Now the water made sense. Not relishing the lukewarm offering from the tap, she raised it to her lips and took a large sip anyway, allowing it to filter around her mouth before swallowing.

"How well do you know Mr. Edwards?" He repeated the question as if doing so would give her the ability to formulate a coherent reply.

She glanced down as she spun the glass on the table. "Not as well as I'd thought."

"Let me rephrase that," the detective said. "How long have you been involved with Mr. Edwards?"

Lilli lifted the glass to take another sip but her hand was shaking so much she set it back down without drinking. "A few weeks. Since around New Year's."

He scribbled in the notepad, then pierced her with his stare. "Can you account for Mr. Edward's time between the hours of six and eight PM on the evening of January first, two thousand thirteen?"

She followed the memory trail back. That was the day she'd gone out with Donna, looking for Jake. "No," she said. "We met up at Trinity, later on. Around midnight, I think."

More scribbling, more staring. This guy definitely took his job seriously. He never let up on the tough-guy demeanor, not even for a second. Lilli could barely breathe. She leaned over and angled her head. Were they still ripping her bathroom apart? Maybe the detective would let her up for a moment.

She raised her hand slightly, then felt silly for doing so.

The detective looked at her expectantly, eyebrows raised.

"I need to use the bathroom. Please."

He stood and marched to the bathroom doorway. "Fenmore. You done in there?"

"Not quite, sir," the officer replied.

"The girl needs to use the facilities. Follow protocol."

"Yes, sir."

Just as the detective was approaching the dining table, a voice came over his walkie-talkie. He leaned toward his shoulder and spoke into it. "Detective Arnold. Go ahead...Roger that." He faced Lilli. "Guess it's your lucky day."

This was his idea of a lucky day? Was he serious? A quick survey of his facial expression confirmed he was. Not even a hint of a grin cracked the stony façade.

"I can use the washroom?" she asked.

"You can use whatever you like." He signaled to his team. "We're done here, men. Let's hustle."

Lilli was frozen to the chair, gawking, transfixed, as the group trailed out in the same rapid formation they'd used to enter. The door slammed shut and she released her held breath. At least this nightmare was over.

She rose to standing and gazed around. The nightmare had, in fact, just begun. Her apartment was in a shambles. No, actually, a shambles would have been a step up from what this was. Devastation was more apt. She would be busy for several hours, not to mention renting a steam cleaner to shampoo the grit out of her carpets.

Normally, tidying up was Lilli's go-to when she was stressed. There was something cathartic about watching the transformation, as though cleaning the house was also purging her soul. Tonight she'd felt as though under siege. Tossing a salad one minute, receiving the third degree from some hard-ass detective the next.

It was straight out of one of the movie scripts sitting on Chuck's desk. Completely surreal. Even now, she had a hard time believing what her eyes had seen and what her heart had felt. Yet it really and truly had gone down like that. A SWAT team *had* burst in. A detective *had* treated her as if she were a criminal. And worst of all, he *had* suggested Jake had done some awful things.

And what of the way they just picked up and left? What was that about? Had they gotten another tip? Arrested Jake? She had no way of knowing and it was giving her a giant headache.

Now, it was officially late—had already been late when the cops arrived—and she still didn't know where Jake was. Did she even want to know? Was he the monster who'd attacked that poor woman on the streetcar line? Was the man she'd fallen in love with capable of such a thing?

According to Brad, yes. But could she believe anything Bradley said about Jake? Should she? And speaking of Bradley, she hadn't heard from him in quite a while, and that too was strange.

Lilli flopped back onto the sofa and began to cry. Really, that's all she had left. She could go over and knock on Brad's door, or even call him, but what if she stirred up more trouble for herself by doing that? No, it was past midnight and Lilli was tired, overwhelmed, and just plain done.

It was a brief but very intense burst of emotion, and when it was over, it was almost as if she had no tears left to cry. She remembered something she had heard once before, that even a person stranded in the desert who had become completely dehydrated and unable to produce any other body fluids still had the ability to shed tears.

Lilli pondered this briefly as she scanned the area for Toby. She hadn't seen him in a while. He didn't like stress either and it often sent him into hiding. She got down on the floor and peered under the sofa. "Toby? Are you under there?" She didn't think so. He would've voiced his whereabouts or crawled out already.

She made the rounds to all of his favorite hiding places but still could not find him. Had the police left her door open at some point and he'd wandered out? Maybe she should go into the hall and look.

She eased open the door and stepped into the dim hallway. The wall sconces that flanked either side of her entry were dark. Just her luck having both bulbs burn out at the same time. She supposed they'd been installed synchronously and had died the same way.

As she turned to go back into the apartment to get her cell phone to use as a flashlight, a deep throaty growl came from behind her and Lilli released a blood-curdling scream.

CHAPTER FORTY-FOUR

THE EAST PRECINCT was humming with activity. It was busy for a Monday night/Tuesday morning. Officer Harris turned as the SWAT team stormed through the doors with Detective Gary Arnold, head of the violent crimes division, leading the army in black.

Detective Arnold scanned the area. "Must be a full moon tonight, eh, Harris?"

He followed the detective's line of vision. It was amazing how the cops could predict the pace of a shift based on the cycle of the moon. Emergency rooms could too. Humans liked to believe they were so unique, and maybe as individuals they were, but put them into a group and the uncommon becomes the norm. "The Algonquin tribes call this the wolf moon," Brian replied.

Detective Arnold chuckled. "You're talking about your woo-woo stuff again." He rolled a finger beside his ear as he said woo-woo. "Besides, ask any beat cop in the country and they'll tell you every full moon brings out the wolves."

"Come on!" A booming male voice emanated from down the hall. "Are there no football fans in this entire place?"

"Move it," the gruff tone of Officer Callaway sounded off in reply. "Ain't no red carpet here, superstar. We are gonna take your picture soon though."

Both men turned to watch as Tom Callaway came around the corner, shoving a handcuffed Jake Edwards in front of him as he went. He stopped and stood with a grin on his face. "Evenin', fellas." He turned toward the lone female officer in the room, bobbing his head. "Lady Beatrice."

"Cut the crap, Callaway," Monty hollered back. "Or should I say Eugene?"

"Not. Fair." Callaway jabbed a finger in Monty's direction, scolding her for using his middle name.

Brian was going to laugh, but then Jake Edwards decided to stir things up a bit.

"You wanna go easy on those cuffs there, Eugene?"

That backfired. Instead of going easy, Callaway wrenched hard, and Edwards' cocky smirk faded into a grimace of pain as his hands were twisted behind him. Callaway handed him over to Detective Arnold. "I believe this is yours."

Arnold turned to face Edwards. "I've got no patience for tough guys like you, Edwards. You're nothing but a washed-up *ex*-football hero. Make that an ex-*almost*-football hero. And don't even get me started on that term. Hero." He jacked a thumb toward his brethren in blue. "Those people you see back there. They're the real heroes. Now, you and me, we gotta talk."

"WHAT THE HELL? You really scared me, Donna." Lilli held her hand to her chest and calmed her breathing.

"Technically, it wasn't me. It was him."

They stepped into the apartment and Lilli reached out to take Toby from Donna's arms. "Okay, I'll meet you halfway. It was his hissing, coming from the height of your arms." The cat relaxed his body and nuzzled in, keeping a suspicious eye on Donna.

"I don't think he recognized me," Donna said as she slipped off her boots and shrugged out of her coat. When she turned around to face the rest of the apartment, Donna's jaw dropped and her eyes went round in shock. "What the flip happened here?"

Lilli sighed. "What happened here rates an actual cuss word, I'll tell you that. And I've said a few myself tonight."

"I don't like to swear." Donna jacked her shoulders up and down. "My dad said a lady shouldn't sound like a trucker."

"Some things deserve trucker talk, Donna. You know how they say truth is stranger than fiction? It feels like I just lived through a bad movie, but this," she swept her arms wide to take in the room, "this is proof of it." Lilli pushed aside a pile of magazines that were strewn across the sofa. "Want to sit?"

Donna bobbed her head and then perched on the edge of a cushion. "So, are you going to tell me what created this proof?"

"Seattle PD's SWAT team and some hostile detective with a search warrant."

"Okay, that does sound like a movie plot. Why you?"

"Not me. Jake." Lilli sat down, still holding Toby, and proceeded to tell Donna what little she knew.

When Lilli finished, Donna summed it up in one word. "Wow."

"Yeah. Wow. I have no idea what happened to Jake. I don't know his side of the story. I don't even know if I want to. I mean, I do, but what if he attacked that woman? Then what? Maybe I shouldn't even be alone with him."

"I don't know what to tell you, Lilli." Donna scooched closer and rubbed Lilli's arm, causing Toby to hop down and scurry under the couch.

Lilli watched him disappear. "The cops must have really spooked him. He's not acting like himself."

"Cats are sensitive, I hear." Donna shrugged. "I'm sure he'll be okay. It's you I'm worried about, Lilli. What are you going to do?"

"I don't know. I don't want to believe Jake did what they suggested. He may be a lot of things but…"

"They must have evidence though, right? I mean, to search your apartment like they did. And SWAT? Has to be a clear threat of danger to get them involved I think."

Lilli didn't want to admit it, but her friend had a point. "Do you think I should break up with Jake?"

"I think you need to be safe and smart. I think you need to talk to him, but do it somewhere public." Donna stood up and extended her hand toward Lilli. "Come on. You need to get some sleep. I'll tidy up around here a bit and you can just go to bed. I'll let myself out when I'm done or else I'll crash in the spare room."

"I can't ask you to do that, Donna."

"You didn't ask. I offered." She nudged Lilli toward the hall. "Now, smile and say thank you and then go to bed."

CHAPTER FORTY-FIVE

AS SHE LAY THERE, having hit the snooze button even though she'd been awake for quite a while already, Lilli felt completely unsettled and afraid. What was she to think about everything? None of it made any sense, even in the rising light of day. In fact, the new dawn had only deepened the surrealism by contrasting with the dark events from the night before.

Was Jake at his parents' house? Had he been arrested? She lifted her cell and pushed the button. No messages. No missed calls.

A light tap reverberated her bedroom door and Lilli's heart leapt into her throat, and then she remembered that Donna had said she might crash in the spare bedroom. It occurred to Lilli that she hadn't even asked Donna why she'd shown up so late last night. She'd probably been helping out at Bucky's. Maybe she'd seen the lights on in Lilli's apartment.

The door popped open and Donna poked her head in. Seeing Lilli awake, she came all the way in, a cup of coffee in her hand.

Lilli reached out and took it. "Perfect. Thank you so much, Donna. Just what I needed." She blew on the steam and then took a tentative sip. Hot and delicious.

Donna perched on the edge of the bed and smoothed back Lilli's hair. "Hey, sleepyhead. Did you get any rest?"

"A little," Lilli said. "Not enough though." She sipped on her coffee and then groaned into the mug.

"What?"

"Work."

"Not to worry," Donna said. "I've already called and told them you weren't feeling well. I said you'd phone when you got up to let them know if you were coming in later or not."

"Oh. Okay. Thanks, I guess." Lilli sank back into her pillows and hugged the warm mug in her hands. She likely wouldn't have called in sick. She would have forced herself to do the responsible thing and go to work, no matter how she was feeling. She'd missed too much lately. But she was relieved that Donna had made that decision for her.

"Oh, shoot." Donna hopped up from the bed and dashed out the door. A moment later she returned, the smell of bacon and eggs wafting in behind her.

"I hope you don't mind," she said. "I took the liberty of making you some breakfast."

"Mind?" Lilli asked. "How could I mind?" She raised her cup. "First coffee, and now breakfast...what's to complain about?"

DONNA HAD BROUGHT Lilli her breakfast in bed, then announced she was on her way out. Lilli hadn't even realized she was hungry, but once the food was placed in front of her she devoured it fully, managing to eat six pieces of bacon, three scrambled eggs—Donna had said she needed protein to keep her strength up—a large glass of calcium-fortified orange juice, and, of course, her coffee.

Herself taken care of, Lilli rose and wandered from the sanctuary of her bedroom. She breathed in the energy of the place. What a difference. With the curtains cast wide open, welcoming a bright stream of sunlight, the place was positively sparkling. Donna had even managed to scrub most of the muddy footprints out of the carpet, obviously by hand. If Lilli didn't know better she might convince herself she *had* dreamt the previous night's events.

Work had been notified, and the place had been tidied. All Lilli needed to do was hop into a nice, warm shower.

She turned on the water and then checked the back of the door to see if her bathrobe was hanging there. Nope. She padded to her room to grab it but was sidetracked on the return route, when a knock sounded on the door.

Had Donna forgotten something? Or was it Jake? And if it was, should she open the door? Would it be safe to do so?

She would determine that after she knew who was there. Standing on her tiptoes she peered through the peephole. Okay. Not who she had expected. A deep breath, a sliding chain, a twisted deadbolt, followed by an open door and a question. "What are you doing here?"

AFTER LILLI TURNED off the shower she joined Brad on the couch. At least he'd had the decency to bring her Starbucks. As she sipped her latte, Brad explained the reason for his invisibility lately. Basically, in no uncertain terms, Jake had "reaffirmed" his promise that if Brad came within two hundred yards of Lilli, he would break his face.

And Brad was quite attached to his face.

He showed her a picture he'd taken with his phone. The aforementioned face, close up, with a black eye and split lip, and he called it Jake's "friendly warning." The date on the bottom edge of the photo was right after her last conversation with Brad. The one where Jake had caught her coming back from his place. Lilli was starting to find Brad's story more credible by the minute. Especially after the last twenty-four hours.

She sat quiet and attentive, still feeling awful about leaving him hanging after their previous encounter. He filled her in on the process so far for treating his bipolar condition. It had been hard, he said, staying away when he *really* needed someone to talk to. He'd had a few ups and downs already, was getting used to the medication, but he didn't like the way it made him feel. It helped with the lows but brought down the highs to the point he felt almost nonexistent.

Finally, Lilli asked the million-dollar question. "How come you risked coming over here now?"

"I ran into that friend of yours. The one you said works at Starbucks—although, I still haven't had the pleasure of being served by her there yet. Anyway, she seemed to know me, and she told me Jake was arrested for assault. I figured it was safe."

"Arrested?" Lilli bolted from the sofa and whirled to face Brad. Then, just as quickly, she slumped back down and dropped her head into her hands.

Brad inched closer and placed his arm around her shoulders, drawing her toward him. She didn't resist the connection, allowing him to caress her back while she processed his words.

"Maybe she was speculating." Brad brushed the hair from her forehead and tapped a gentle kiss there.

"Maybe. But it makes sense," she raised her face and met with his eyes, "after what happened…" Brad's sustained eye contact was ripe with expectation, so she continued. "Last night. It was awful. This detective barged in and then ushered a team of commandos into my apartment to shred my life apart."

"Commandos?"

"Okay, technically they were SWAT, but I *was* under siege." She leaned forward to reach for her coffee, shrugging out of Brad's embrace.

"They were looking for evidence against Jake?"

"Yeah. But then—" she downed a huge gulp, "then the detective got this mysterious call and *bam!* They left. Didn't bother even shutting the cabinet doors, left everything asunder."

"Asunder?"

"What? It's a thing. Never mind. The point is—the call. They must have been telling him they'd arrested Jake. That's why they left the big mess."

"Mess?" Brad gazed around the space. "You get any sleep last night?"

"I did actually. Sort of. Donna cleaned everything. She's the one who likely stayed up all night." She followed the path his eyes had traced. "She's a good friend." Lilli faced him, and his eyes matched with hers. "So are you, Brad. And I'm sorry about what happened with Jake. I should have checked on you. I felt bad, but there was just so much going on."

"Shhh."

A little shiver filtered down her spine as he swept the backs of his fingers along her forehead and down her cheek, tucking an errant lock of hair behind her ear. His expression was so penetrating, for a moment, Lilli thought he was going to kiss her.

"I was okay," he said. "It would have been better with you by my side, but I understand. You believed Jake. Why wouldn't you?" Brad rubbed the corner of his mouth where a small red mark persisted as a memento of Jake's friendly warning. "Trust me, I know how convincing he can be."

Lilli ran her own hand along his face. "Oh, Brad—"

The pounding on the glass patio doors snapped both Lilli's and Brad's attention toward them.

It was Jake. And he looked pissed.

CHAPTER FORTY-SIX

MONTY HAD WANTED to talk to him after work, so, when their shift ended, they went to grab a bite to eat. As they wandered back to the car, loaded down with a tray full of burgers, fries, and milkshakes, Brian shook his head. "I can't believe I let you talk me into eating here."

He looped around to the driver's side of his SUV, while Monty hopped in the other. Leaning through the open door, he handed her the tray while he climbed inside.

She grinned at him, a large bite of a quarter-pound Dick's Deluxe already occupying her cheeks. She spoke around the mouthful of cheeseburger. "Dick's Drive-in is a Seattle classic, Bri. It was named 'America's most life-changing burger' for a reason." She swallowed and ripped off another chunk. "God, this is good." She wiped her chin with a napkin and thrust a wrapped burger toward him.

He accepted the foil bundle and regarded it with suspicion. "We coulda had sushi," he said.

"Sushi-schmushi." Monty shoved a wad of fries into her mouth, then mumbled something that sounded like "Fresh not frozen." He assumed she meant the beef. She gulped the food down her throat and nudged him. "Come on, Brian. Give yourself over to the burger experience. Life changing. Imagine that. Let it change yours. You can eat like a fish later."

"Like a fish?"

"With the sushi. Fish eat other fish. Raw."

"Oh." He peeled back the wrapper and raised the double-patty burger to his open mouth.

She jabbed his hand closer so that the burger touched his lips, smearing mayo and pickle relish all around.

He bit into it and then snatched the napkin from her outstretched hand, as dribbles of sauce and burger juice rolled over his chin. He swallowed, bobbed his head, and then took another bite.

She popped him in the shoulder. "See. Delicious." She punctuated the statement with a loud slurp on her milkshake.

"Fine," he said, "it's kind of all right."

"Kind of all right?" She slugged him again, causing him to drop a huge glob of mayonnaise on the steering wheel.

He shook his head, but before he could wipe up the spill his phone was vibrating. He checked the caller ID. It was his brother Stephen.

"Behave," he warned before he answered his brother's call. "Hey, Bro. What's up?"

"Just hung up from Mom. She told me to call to make sure you're coming for the party."

"Super Bowl Sunday, Mom's birthday—wouldn't miss it." It was a not-too-subtle dig. Brian was the only one of the three sons that made it every year. "Already booked it off. Coming up on the thirty-first and heading back on the sixth."

"I'll be there to greet ya."

"Hey, Stephen, did Mom say if she wants me to bring anything?"

His brother chuckled. "Yeah, kid, she wants you to bring something—a girlfriend."

"That's hilarious." He drew out the middle of the word for added emphasis.

It was a favorite topic around the Harris dinner table whenever Brian visited—at least since his engagement to Cynthia had tanked and Brian had not found a suitable replacement. Stephen was a player, so he got a pass. Bobby was voted "most likely to be married to his career" so that earned him one too. But speculation abounded regarding when Brian would settle down with a nice girl, get married, and have his 2.1 kids and a dog. For a new-age thinker, his mother could be rather old-fashioned at times.

Stephen finally suspended his laughter. "At least bring that sexy partner of yours. I might as well have a date."

"Monty?"

She leaned forward at the mention of her name.

"Hell yeah, Monty. You got another sexy partner I don't know about?"

"No. Just her. But she's out of your league, Bro."

"Whatever," his brother said. "Just ask her."

"We'll see."

Brian ended the call, and Monty immediately jumped into the fray.

"I heard my name. Why did I hear my name?"

She was poking him in the shoulder. He hated that. She knew it. More poking.

He brushed her hand away. "What are you? Six?"

She stuck her tongue out at him. "Is that six enough for you?"

"More than." He shoved some fries in his mouth and then sucked on his milkshake to buy time. The last thing Monty needed was his brother Stephen hitting on her. Stephen was pure dog. He'd left his scent on every available cheerleader-tree in high school, and his adult territory had been marked far and wide. He excused his womanizing ways and emotional unavailability, claiming commitment would jeopardize his ISA job within HUMINT—Human Intelligence. If he let them in, he'd have to kill them.

Brian finished chewing and turned to Monty, hoping she had moved on. Her face told him she hadn't. "Fine," he said. "My brother was teasing me, asking me to bring you to our yearly Super-Bowl-slash-Mom's-birthday bash."

Monty burst into laughter. "With you? Like a date? You wish, Harris."

"Gee, you're hilarious too. Maybe you two are meant for each other."

"Us two, who?"

"You and my brother."

"The cute annoying one or the sweet brooding one?"

"Stephen is the *older* annoying one. Bobby is younger. He's the brooding one."

Monty appeared to consider it as she slurped on her shake. "I'll pass." She shot him a grin. "Stephen seems a little *too* charming, and the other one, Bobby, he's too young for me. Besides, I have some big news."

News? Now he was interested. He met her gaze and waited for her to continue. When she didn't, he rolled his hand in a circular motion, encouraging her to go on.

"Fine, Captain Curious, I'll tell you." She spoke the words as though she was reluctant to say anything, but Brian could tell she was practically bursting at the seams. "I passed phase two. Got my conditional offer yesterday."

"You did? Wow. Congrats. What happens next?"

"Background. I'm filling out the forms tonight. Then the interview, drug testing, polygraph. They'll probably want a dialog with you too. Give me a glowing review, will ya."

Time for him to grin with mischief. "You want me to lie to the FBI?"

Another shot to the shoulder. "I see hilarity runs in the family."

CHAPTER FORTY-SEVEN

"COME ON, LILLI. You can't mean it. I didn't do those things they accused me of. If I had, do you really think they would've let me go?" After hours of talking, Jake still pleaded with Lilli to not break up with him. "I've been through hell you know."

"Oh. I see. And what do you call what I've been through? Do you think it's been easy for me?"

"I didn't say that, but..." Jake shot a glance toward Brad, who was parked at the dining table with headphones in his ears so he couldn't—technically—hear the two of them talking.

Jake had been adamant that Lilli speak with him in private, but Lilli had been equally determined not to be alone with him. Brad had taken her side, refusing to leave, finally agreeing to don the headphones and listen to some loud music so they could at least have some semblance of privacy.

"But what, Jake? I need a break. Ever since we started dating, life has been all drama. Yes, some of it was good, but the rest? I can't take it anymore. My life is upside down. Maybe after things settle, after they've put this streetcar attacker in jail—whoever it is."

She stood and marched to the door. "We've said all there is to say. Twice. Please go." She opened it and gestured toward the hall. "Now."

"Baby, please."

His eyes were full of torment, and a part of Lilli wanted to reach out to him, but she had to be strong. Right now she couldn't be sure what was truth and what was fiction. A clean break would be best. She had let the demise of her relationship with Brad drag on too long, and she refused to make that mistake again.

"Now, Jake." He didn't budge. "Please? I want to be alone."

He stood, large and looming, as he came toward her. The fire in his stare had been reignited. "Alone? Or with Brad?"

"Just what are you accusing me of?" Lilli opened the door farther. "Never mind. I don't care. Just leave."

He didn't. "God, Jake, do I have to call the cops or what?"

"Go ahead. I'm not leaving until you forgive me. Everything you heard was lies. I didn't do any of that stuff. I swear."

Lilli squeezed her eyes tight. She didn't want to see his face. Didn't want to feel her feelings. What she wanted was to scream. Primal like. When she opened her eyes again, he was facing Brad.

"This ain't over, Vanderson. I made you a promise. Don't forget it."

"I know what you mean by that, Jake. I saw the pictures of what your promise did to Brad's face."

Jake began to laugh. It started as a soft chuckle but morphed into an almost maniacal cackle. "What I did? Yeah. That's rich. Did you know lover boy here joined Bucky's Gym too?"

Brad pulled the headphones out. "That's right, Edwards, I did. Self-defense."

When Jake still made no move to leave, Lilli pulled her phone out and dialed two digits. "Only one left, Jake."

He leaned over and hit the number one. "Not anymore."

When the operator came on the line, Lilli stuttered, trying at an incoherent reply. What was she supposed to say? Did she want to go through with this? Call the cops? Jake would be in an awful lot of hot water if she did.

Before she could formulate her response, Jake yanked the phone out of her hand and spoke into it. "Jake Edwards here. Sorry to have bothered you fine folks. Turns out we won't be needing your services after all. I was just leaving. Have a nice day." He handed the phone back to Lilli and stomped out.

BRAD LEFT SHORTLY after Jake did. It was for the best. Lilli really did want to be alone. Hours passed. Tears were shed. Promises had been broken. Dreams had been destroyed. Where would she go from here? Lilli couldn't answer that.

She spent the rest of the day pacing the house and thinking. She would have scrubbed and polished a few things but Donna had managed to do everything for her already.

As it neared bedtime Lilli ran a hot bath, hoping that it would relax her enough that she could sleep. She didn't want to miss any more work.

When all was said and done and she crawled into bed with a purring Toby, she'd reached few conclusions. It had to be over with Jake, at least for now. He'd changed so much since his injury.

Or had he? Maybe he hadn't "changed" at all. Maybe he was just unable to keep the real Jake hidden any longer. Even if the things the detective had told her about Jake were untrue, she wasn't happy. Not really. Sure they had some great chemistry, but maybe that's all it was.

Her life had become a jumble of emotions and she just wanted to feel normal again. She didn't want to fall back in step with Brad either. That would be nothing more than emotional subterfuge. It was time to stand on her own two feet.

But how would she do that? Where? She believed that Brad meant well, these days at least, but being near him would only encourage his closeness and, even if that was what she needed, it was putting his safety at risk, wasn't it? She could throw herself into work. It was good to keep busy. But would she focus enough to do justice to her job? Could she?

She had good friends—Charlie, Cassie, Annie, and now Donna too—but did she want to involve them in all this? No. She did not. Moving in with one of them was off the list. She could go back home, back to her family. But if she did that and Jake was proven innocent, then what? She might give up on something that only needed time.

Finally, unable to stop her mind from spinning in a vortex of what-if scenarios, she put her headphones in and turned on her iPod to listen to an audio book. Deepak Chopra. His voice always soothed her to sleep.

CHAPTER FORTY-EIGHT

"WHAT ARE YOU GONNA DO?"

Lilli was on the phone with Annie, unsure how to answer her question. "I don't know, Annie. Chuck has a cabin in the Cascades and he said it's empty right now. Told me I could go stay there for a week, maybe more. As long as I needed to, he said.

"I think that sounds like a good idea. What did Cassie and Charlie say?"

"Same."

"Well then?"

"I don't know. Maybe."

It would be quiet out there, and she needed some of that. In the three days since she'd broken up with Jake, she could swear he'd been following her almost constantly. She couldn't prove it, but she had that feeling a lot, the one where her spine went all tingly, as though someone was behind her. It wouldn't surprise her. She had been certain he'd been lurking in the shadows, even before she ended their relationship.

Lilli's computer dinged with an instant message from Chuck. He was asking again about the cabin. Basically telling her that he had booked her off from January twenty-eighth to February eleventh. Then he inserted a smiley-face emoticon and said he didn't want to have to fire her if she didn't go, followed by LOL.

But was he joking? Maybe he was only partially serious. Her work had suffered. She couldn't deny that.

"Maybe it's in my best interests," she said.

"What is?" Annie asked. "Getting away?"

"Yeah." Lilli told Annie about the message she'd just received from Chuck.

"You're always asking for signs. I think that was your sign, Lilli. Take it. No one will bother you for two weeks. Sounds like heaven to me."

Lilli's cell vibrated on her desk. There was a text. It was from Jake. He missed her and wanted to see her. "All right. That's it," she said to Annie. "Jake just sent me another text. I'm getting the hell outta Dodge."

"Good girl," Annie said. "But first, you need to let your friends take you out to dinner for an early birthday celebration."

"Okay, but not tonight. Tomorrow."

Annie agreed and told Lilli she would get in touch with Charlie and Cassie to set it up.

"One more thing," Lilli began, "it can't be anywhere that Jake would go."

"Done." Annie hung up, and then Lilli replied to Chuck's message, with a single emphatic word: Yes.

Then she typed another message thanking him and apologizing profusely for needing a vacation in the first place. Before she could even press send, Chuck was in her doorway, dangling keys from his finger. The wide grin on his face telling her that she didn't have to apologize. He was happy to do it.

AFTER WORKING EXTRA hard the rest of the day so she could wrap a few things up before leaving town, Lilli finally climbed into her Jeep to head home. As she started the engine her phone alerted her of an incoming text. Jake again. He wasn't going to leave her alone, was he?

She had made the right decision, but maybe she should have decided to leave sooner than Sunday. She couldn't though. She needed to do too much beforehand. She needed to find someone to look after Toby. She should speak to her mother—suck it up and do her best to keep her emotions hidden from the woman who knew her too well. She'd been ignoring her mom lately and felt bad about that, but there was simply no way she could fool her.

"Shake it off, Lilli," she mumbled. She'd promised herself no more thoughts of Jake today. She pulled out of the garage and into the cold obscurity of the Seattle night. The roads had slickened up since earlier in the day. The weather had warmed while the sun had been up, but now that it was down, the melted snow had turned to black ice. She took her time, driving cautiously, careful to allow plenty of room between her and any cars in front.

As she came to a stop at the next light, she noticed a car about a block behind her. It was barely inching along, going far too slow, even for the weather conditions. She squinted at the image in the rearview. Looked like a sliver sedan. Jake?

The thought made her angry. How dare he stalk her like this? Then that thought scared her. Is that what he was doing? Stalking her? She hadn't put it quite in those words before, and she didn't like the way they sounded now.

The light turned green and the car was still too far behind her to see it clearly. She took her time accelerating, hoping it would catch up a little. It was close enough now that she could tell it was a Honda, but she couldn't make out the driver. It was almost like there was no one behind the wheel.

That's when she realized there was someone there, but they were crouched down low so that barely their eyes showed over the dashboard. It had to be Jake.

She squinted against the glare of the headlights bouncing off the slick ice. Was it him?

She wasn't sure, so she drove slowly, all the while checking her rearview to see if the car remained behind her. It did, so she made a series of right turns. She'd read online that it was a good strategy if you thought you were being followed. The advice said that if the car behind you did the same, then you should head to the nearest police station. After the silver Honda completed the third right turn, she decided to do just that.

East Precinct was about two miles away. She drove calmly, in spite of the fear rising in her throat. She crossed Broadway on East Pine and could see the safe haven of the police station ahead. She swallowed hard and took a deep breath.

The light turned yellow as she approached and, rather than go through it, she stopped. The vehicle tailing her hadn't anticipated that and was only a couple of car lengths behind her now. It seemed to be hesitating, but traffic was more congested here and a marked police car was right behind the silver sedan. It had no choice but to pull right up behind her. This enabled her to make a better assessment and, in spite of the fact that he was crouching behind the wheel trying to hide, she got a good view of the driver too. It was Jake.

The light changed to green and Lilli made her turn, signaling and pulling into a spot on the street marked Police Vehicles Only. This way she was sure to attract attention. Jake stayed in the left lane and passed her. What was he doing now? He slowed as he drove by, then he sat up straight, waved and smiled—if you could call it that. It more resembled the predatory sneer of a wolf.

A light knock came on Lilli's window and she turned to see a uniformed cop standing beside her. She rolled it down, prepared to tell the officer about Jake and why she'd pulled into the reserved spot. When she leaned over and the cop leaned down, she realized it was the officer who had investigated when Bradley had broken into her apartment.

"Is there a problem, ma'am? Everything okay here?"

She nodded.

"You do know this is police parking only."

"Yes, Officer. I was being followed. I read that I should head to a police station, so I did. I thought parking here would bring the cavalry rather quickly. I suppose I was right." She offered a smile and when she did he seemed to recognize her too.

"I know you," he said, pointing a gloved finger. "Bamboo. My partner and I were out to your place a few weeks ago."

"Yes, that's right," Lilli said.

"Is that fellow bothering you again?" He stood and surveyed the street.

"No, I...it's someone else." Just saying the words aloud made her cringe. Was she a crap magnet or something? It was starting to sound like it. She offered another smile, hoping it would soften the words. "I know how that sounds, but I'm really not crazy. I promise. I just make bad choices in boyfriends." She shook her head. "I'm working on it. Anyway, he drove off now, so..."

He allowed a smile now, as a statuesque, uniformed woman—far too beautiful to be a cop, Lilli was certain—joined him at the window. "Problem, Officer Harris?"

He shook his head. "No. Things are under control here, Officer Montgomery."

Lilli smiled hopefully and offered a small wave to the female officer.

Officer Montgomery leaned in to get a better look, nodding her head. "Ma'am."

"I was being followed," Lilli said, feeling as though she needed to explain.

For a brief moment, Lilli was sure she saw something flash across Officer Montgomery's eyes. She wasn't sure what, but something had dawned on the woman. Maybe she had seen Lilli through the windows that night and she recognized her too.

She stood and tapped the roof. "All right, then," she turned to Officer Harris, "since you got this under control."

He nodded, and she headed into the precinct, while Officer Harris leaned back down to the window. "Did you want to file a complaint?"

"No. I think my pulling in here scared him off. Hopefully he won't bother me anymore."

"If he does, you've got my number." Officer Harris pinched his lips together as though he were trying to stop a smile from forming, but the sparkle that reached his eyes confirmed Lilli's assessment.

"Nine-one-one, right?"

He allowed the smile this time and then backed away from the vehicle. "Have a good night, ma'am. Drive safe."

"Thank you. I will." She started the Jeep and then pulled out, watching Officer Harris in the rearview as he stepped toward the precinct doors.

CHAPTER FORTY-NINE

BRIAN STRODE INTO the precinct and shook the light dusting of snow from his jacket. His partner was in the bullpen staring down the pot of coffee. She glanced up when he walked in. She had that expression on her face. She wanted Starbucks. Not this thick sludge that the precinct tried to pass off as coffee.

He zipped his jacket up again and turned to head back out, darting a fleeting look behind him. As expected, she followed with a smile on her face. He pushed the door and went through, letting it fall shut. Female cops hated it when their male counterparts treated them like ladies. There was to be no holding of doors, no pulling out of chairs, and definitely no preferential treatment when chasing down a perp. Oh, and they had to buy the donuts once in a while, same as the men. Fair was fair. They'd worked hard to fight stereotypes, they said, and anything less than equal treatment and equal expectations just wouldn't fly.

Brian didn't have the heart to remind Monty that he wouldn't have trudged back out in the snow for one of the guys. He was planning to have green tea tonight, and that he could make here if he had to, so no worries about burnt offerings from the bullpen. Truth was, he did it because a Monty with no coffee was a grouchy Monty.

Once outside they turned to each other. "Did you notice anything about the girl in the Jeep?" they blurted out simultaneously.

"You go first," Monty said.

Brian zipped his jacket all the way and then tucked his hands into his pockets as they headed up Twelfth Avenue. "The girl. She's the one from that domestic call a while back. Madison Gate apartments. Remember the cocky Brad Pitt wannabe?"

"Oh yeah. Right." Monty pulled on her gloves and zipped up too. "I never saw the girl though. Was that her?"

"Yeah." They turned the corner onto East Pike Street. "Wait. If you never saw her, how did you recognize her?"

"I didn't. Not exactly." Monty walked between the brick columns ahead of him, pulling the door open as two hipsters meandered out, clearly in no hurry. She tapped her foot impatiently, holding the door, Brian guessed, about thirty seconds longer than she would have liked.

Inside, the aroma of freshly brewed coffee reached out to them. It was almost enough to tempt Brian into a Caffè Americano. Almost.

Monty gazed up, reading the menu.

"I don't know why you always do that," he said.

"Do what?"

"Scan the menu. You always order the same thing."

"But you never know when that might change." She smiled at him then stepped to the counter and ordered a venti Caramel Macchiato.

Brian sidled up to her and ordered a venti Zen tea.

She raised her eyebrows to him. "See, you're just as predictable as I am."

He'd see her eyebrow lift and raise her a cocky grin. "Scratch that," he said to the barista. "Make mine a Caffè Americano. Grande."

She laughed. "I see you're Captain Adventure tonight. Fair enough." Her eyes went up to the menu. "I'll change my order too." Then back to the barista. "Make that a Hazelnut Macchiato. Same size though—venti."

Brian attempted to disguise his grin but failed miserably. "You do know the only difference between those two is the drizzle on top, right?"

She looked at the barista and the girl nodded her confirmation. Monty sent a sheepish grin his way. "Well played, Harris. Well played."

They moved off to the side to wait for their drinks and Brian leaned against the window. "What did you mean when you said you didn't exactly recognize the girl in the Jeep?"

"I didn't know she was the one from the call. Did you see her face? Her hair? She looks just like the girl that was attacked on the streetcar line. They could be sisters."

"How do you know?"

"Don't you read the memos, Brian?"

He shrugged. "Most."

She challenged him with her eyes.

"Okay, some."

The barista set their cups on the counter and called them out. The two officers grabbed their beverages and looked around for a table. No sense taking them back to the station. In this weather the coffees would be cold by the time they arrived. About to accept their fate and venture back out into the falling snow, a corner table opened up.

"Aren't they the same hipsters we passed on the way in?" Brian jacked his thumb toward the two guys heading through the door.

"They aren't hipsters, Bri. Hipsters get their java in dimly lit, one-off cafés that serve organic fair-trade coffee."

"Huh?"

His partner laughed. "Hipsters, according to the general consensus, are anti-mainstream, Brian, and Starbucks is totally mainstream. Especially in Seattle."

"Thanks for the life lesson."

"That's what I'm here for."

They navigated the narrow space in between customers, stepping over an array of laptop and iPad cords snaking across the floor to the wall outlets behind the tables. Heading to Starbucks with Monty was always an adventure. He would miss her—and her life lessons—when she left to join the feds. They'd been working together for almost three years now and it was a good fit. His mother accused him of not looking for a girlfriend because he didn't feel the need for female companionship with such a beautiful partner. It wasn't like that though with him and Monty. He thought of her more as the sister that he always wanted but never had.

LILLI HAD MANAGED to drive the rest of the way home without further incident. She'd been quite positive that Jake had given up on following her—at least for tonight. Still, there had been a part of her that was resistant to going to her apartment right away. So, she'd sat in her parking spot for a few minutes contemplating the decision.

After a quick glance behind the seat to confirm her gym bag was still there, she'd opted to go for a workout at Bucky's instead. It had felt like the right thing to do. Her boxing lessons had been coming along nicely, even though she hadn't had as many as she would have liked. She'd been feeling much more confident in her self-defense abilities, and, the way her life had been going lately, that couldn't be a bad thing.

The gym hadn't been too crowded and she'd even done a little sparring with Bucky himself. He'd told her, again, that she was a natural, and had asked her about entering a competition. Lilly had declined, saying she had to get some things in order before she took on more responsibilities. As far as boxing was concerned, right now, Lilli's only goals were working up a good sweat and learning a few defensive maneuvers.

Tonight she'd accomplished both. Two hours later, as she stood under the shower in the empty locker room, she savored the pelting of the hot water raining down on her back and she allowed her depleted muscles to relax. Her exhausted brain too. Lilli closed her eyes and took three slow, deep breaths.

It was so quiet. Peaceful. She decided she liked the gym at night. It was a much better experience than during peak hours. Less people. Less distractions. More hot water. She wondered how long she could stay in there before Bucky came and kicked her out.

Lilli closed her eyes once more. She'd really needed this. All of it. The workout. The solitude. She began to look forward to going to Chuck's cabin. If it was half this peaceful there she would come back a new woman.

She pictured a snow-covered mountainside, sipping wine in the hot tub, reading a good book, listening to the sounds of—what? She didn't know. Surely the crickets didn't chirp in the winter and there shouldn't be too many critters around to make any noise. Maybe she would have the sounds of absolute stillness. That idea appealed to her. Although, she might be wise to take along a white-noise machine in case it was too quiet. After living with the bustling echoes of big-city life for so long, she might find the stillness of seclusion to be too much. Even now, although it was quiet in the gym, there was the constant hum of life all around her. The steady buzz of the fluorescent fixtures overhead. The random clanks of the radiator kicking on.

In the city, even silence had a sound.

Turning off the water, Lilli resigned herself to getting out of the shower, but as she did, the lights in the change area flickered a few times then went dark. Had Bucky forgotten she was back there?

A single circular bulb shone from up in the far corner, but it was too dim to see much of anything. She called out but received no response. As she slid back the curtain, the rings clinked on the metal rod. She reached out and felt around for her towel. Where was it? It should be hanging on the hook right outside her stall. She felt the other side. Nothing. She bent down to the floor and moved her hand side to side, coming up with nothing but puddles of water.

Goose bumps spread across her naked body, but were they from the sudden cold or from the fear that was beginning to take hold of her?

She cocked her head to decipher the sound she was hearing. What was it? A shuffling of feet? Maybe. But who was it? She'd thought Bucky was the only one left besides her. So it had to be him. Right?

Lilli opened her mouth to speak, but something inside her told her not to utter a single word. She cemented herself to the spot, wanting to pull the shower curtain around herself but knowing it would scrape against the metal bar. Instead she crept into the farthest corner of the stall, pressing herself against the cold tiles and wrapping her arms around her shivering body. Her teeth began to chatter and she clenched her jaw to mitigate the noise.

God. She really did need to get away. She was a wreck. Panicking at little things. Assuming the worst. It was probably just as she had thought. Bucky forgot she was back there and turned off the lights. Now he was likely shuffling around doing his closing routine. She should just call out to him. Let him know she was still here.

Again, Lilli parted her lips and began to form the word "Hello" but the sound of it froze in her throat.

CHAPTER FIFTY

FUCK IT'S COLD. I hate the freakin' winter. You don't realize how much it gets to a person until you've been trapped with your back flattened against an icy brick wall, standing motionless, not even breathing. I live in the shadows, watching through the window. Waiting. Blood pumping inside my head—*swoosh, swoosh, swoosh.* Pulse pounding so hard I think I'm going to pass out. All so that I won't be discovered. Not before I'm ready to be.

If she found out the truth about me now, she would never forgive me. I can't have that. Not when I am so close to the end.

It's wonderful that it gets dark earlier though. That gives me an early start on things. But the cold makes it hard to stay outside for too long at a time. Damn Seattle weather. If it's not raining it's snowing instead. Don't even get me started on the snow. I have to make a thousand more footprints everywhere just so my marks are not obvious. Plus, I can't go right up to her window or she'll see my tracks. I can go indoors. But then I can't see. Although, I can hear better and that's a nice change. I like that. I could listen to her all day. There's so many things I love about her. The way she giggles watching TV, all alone—well, she thinks she's all alone—but she just giggles randomly at silly things.

And all night. The way she makes that cute little snoring sound when she sleeps. Or the random murmurs that come out when she's dreaming. Of course I have to go all the way inside for that. And that can be risky. She almost caught me once. Stupid cat.

Don't get me wrong. I'm not saying it isn't worth it. That familiar feeling of adrenaline surging through my veins, it gives me comfort.

The excitement of the hunt—that's what it's all about. I like having a little secret. Truth be told, I like being the cat to her mouse. But I'm a feral beast. A hunter stalking my prey.

Yes, there were others before her, but she's the best mouse yet. She's a smart little mouse. I like that. She's feisty too. The way she drove straight to the police like that. She likes to challenge people. She gives me a rush like I haven't felt in a long time. No one else has come close to giving me the same thrill.

And as for those sounds I love to hear her make…the final little squeak she gives me…that will be a symphony to my ears. So worth it.

I thought she was going to go straight home after her East Precinct diversion, but she didn't. She came here. To the gym. It's so cute the way she throws those girly punches when she's sparring. As if that right cross could do me any harm. Ha! I had fighting bred into me, beat into me. Thanks, Dad. No. Seriously. I am grateful for all the shit he beat out of me as a kid. Cause boy oh boy, look at me now.

I'm on a roll. In it to win it, and all that.

And because that's true, it's time for me to leave. I've had my fun. For now. Even though, outside, in the dark, I know the wind has picked up. The blustery snow was already falling heavily when I arrived here. Visibility was almost nil. My work will likely be done for tonight. I can handle that. I just have one thing to do first…

Come on, Lilli. The lights are out…why aren't you leaving?

CHAPTER FIFTY-ONE

IT'D BEEN QUIET for long enough, and she had been freezing for too long, so Lilli decided to venture over to the light in the corner, hoping to find her clothes and get dressed. Her heart was racing and the hairs were on end all over her body. The cold and the nakedness didn't help with that.

She felt her way along the chilly tile until she came to the short hall that led to the rows of lockers along the back wall. She could almost make out the silhouette of the bench where she'd set her gym bag. That meant her clothes should be in the locker adjacent to it.

She kept blinking her eyes, striving to find focus as she inched her way there. The next step had her almost losing her footing as she stepped on something unexpected. Her towel? She bent down and held it up toward the bulb in the corner. It appeared to be just that. But how did it get over there? She was certain she'd taken it with her to the showers, hung it on the hook. Either way, she was freezing so she wrapped it around her. If it turned out to belong to someone else, so be it. At that moment she didn't care.

The towel was damp from the floor but it was still a welcome shelter against the drafty room.

Pay dirt. She had her gym bag and her locker. Now, if she could find the small key at the bottom of her bag. As she fumbled for it a loud crash bellowed from outside the locker room. Lilli's back went stiff, but relaxed a moment later when she heard Bucky muttering. He must have dropped something.

She really did feel like she was losing it. Seeing shadows around every corner. Thinking every dark room held some kind of monster.

Lilli gave her head a shake and then pulled on her workout clothes. She would find the key and come back for her other clothes later.

What she needed right now was to unwind. And she had just the thing. Donna had given her two Xanax the other night, after the SWAT invasion, but she hadn't taken both. She still had one in her bedside table drawer and she would use it tonight. It felt like the only way she'd be able to chill out.

A HYPER-VIGILANT drive home, again, and Lilli was thinking of one thing. Popping that Xanax and going to sleep. She would figure out what she would do with Toby tomorrow. She was certain one of her friends would agree to take care of him.

She yanked her purse off the seat and scurried to the building, darting glances all around her as she ran. She hated feeling like she was being watched. Followed. It was turning her into a stressed-out crazy woman. Thank God she only had one cat.

After dashing through the hallway, keys in hand, Lilli zipped through the locks and just as rapidly latched them behind her. She leaned her back against the door and heaved in a giant gasp of air. She'd made it.

As she glanced down to slip off her shoes, there was Toby, staring at her as though he were thankful she only had one cat too. She bent and picked him up, nuzzling her nose to his furry head. As she scratched him under the chin, he wriggled free and hopped to the floor, leading her to the kitchen.

"Food. Is that all you think about?" His eyes were round and black from the extreme dilation in the dark, giving him a wide-eyed, innocent demeanor. It made her smile as she went to the cupboard and grabbed a scoop full of kibble.

The next stop was her bedside table drawer and maybe a warm bath.

LILLI STEPPED OUT of the tub, feeling like a raisin after all the time she'd spent in water tonight. But the heat of the bath had done what she'd wanted it to. It had helped get the tranquilizer she'd taken into her bloodstream fast. At least she was a tranquil raisin.

She wandered around the apartment, making sure there were no gaps in the curtains and blinds where anyone could see inside, then she checked all the door and window locks. After that she made a cup of tea before she climbed into bed and turned on her reading lamp. Lilli tucked the blankets up to her chin and then cracked open a new novel she'd been waiting to read. Just a few pages and she'd feel ready to drift off.

She sipped her tea and followed along in the book, but she couldn't keep her mind focused on the story, finding herself rereading several passages in a row. She slapped the book shut without adding a bookmark. There was no point since she would need to start at the beginning again.

At least her eyes were getting heavier and she was beginning to feel not too shabby. Maybe she would visit her own doctor and get a prescription for these pills. Just a few. To help her get through all this. It couldn't hurt.

She could hear the wind whipping around outside, blowing snow everywhere she was sure. Not even Jake would be crazy enough to be outside watching her on a night like this. She reached over and snapped off the lamp, then she snuggled down deep under the blankets, pulling them all the way up so only her eyes and nose stuck out.

CHAPTER FIFTY-TWO

SATURDAY MORNING Lilli peeled her eyes open a crack to look straight into Toby's purring little face. He stood, all four paws on her chest, periodically tapping her cheek with a partially extended claw. "Feed me. Feed me," he was saying in his not-so-subtle way.

Lilli wanted to move him so she could roll over and go back to sleep, but his face was so darn cute, and the way he ensured gentleness, using strictly just enough claw to wake her without hurting, convinced her otherwise.

"All right, Toby, you win. I'll get up. But I'll have you know I don't want to."

Her cat hopped off her chest, and Lilli reached way back and stretched as far as she could, twisting her spine so the stiff vertebrae would release. Her body ached from the workout the night before, but in a good way, and her head felt fuzzy from drugging herself, although, not so much in a good way.

In spite of taking the tranquilizer it had been a tormented night full of pitching, tangled blankets, and peeking through sleep-hazed eyes to battle with the shadows that cast around her room, changing position according to the moon's path across her window.

Several times she would have sworn those amorphous, ambiguous images moved of their own volition. But every time she blinked and refocused on them they affirmed themselves. Just a pile of clothes draped over a chair. Simply the giant teddy bear Jake had given her as it sat sentry in the corner, smiling and wearing a mini Seahawks jersey, number eleven. Innocent items that her overtaxed mind had contorted into malevolent mirages.

She rubbed the sleep from her eyes and took in the area. The bright white glow that illuminated the backs of her curtains told Lilli that it had either snowed overnight or was still snowing now—it also provided sufficient light to validate the benign nature of all the shadow monsters that had haunted her slumber.

The carpet felt cool to her feet as she struggled out of bed. In fact, the entire room felt drafty, the crisp scent of winter lingering in the air. Movement in the corner caught her attention and she spun her head in that direction. The curtain had moved. She was certain of it. Surely the window was not open. She'd made the rounds before bed, checking all the latches. Everything had been locked up tight.

She slid her feet into her slippers and padded, first toward the window, which was indeed locked, and then toward the partially open bedroom door. As she reached out to grasp the handle something sucked the door outwards causing it to bang shut.

Lilli's heart took up residence in her throat and the surging of her blood pumped a deafening beat in her ears. She looked down to see if Toby was still waiting at her feet but he was not. He must have slinked through the small opening right before it had slammed.

She forced herself to breathe, the air slipping in through her nose and then rushing from her mouth in shuddering vacillation. She counted down from ten. Okay. Logic would say that Toby had somehow created a vacuum effect as he crept through the opening, drawing the door out. That's all it was. Still, Lilli surveyed the room, looking for anything she could arm herself with…just in case.

"YOU THINK I'M INSANE, don't you?" Lilli tucked her legs beneath her on the sofa as Toby hopped up to join her.

She blew on her steaming mug then took a sip. This was a two-coffee morning. If she hadn't made plans for an early birthday dinner with her friends, Lilli would've considered leaving for the cabin a day early. What she needed was nothing. No looming shadows, no drafty hallways causing bedroom doors to slam. She needed a break. A reboot.

But before she left she would remind the apartment manager about the front door sticking open. It had caused her more than her share of problems already.

Toby curled himself in the bend of her legs and proceeded to wash his face as she cradled the warm cup in her hands and made a mental checklist of all the things she needed to do before she left.

When that didn't prove a sufficient distraction, Lilli decided to start packing for her trip. It was something concrete. Something she could control. As far as calling her mom and finding someone to take care of Toby, she would do the latter at dinner tonight and the former via Bluetooth while en route to the cabin. That way if her mother picked up on any underlying stress in her voice, Lilli could attribute it to being distracted with driving.

BEFORE SHE KNEW it, the better part of the day had passed. After her shower Lilli stood in the doorway to the spare room and took in all she'd accomplished. She had two big suitcases as well as a smaller carry-on packed and ready to go. Likely way more than she needed, but since she wasn't sure exactly what to expect, she prepared for everything she could think of.

This trip was really coming together. Everything was falling into place. Now she just needed to finish getting ready to go out. She would meet her friends at Lecosho, halfway down the Harbor Steps, over on University Street. Lilli had never been there before, but both Annie and Cassie had, on separate occasions, and they both raved. On the plus side, it didn't seem the type of place that Jake would go, at least not without a date.

Reservations were for six PM, and Lilli found she was actually looking forward to it. More than she had thought. Filtering through her closet, she couldn't decide what to wear. Lucky for her she'd mostly packed casual clothes for the cabin, so she had an entire wardrobe of choices. Finally she settled on a long sweater over black leggings, tucked into black suede boots. She adorned herself with a few silver pieces of jewelry, slipped on her coat, and then double-checked all the locks before scanning through her windows and then dashing outside to her Jeep.

A SHORT WHILE LATER, Lilli climbed the Harbor Steps. Lecosho was bustling and brightly lit, lined on three sides with huge windows. She could see that her friends had already arrived and were sitting and chatting at a table near the half-wall that separated the open kitchen from the eating area. As she entered the sprawling restaurant, a hostess approached, and Lilli pointed to her friends. The woman showed her to the table and brought her a glass for the wine that the girls had already ordered.

The dark stained wooden tables and upholstered banquettes accentuated the long lines of the flowing space. Lilli admired the ambience and décor as her friends took turns standing to give her a hug and wish her a happy *early* birthday.

The server was waiting in the wings and poured Lilli some wine as soon as she settled into her chair. After she explained the house specialties, the girl excused herself, saying she would be back shortly to get their orders.

Lilli and the girls made small talk while they perused the menu, finally deciding on a cheese plate and the charred baby rainbow carrots to share as appetizers. Then, by the time the waitress brought the apps, the girls had all made up their minds on the main courses.

It was time to drink wine, relax, and kickback with her good friends. Time to forget, for at least the next couple of hours, all about Jake.

CHAPTER FIFTY-THREE

DON'T THEY LOOK COZY? Smiling and laughing. What a happy little foursome they make. Bitches.

They're celebrating something. But what? Wouldn't they all be surprised if I walked up and joined them. Clink, clink, ladies. Yes, I know I wasn't invited, but let's all toast to my arrival just the same.

None of you have to worry your pretty little heads though. I'm enjoying the show from outside. The bitter cold from yesterday has died down a bit, and all these people hustling around are giving off a nice bath of body heat, so, yes, I am quite content to stay here.

For now.

But wait. What's this? Lilli has gotten up from her place beside Annie and she's leaning over the bar talking to some shaggy-headed blond bartender. Come on, Lilli. He can't be more than twenty. God. Does she need to seduce every guy in Seattle? Does every man alive have to look at her that way?

Go ahead, kid. Smile, flirt, shake that cocktail mixer. Blend a special little Shaggy-tini that Lilli will think is positively *to die for*. What you don't understand—what no one seems to understand—is that she's mine. I need her to complete me.

I have been searching for my other half—my better half—so fucking long. I have been searching for her. And make no mistake. I will not go home empty handed.

This is my destiny. It is her destiny.

So, move on, Shaggy, move on. She's not available, in fact, very soon now, Miss Lilli Brooks is going to be *off* the social circuit.

Permanently.

CHAPTER FIFTY-FOUR

LILLI WAS SO LUCKY. She had such wonderful friends. Sometimes she didn't know what she would do without them. They were her sounding board, her cheerleaders, her shoulders to cry on, and her compass in times of confusion. And right now they all agreed on two things—she needed to get away and going to Chuck's cabin was the perfect solution.

Although, all three had hesitated when she'd asked about Toby. She could see they all wanted to help her out, but their busy schedules and less than pet-friendly apartments put a wrench in that.

But luck had stepped in again when she'd run into Donna—literally—on the Harbor Steps. She'd offered to take care of Toby, but would have to do it at Lilli's place. She said her roommate was allergic. Lilli hadn't remembered Donna mentioning a roommate before but she wasn't about to question it. The last piece of the puzzle was in place now and Lilli was relieved that she wouldn't have to take her cat to the mountains with her. Plus, she had someone she trusted keeping an eye on her apartment while she was away.

Now, as Lilli pulled into her parking spot, on edge after yet another overly attentive drive home, she was ready to get to bed early so she could head out at sunrise. She snatched her purse off the seat and pressed the key fob to lock the door. Then, as she turned to dash into the building, she ran into Brad. Not quite as literally this time. Thankfully. He was a much more solid target than Donna was.

"Hi, Brad. How have you been?" Lilli had been meaning to call him since the other day when he'd played referee during her visit with Jake. She supposed he'd been staying away again since Jake had only been questioned in the attack, not actually arrested. She couldn't blame him.

He shoved his hands deeper in his pockets and shrugged. "I been okay. I guess. You? Edwards leaving you alone?"

"Sort of. Not really." She nodded toward the building. "You wanna walk me inside?"

He showed his agreement by heading toward the door, which, as had become the norm lately, was not even closed all the way, let alone locked.

Lilli sighed and stepped inside after Brad. They walked to her apartment in silence and she opened the locks on the door. Lilli figured they were both probably thinking about the same thing—Jake Edwards.

Should she invite Brad to come in? She didn't even know how to make simple choices anymore. She couldn't stop questioning her own judgment lately.

He saved her the decision.

"I know you're heading out somewhere tomorrow, so I won't keep you. Just wanted to make sure you got in safe."

"Thanks, Brad, I appre—wait. How do you know I'm going away?"

He didn't answer.

"Brad?"

"Okay. I was out for a walk and I saw you through the window, packing your suitcase—before you closed the curtains. It made sense, after all Edwards has put you through. I can't blame you for taking a vacation. That's kind of why I happened by just now. I wasn't sure if you would be gone for a week or forever. So I wanted to see you one last time. Just in case."

"I'd never be gone forever, Brad."

"Maybe. Maybe not. You might decide it's better wherever you're going. We can never know when it might be the last time we see someone, Lilli. Sometimes there's just no going back."

As she stood in the threshold, emotion whelmed inside of her, then surged forth as she flung her arms around Brad's neck and hugged him tightly. "I'm so sorry, Brad. For everything."

He slipped his arms around her too and returned the embrace. "I'm the one who should be sorry, Lilli. My Dad…this disease. I'm ruined. But if I hadn't been so stupid, you and Jake—never mind. Just know I'll always love you, Lilli." He kissed her on the head and ran his fingers down her arm until he grasped her hand. "Even if I never see you again." He brought it to his lips for a moment then let it filter away as he turned to leave. "Good-bye, Lilli."

"Good-bye? Brad? Wait."

But he didn't. He kept walking, head down, hands shoved deep into his jacket pockets.

She didn't have a good feeling.

LILLI ALMOST CHASED AFTER HIM. Something didn't feel right with Brad. He'd said he would always love her, and the truth was, a part of her would always love him too. The timing wasn't right for them to be together. Maybe it never would be. So much had happened in such a short time. Life had a way of changing people—for the good and the bad.

She entered the apartment and closed the door behind her, running her hand along the back of it, as if by doing so she could touch Brad, let him know she wasn't leaving forever. She would come back, be his friend, help him through this.

She leaned her forehead against the door and breathed out a deep sigh. A single tear drifted down her cheek and landed on the carpet at her feet. "Oh, Brad…"

"How is lover boy anyway?"

Lilli screamed and spun around. "Jake? What are you doing here? How did you get in?"

"You were out and I wanted to talk to you. I decided to wait." He shrugged as though it were perfectly normal for her to find him there, stretched out on her sofa, arms draped across the back, feet crossed and resting on the coffee table in front.

Lilli studied him. She couldn't get a read on his expression. Every neuron in her brain seemed to be firing all at once, imploring her to run while she had the chance, but her heart put its two cents in and she hesitated. He hadn't answered her question.

"I asked how you got in my apartment." She crossed her arms and stood her ground. This was her home. Her refuge. No one, not even the great Jake Edwards, was going to run her out of there.

He maintained his position. A wicked sneer replaced the crooked grin she used to love. The light that had sparkled in his hazel eyes was now dimmed by an unknown force.

"Either answer me, Jake, or leave. If you don't I will call the cops and have you arrested for break and enter."

Jake's smirk didn't fade. "Go ahead and try. I let myself in with the key you gave me."

"I didn't give you a key."

He rose off the couch and advanced toward her, dangling a set of keys. "Sure you did. Remember? 'Just slip it under the door when you leave, baby.' I believe those were the words you used."

"You made a copy." She rushed forward in an attempt to grab the keys, but he yanked them up and out of her reach. Instead she used momentum and her outstretched arms to shove him as hard as she could.

He didn't budge, but his eyes sparked with electric adrenaline. And then he chuckled. "Seriously? Is that all you got? I thought you've been taking boxing lessons."

That was it. Her open palms clenched into fists, she surged with a jolt from her own adrenal glands, and began wailing on him. "I. Hate. You." Each word came out as a single distinct entity, punctuated with a blow to his chest.

He stood there and took it, not flinching, not reacting in any way, which only served to make her angrier. "You broke in to my apartment, Jake." She pounded on his body, each strike amplifying the next, until, finally she tired and gave up.

She stepped back and he stared at her, deadpan. "Actually, I didn't *really* break in now, did I? I used my key, right? So…"

"So what, Jake? It's still breaking in when you are not invited. God! You make me so…so…" Lilli collapsed against the wall, the fight drained away.

"What do I make you, Lilli?"

"You piss me off. That's what you do. I am so angry with you."

"If you're angry it means you still have feelings for me."

"I don't, Jake. I don't love you."

"I didn't say love. But you just did." He closed the distance between them, placing his arms on her shoulders. "Admit it, Lilli. You do still love me."

She shook her head wildly, but did not infuse the denial with words.

He leaned down as though he was going to kiss her.

Her head was spinning, her heart was twisting, and her body felt weak. As his lips grazed the surface of her own, she found her voice.

"No!" She turned her head to the side. "No, Jake. I can't. I don't—just go."

"No."

"No?"

His face softened, his shoulders dropped, and he backed up, allowing her to move away from the wall.

"I'm sorry. I shouldn't have done that. You talk. I'll listen. But don't make me leave. Please? We can work things out."

"No, Jake. We can't work anything out. I don't know who you are anymore. I don't think I ever did. It's over…accept that."

"Except what?"

"No, Jake, you have to *accept* that—we're not getting back together. Not now. Not ever." She thrust her arm toward the door. "Please, just go."

He didn't move.

His eyes glazed over.

His shoulders no longer slouched forward and his expression hardened. "I don't want to go."

He took a step toward her. She, one back.

"Jake, you're scaring me." Lilli scanned the area. Where was the telephone? She'd left it in her bedroom, and her cell was in her purse, which she'd dropped by the door. The landline in her room was the best bet.

She stepped to the side and then back, toward the hallway. "Sure, Jake. You're right. Let's talk. Hang on. Wait there."

She walked casually, which was a struggle when her legs wanted to run.

"Interesting." He was right on her heels.

"What?"

"Nothing."

"Jake, I said to wait there. I just want to change into something more comfortable."

"Right." His voice deepened, taking on a gravelly tone. "I don't want to wait here. I'd rather follow you."

That might have been funny under other circumstances, but right now there was nothing humorous about it. The fact that Jake could be so flippant about stalking her didn't sit well. Lilli's fear amped up. Fight or flight kicked in with fervor, and she sprang toward the bedroom and snatched the phone off the dresser.

Only now she was cornered.

"Put it down, Lil."

"No, I—Charlie is on her way over. We had dinner, and uh, I should call her. Tell her not to come."

"I said put the phone down."

Her breathing echoed in her ears, adding acoustic melody to the pulsing drone of the blood rushing in her head. Her heart felt like it was going to thump right out of her chest and take flight like a caged bird set free. What options did she have? Not many. She took the risk and began to dial. "I'll tell her we're talking…working things out. She'll understand. She wants me to be hap—"

He lunged at her, knocking the phone out of her hand.

It slid across the floor and skidded under the bed.

"Jake, stop."

"Don't tell me what to do. I am sick and tired of people telling me what to do." With little effort he threw her onto the bed, then pounced, pinning both her arms above her head.

"Please, Jake. No."

The beast rose up in him. It was evident in his eyes. In the sudden feral hunger etched into his face. "You can't deny me any longer. Jake Edwards always gets what he wants. Do you understand?"

She nodded her head. A feeble motion, relinquishing control. "Please don't hurt me."

CHAPTER FIFTY-FIVE

"YOU DID WHAT NOW?" Brian pulled the squad car to the curb, left it idling, and turned to his partner.

Monty shrugged it off. "I called your brother."

"Stephen?"

"No. Bobby."

"Now why would you go and do that?" Brian hadn't anticipated her pulling such a move. In retrospect, he should have. Coulda, shoulda, woulda.

His brother, Supervisory Special Agent Bobby Harris, worked out of the DC field office. He was FBI. Just like Monty was going to be very soon. Brian did not ever want his partner finding out that he had pulled a few strings with the feds on her behalf. She wouldn't walk away from the assignment if she knew—it was too important to her— but she would find a way to make his life hell. If there was one thing about Monty, she could do it herself, or so she habitually reminded him. It was part of the whole don't-treat-her-like-a-girl thing they'd agreed he wouldn't do. Ever.

Yet he had.

Sure, she could have made it on her own merits. In fact, she did. He just greased the wheels a little, sped up the process. Not because he wanted to get rid of her. On the contrary. He would miss her greatly and couldn't imagine breaking in a new sidekick. He just knew how much this meant to her. She deserved it. She was smart as hell. Too smart to spend her time flagging down speeders on the I-5 Express.

Maybe she had a big old chip on her shoulder he wanted to see her knock off too. But mostly, it was because she'd be good at it. And the country needed more agents like her. So, really, he wasn't even doing it for her. He was doing it for his country.

She lifted the paper coffee cup to her lips. A casual move designed to show him that it was "no biggie." Then she offered him a subtle shrug of a single shoulder to reinforce the coffee move. "I thought I should tell him."

Okay. Maybe he could relax. Perhaps she hadn't found out. But what could she possibly have to tell Bobby? "All right. I'll play along. Tell him what?"

"That you are a horrible partner and he should pull some strings to get me on his team after I graduate the academy." A wide grin pushed her cheeks into rosy globes, lighting her eyes with mischief from within. She was toying with him.

But did she know? It was too soon to show his hand.

"Yeah. You should definitely do that." He could call her bluff. Assuming it was a bluff.

"Okay fine. You got me." She slapped the dash with the gloves she held folded in her hand. "I called him because I thought the feds should know."

Brian groaned and turned his shoulders to face her square on. "Beatrice—"

"Uh, uh, uh." She admonished him with a wagging finger.

"You earned that one."

"How?"

"By making me work so damn hard for the four-one-one. Now, just tell me why you called the SupSpAg. What do you need with Bobby?"

"Well, I thought SSA Harris, your brother Bobby, should know about the Jeep girl's resemblance to Haley Cole."

"Who?"

Monty sighed as though he should be able to decipher her verbal hieroglyphics better than that. "The Jeep girl—aka the one from the domestic at Madison Gate, and Haley Cole—aka the girl attacked on the streetcar line."

He nodded his understanding. "Was that so hard?"

"Careful, Harris. You don't want me to suddenly forget the rest of the story, do you?"

"My apologies, Officer Montgomery. Do carry on."

"Well, they brought in that washed-up football player—"

"Jake Edwards?"

"Yeah. Him. Anyway, sure they released him after questioning, but Arnold told me he's still at the top of the suspect list. They just need proof."

"And?"

"And, since Jake Edwards is dating the Jeep girl."

"Lilli Brooks."

"You remember her name?"

He shrugged. Photographic memory his father called it. A gift from the universe his mother called it. Either way, he didn't often forget stuff.

Monty showed him every one of her gleaming white teeth, she was smiling so big. Then, she popped him on the arm. "I think someone has a cop-crush."

"It's not a—never mind, she's pretty okay. That's all. Besides, my love life—or lack thereof—is off limits. Like your name. Beatrice Puanoni Montgomery."

"Ooh. You're bringing my Hawaiian middle name out of your arsenal. I think I pressed a hot button."

Brian crossed his arms and faced forward. "Finish the story."

"Okay, okay. So, Jake Edwards is dating the Jeep girl—you would know this if you bothered to read the paper, Bri—and Jake Edwards is a suspect in the attack on Haley Cole. Lilli Brooks and Haley Cole look like they could be sisters, ergo…"

He rolled his hand for her to continue.

"Ergo, this is something the feds might want to look into. Maybe we've got a serial on our hands. So, I called your brother."

She took a large swig of coffee, punctuating the fact that all of this should have been obvious to him.

CHAPTER FIFTY-SIX

TWELVE THIRTY AM and there was no water hot enough to take away the deep gut-wrenching sickness she was feeling. By the time Lilli had realized she'd made a mistake by running to her bedroom, it was too late. The consequences were already in motion.

When Jake had been on his way out the door, through silent tears she'd asked him why.

His answer had been simple. He'd wanted to know what it would feel like to take it without permission.

When he'd shut the door behind him—even locking it—leaving Lilli as she was, with her clothes and her dignity in shreds, she'd decided it would be best if she just accepted that she really didn't have control over her life.

How could she ever really know if a choice might come back to haunt her, invading her peaceful existence so intensely that it would leave her broken?

What had happened went beyond physical exploitation, beyond psychological too. Jake had ripped out the very essence of her being. The question wasn't if she'd ever trust another man. It went so much deeper. The question was, would she ever trust herself again?

Time may heal all wounds, but some need more of it. More time. More healing.

Lilli couldn't rely on Jake to let her have either.

As much as she'd tried to walk away from him, she could not. Jake was there at every turn. Literally. She'd proven that hadn't she?

His obsession was no secret. There was no going back.

She wouldn't call the cops. What could she say? This was all her fault. She'd given him the key. While Jake had torn the clothes from her body with vile intent, and he'd bound her wrists with the force of a single hand, and he'd ravaged her soul into a million jagged shards of broken glass—he hadn't finished the act. He'd released her. Zipped up and left.

Although, what caused him to resume his human form she did not know. Knowing that might have helped.

So Lilli let it go.

Having to tell would be the same as living through the experience over and over and over and over. It wasn't worth it. She sunk down in the tub, almost completely submerging herself, as her tears became one with the bathwater.

A SIX-AM WAKEUP CALL had jolted Lilli from her hour-long slumber on the sofa. The moment her eyes had opened, her brain had engaged, and the minute that happened she'd begun to sob, as the flashbacks resumed their tormenting cycle through her mind.

Finally, she had pulled herself together. All that had stood between Lilli and her great escape was about thirty minutes and a ton of makeup. She could handle that. And she did.

Now, her bags were by the door, her cell phone was charged, and the Jeep was gassed up. She was ready to go. Lilli did a final check to make sure she had written everything down for Donna. Yup. A page and a half of detailed instructions on what to do when, and what goes where.

She rose and smoothed the sitting marks from the edge of her freshly made bed. She'd been the only one in the laundry room at three AM, but her bedding was bleached and pristine.

She bent down and lifted Toby into her arms. She had to hold herself back from hugging him too tight. A few tears slipped down her cheek and dampened his fur. She wiped the remnants away with her fingertips, then raised his chin to look in his eyes. He'd been there. He could tell something was different about her. Something broken. But Toby wouldn't judge her. No. He was an innocent witness to a crime not fully realized.

Or was it? The damage was the same.

She placed a kiss on his nose and set him down. "Don't worry, Toby, Donna is gonna feed and pet you while I'm gone." She scratched him under the chin. "And don't hate me for leaving you behind. I have to do this. Alone. But I'll miss you. I will. And don't you go thinking Donna is your new mommy. I'll be back." She stopped to take a deep soul-shuddering breath. Donna would be there any minute and she refused to let herself cry again. At least not yet. She'd save that for the three-hour drive to the Cascades.

Toby meowed his disapproval before sulking away down the hall.

"I'm coming back," she shouted after him as she dragged her suitcases closer to the door.

She pulled out her cell and dialed Brad. She still didn't like the way he'd left her the night before. She should at least say good-bye. After four rings it went to voicemail. She hung up and tried once more. Same thing.

The buzzer to the front door sounded and Lilli left a hurried message, then pressed the button to let Donna in. She supposed the manager had finally fixed the sticking lock. Better late than never.

A quick rap on the apartment door and she slipped her cell back into her purse then checked the peephole, just to make sure. Yup. It was Donna. And she looked as tired as Lilli felt. Maybe more, if that was possible.

She began a verbal dissertation of the written one she'd left on the dining table, seeming to overwhelm Donna. That is why she'd written it all down, after all, so, fine, she wouldn't reiterate now. Just trust.

Even if she couldn't trust herself, at least she trusted her friends. Toby was in good hands. And each of the girls had promised to stop by and check at least once while she was gone, just to give her more peace of mind. While she hadn't known Donna long, she'd proven her loyalty to Lilli. In the few weeks they'd been friends, Donna had been a constant source of support, always going above and beyond. Lilli supposed she could say she'd made at least one good decision lately.

She said her fifth good-bye as Toby sulked in the bedroom and Donna shooed Lilli out of the apartment, assuring her that everything would be taken care of. She should focus on her trip. Driving conditions on mountain roads could be unpredictable at this time of year, and she warned Lilli to drive safe.

Still, as she placed her bags in the back of the Jeep, Lilli wasn't taking any chances, scrutinizing every corner and every shadowy hiding place up and down the street. There was no sign of Jake or his car. She closed the back, hopped in, buckled up, and pulled out.

Once she was safely on the I-5 heading south, with no sign of any vehicles anywhere near her, she finally allowed herself to exhale. Surprisingly, she didn't cry. She had intentionally sabotaged her tears by loading up on happy-music CDs. As long as she was listening to feel-good tunes, she could keep her mind where it needed to be.

The scenery began to change and soon the sides of the roads were lined with looming coniferous trees reaching their spiky boughs to the sky.

She put on her headset and called her mother. It was the perfect time to do it. She was full of positive vibes. That's what would come across the phone lines. She would leave her mother with a sense of peace, the same peace Lilli was feeling.

Before she knew it, she was exiting onto US-12 and the terrain went from flat, to hilly, and finally became mountainous. She was approaching Mount Rainier and her excitement was building. Everything in her told her this trip was her destiny. She felt life pulling her forward, urging her on. Solitude and self-reflection were beckoning her. She could sense the transformation waiting to happen. Freedom was a short distance away, even if it would only exist for a little while.

CHAPTER FIFTY-SEVEN

LILLI WAS CROSSING Main Street on US-12, entering the town of Packwood. There was a sign ahead that read: *Butter Butte Great Coffee and other Fun Things!*

How could she say no to that? Lilli made a mental note to go and visit the little shop in lieu of her daily Starbucks. Assuming Chuck's cabin wasn't too far away.

She drove by the Packwood Inn. A quaint looking motel that advertised a discounted room rate called the Hunter's Special. It made her smile. It was a simpler way of life around here compared to the hustle and bustle of Seattle living. She wasn't sure if she could handle it for the long haul, but for the short term, yes, Packwood and the beautiful Cascade mountain range would do quite nicely.

Beside the motel was Blanton's Market. Lilli would have to stop there to load up on groceries. She was famished and wanted to grab a bite to eat first, maybe confirm cabin directions from a local. Right now the only question was did she want to play it safe with Butter Butte or was she feeling brave enough to go for a real meal at the Blue Spruce Saloon and Grill.

Both sounded intriguing. Butter Butte promised fun things and Blue Spruce had the word saloon in the name, which conjured up all sorts of imagery.

Maybe she would flip a coin. Why not? She was on an adventure after all. Going with the flow. Following her destiny.

She pulled over to the side of the road and fished in the console for a quarter. Heads she'd go to the café and tails she'd try the saloon. She closed her eyes and flipped the coin. Tails.

She hesitated. Maybe best two out of three? Of course, she could always add the Hancock Wildlife Art Gallery and Café to the list. It was nearby as well. No. She would have plenty of time to come into town and visit each one of these cozy venues. The coin had spoken and tails it was.

Lilli disengaged the parking break and drove the short distance to the eatery. With the faded blue hue on the building and the barn-door entrance the word saloon seemed an apt description for the place. The sign on the building advertised cocktails, pull tabs, pool tables and good food. That'll do.

She took a deep breath.

New situations never failed to launch an army of butterflies straight into the pit of her stomach, but she was an adventurer now. She needed to think like one. Besides, nobody here would know her, let alone ever see her again. If she felt shy and awkward, so what.

She could handle this.

One more deep breath and a tug on the barn door. It was surprisingly busy for a cold Sunday afternoon. An eclectic mix of young and old—minors were welcome until nine PM—it appeared to be a friendly bunch, with people chatting and laughing with those seated nearby and standing around the pool table clutching their cues.

A bold yellow sign welcomed her to the Blue Spruce. She did feel welcome. Nervous, but welcome. Her eyes barely had time to adjust to the change in lighting before a woman approached her, smiling as wide as the Cascades, with a spark that not only reached her eyes but overflowed them.

"Welcome to the Blue Spruce." She gestured to the sign. "And welcome to Packwood. Sit where ya like. Squeeze in if ya have to. We're all family here. Some are just family we haven't met yet."

Lilli found a table in the back corner near the washrooms. As much as she wished to blend in with the crowd, Lilli knew she didn't. Not only was she dressed like a city girl, but the crowd here all emanated a sense of belonging. Like the Blue Spruce was a home away from home. Norm from the TV show *Cheers* would feel comfortable here.

She ordered a cheeseburger and salad without looking at the menu, and, as she waited for her order, Lilli carried out an extended examination of the interior, which was almost exactly as she had expected—dark wood paneling, pedestal tables with a mish-match of stacking chairs and barstools, a small stage set up in the corner, and, of course, an abundance of neon signs touting everything from *Miller Lite* to *GO DAWGS!*

She smiled when she read the sign tacked onto the breaker box near the coffee machines warning her that playing pull tabs may lead to extreme excitement. Maybe she could use some extreme excitement.

However, one sign stood out as her favorite. It was the one hanging right below the huge Seahawks bird that promised a giant TV, as well as food and prizes on Super Bowl Sunday. If for some reason she couldn't get the game up at the cabin she could always come here.

THE BLUE SPRUCE had been a little overwhelming for her, with the abundance of people who all seemed to know each other and the comradery that trickled between the tables like specks of dust on the sunbeam streaming through the front window.

Lilli had been anything but alone while she'd dined, inundated with conversations that all began with "You're not from around here are you?" That query was followed by a variety of topics, concentrated on where she had come from, how long she was planning to be around these parts, and warning her to make sure she stayed away from Bud— he fancied himself the town Lothario and was not to be trusted. He'd break her little heart apparently.

A chorus of "Come on back" followed her out the door and into the street, which was glowing bright from the sun reflecting off the snow. Squinting, she fished in her purse for her shades.

Lilli was tempted to walk up the road to the market, but since she didn't want to be making the trek back laden with groceries, she opted to drive. Just beyond the motel was the market, where she pulled in, hoping they were open on a Sunday.

She was relieved to see they were. Twenty-four hours a day. As she gazed across the street she was gifted with a pristine view of the snowcapped mountains she had come here to shelter herself within. It made sense that they were open. They must cater to the winter tourists—skiers, snowboarders, and don't forget the hunters.

Blanton's had an old-fashioned, family-run feel, but with the backing of IGA they had a pretty decent selection, and Lilli was ready to stock up. She wandered the aisles, friendly shoppers and employees alike greeting her at every turn. Soon, she had accumulated likely more than she would need during her stay. Much of it was dry goods or could be frozen if she didn't use it.

A plump, pleasant woman with red hair and rosy cheeks offered her a welcoming smile as she rang up Lilli's items and chatted about the town. As a young man of about fifteen bagged up her purchases, Lilli asked the cashier for directions.

"Oh!" the woman exclaimed as though Lilli were heading straight to Buckingham Palace. She turned to an older gentleman who was stacking cans of Campbell's Tomato Soup on a center display. "Hank, this young lady is heading up to Willow Lodge." Her smiling face flashed back to Lilli. "I'll have Billy throw in some firewood. On the house."

Lilli began to protest, pulling her wallet back out, but the woman insisted. "Nonsense. You've already paid. If you run out just give us a holler and we can deliver some more. It's a big place, but the power can be unpredictable this time of year. If you lose your electricity, keep the fires burning so the pipes don't freeze up."

"Good to know. And thanks for everything. I'm looking forward to my stay. Chuck invited me up to get away from the city for a few days. He forgot to mention firewood. I appreciate this so much."

"Mr. Willows is joining you?"

"No, I meant he offered it to me. To get away. I, uh, need some alone time." Lilli felt her cheeks warm and she reminded herself to shut her piehole. She had to do something about her habit of running off at the mouth.

The cashier blushed a little too, and Lilli was surprised the woman's cheeks could get any redder. "I'm sorry, dear. None of my business. It's okay to tell an old lady to butt out."

"Oh. No. That's perfectly all right. You weren't prying…I just…" Lilli shrugged. "Man troubles, you know…"

"Oh yes, I understand." The woman gestured for the bag boy to help Lilli with her groceries. "Just be careful out there alone—a beautiful young woman like you…"

"You mean Bud?" Lilli smiled at the remembrance of the abundance of warnings she'd received earlier.

The cashier chuckled. "I see you've heard about the town's Romeo, but no, aside from Bud—who's likely pretty harmless actually—there aren't any other cabins near the lodge. Not ones that have full-time residents anyway. Some are rented out to tourists, but if you get yourself stuck in a snowbank you'll be shouting for an awfully long time before anyone hears you. Better to be safe than sorry. Don't go out too close to dark, bundle up, and leave yourself some markers if you venture out on a hike."

"Thanks again for the directions. I think I might be the last remaining person without a GPS in my car." She moved toward the door, Billy the bag boy right behind her.

"Wait a minute." The woman came from around the counter and handed Lilli a can of bear spray. "You might need this," she said.

Lilli glanced at the can. "Really? I thought bears hibernate all winter."

"You'd be surprised," the woman replied. "Grizzlies are lighter sleepers than black bears, they can wake up early—hungry too. Now, some will tell you that grizzlies disappeared from the Cascades decades ago, but most locals can fill your ears with stories about sightings—either grizzly or sasquatch. Saw one myself few years back."

Over by the soup Hank began to chuckle.

"A grizzly, not a sasquatch," the cashier corrected with a subtle grin. "And never you mind there, Hank. Big old male griz came right up to the house, foraging for food. Weather was warm that February."

"That's good to know. How much?"

"It's on the house too, dear. Just don't tell Hank." She winked. "Keep it handy, in case you need it."

"Thanks, but you don't—"

"Course I don't." The woman beamed. "Now go. Have a wonderful *alone* time. And don't forget to come on back."

With the back seat full of groceries, Lilli headed up the mountain toward the cabin. She felt on top of the world. The beautiful snowcapped peaks and the endless blue sky, dotted with fluffy white clouds, served to invigorate her. This was going to be great.

LILLI MADE THE JEEP work at capacity—even with four-wheel drive, it still struggled on the icy incline—but soon she saw the long driveway. Or, at least, she saw the fence that lined a length of winding terrain that Lilli assumed was the driveway. So much fresh snow had fallen recently that there was not a single track to blemish the pristine carpet of glistening white. She almost regretted having to do so herself.

A large sign announced she was, in fact, at Willow Lodge. From what Chuck had said she'd expected a cozy little retreat, but this place justified the cashier's response to Lilli's mentioned destination. Although the many front windows were now dark, Lilli envisioned it at night, brightly lit against the mountainous snow-kissed backdrop. It would be stunning. Surrounded on three sides by majestic pines, the place was nestled cozily into a giant glittering white pillow and looked to be at least six to eight thousand square feet of living space.

Never mind the hiking trails, she might get lost in the cabin. Maybe she'd need to leave markers as she wandered the halls. Lilli briefly wished she had brought Toby. Having a little feline company might have been good in a place as vast as this.

She engaged the parking brake and stepped out onto the ground—then sunk almost to her knees. The snow was deceptively deep. Without a point of reference she'd had no way to tell. Shoveling a path would be high on her list of priorities. Especially before it got dark, which it would be soon.

For a moment, she stood and gazed at the beautiful home. Two stories high with multiple balconies, made of stone bricks and wood, it was rustic yet luxurious. She was so privileged to have this opportunity. Chuck was a good friend, and she would have to thank him properly when she returned to work. He was a good man too—it was reassuring to her that there were at least a few of them out there. Maybe someday she would find her own. But one thing was certain, she would not make the mistake of rushing in blindly ever again.

She breathed in the crisp mountain air. Everything around her was so still she almost felt transported to another dimension. It was eerie and calming at the same time. She rummaged through her purse to find the set of keys Chuck had given her, but came up empty handed. What if she'd forgotten them?

About to panic, Lilli remembered that Chuck had told her there was a key hidden under one of the rocks in the front garden—but with all this snow how could she even find a rock, let alone a key? As she stood there, knee-deep in snow, she mentally went back over all the steps she'd taken while packing. She visualized each bag and what she'd put in them.

Getting cold, she decided to sit in the warm Jeep while she figured out what to do or where to look. As she inserted the key in the ignition she spotted the one for the cabin. It was right in her hand, attached to her own keychain. Now she remembered clipping it there so she wouldn't forget.

She climbed the snow-covered front steps, unlocked the door, and scanned for a broom or shovel. There it was, a few feet away from the door. She dug a path from the door to her Jeep and then made a few mad dashes, bringing her suitcases and groceries to the entryway. Once actually inside she let her shoulders relax and traced her eyes around the grand foyer.

"Wow," she said and her voice echoed around the empty space. For the next week to ten days, this would be her sanctuary.

CHAPTER FIFTY-EIGHT

THE KITCHEN WAS stunning, richly appointed in wood, slate, stainless steel, and granite. After putting her groceries away she stuck the peeled end of a banana in her mouth and set out to explore the rest of the cabin.

First she wandered around the main floor. It had all the expected amenities and more. The living room was furnished in dark brown leather with a massive flat-screen TV mounted above one of the two stone fireplaces. There were three distinct sitting areas, each designed with a purpose—reading, watching TV, relaxing in front of the fire with floor-to-ceiling windows to take in the spectacular view.

Down a short hallway from there she came upon a large fitness area. She entered and found that a two-story window looked over an indoor/outdoor swimming pool. It was empty right now, but she imagined it must be fantastic in the summer months. This room fed onto yet another balcony, which was huge, with stairs that led down. The hot tub was here along with an outdoor grill.

Yup. She might never go back home. This was too perfect.

After backtracking to the main foyer, Lilli picked up two of her suitcases and headed up the winding double-L staircase, stopping on each landing to adjust her grip on the bags.

At the top, she set the heavy luggage down and wheeled them as she peered into each of the doors lining the long hallway. She'd counted at least eight luxurious bedrooms when she got to the end of the hall and turned the corner. The room at the end of this short span had double doors. She wondered what it could be. Perhaps a den or library?

She flung open the two doors and gasped. This was clearly the master suite. And it was that. More than a bedroom, this one went on father than her eyes could see from the entry. There was a seating area with a sofa, loveseat, and two large over-stuffed chairs that faced a TV and fireplace. On either side of this wall was a short open passage that led to another part of the room. There she found the center of attention—a huge dark wood canopy bed perched upon a colorful flat-weave Navajo area rug. Beyond that she discovered the luxurious bathroom that housed a deep, claw-foot tub, a separate double-sized stall with a half dozen shower heads coming from various directions.

Yes, Lilli was breathless.

She shuffled to where her bags were parked near the armoire, but it was the bed that was drawing her. She went to it and caressed the shiny, dark wood and then she fluttered the gauzy white cotton canopy through her outstretched fingers. Decadent. She fought the urge to flop down onto the fluffy down duvet.

Lilli felt like a princess in this room—and she was a woman who didn't believe in fairytales or Prince Charming. But she did want to cuddle up in this room and make it her oasis for the next several days. Still, she couldn't help feeling as if she should choose one of the more modest rooms.

She remembered the words Chuck had said to her when he'd given her the keys. "Make yourself at home. It's there to be enjoyed. You can even run around naked if you want."

That last part had made her smile. He'd meant it when he'd said she should make it her home. Knowing Chuck, he had also meant it when he'd told her she could run around naked. It was far too cold for that though, neighbors or not.

Lilli sighed the guilt and unworthiness out in one huge breath, then sat on the end of the bed. She was worthy and she deserved this. She definitely needed this. She hopped up and crossed to the armoire where her bags sat. She pulled out two copies of *Vogue* and the most recent Lisa Gardner novel and placed them on the chair closest to the fireplace. Perfect.

It had somehow managed to get dark while she'd been touring the place, so she scooted downstairs, made a quick sandwich, checked that she'd locked the front door, then grabbed the last of her things and took them up to her temporary new bedroom.

Just the sight of the room again gave her a sense of tranquility. What a welcome respite from the bustle of Seattle—from Jake and

Brad and all the drama. It was quiet. Still. There were no sounds besides her breathing. Music to her ears.

She drew the bottle of wine from her bag and then lit a few candles while she ran the water in the tub. All thoughts of stress floated away on the wisps of lavender-scented steam wafting through the air.

As she sank under the thick bubbles and stared out at the pitch-dark of night, all became right in her world again.

CHAPTER FIFTY-NINE

SHE CAN RUN, but she can't hide. Ever since we were little we've both known that. But the time has come to finish what we started. One way or another.

She promised me forever and she had no right to leave me. No right to make me go through everything alone—without her. She will come back to me. I cannot continue to exist any other way.

Yes, there are two sides to me, but still I am an incomplete person. I need her and she needs me. Even if she can't remember that. There is no one else like her. I've seen the imposters. But they weren't her. They only looked like her. And I had to make them pay for trying. I'm sorry if that's wrong. I didn't want to turn out like this. He made me into a monster.

Do you hear that, Dad? You made me this way. This is your fault. You made her leave me. You thought you could destroy me too. But guess what? You can't. You can't break me!

Because I have her right where I want her. And she's my life. Not you, Dad. She is shiny and pretty and glowing. You are a creature of unspeakable evil. And she is...

Perfect.

She will fix me and make me whole.

This is our destiny. We will be together again. Like it was always meant to be...before you took her from me.

CHAPTER SIXTY

"HEY THERE, BRO. January thirty-first. Right on time." Stephen held out his closed hand, waiting for a fist bump.

Brian offered one. Reluctantly.

His brother chuckled. "That's not how the Harris boys do it. Come here." Stephen pulled him in for a hug. But rather than the standard manly back pat before release, keeping in true Stephen style, he blurred the gesture of affection with his time-honored tradition—a rough noogie to the top of Brian's head.

He'd been on the receiving end of his brother's noogies at least since birth—maybe before. If that had been possible, Brian was certain that Stephen would have found a way. Stephen was just shy of four years older than Brian. Bobby came in third, just under a year younger.

As young lads they played together in the same sandbox, but as grown-ass men, the game had changed. Drastically. Brian suited up as the local arm of the law, representing the civies. His two, very different, brothers played on the federal side. Different federal sides. Their parents were proud—especially their cop-blooded dad—but family get-togethers such as this were the epitome of a logistical nightmare.

When each had joined their respective teams, their mother had extracted a promise that they join forces once a year for her birthday. If it landed on a Super Bowl Sunday, well, that was called added incentive. Each of the brothers had played a little ball growing up. Many of their mother's fondest memories were associated with the Friday night tradition.

Brian kept his promise every year, while Bobby and Stephen had broken a few—family life was more of a job hazard at the federal level, whether US Military or Department of Justice. That's another reason Brian preferred his career choice. He could still catch bad guys, still make a difference, but he was able to have a life. Or, at least, he could have one someday, when he allowed himself to take the risk. He might start with a dog. They were man's best friend, right? He'd never heard of a dog breaking a guy's heart. But women…they were another story, and Cynthia had done a real number on his. She'd broken it once, glued it back together, smashed it into a million pieces, and then danced on the shards.

No thank you, ma'am.

It would take more than a pretty face to get Brian to boat down that river again. It would take a girl with a lifejacket and a compass. If she had two left feet, all the better. No dancing.

AFTER DINNER AND a nice visit with his family, Brian headed back to his room at the hotel—his parents had downsized when they'd relocated after Dad's retirement. This arrangement worked out well. It gave him time with his mom and dad but also afforded him solitude when he needed it. The bonus? Hanging out with his brothers away from the family dynamics, drinking a few beers, shooting some pool, talking about the job—only what they were allowed to share without needing to kill each other after. Case details were off limits, but they could discuss the way they felt at the end of the day. Necessary on the paths they'd chosen to walk. Everyone needed to defrag their brains once in a while, but those that dealt, day in and day out, with the seedy underbelly of civilization needed it just a bit more.

Every now and again their father would sneak out and join them. He thought he'd convinced their mother that his mind never wandered down mystery alley anymore, now that he was retired PD, but she knew. She always knew. But she loved their father so much she made them all swear to keep up the charade. It made their father happy, she said, that and watching crime-show marathons while seated in his recliner.

Tonight it was just the three of them.

Stephen and Bobby arrived sequentially, in the reverse order of how they came into the world. Bobby first, followed by a delayed Stephen. He'd likely been grooming himself for too long, or got caught up with a DID—damsel in distress. Stephen had an eagle eye for beautiful girls who seemed to need a big strong man. And he used it. Every chance he got.

Brian and Bobby were into their second beer and their third game of eight ball when a grinning Stephen sauntered in to join them. Brian managed to fend off the noogie attack, while Bobby wasn't so lucky.

After a brief, yet unsuccessful, attempt at retaliation, Bobby handed his cue to Stephen and sat down while Brian and Stephen went head to head. Winner take all—meaning the loser paid the bar tab.

THEY CLOSED THE place down, which was a rare occurrence for Brian and Bobby—Stephen not so much. They'd shared pints, plans, play, and a good dose of pestering, while ultimately Brian and Bobby had been stuck paying the bar tab. Not because Stephen was intentionally stiffing them, but because, as was often the case, a fair-haired maiden was in need of a dragon slayer.

Tomorrow was Friday, and Brian planned to spend the day with his mom, drinking green tea, looking at photos, and talking about life. She would read the leaves in his teacup, which, no doubt, would offer her a clear and impending portent regarding Brian's soul mate.

Then on Saturday he and Stephen would go down to the store to help their dad out, while Bobby kept company with Mom, likely receiving his own tealeaf omen.

And Sunday? Well, that was The Big Day. It was one of those rare occurrences where the planets aligned—or so their mother would proclaim—and not only did her birthday fall on game day, but she had all three of her sons there to celebrate with her. At the Harris household it didn't get much better than that. Unless she had a kitchen filled with three beautiful daughters-in-law too. And maybe a grandkid or two on the way.

CHAPTER SIXTY-ONE

LILLI CLEANED UP her lunch dishes and took her tea to the bedroom to sip it in front of the fireplace there. She'd figured out how to get the wood burning, finally, and had been making good use of the skill ever since. She'd been wise to acquire the ability too, for the power had threatened to go out a few times already.

She made a quick call to the cashier from the market, who she'd learned was named Bernice, to confirm that Billy was to be bringing her some more firewood this afternoon. Bernice affirmed, and Lilli could now relax.

Just two more sleeps until the Super Bowl…and her twenty-sixth birthday.

Hard to believe it was Friday already. The days had flown by, between reading, soaking in the hot tub, and exploring the area nearby—accent on the nearby part. She didn't want to venture too far away, thanks to Bernice's warnings.

Tomorrow she would drive into town to see some sights and shops, as well as pick up some stuff for Sunday. She wanted to treat herself to all her favorite things as she watched the game and celebrated a solitary birthday—just the way she wanted it. She might even hit that art gallery she'd seen and check out the local artisans' handiwork. Maybe buy something for her apartment, something that would remind her of this wonderful experience.

Lilli curled up on the chaise in front of the fire, pulled the wool blanket over her lap, and cracked her book open to where she'd left off. As she blew on the steaming hot tea, she gazed out at the winter-white landscape, no longer pristine but littered with her footprints, as well as a giant snowman she'd built on the third day while she was getting in touch with her inner child. It was a shame she would have to go back in a few days. The state of relaxation she'd been achieving here was unprecedented. She could get used to this. Definitely.

LILLI AWOKE SEVERAL hours later, with a stiff neck and a sense of total disorientation. She'd opened her eyes to find thick, black nothingness.

Where was she?

Then she remembered. It had been daylight when she'd come up to read. She must've drifted off, and now, with the fire burned out and the sun gone down, she was blinded by the purity of the primitive darkness this far from civilization.

She reached her hand out to where she anticipated a side table, easing forward until she touched the cool metal base of the lamp. She slid her fingers up until she found the switch, but was greeted with a hollow click. Maybe it was unplugged.

Lilli brought her feet down to the floor, which had cooled significantly with the fire extinguished, and then inched her way across the floor in the direction she believed the bathroom to be. With arms outstretched and her other senses on high, she was adjusting to temporary sightlessness.

Once she discovered an opening and confirmed through touch that it was the doorframe, she slid her hand along the wall until her fingers met the switch plate. Twice up and twice down. Nothing but futile darkness. Okay. Power was out. If she could find the breaker panel, maybe it was a simple case of a blown fuse. A simple fix. Was there a breaker panel? She didn't really know how these things worked out here, away from the infrastructure of the city. Was the cabin dialed into the local power grid or did it operate on its own generator? Maybe this was beyond her skillset.

Lilli's heart began to hammer in her chest, in spite of her attempts to remain calm. She was in the darkest dark she had seen in a long time, maybe ever, and in unfamiliar surroundings. She hadn't spent enough time here to have any kind of internal sense of where things were or how many steps from one place to another.

Her cell phone. She could use it as a flashlight. Lilli inched forward, hands outstretched and floating side to side, until her fingertips grazed the slick, cool patent leather of her Coach bag sitting on the bedside table. She fumbled for the opening, but in doing so she tipped the bag over, scattering the contents on the floor. In the dark.

She dropped down to her hands and knees and traced her palms in a grid pattern along the rug. Wallet, cosmetics bag, lip balm, nail file, some kind of crumbs—yuck. Bingo. She had it. Her fingertip determined bottom from top and then connected with the center button. She pushed it several times, but nothing. The battery must have died from constantly searching for a signal out here.

She collapsed forward in defeat, the excitement at finding the phone quickly replaced with a sense of despair. Eyes wide open yet she couldn't see a darn thing. There were no streetlights to shine in the windows. Not even a moon as far as she could tell. Nothing that would provide her with even a hint of illumination.

She quickly came to the conclusion that absolute darkness was the same as a closed-in space. The silence was pressing in on her. The claustrophobic pace of each breath was ratcheting up until the sound of her respiration became a thunderous rumble submerged within the blackened veil of night.

One option. She had only one. Think clearly. Willing herself to calm, Lilli rose to her feet again and edged her way to the end of the bed, toward where she thought the dresser would be. She remembered noticing an oil lantern there. Matches had to be close by.

More measured, incremental movements with extended arms, but she came upon the heavy bureau sooner than she'd anticipated. A *crack*—or maybe it was a *crunch*—came from her toe as it made a hostile connection. Either way, the pain was intense. Lilli yelped in agony, breaching the cocoon of silence. Oh crap, that hurt. Biting her lips together, she bent down and grasped her injured toe, holding it tight against the searing pain.

Once the throbbing pulse died to a stinging whimper, with a slight gimp, she continued her search. Relief splashed over her when she found the lantern, as well as some matches, right where she'd thought they would be.

She struck one on the side of the box and shadows ignited all around her. Lifting the glass top, she carefully placed the lit match at the wick's edge. The lantern flickered, but sprung to life, casting a yellow wash of light.

Lilli could exhale.

She carried it out of the room, around the corner, and hobbled down the hallway to the massive staircase. The raw sensations in her foot would make this challenging, but she could do it. As she made slow progress, step by aching step, she began to admit the unlikelihood of finding a breaker box tonight, assuming one existed.

She was hungry and cold. So she had two priorities. Heat and then food.

With the power out, the furnace wouldn't kick in, and she was out of firewood. Unless perhaps Billy had brought some after all and had left it outside when she didn't answer the door.

Fingers crossed.

Lilli navigated her way to the front door with nothing but the glow from the lantern to guide her. When she opened it, a gust of cold wind threatened to extinguish the lantern, but she managed to shelter it. Reluctant to hold her precious light source too far out for fear of another blast of air, she kept it close. Stepping a foot onto the porch she scanned the entire area. No firewood.

Maybe the market had gotten too busy to let Billy leave. Or maybe he'd run into some bad weather on the way up.

She squinted into the darkness, trying to discern if there were any fresh tire tracks leading up the driveway. She thought she could make out two sets, but with the blowing snow there was no way to be sure. Perhaps he had brought it but had taken it to the back. That made more sense. There was a fire pit there.

With any luck the lantern had enough oil to keep burning, at least until Lilli could get to the back door.

As she meandered through the massive cabin Lilli limited her awareness to the area immediately in front of her. Every time she tried to look beyond the lantern's glow, an icy chill flashed down her spine. Well lit, the lodge was an exquisite oasis, but the murky ambiguousness that loomed outside of the five-foot radius of luminosity felt menacing and more than a little intimidating.

With a tight focus she managed to pilot her way to the door that led onto the large back deck. Careful to avoid the flashing current of air, she eased it open and poked her head out. A sudden, loud crash nearby had Lilli slamming it shut and panting for breath, her back pressed firmly against the door.

It was just the wind. Just the wind.

Still, Lilli was fused to the spot, her feet unable, or unwilling, to take her anywhere else. With the lantern's glow she felt visible. Vulnerable. But if she snuffed it out, it would plunge her into inky obscurity. That seemed worse.

She could hear the wind whipping around outside and began to feel brave enough to try again. There was no one here except her, and maybe an errant raccoon on the deck. She needed firewood or she was going to freeze without heat. So would the water lines.

This time she would prop the door open with a broom handle so she could set the lantern on the floor where it was sheltered from the burgeoning storm. She would dart out and in so quick that silly raccoon wouldn't see it coming. If there was firewood, great. If not, plan B.

She could execute the entire reconnaissance mission inside of twenty seconds if she did this right. Count to three, set lantern down, unlock the door, place broom at proper angle, out, in. No problem.

Boom, boom, boom. She could handle this. Now, go.

CHAPTER SIXTY-TWO

LILLI WAS RUNNING down a dark corridor. Something, or someone, was after her. There was a deep panting resonating behind her, and her own breathing was coming in rapid gasps. The booming was getting closer too—heavy footfalls thudding on slick marble tiles, echoing off glass walls. The uneven clicking of her own high-heeled boots.

Ornate pewter candle-sconces adorned the walls at six-foot intervals, the crazed flickering created terrifying shadow monsters, reaching out to grab her, take her, pull her down.

She couldn't give in. Wouldn't.

She willed herself to go faster. Faster. Faster.

Run, Lilli, run!

She tasted blood at the back of her throat—an asthma attack. It only ever happened when she was sprinting hard, but she couldn't stop. Keep running. A stitch twisted like a knife in her side.

Lilli gasped. Lost her footing. Her feet tangled behind her and she careened forward onto her hands, hitting the polished marble. Hard.

The panting and booming were closing in. There was no way out.

Suddenly surrounded by a visceral buzzing, she was completely immobilized, powerless to save herself. Lilli opened her mouth to scream but she was muted by her dream prison. Only a hollow gurgling sound emitted from behind panicked frozen lips.

The scream finally pierced her consciousness, ragged and forced, and Lilli bolted upright in the bed, her eyes adjusting to the dim lantern flickering in the distance. Panting, sweating, and shaking from the terror of her dream, fear and confusion was slowly replaced with the knowledge that she was in Chuck's cabin.

She breathed in and out, deeply welcoming oxygen into her lungs, trying to get her bearings. She snaked her forearm across her forehead, clearing the perspiration, and then hugged the blankets tighter around her shivering body. Her t-shirt was soaked through and the cool air was quickly evaporating the sweat on her skin, leaving her trembling.

Lilli stepped out of bed with the intention of dashing to the fireplace, but grimaced when she put all her weight on her left foot. She remembered the dresser toe-stubbing incident and cringed again.

Finally, she stoked the embers before placing several chunks of wood in a crisscross pattern. How relieved she'd been last night when she'd discovered the toppled over pile of firewood on the deck, answering two questions at once. Yes, Billy had dropped off the wood, and no, it wasn't an errant raccoon—or any other woodland creature that had crashed outside. It was a pile of poorly stacked firewood.

She tore a few more pages from last month's issue of *Vogue* and lit them with a match before slipping them into the center of the wood pile.

She limped back to the bed and slid deep inside the huge pile of blankets she'd collected from the other bedrooms last night. No wonder she'd had such a horrible nightmare. She shook it from her mind, mentally resetting herself for the day ahead.

Soon the fire would kiss warmth back into the air and she might venture into town for a coffee, assuming the power wasn't yet restored. As a shiver danced through her body she concluded that it had not been. There would have been heat. A quick flick of the switch on the bedside lamp confirmed it. But she'd made it. Alone. Lilli the adventurer.

She gazed out the window to see the slightest trace of orange peeking over the horizon. It was a brand-new day. And tomorrow was her birthday. The adventurer was turning twenty-six. Alone. But that was how she'd wanted it, right?

Without warning, thick, warm tears heated a path down Lilli's temples and into her hair. She didn't bother to wipe them, just pulled the blankets up and allowed herself to drift back to sleep, the salty liquid creating a damp spot on the pillow before crystalizing in the corners of her eyes. Soon, the bad dream—and the sad reality—faded away.

THE BRIGHT FINGERS of the morning sun had risen higher into the sky and were prickling at the backs of Lilli's eyelids when she awoke again. The dawn made no apologies at this early hour, and neither did the bright reflection bouncing off the snow. In spite of the cheery façade beyond the windowpane, Lilli still felt groggy and out of sorts. More than just needing her morning coffee, something was bothering her, but she couldn't quite put a name to it.

Then it came rushing back to her. The nightmare. The frozen scream. She'd heard about sleep paralysis. What an awful sensation that was. She didn't think she would forget it anytime soon.

She padded to the bathroom, favoring her injured toe, and flipped the switch. Nothing. She hadn't really expected ignition, but since there was still no electricity, she'd need help from town. And coffee. Coffee would be good.

RESIGNED TO DRIVING into town *sans* caffeine, Lilli bundled up, squeezing her slightly swollen toe into her boot, and ventured out. She would grab coffee and breakfast and then stop by the market to see if Bernice could hook her up with a handyman of some sort.

She hesitated outside of the idling Jeep to take in the beauty of her surroundings. It really was peaceful out here—nightmares and power outages aside. She pulled in a huge breath of moist, pine-scented air. Did it again. Lilli felt her shoulders drop, her jaw ease, and her heart sing.

As the Jeep carried her down the mountain road, a new smile on her lips, she decided that going into town for breakfast wasn't all bad. Everything happened for a reason. She got to see the breathtaking scenery again and even a couple of deer grazing by the side of the road. A mama and a baby.

As the trees and winding roads gave way to pedestrians and quaint little shops, Lilli's appetite grew. She was so hungry she was getting queasy, and her head was beginning to ache from lack of sleep—and caffeine.

She noticed a small eatery she hadn't seen the other day. It was called Auntie Dorothy's Diner. She wondered if there was actually an Auntie Dorothy. As she sidled into a booth, her stomach was grumbling so loudly she was certain she could win an eating competition against any man in a plaid, lumberjack shirt within a pancake's throw of her table. In fact, she couldn't remember ever being this hungry.

As Lilli shrugged out of her coat, a tall woman with short dark hair and a face-illuminating smile tipped over a plain white coffee cup, *clinking* it onto the saucer. "Want coffee, hun?" She had pot in hand, ready to pour.

"Boy, do I."

"I like an enthusiastic response."

Lilli returned the woman's smile. "I haven't had my morning cup yet."

"You want me to leave the pot?"

"Sure—no, actually. Sorry. As tired as I am, my stomach isn't feeling great this morning. I may not make it to a second, let alone third, cup. My tolerance seems to have diminished recently." Lilli rubbed her growling abdomen. "I'm craving bacon and eggs though, and starving, so you can bring me a large serving of those."

"So, no menu?" The waitress gestured with the plastic-covered breakfast list.

"No, but you can add a side of hash browns and toast to the bacon and eggs, please."

"Little thing like you…can't see where you're gonna put all that food." She waved a hand and winked. "You need anything else, just holler. The name's Dot."

"Thank you, Dot." Lilli inhaled deeply as she stirred the cream and sugar into the steaming hot, delightfully fragrant cup.

After a couple of good-sized gulps of coffee, Lilli removed her cell phone and charger from her purse. She glanced under the table. It was her lucky day. There was an empty electrical outlet within reach. When Dot returned with a heaping plate of food, Lilli asked if she could plug her phone in to charge.

"You help yourself right to it," Dot said, reaching out to refill Lilli's coffee, pulling up short. "That's right, just one." She turned and headed toward the kitchen, but stopped when Lilli called her name.

"Maybe just half a cup?" Lilli flashed the waitress what she hoped was a suitably sheepish grin. "I didn't sleep well last night. If I have to pop a couple of Rolaids, so be it. Besides, the coffee is really good. Reminds me of my mom's. She puts a little bit of—"

"Cinnamon in it," Dot finished Lilli's sentence.

"Yes, exactly."

Lilli slid her cup toward the edge of the table, and Dot topped it up, then reached into her apron pocket and dropped a couple of creamers on the table. "Enjoy," she said. "If you need those Rolaids, let me know. We keep a big bottle behind the counter here for Ricky's chili nights."

"Thanks, I will." Lilli plugged her phone in and then dug into the greasy and delicious food. As she devoured it in record time, it occurred to her that she didn't know where she was putting all this food either. She'd had an incredible appetite since arriving here. Must be the mountain air.

CHAPTER SIXTY-THREE

LILLI SPENT MORE time in town than she had intended. Needing to burn off some of the coffee and breakfast, she walked around browsing the charming shops and boutiques along Main Street. Completely enamored with the quaintness of it all, she couldn't resist purchasing a few folksy handcrafts for her apartment, most notably, a carved wooden cat that reminded her of Toby. She also indulged her sweet tooth, buying a pound and a half of homemade fudge.

Instead of crossing and walking back along Main Street, Lilli turned the corner, curious to see what was off the beaten trail. Serendipity struck halfway down the block in the form of Tom's Mercantile and Hardware. Perfect. She would go in and ask about the power. Maybe they could help solve her problems.

A little bell jingled her arrival as she stepped through the front door into a quirky collection of hardware and sporting goods, both new and antique. As Lilli browsed, fascinated with the old-fashioned tools, a man looked up from an aisle over, where he was with another customer.

He was respectably tall, although, not nearly as tall as Jake, lean and muscular, handsome, with tousled hair—the type of style that appeared as though he'd worked at making it look as though he hadn't done a thing to it. Dressed casually in jeans and a button-down shirt, he didn't appear to be a local, yet here he was, clearly working in a local store.

He let out a whistle. "Must be my lucky day. Two gorgeous women needing help in Tom's Mercantile at the same time. This is a history-making day here in good old Packwood." He turned to the blushing elderly woman beside him, draping his arm across her shoulder in a lighthearted, flirtatious way, causing her to giggle. "One moment, beautiful Gladys."

He approached Lilli, hand extended. "Hi. The name's Stephen."

She reciprocated the greeting, but as she was saying her name, he turned her hand over and placed a delicate kiss on the back. Yes, he was a charmer. If he hadn't introduced himself as Stephen she would have guessed he was the infamous Bud everyone had warned her about.

He spread his arms wide. "Welcome to my father's store. I have to ask, though—did a gorgeous creature, such as yourself, get separated from ski-bunny patrol or did you have a hardware-related need requiring the talents of a man," he cleared his throat with a loud *ahem* and splayed his hand across his chest, "such as myself?"

He was charismatic, Lilli had to give him that. And she'd noticed that the ring finger on the hand pressed against his wide chest was noticeably free from adornment. A single guy like him in a town this size…he must have the ladies lining up at his door on a daily basis.

"Stephen, are you flirting with Gladys again? Leave that poor woman alone. No means no." The deep voice came from the back room. It appeared Stephen might have some competition for the title of Packwood's most eligible bachelor.

"My brother," Stephen mentioned as an aside. "Yo, PD. I wasn't talking to Gladys. There's another pretty girl out here needs help. You're welcome to join the party."

"I'm coming, Bro."

So, they were brothers. Safe bet then that this PD fellow was as good looking as the warm tenor of his voice implied.

He started into the front of the store but stopped and turned in the doorway, his back to Lilli. "Yeah, Dad, I'll tell him."

"You want to help the delightful and effervescent Gladys with her plumbing issue, PD, or you want to help the new girl in town?"

"New girl?"

He spun toward her, looking down while he brushed his hands along the front of his jeans. Then, as he filtered his fingers through his cropped blond hair, he met Lilli's eye contact.

"You?" They spoke the query simultaneously.

Stephen darted a look between Lilli and his brother. "You two know each other?" he asked.

"This is the new girl?" his brother questioned.

WHAT ARE THE odds that she would walk into a small-town hardware store looking for help and run into a familiar face? She'd been right when she had assumed there were two handsome, unmarried men in town.

Stephen and his brother had played rock-paper-scissors to determine which one would drive up to the cabin to help restore her power. They'd made it to best eight out of twelve before Gladys spoke up and told Stephen to do the honorable thing and step down. After a small amount of brotherly banter, it had been agreed. Stephen would stay at the store helping their dad and his brother would come to the cabin to help Lilli.

Their mother had stopped by as they were about to leave. Introductions were made—their mother had been very curious about "the new girl" too—and then Lilli had gone on ahead.

The cabin had chilled significantly while she'd been in town, so, after Lilli unloaded her purchases she went to the living room to light the fireplace. Her savior would arrive soon, but she couldn't wait for the furnace to warm things up. She needed more wood and some kindling, so she snugged her thick sweater around her waist and went out onto the deck.

She glanced at the pieces of wood that had fallen from the stack the night prior. "I can't believe I was scared by a pile of sticks."

"Talking to yourself?"

Lilli startled at the sudden male voice behind her.

"You've only been out here for a week and you're already going loopy?"

She twirled around, dropping the bundle of kindling. "You surprised me."

"Sorry. Didn't mean to sneak up on you." He had an insulated bag in one hand and six-pack of Coke in the other. "Mom insisted I bring you sustenance. She figured if you had no power you hadn't eaten. So…" He raised his full hands.

"Thank you, Officer Harris."

"If you call me that again," he smiled, causing his eyes to follow suit and twinkle with light. "It's Brian, Bri, or, hey you, but no more Officer Harris. Now, if you would kindly point me in the direction of the kitchen, I shall follow my mother's strict orders to feed you first."

"You don't have to—"

"Are you trying to get me in trouble with my mother?"

"No. I—of course not."

Brian was grinning at her.

"Oh," she felt her cheeks warm, "you were teasing me."

"Guilty." He looked at her with expectation blooming in his eyes. "So…the kitchen?"

A TWIST OF FATE. That's what it had been. As Lilli began to draw herself a warm bath she still couldn't believe that, here in Packwood, she'd run into Officer Harris—no, wait, he'd told her to call him Brian. That might take some getting used to. Maybe she'd call him PD the way Stephen did. She assumed it stood for police department. Either way, she couldn't believe her luck.

Not only did he get the power restored for her—he'd said it looked like an animal had chewed at the wires—but he'd fed her some delicious homemade chili his mother had prepared. And fresh garlic bread. He'd stayed until the furnace had warmed the place sufficiently, and he even made a few adjustments to the satellite dish so she wouldn't miss the big game. If she was in any other place emotionally, she might consider him a good catch.

However, as things stood—and he was a witness to her luck with men—she would need some time before she considered any relationship. Although, dating a cop might give her some peace of mind.

But no. She was not ready. Her bath was though. And her iPod should be charged too.

Lilli made her way down to the kitchen where she had plugged it in while Brian was dishing out the food. A little Ella Fitzgerald would be a perfect addition to the waiting bubble bath.

As she turned to go back up the stairs a knock came on the front door. Brian had been gone for almost forty-five minutes. Had he come back? He must have. It's not like she was in the city with people coming and going. There was no one else out here. No one that knew she was here.

CHAPTER SIXTY-FOUR

WHY WAS JAKE HERE? And how had he known where to find her? He breezed past her and into the foyer. Caught unaware, there was no way she could have stopped him. "We need to talk, Lilli."

"Okay." What choice did she have? "But how—"

"I have my ways." He shook the snow from his leather jacket and let out a low whistle as he stomped his feet. "Some place. Chuck sure knows how to live large."

Lilli scanned the area. Where was her cell? She should have it with her, even if the signal was unpredictable. In the kitchen, charging some more. She needed to lure Jake in that direction. "Do you want something to drink?" she asked.

"No."

"Oh. Okay. Well, I'd like some tea, so…" Lilli started toward the kitchen, but Jake grabbed her arm and yanked her back.

"I said no. We need to talk."

That wasn't a good sign. Lilli would not react. She refused to show fear. It would only give Jake something to feed off of. "Okay, then. Let's go sit." She gently but firmly drew her arm from his grip, and he let her.

"Fine. You go first."

The living room would be the safest choice. She was still within a reasonable distance to get to her cell phone and there were two directions in which she could run if she needed a quick egress. All her senses were tingling as she walked in that direction. Her brain synapses were firing like crazy and her heart was racing to beat the wind.

It was as though she could feel Jake's energy fusing into her from behind. It wasn't a good energy. As much as she tried to remind herself that just a short while ago she had been madly in love with this man, an even shorter while ago the same man had been a single thrust away from raping her.

Her sense of foreboding was increasing exponentially with every step. Lilli forced her breathing into as stable a pattern as she could muster. Everything would be okay. She would handle this.

It was as though all warmth had been siphoned from her being in a single sucking draw. With teeth chattering Lilli stopped in front of the fireplace and lifted the poker to stoke the diminishing embers within.

Jake seized her and whirled her around to face him. "Why'd you do it, Lilli?"

"Do what?" He towered above her, but she tried to search his eyes for answers. They were blank and hostile. What did he think she had done?

"Don't play dumb blonde with me. You know what I'm talking about."

No. She didn't.

"Why did you tell the police you saw me attack that woman?"

"Jake, I—"

"Shut up! Shut up! Shut up!" He had both hands on her shoulders now and began shaking her as though she were a cage he wanted to escape from. "I know it was you. It was you, Lilli. Why?"

"No. I wouldn't ever—why would I do that, Jake? I loved you."

He thrust her backward and she landed against the mantle, whacking her head on the edge.

As she regained her balance, Lilli reached up to the back of her head, her hand coming away tainted with blood. Her eyes widened as she stared at the sticky redness dripping from her fingertips. "I'm bleeding." It was a stupid thing to say. Anyone could see she was. She just couldn't believe it.

Jake rushed at her and she cringed, bracing for another attack, but instead he pulled her to him and held her tight, smothering her face in his chest. "I'm sorry. I'm so sorry." He ran a hand down the back of her head. "Your hair. Your pretty hair. It's all red. Oh God. Oh God."

She tried to speak, but her mouth was pressed tight against his chest and his arms were wrapped so snug around her she couldn't budge. She pulled a small breath in through her nose and mumbled into the fabric of his shirt.

"What?" He released his hold a little.

"I said I can't breathe. But I can now."

"I'm a monster. I am. They were right." Jake was shaking his head so harshly that Lilli was tossing to and fro.

"Who was, Jake? Right about what?"

"I didn't do it, Lilli. You gotta believe me. I didn't hurt that woman on the streetcar line. But look at what I've done to you." He straightened his arms now and drew her back and away from him, looking at her with such powerful force that she felt both fear and compassion simultaneously. Then he yanked her to him again with equal strength, his muffled sobs getting lost in her hair.

He released her and staggered backward, collapsing onto one of the sofas. His head dropped into his hands, shaking, shaking, shaking. "No. No. No. It's all wrong. This is all wrong. This is not how it was supposed to be. This is not what I had planned." He raised his eyes and fixed on hers as she stared at him. "You were supposed to be the answer to everything."

She risked coming a little closer, torn between fear and empathy. Jake was big, and angry, and scary…but he was also broken. She hadn't been the one to break him, though. His father had done that, and she could not undo that damage.

What kind of a man takes a perfectly good child and casts him in his own image of hell? The answer was simple—the kind of man that Jake's father was.

With Jake's rampage defused, at least temporarily, the searing pain at the back of Lilli's head stampeded to the foreground, taking the place of fear. She needed to tend to the bleeding, maybe get some ice.

She remembered seeing a first-aid kit hanging on the wall in the fitness room, so she turned away from Jake in order to go there. She heard him get up from the sofa, but she continued pacing forward, slowly. He was closing the distance between them. She could feel it and hear it.

All of a sudden, he screamed her name and then his body crashed into hers, knocking her to the floor.

Her vision blurred in and out of focus, and then everything went black.

CHAPTER SIXTY-FIVE

WELL, WELL, WELL. It's twelve-oh-one. February third. I guess I should wish you a happy birthday. I'd toast the occasion but I haven't uncorked the champagne yet. I will though.

Soon.

Another year older but not the least bit wiser. Oh, Lilli. Sweet, stupid, trusting, Lilli. Maybe next time you'll know better and check who's outside your door before you open it. That'll teach you. But I bet you thought your Mr. Fixit was returning. You let him restore the electrical and I bet you were hoping he'd come back and hardwire your breaker box too. I would have put a stop to that. And quick.

I think I've proven myself in that department.

You forced my hand today. You were supposed to be alone up here. No visitors. And now look what you made me do—problem solved. You pretty unconscious thing…what am I going to do with you?

I had everything worked out. Planned to perfection. You had to go and mess it all up. You had to invite him in, didn't you? What did you think you would accomplish? All you did was make me angry. I don't like to be angry, Lilli. Bad things happen when I'm angry. But don't worry. He'll live. For now.

It was supposed to just be you and me. So simple. But no.

Now what?

I need to think, that's what. And I need time. Time to plan. Time to prepare. Time to get what I came here for.

And for that, I need rope. Lots of rope.

CHAPTER SIXTY-SIX

WHEN SHE AWOKE her head was throbbing and her neck and back were killing her. It was pitch black. And damn it, why couldn't she move? Lilli worked to get some sense of cohesiveness inside her mind, but everything felt so fragmented and patchy.

Not only was her recognition blurry, but so was her memory. Why the hell couldn't she move? It was starting to piss her off. As her head dipped forward again, bobbing unsteadily from side to side, it felt as though she was going to vomit. Yes, she was gagging and would throw up any second.

No. She was gagged. Something was wrapped across her mouth and tied at the back of her head.

Her head. It had been bleeding, and then…and then Jake. He'd lunged at her. Attacked her from behind.

She should never have turned her back on him. Should never have opened the door without checking first. She should have known better.

Slowly her awareness returned, bringing with it the sick realization that she was not only gagged, but bound to a chair.

Lilli tugged her arms and legs to test the strength of the bindings. They held fast. Jake had done an impeccable job of securing her to the chair. Of course he had. He'd obviously come prepared.

She had no idea how long she'd been out. It had been at least an hour, maybe more. And that meant that February second had turned to February third. Her birthday.

It started with one salty drop, skimming a solitary path down the surface of her cheek. But before long she could feel the warm wetness turn cold as her tears became imprisoned in the strip of fabric designed to silence her screams. It was a glaring reminder. A reminder that choices mattered. They mattered. And hers had been faulty. Wrong.

They had been so wrong, in fact, that they might be the last choices she would make in this life.

More tears came and joined the brigade. Weeping turned to sobbing, which turned to outright bawling. Soon, her nose was leaking worse than her eyes, the urge to wipe it so strong Lilli was becoming agitated.

That turned out to be a good thing.

Anger was a strong motivator. She would cry no more. Lilli filled her lungs to capacity three times, exhaling with the purpose of becoming the predator, no longer the prey. She began to use what part of her Jake could not enslave—her mind. She began to think. To analyze. To plan.

What was Jake going to do with her?

Whatever it was, it was unlikely he planned on taking her home. Ever.

The minute he did, he would be arrested for what he'd done to her. Maybe stalking hadn't been enough, and maybe even the almost-rape would not have been enough, but this...

Was it kidnapping if you held your hostage in a place they had gone willingly? It shouldn't matter, should it? He had attacked her, knocked her unconscious, and then bound and gagged her. That had to be enough to earn him an orange jumpsuit.

No, he had no plans to release her.

But what would he do with her? Had he thought that far ahead or was he operating on the fly?

Clearly he had no qualms about harming her. The way he'd charged at her right before she'd blacked out was testimony to that.

So, what did she know?

She knew that Jake was bigger than her. Jake was stronger than her—at least on a physical level. But Jake was not smarter than her. And he was emotionally, mentally, unstable.

That was her advantage.

First, she would test the ropes. See if she could get enough wiggle room to work the knots loose around her wrists. If she could do that she could unbind her legs and escape.

Jake must have tied her up and then gone to sleep, thinking he could relax. This should buy her at least a couple of hours. Lilli sat up as straight as the ropes would allow, dropping her shoulders low, then moving them up and down in slow deliberate motions.

The friction began to gnaw at her flesh. The ties were burning into her skin, creating a raw and painful canvas for her efforts. But no matter. She could handle this. She had to.

Besides, she was certain they were slackening up, even if a little. She curled her fingers up, trying to reach the knots with her nails. She would pick at each woven strand on the rope if she had to. She began to contort herself every which way, bending this way and twisting that, her fingers stretching, curling up, scraping the surface of the rope.

The heat and deepening wounds were crying out to her—fiercely. Ignoring their calls was no longer working. She relaxed her efforts and took a break. If she did escape, she would need her energy.

Not if.

When.

When she escaped.

Lilli had never known the meaning of the words *give up*—go ahead and ask her mother. And she wasn't giving up now. She was taking a strategic break.

She'd be damned if she was going to spend her twenty-sixth birthday like this.

Screw you, Jake Edwards.

CHAPTER SIXTY-SEVEN

THERE'S A MEMORY I have. It's one of many, but this one, this one stands out.

It was the first time that everything changed.

I remember the suffocating darkness of the closet. I remember how my breathing took on a life of its own. Hard, fast, shallow. Loud. So loud.

But no crying. Big kids don't cry. I know that because Dad told me.

It was the day I learned to wait. To be patient. Patience always pays dividends.

I remember the stifling heat in that closet. I can even taste the blood from biting my tongue when he'd hit me instead of my sister— my reward for having had the *cajones* to step between him and his intended target. The big and menacing versus the small and weak. That's how Dad liked it.

She'd been there. In my lap. Crying, diluting the silence of oppression in that closet-prison. I'd told her to shut up. He was going to hear her.

I regret that now. I should have been nicer to Tabitha.

I hadn't been able to decipher what was going on outside the room, down the hall, but the screaming had stopped. I'd been convinced of that.

But unclear if it was good. Or bad.

Had he gone? Had he given up?

I remember how the not knowing had served to deepen the sickening hole in the pit of my stomach, how I'd reached out my hand then, tempted to push back the row of clothes and ease the closet open. Just a little. Just enough.

But no.

No.

I'd known better. Even then.

Of course he hadn't given up. He wouldn't.

Ever.

I'd known that then too.

I remember how each breath I took rose in a crescendo to the next, building to a deafening rhythm, until the pounding of my heart became a wild jungle drum, warning me of the imminent danger.

I'd held my breath so long I'd almost passed out. But as much as I'd wanted to be free of the situation, I couldn't have done that. Not with her there, slumped awkwardly on my lap. Shivering. Barely breathing.

My sister.

Tabitha.

The weight of her body had increased as the seconds had ticked on.

And the blood.

There'd been so much blood.

The warm, thick stickiness of it had soaked my pajama bottoms. I can't stand the smell of copper to this day. If a store clerk ever hands me pennies for change, I always say keep it. Just keep it.

"Remember," my sister had murmured to me that day, on a single breath. "There are only two times we're going to be together—now and forever. We have a deal."

She'd linked her little finger with mine and had whispered the last words I ever heard her say. "You pinkie-sweared."

Then her hand fell away. The shivering stopped. I remember how her body had jerked—the way we sometimes do just before we fall asleep. In that moment I'd known.

We would never be together again. Not now and not forever.

But then I found her.

CHAPTER SIXTY-EIGHT

THE SUN WAS high on the horizon when she came to. All the exertion, and possibly the blood loss, had caused Lilli to black out again.

She'd lost a lot of time. Damn it.

Jake might show up at any moment and she needed to escape.

At least now she could see. But she barely had the drive to lift her head from the wilted position it had taken.

It hurt like hell just to try. Her neck was fused that way.

Lilli sucked in some air and harnessed her inner strength. She managed to pull her head upright. A slow scan left and right. Nothing that hadn't been there in the light of the previous day.

A soft chuckle arose from somewhere behind her, escalating to what could only be described as a cackle. But her head wouldn't turn that far. All she got was a glimpse of blond hair.

The approaching footfalls filled in the blanks. The hyena laugh stopped as the source of it stepped in front of Lilli's chair. She felt her eyes widen as her brain attempted to download sufficient information to comprehend the incomprehensible.

"Weren't expecting me huh?" Her captor took a bite of an apple, then spun Lilli's chair around. Jake was a few feet away, tied to another chair, and he appeared to be unconscious. "I bet you weren't expecting him either. Maybe next time you'll check before you open the door." A loud snicker, followed by an aggressive chomp, ripping off another bite of fruit. "But don't worry about him. He's not dead—yet." A wild smile. "I had to slip my competition a little something." A gesture toward Jake's slumped form. "I mean, you can see why. He's fucking huge. Rohypnol is an awesome drug. So versatile."

Her captor walked away now, laughing and crunching on what was left of the apple.

CHAPTER SIXTY-NINE

BRIAN ARRIVED IN his mother's kitchen to the smell of sizzling eggs, pancakes, real bacon, and *fakon*—his mother's vegetarian version.

He shrugged out of his jacket and slipped it over the back of a chair before he crossed to his mother and picked her up in a big bear hug. "Happy twenty-ninth, Mom." He set her down and kissed her on the cheek.

"Again," came his father's voice from the other room.

"Hey, Pop." Brian sauntered to the living room where his father and Bobby were already parked in front of the TV watching the pre-game show. "Bobby."

"Brian." Bobby raised his coffee in salute. "Couldn't hang around the motel once I was awake. Sorry I didn't wait."

Brian waved it off. "You guys eat?"

Bobby nodded, and his father rubbed his round, full belly. Affirmative.

"I guess I better get in the kitchen and snap up some of the real bacon." He made a face. "Fakon—*blech.*"

He strolled back to the kitchen and grabbed a plate from the cupboard. As he reached over to snatch a piece of bacon off the frypan, his mother slapped his hand with the spatula.

"Sit. I'll bring it."

Brian wrapped an arm around his mother's waist, giving her a side hug. "You rock, Ma."

"Yeah, yeah." She loaded up his plate and set it in front of him.

He noticed that she had given him the last of the bacon. "What about Stephen?" he asked.

His mother waved the spatula toward the door. "He's come and gone already."

Brian was shocked. "Stephen? Our Stephen?"

She nodded and placed some veggie bacon on her own plate.

"Tall guy, not quite as handsome as me?"

"One and the same. But you boys are equally handsome if you ask me."

"So, if he came, where did he get to?"

His mother sat down across from him. "Now, don't be mad at me."

"Ma? What did you do?"

"I told him to go up to Willow Lodge and bring that nice girl to din—"

Brian jumped up from his chair, almost knocking it backward. "You did what?"

"You told me it's her birthday today too. We're kindred spirits. And no matter what she might have said, no one truly wants to be alone on their birthday." She gave him that look she wore whenever she had acted impulsively about something. "So, he went."

Brian grabbed his jacket and thrust his arms into the sleeves. He'd be damned if Stephen was going to get his hands on this one. Maybe Monty had been right. Maybe Brian did have a cop-crush on Lilli Brooks. And maybe he hadn't known that until he'd spent time with her last night. She'd seemed so vulnerable. Tried to hide it, but it was there, just below the surface. He'd never take advantage of that. But his brother might.

He headed for the door, then turned back, kissed his mother again, shoveled a forkful of eggs into his mouth and snatched the last piece of bacon from his plate. "I'll be back," he mumbled through the food.

As he pulled the back door shut behind him, his mother was, not so successfully, hiding a smile behind her teacup.

She'd known exactly what she was doing. He shouldn't be surprised. She always did. And he always fell for it.

Still, if he hurried he could catch up to Stephen. Hopefully the weather, and the roads, cooperated.

CHAPTER SEVENTY

HER CAPTOR HAD left Lilli alone for...she didn't know how long, but the sun was high in the sky now, telling her it must be almost noon.

She had a clear view of Jake, but he still hadn't come to, and her captor had not returned.

If only he would wake up, maybe they could find a way to work together. Lilli began to fear the worst—she might not make it out of this alive. At least when she'd thought Jake was responsible she was dealing with a known unknown. But now, with the twist of finding him also bound to a chair, and drugged no less, she couldn't even fathom what the unknown unknowns were.

If you had asked her who could do this to her, sure, Jake would have topped the list. But she never saw *this* coming. Maybe she should have. Maybe there had been signs. Still, she couldn't think of any and had no clue what to do. She'd figured she could reason with Jake, or at least talk him into a situation where she might have the upper hand. But what would she do now?

Her best bet was to wake Jake up. She needed his help.

God! What kind of monster would do this to someone? And what else was a person like that capable of?

Lilli began to scoot her chair across the floor. All she could manage were tiny little increments, and each one made a horrific scraping noise on the wooden floors. After a few moves without anyone showing up, she surmised that she and Jake were either alone in the cabin, or the maniac was far enough away.

She began to hop and push with everything in her, and she seemed to be gaining momentum. Until her chair tipped over and she landed sideways on the floor. Crap. What now?

Jake moaned a short distance away and she arched her neck to try to see. His head was lolling side to side, swaying around drunkenly on his neck. His eyes began fluttering, and she willed him to wake up and look at her.

She made a garbled shouting noise around the gag, hoping to get his attention. It seemed to work. His eyes opened all the way, but he was looking straight, and around, but not down, where she was on the floor.

Lilli jerked her body, dragging the chair a little. It was enough to make him notice her there. She implored him with her eyes.

At first he didn't seem to register what was going on. His eyes were open but appeared vacant, confused.

Come on, Jake. See me. I need you.

Slowly the animation returned to his expression. Reality was dawning on him. When he seemed to finally clue in, he made a move as though he was going to stand, but being bound to the chair he couldn't. His chair thudded back, then rocked, and the force of Jake's weight almost carried him backward.

Once he settled, Jake sat motionless for a moment. Was he thinking of a plan? She couldn't read his intention. And they needed to communicate. But they couldn't. At least not with words. If telepathy was a real thing, Lilli prayed it would work now. It was their only hope. They needed to function in synchronicity.

Lilli worked the situation through in her mind. Jake was upright and she was stuck on the floor. He couldn't untangle her bonds because he couldn't reach them. So what did that leave?

It left her freeing him somehow. And trusting him to then save her. If she wiggled over and managed to get her back toward his feet, maybe she could move her hands enough to get those knots undone. Then, he could use his feet to try to lift her chair back up. And then if they could get back to back...

But before she could try, the monster that *had* done this to someone—two someones if you counted Jake—came sauntering back into the room.

"I see you're awake, Jake. And you," she turned to Lilli, "you have gotten yourself into a mess now haven't you?"

The next thing Lilli knew she was being thrust upright, the gag yanked out of her mouth and left to dangle around her neck.

She seized the opportunity to spill the words she'd been forced to keep silent before. "Why did you do this, Donna? Why?"

"Why?" The woman who Lilli had believed was her friend began to pace the room like a caged beast.

"What did I do to deserve this? I don't understand."

"What did I do? I don't understand," Donna repeated Lilli's words, her voice laden with a mocking cadence. "So sweet and naïve, aren't you? It's not cute anymore, okay. I took all the hits for you. I did so much for you, and how do you repay me? Do you have any idea how much planning went into all this?" She swept her arms in a wide gesture. "I had to work hard for all this. But you? You flutter your eyelashes and the world falls at your feet. Everything is so fucking easy for you. Men, your career, everything! One look at you and everyone, and I mean everyone, is under your spell. I'll admit it, when I found you, when I realized that we still had a chance to be together forever, I was under it too."

She lurched toward Jake, stopping dead center in front of him, her arms crossed and her face taking on the appearance of a snarling ferret. "Take this one." She kicked at his chair. "All I had to do was mention where you were, and he came running."

"You told him I was here? When? Why?"

Donna ripped the gag from Jake's mouth. "Tell her, Jake."

He shook his head with vehemence and refused to speak.

Donna slapped him across the face. "Chicken shit."

"Tell me what?" Lilli's eyes darted from Jake, to Donna, back to Jake.

"Whatever Donna tells you, it's a lie. She tricked me."

"What are you talking about?"

Donna broke into a fit of laughter. "I told him when we were in bed—your bed—after we had sex."

Lilli was in shock, unable to form a fitting response. Regardless of what they had been through, and what Jake had done to her, she would never have expected this. Donna was not exactly Jake's type. A sickening weight sunk all the way from her throat to her stomach. Her gaze was frozen on Jake, awaiting his justification.

His eyes became lasers, imploring her to understand. "It wasn't like that. I thought it was you."

"Shut up, Jake!" Donna backhanded him, causing his head to snap sideways. "You liked it."

"I was drunk."

She hit him again. "I told you to shut the fuck up." She sneered and yanked the gag up over his mouth. "There. That's better. And don't flatter yourself, Jake. You were just an experiment. What we did, it had nothing to do with you. It had to do with her." She spun around and stepped toward Lilli. "I wanted to see what it feels like to be you. Speaking of which, what do you think of my new hair color? I think I look good as a blonde. Just like when we were kids."

Donna snaked out a foot and used it to drag a side table over. She sat on it and leaned forward. "Now, where were we? Oh yes, that's right. You wanted to understand. And you get everything you want, don't you? So let's go ahead and enlighten you—you do still want that, yes?"

She did want to understand. She needed to. Plus, the longer she kept this madwoman distracted and talking, the more time she and Jake had to formulate an escape. Although Lilli would not risk matching eyes with Jake, she prayed he would pick up on her thoughts and give her some kind of signal behind Donna's back.

Lilli was quiet.

That seemed to make Donna angry. She leapt off the table and grabbed Lilli by the hair, yanking her head up and down. "Say yes. Yes, please, Donna." She snapped Lilli's head back and forth. "Say it!"

"Yes! Yes, Donna. I want to understand."

"Please!"

"Please?"

"Good girl." She smiled, genuine happiness radiating from the expression, and perched, again, on the edge of the table. But then, her features took on a glazed and faraway countenance. "I thought he'd killed you. I thought you were gone forever. I lost everything that day. But it wasn't lost. You were just a child then—but your eyes, your hair, your aura. I knew it was you the minute I laid eyes on you. You'd kept your promise after all."

What was she talking about? None of this made any sense, but Lilli played along. It was her only hope. "Yes, Donna. I kept my promise to you."

That seemed to make her happy. Donna reached out and stroked her hand along Lilli's hair. "You always were the pretty one. I think that's why you were his preferred target. I tried to stop him. I did. I always put you first. Everything. It was always for you." She brought her arm behind the chair and grasped Lilli's hand. "Remember, Tabitha?" She linked their little fingers together. "We pinkie-sweared."

CHAPTER SEVENTY-ONE

DRIVE LIKE A MADMAN. That's what he'd had to do to catch up to his brother, but he'd succeeded. Thank God he knew these mountain roads as good as he did.

Brian flashed his high beams, hoping to get Stephen's attention. Nothing. He flashed again, giving the horn a double-tap for extra measure. The brake lights on their dad's pickup glowed red. It had worked. But there was no shoulder to pull over onto so they would have to keep driving until it was safe to stop.

He fished in his pocket, searching for his cell phone. He hadn't wanted to call earlier because the last thing he'd wanted to do was stoke Stephen's competitive fire. It would have only served to encourage his pursuit of Lilli.

Even if Brian probably wasn't going to act on his crush, he still didn't want Stephen to have her. With the little he knew about Lilli Brooks, he could determine that she didn't need the type of complication Stephen would provide.

Where was his phone? He always kept it in the left pocket of his coat. But it wasn't there. It must have fallen out when he'd yanked the jacket off the chair in such a hurry.

Keep driving it was.

A few miles up the road there was a ranger station. A substation really. It served more as a base for search-and-rescue ops when some jackass inevitably went off the trails. But all Brian needed was sufficient space to pull over and chat with his brother.

"GOOD BOY, STEPHEN," Brian mumbled to himself as his brother pulled into the area outside the ranger station. He left his mom's SUV running and hopped out, zipping his coat against the chill.

"What up, PD?" Stephen was grinning in that way he did whenever he felt he was winning at something.

Brian had been concentrating so fully on driving fast that he hadn't had a chance to play the conversation in his mind beforehand. What was he going to say? He cleared his throat and thrust his hands in his pockets, then stepped toward his brother.

"Thought you might want company." That was a stupid thing to say. He braced himself for Stephen's smartass reply.

"Company? When I'm about to go rescue a lovely lady from a remote cabin and whisk her away to spend the day with the Harris clan? Why, she'll be so grateful she might have to throw herself at me in appreciation. You know I've never needed help with the ladies, Bro." Stephen walked toward Brian, wagging his finger. "Ahh, I get it. Yes. My *little* brother is jealous. You want this one for yourself."

God his brother could be infuriating. It wasn't like that. Okay, maybe it was, but still.

Stephen's face lit into a mischievous grin. "Race ya!" Stephen darted back to the pickup and hopped inside. He had verbally slapped Brian across the face, issuing his request for a duel and Stephen was set to win.

Brian rushed to the SUV too. This thing was on. Damn Stephen. He was so immature sometimes. No! The door had locked—with the keys inside and the engine running.

Brian hustled toward the pickup, waving his hands. "Stop the truck!"

His brother looked like he was going to drive on by, but at the last second he slowed and rolled the window down. "Throwing in the towel, PD? I mean, you must know you don't stand a chance."

Brian bent down and pressed his hands against his thighs, panting a couple quick breaths, the sudden rush of cold mountain air stinging his lungs. "No towel throwing." Another gulp of oxygen. "SUV locked. Keys inside."

"Get in, fool."

Brian shot around to the passenger side and hopped up into the truck. He wasn't sure if Stephen was grinning like the Cheshire variety of cat or the one that ate the canary. Either way, Brian would not live this one down, that was guaranteed.

He buckled in as Stephen threw the truck in gear and spun onto the roadway.

"Mom's gonna kill you," he taunted.

Brian gritted his teeth. "Drive, Stephen."

"Just sayin'." His brother grinned some more. Cheshire, definitely Cheshire.

CHAPTER SEVENTY-TWO

"WHAT ABOUT JAKE?" Lilli asked as Donna led her down the hallway toward the kitchen.

"What about Jake?" Donna mocked. "Who gives a flying fuck about Jake? He's a creep. You don't still have feelings for him do you? After what he tried to do to you the last time you were together? God, Tabitha, he almost raped you."

She stopped her forward motion and turned to face Donna. "How do you know about that?"

"Tabby, Tabby, Tabby. Haven't you figured it out yet? I thought you were a bright girl." Donna shook her head and shoved Lilli onward. "I was there. I was always there. I watched you sleep. I watched you *everything*."

Donna was tugging on the ropes, using them as a grip to push Lilli forward. The action was chafing at the abrasions from her earlier attempts to escape. Lilli bit her lips together and fought against the pain. She needed her wits about her. The one thing she was certain of was that Donna was not playing with a full deck. And crazy people were unpredictable.

"I have to go to the bathroom," Lilli blurted out. "Please?" She added the last bit in an attempt to placate. Whoever this Tabitha was, it was clear she'd been important to Donna. Maybe she could use that to her advantage. "I promise I'll be good." It seemed like the right thing to say.

And it was. Donna stopped moving and turned Lilli to face her. "You promise?"

Score one for Lilli. It seemed that in this original relationship, Donna was the Alpha. Made sense. Lilli worked at appearing wide-eyed and innocent, bobbing her head up and down. "Uh-huh."

"Okay."

That was easy.

"Come on." Donna turned away from the wine cellar door and headed back toward the half-bath near the dining room. She stopped outside the open door. There was no window. No escape.

Lilli studied Donna's face. She had one chance to get this right. She blinked her eyes, appealing to Donna's nurturing side. "I need my hands, please?"

Donna scrutinized Lilli's intent, reading her for clues. She peered into the windowless bathroom, nodded once. "Okay. But you have to be quiet. We don't want him to hear us."

Jake? Lilli couldn't see what difference it made if Jake heard them, but she went along with it anyway. "Quiet as a mouse," she promised.

Donna pushed Lilli into the small bathroom and then blocked the doorway as she loosened Lilli's ties. Keeping the ropes in her hand she waved a finger. "Behave."

Lilli nodded and Donna pulled the door shut.

"Don't lock it though, or I'll kill you now. Do you hear me, Tabitha?"

"I promise," Lilli said.

She knew Donna would have her ear pressed against the door, maybe even open it, so Lilli pulled her yoga pants down and sat on the toilet. She hadn't had any water in hours and she hoped her body had manufactured enough urine to not arouse suspicion.

After a few moments, thankfully, Lilli managed to go. She didn't have much time to formulate a plan. Her wrists were burning and her head was splitting from where she'd hit it on the mantel. As she stood in front of the mirror and turned on the faucet she got her first vision of herself since all this began.

Hell would be a step up from how she looked.

Come on, Lilli. You can handle this. Think.

There was no way Donna would agree to keep Lilli's hands unbound. What were her options? Then it came to her and she opened the door, thrusting her arms out in front of her. "I'm ready."

Donna seemed impressed at Lilli's compliance and did not question the forward placement of the ropes.

Good.

As Donna refastened the restraints, against the searing pain, Lilli held her wrists slightly apart, hoping the action would go unnoticed.

It did.

Score another one for Lilli.

Now what? This was going to be a go-with-the-flow type of thing. Lilli needed to think and act on the fly. Her next move was dependent on her captor's next move.

As they wandered back toward the wine cellar, Lilli calculated that she didn't have much time. It seemed likely that Donna planned on barricading her in the cellar, at least for now. She remembered her bruised toe from the other night and pretended to trip. "Ow!"

Donna relaxed her pressure on Lilli's back. "What's the matter?"

"My toe. I stubbed it hard in the bathroom. I can't walk."

Annoyance and distrust flared in Donna's eyes as she came around to the front, bending down to the floor. "Let me see." Donna rolled Lilli's sock down and off her foot, examining the swollen toe. "This doesn't look fresh."

Lilli had one chance to get this right.

As Donna rose to standing, Lilli steadied her stance and brought her bound hands as far back as she could, then, twisting her hips to generate more force, she swung her arms like a club. A loud *thwack* confirmed she'd connected with her intended target—Donna's temple. As the woman's head snapped sideways, a blank glaze came over her and she dropped to the floor.

Yes. Thank you, Bucky.

She didn't have much time. It was awkward with her hands tied, but Lilli hauled Donna's unconscious form to the wine cellar and shoved her inside. She performed a quick scan to find something to lock the door.

A kitchen chair.

She dashed to the table, but spotted the knife block on the island. She snatched out a blade and studied it. How the hell was she going to cut the ropes off? She smiled and lifted the handle to her mouth. Vising it between her teeth she began to saw back and forth. Carefully.

Once free she dragged one of the wooden chairs and jammed it under the wine cellar doorknob.

As she turned to hurry back to where Jake was, she smelled fire. It was more than crackling wood in the fireplace.

She sprang forward, hitting a wall of smoke as she entered the living room. Through the haze she could see Jake's panicked eyes directing her toward the fireplace. A stream of fabric trailed out and onto a pile of newspapers and magazines. The flames were licking out all around, getting higher by the minute. Soon the room would be completely engulfed.

Lilli began to cough. But she still had the gag hanging loosely around her neck. She pulled it up and over her nose and mouth. It wouldn't protect her for long.

Jake's breathing was raspy and hoarse. His skin color didn't look right.

She worked frantically at the ropes around his wrists. The knots were too tight. She went for the ones binding his legs to the chair. Same thing.

The fire was bearing down on them. Lilli could feel the intense heat as though it would fuse her flesh to bone.

Jake moaned, bringing her attention up to his face. He was about to throw up.

She jumped up, yanked the gag from his mouth, then darted sideways just as vomit spewed forth.

If they didn't get out of there right now, they were both going to die.

No. No way. Lilli refused to go out like this. But she couldn't leave Jake behind. No matter what crimes he might be guilty of.

"Come on, Jake. We've got one chance." Lilli dashed behind his chair and leaned it against her. He weighed more than twice what she did, but somehow Lilli supported the bulk with her back and legs, she grunted and began to drag the chair. The heavy burden fought against Lilli's good intentions as she made incremental headway toward the foyer.

The flames shadowed the path she took, shooting toward them, taunting with their advancing progress. As she reached the front door she heard a rattling coming from the back of the house, followed by a crash. Had Donna come to and escaped from the wine cellar?

Lilli set Jake's chair on the floor and thrust open the door. She had to move fast. The oxygen entering the cabin would increase the flames drastically.

There was one more problem. The threshold of the door. She would have to lift the chair over that.

Through the smoky haze Lilli thought she saw Donna's shadowy form advancing toward the door, thought she caught the glint of something metallic. The knife.

No. She had to be hallucinating. She'd jammed that chair tight. There was no way Donna would get out on her own. That thought made her gut twist with guilt. Donna was going to die and it would be Lilli's fault. She couldn't think of that right now. Lilli closed her eyes and pulled her strength from within. She had to handle this.

Three. Two. One.

She grunted and heaved, hoisting the chair over the low doorstep.

With her back to the outside, Lilli misjudged her footing and caught a patch of ice. Jake and the chair crashed into her, sending her flying down the porch steps. She hit the ground with a thud, the air whooshing out of her from the force. Heard someone scream her name.

Donna?

The burning pain from Lilli's head wound came at her with a vengeance. She had to get up.

Couldn't get up.

The trees in her line of sight began to sway obscenely. Lilli raised her head a few inches from the ground. Then the world disappeared.

CHAPTER SEVENTY-THREE

LILLI'S EYES FLUTTERED. Open. Closed. Open again. She couldn't move. A stinging, tingly pain gnawed at her shoulder blades, and the gash at the back of her head was shrieking like a banshee, competing for her attention.

Where was she?

Movement off to the left. A shadowy form. Another person. Not big enough to be Jake.

Lilli pushed her eyes so far to the side that she began to feel dizzy, but she managed to make out a few details. The looming shadow figure was a woman. Blond hair. Ponytail.

Out of focus.

Please, no...

If it wasn't Jake...that left only one other person up at the cabin. Donna!

No. No. No.

Lilli hadn't been imagining the vision of the crazy woman staggering through the darting flames. Now Lilli was helpless. Captive. Again.

Adrenaline taunted her to sit up, but every part of her, including her head, was bound to something hard, flat, and stiff. And something was covering her mouth and nose.

A strong hand pushed down on her chest. "Don't move."

Please, please, please.

Lilli blinked her eyes, willing them to focus. She was going to pass out.

The blonde came closer, leaning into Lilli's direct line of sight. "You can't move. You're strapped down."

Lilli's eyes began to adjust.

"Relax. Everything will be all right. You're in an ambulance."

If this woman wasn't Donna, then who was she?

She removed the apparatus from Lilli's face. Flashed a light in each of Lilli's eyes. "Do you know why you're here?"

Lilli couldn't respond. Her throat was raw and her head was killing her. Everything was killing her. A thousand points of pain, all over her body, fighting for dominance.

"My name's Denise," the woman said. "I'm an EMT."

"Jake?" The word scraped from her throat, through the glass-shard pain.

"The man who was with you? You saved his life. They've flown him to Seattle in a medevac helicopter."

A knock came on the side of the ambulance. "Can I join the party?" It was man's voice. Lilli recognized it.

Denise nodded, and the familiar voice brought with it a familiar face. It was Officer Harris—Brian. The smile he wore encompassed him entirely, lighting his eyes and rounding his cheeks. She realized he had dimples.

Lilli was about to say something, but he rested a finger over her parting lips. "Don't try to speak. You've been through a lot. We've got another chopper about to arrive to take you to Seattle. Don't push yourself right now, even though you're clearly tougher than you look—you did manage to overcome a man twice your size and tie him to a chair. Although, not many victims would go to the trouble of saving the bad guy."

Lilli tried to shake her head. Strapped to the board. Bad move. It hurt. "No," she rasped. "Not Jake." Lilli began to cough and the EMT put the plastic device back over her mouth and nose.

"You need more oxygen," she said.

Brian pulled out a small notepad and a pencil. "I can see you're determined." He turned to Denise. "Are you able to free one arm?"

She nodded and released Lilli's right one.

Brian handed her the pad and pencil. "Write it down."

It was a struggle but Lilli pushed through the pain, scribbling *Donna Parker bad guy inside cabin*. She handed it to Brian.

He read it, then shook his head. "My brother and I were pulling up when you came through the door. We saw you fall. Just you and

Edwards made it out. The cabin was completely destroyed by the fire. No one could have survived inside."

His eyes searched Lilli's. He could read her concern. Brian placed a gentle hand on her shoulder. "Just to be safe, I'll let the crew know that we want to be notified when they find her remains." He gestured *just a minute* and then stepped out of the ambulance.

She heard him talking to someone outside, but couldn't decipher what they were saying as the *thwup, thwup, thwup* of helicopter blades drowned all other sounds.

While he was gone, Denise took Lilli's vitals again and made some notes on a chart.

When Brian returned, his expression was unreadable. "Two things," he said. "One, your chopper awaits. And two, I've informed local authorities, and the fire marshal will notify Seattle PD when they've finished the inspection. But *you* are not to worry about that right now."

He stood and went to the door, hopping out again. "All right, boys, load her up. And save room for me. I'm coming along."

Two men entered and carried her out of the back of the ambulance on the stretcher. Brian was standing a few feet away, talking to Stephen, but when they saw her, they both approached.

Stephen was grinning at her. "Leave it to the new girl in town to create a bigger fuss than the Super Bowl." He turned to Brian. "Take care of her, PD. Keep us posted. Oh, and thanks for leaving me to tell Mom her SUV is running out of gas at the ranger station."

Brian clapped Stephen on the shoulder. "My pleasure. In exchange you can have my slice of Mom's birthday cake." The brothers exchanged a look, then turned to Lilli. "Happy birthday," they said in unison.

"Don't do it, PD." Stephen wagged a finger at Brian.

Brian raised his hands in question. "What?"

"Whatever you do, don't sing the birthday song—or any song for that matter." Stephen faced Lilli now. "The man couldn't carry a tune even if it had built-in handles." He slugged his brother in the arm and winked at Lilli. "We should definitely get together again sometime. Next year? Same time. Different place."

Brian flashed his eyes at Stephen. There was some hidden communication there, but Lilli couldn't say what. Although, Stephen seemed to read it clearly, raising his palms in surrender as he stepped back.

Brian joined him, and the medevac EMTs loaded Lilli onto the waiting helicopter. The brothers shared a few words and a handshake that turned into a hug, followed by a noogie to the top of Brian's head.

They settled her into the chopper, and then Brian hopped up and took a seat beside her. His eyes were full of compassion—and something more. What, Lilli didn't know, but it was clear he was going to see this through all the way to Seattle. Still, Lilli wondered how he came to be at the cabin.

"Brian?"

He leaned over so she wouldn't need to speak too loudly. "Yes, ma'am."

"You were at the cabin. Why?"

He flashed a mischievous grin and pretended to tip an imaginary hat. "Just doing my job, ma'am."

EPILOGUE

BRIAN WAS OUTSIDE her room talking on the cell phone his partner had delivered to the hospital before they'd arrived. He'd been standing vigil over Lilli since the chopper had lifted them off the mountain. She wasn't sure what to make of it though. From her side or from his. He seemed to be somewhat attached to her, but in a detached sort of way—if that made any sense.

She supposed it did. Lilli figured that would be the way she would approach the next man after all she'd been through. Not that she thought this cop saw her as a potential mate. Maybe he did. But even if, Lilli herself was not ready to see the potential in anyone.

The door slid open and Brian peeked around the edge of it. "Got some news," he said. "The inspector went through the cabin—briefly. Thought he'd do a quick look around as a professional curtesy. He'll go back to sort through the mess in more detail, but figured a body would be easy to see."

"And?" Lilli was holding her breath, afraid to hear the answer. After all, Brian had said he had news. Hadn't said what kind—good or bad.

"And, sure enough there was a woman's body found in the wine cellar, just like you'd said. Burnt beyond recognition, of course, but I think we'd be betting safe on this one. The woman that did this to you…she's gone. She can't hurt you anymore."

Lilli bobbed her head. Relief washed over her in the form of a single drop of saline skidding down her cheek. She swiped at it before he could notice.

Brian took her hand, then let go as though he had crossed a line. "Sorry. That was a little too familiar of me. I apologize. You've been though a lot. I don't mean to complicate—"

"It's all right." She managed a grin. "No one complicates my life better than I do."

She caught the beginnings of a return smile tugging at his lips, but a knock on her door pulled her attention toward it. A nurse entered with a caddy in her hand. She sent her eyes to Brian and he seemed to get the message. He excused himself and left Lilli alone with the nurse.

"We need to take a quick blood sample before we send you to radiology to get the bump on your head looked at."

"Blood? Why?"

"Just to confirm you're not pregnant." She stretched out Lilli's right arm and ran the pads of her fingers along the veins. "Got one." She tied a rubber band around it. "Make a fist."

Lilli did and the nurse pulled the cap off the syringe and positioned the needle above the vein.

"Little poke."

Looking away from the needle—and the blood—Lilli took a deep breath and waited, releasing her fist when the nurse instructed her to.

She flicked the vial, wrote on it, and placed it in her caddy, turning to Lilli with the chart in her hand. "When was the date of your last period?"

Lilli worked at remembering, but so much had gone on in these last few weeks she'd lost count. "Just before Christmas I think. Maybe around the twentieth."

"December twentieth?"

"I think."

The nurse placed a hand on Lilli's shoulder. "Then we better get this blood off to the lab pronto."

"Why the hurry?" Lilli asked the question but immediately wished she could take it back. She didn't want to hear the answer. If her last period was before Christmas and it was now February third...Lilli was at least two weeks late. "Never mind."

The nurse offered Brian a smile as she went out and he came in. Clearly she thought he was the fath—Lilli couldn't bring herself to finish that thought. No fathers. No babies. No. Just no.

"Delivery service brought these for you while the nurse was in here. I signed for them." He handed her a beautiful bouquet. Several white lilies surrounding a single red one. "There's a card here," he said, handing her a small envelope.

Lilli set the flowers on the rolling table and slid the flap open, pulled the card out and read. A wave of nausea swept over her and Brian's face registered the shock she was feeling.

"What is it?"

Speechless, she extended the card to him.

His eyes scanned it and he read it aloud. "Oh, Tabitha, what have you done?" A curious light flickered over his face as he turned to Lilli. "Who's Tabitha?"

~*Gratitude*~

Thank you so much for purchasing and reading my story. Your opinion is of great value to me as a writer. I hope you enjoyed it, but even if you didn't, I welcome your honest feedback and review.

Acknowledgements

My gratitude to my Muses, first of all, for without them these lines would be blank. To the Universe for leading me down the path of my highest excitement, providing for me to follow my bliss.

Thanks to my husband, Miguel, for believing in me, understanding my processes, being my co-brainstormer, and furnishing me with an ongoing supply of chocolate, surprises, and great ideas.

To my children, Ty, Josh and Emilio: Ty, you have always been at the head of my fan club. Your strength and belief in me has helped me move literary mountains (and other mountains too!) Josh, you have taken care of so many things in order to support my dreams. Your positive attitude, spending time with your little brother, helping around the house, fixing computer issues, patiently teaching me how to use Photoshop (then teaching me again when I forgot), as well as putting your creative touch on the cover design for this novel, not to mention reminding me to take care of myself sometimes too. And, Emilio, your mere presence in my life every day is like a beacon of joy. You asked me if writing books made me happy, if I loved my job. Yes it does and yes I do. Even better is the knowledge that seeing me almost constantly at my computer showed you my passion for words in the most positive way, and has inspired you to write your own books (at six!). In fact, you are writing one as I type these words. ("The Snowman: The Snowman Melts.") I can't wait to see what happens! Also, I have to mention the furry adopted member of our family—my little rescue Chihuahua from Las Angeles: Zuzu, you are the best little dog any family could ask for. Thank you for being part of our lives.

To my stepsons Jeren and Sherwin, you are always excited when I show you something I published—that means more to me than you know. You keep your little brother happy and entertained on the weekends, giving me space and time to write. I am glad you are part of my life.

To my parents: You are the originators of my fan club. You taught me that I could do anything, and were patient while I tried…and tried again. And sometimes again. Because of you "I can do it myself." To my sister, Sherry, you have helped me in so many ways throughout my life, but most relevant to this, thank you for all the vocabulary lessons (even though sometimes my friends stared blankly and teachers thought I had cheated on essays because of all the big words I used) and thank you for all the puppet shows and story time. To my brother, Gord, you gave me the incentive to stand up to peer pressure (and the twenty I won in the bet) and when I was terrified to get back on my bike (after falling and laying in the road, momentarily paralyzed—I'll never forget that day) and the neighborhood bullies teased me as I walked my bike in circles around the block, you stood up for me until I was brave enough to hop back up and ride.

Special thanks to "the big four." My girls: Kimberly Bartko, aka Cassie; Tracey Myles, aka Charlie; and Annette Pierce, aka Annie—my life has been so much better with you three in it. Thanks to your inspiration, Lilli Brooks had three equally amazing friends to lean on. And to my guy: Stephen Woodward (the talented stylist/owner of Salon Sugar Calgary and my best guy friend, whose charm, handsomeness, and Harley-riding, bad-boy persona was inspiration for his namesake in the book—although, I have taken "creative liberties" with the rest of Stephen Harris's character traits…) Thank you, Stephen, for making me look my best and for always "giving it to me straight"—and sometimes with a little wave. The four of you add up to over a hundred years of best friendship. I love you all.

Special mentions

A special thanks goes out to fellow author, and my former mentor at Winghill Writing School, Joan Hall Hovey. Your writing inspires me, and your guidance set me on the path of "Serious Writer" and for that I am eternally grateful.

My cousin Kim Ward, thanks for allowing me to add your wonderful memories of our grandmother to my own.

To Sara from Starbucks (as well as the rest of your crew) thanks for keeping me caffeinated and providing me with "office space" on an almost daily basis.

Thanks to Russell Wilson, the *actual* quarterback for the Seattle Seahawks—your post-Super Bowl words are written in crayon on my shower stall wall (my "vortex of creativity"), where I see them daily: "Why not me?"

Thanks to the Four Seasons Seattle for providing me with pictures, links, and information for my New Year's Eve scene—any factual errors are mine and mine alone (sometimes we writers need to "tweak" the truth a little.)

Thanks to Google for facilitating my research by making all my "virtual" travels interesting and enjoyable. Keep up the good work. (Again, any factual errors are mine and mine alone.)

Gratitude to the good people and fine establishments (both real and imagined) in Seattle and Packwood.

And, last but most definitely not least, thanks go out to the rest of my family and all of my friends, with big gratitude to my loyal readers/supporters—you all rock!

About the Author

Lisa Martinez has published several magazine articles as well as works of fiction. One of her favorite surprise moments as an author was when she discovered that a "quiet little story" she'd written was being used by a teacher at a college in Buenos Aires, Argentina as part of her course training Language Arts teachers.

With a passion for realistic details, research is high on her list of "fun things to do." When posed the question of whether or not she would give up writing in exchange for ten million dollars, the answer, for her, was obvious—absolutely not! "There are a few things in life that I would never give up," she says, "my family, my friends, words, and, of course, chocolate."

Contact the Author

Web: www.lisadawnmartinex.com
Email: mail@lisadawnmartinez.com
Social:
www.facebook.com/LisaDawnMartinez.Writer
@LisaDMartinez

www.ingramcontent.com/pod-product-compliance
Lightning Source LLC
Chambersburg PA
CBHW050919250626
47155CB00001B/299